ENDORSEMENTS

"I have known George for more than ten years from a Bible study comprised mainly of physicians. (It's the safest place to be on a Tuesday night in Berks County with a heart surgeon, orthopedic surgeons, internist, artery, and kidney guy.) George is somebody who walks the talk. He has incredible integrity and love for his fellow man. On top of that he has amazing, if not hilarious, ways of describing things. But like many of us, he wasn't always a stand-up guy. Like many of us, he was on the fence for a long time. I didn't know him back then, but I can identify with the person George describes himself being at that time. I was a lot like it.

"He has wanted to write a non-religious book for people who may be on the fence, or distant believers, that they may be blessed with the Holy Spirit. Personally, as a writer, I felt this task to be nearly impossible to do in book form. Once I read *The Last Soap Opera Before Sunrise* all the way through, however, I had just one thought: By God, he's done it."

—DR. JAY CARTER, best-selling author of *Nasty People*

"George Mattmiller has crafted a protagonist who is instantly recognizable, sympathetic, and occasionally cringe-worthy all in one. In other words, the character I came face to face with in *The Last Soap Opera Before Sunrise* reminded me a lot of me!

"The star of this fast-moving story is Vance Chelan, a workaholic television executive who embodies all that the world admires, envies, and fears. His astonishing collision with God chases him through plot twists to a wholly satisfying and hopeful conclusion.

"I feel certain that today's career-centric men and women who one day wake with a start to find themselves in a spiritual desert will love this book. I plan to take an annual trip into its pages to remind me of who I had been without Christ and the brand new person Jesus turned me into.

"I highly recommend this novel for being uniquely American, exceptionally rewarding, and capable of kicking off a revival among all kinds of people in all kinds of places. Kudos to George Mattmiller for a wonderful look into what life with our Savior Jesus Christ can be!"

—DALE W. DAVIDSON, host, *Las Vegas Tonight*

The Last Soap Opera Before Sunrise

George Mattmiller

Carpenter's Son Publishing

The Last Soap Opera Before Sunrise

© 2021 by George Mattmiller

Published by Carpenter's Son Publishing, Franklin, Tennessee

Published in association with Larry Carpenter of
Christian Book Services, LLC
www.christianbookservices.com

Scripture is used from the The Holy Bible, Today's New International Version® unless otherwise noted. Copyright © 2001, 2005 by Biblica®. Used by permission of Biblica®. All rights reserved worldwide.

Edited by Robert Irvin

Cover Design by Damonza.com

Interior Layout Design by Suzanne Lawing

Printed in the United States of America

978-1-952025-18-1

To Pastor Bob Rieth, founder of Media Fellowship International, who, along with the power of the Holy Spirit, brought us all together and helped make us changed people.

Contents

CHAPTER ONE

Dead Thoughts
at a Funeral

*E*ven I had to admit this looked bizarre: a guy in a pinstripe suit scaling a sixty-foot extension ladder up the side of a mansion currently under construction. I could have checked in with the foreman and gone upstairs the conventional route, but that would have blown my cover. Besides, the conventional route was never my style.

I meticulously ascended each rung of the fully extended ladder, not wanting to announce my presence. Hopefully the footing was firm. If this contraption gave out it would be all over. I'd probably die on the spot—and then what? Oh well. *RIP*, as they always say. And what does that really mean? Running In Place? Radical In Pajamas? Rears In Peoria?

The ladder flexed more freely the higher I climbed; insecurity roiled in the pit of my gut.

Closing my eyes, clutching the metal rungs, I dragged myself along the jagged stone face. Cargo vans and pickup trucks grew small on the parched ground below me. Each step became more labored. Sweating buckets, my palms were like greased eels.

Amid the cacophony of screeching saws and hammer blows, I paused to catch my breath. I wasn't exactly out of shape, just not used to this level of cardio insanity. In my mid-thirties, I was a fairly solid 185, about ten pounds over my college football playing weight. I made a mental note to hit the stair climber harder the next time I was at the gym.

The bathroom window was a few rungs up and, thankfully, wide open. I'd always heard you weren't supposed to look down from heights, but I couldn't help admiring the symmetrical fields of the neighboring winery.

"You got a happy clog, baby! Your throne's a regular cherry, cherry, chariot!" Jules, the "Rock 'n Roll Plumber," was in rare form. Known for his MTV-style commercials, he had become a legendary local personality with national aspirations. To Accounts Receivable at my television station, though, he just represented a glaring liability. A notorious slow-pay, Jules was rapidly becoming an RIP in his own right: a Rude, Insolvent Plumber.

As I pulled even with the sill, I spied him in the corner of the sumptuous master bath, his back to me. Here I was, Vance Chelan, a moderately successful television executive, about to ambush a celebrity plumber. Did this qualify as "just another day at the office"?

"You need a regal throne for the higher, the higher, the higher place of bliss!" His painful vocal rendition echoed off a bank of bare drywall, jarring my senses. At least it muffled the clumsy way I squirmed through the window.

Installing the flange for a bidet—the popular Whispers in the Valley model—he had no clue of what was about to befall him.

"Buckle up, Jules!" I said as I dropped over the ledge. "It's gonna be a bumpy ride."

He froze.

I vaulted the King Cobra Royal Pneumatic Flush toilet and lunged for him just as he whipped around on a sheet of cardboard protecting the marble floor. Dropping his pipe wrench, he sidestepped me and bolted for daylight.

Summoning my former gridiron skills, I grabbed a fistful of his purple-dyed mane and clamped an arm around his straining gut. Riding him past the custom-made platform tub and granite-topped vanity, I tackled him atop the paint-smeared subfloor of the expansive master bedroom where he writhed like a wounded antelope.

"Man, are you nuts?" Jules gasped. Wincing, he turned his head on the particleboard like I'd just cuffed him. "What're you trying to do to me?"

"I barely recognize you without the pink spandex," I heaved.

"I know why you're here. I don't need to be read the riot act."

"Oh really? You know how bad it's gotten? You know how I've covered for you, putting myself on the line for you?" I wobbled to my feet. "Not to mention the fact I discovered you in the first place." I looked for a place to spit. "And this is the thanks I get."

"You think I've got it easy?" He rolled onto his back.

Sucking wind, I dusted off the knees of my suit pants, hoping the antique white overspray wouldn't leave a stain.

"I'm dealing with a copyright infringement claim on my new jingle," he wheezed. "You know, 'Butt Crack Blues'. It's all bogus but lawyers aren't cheap."

I thought about how stupid that statement sounded: a plumber worried about copyright infringement. "That's not gonna cut it anymore," I said. "My owner is breathing fire. Unless I return to the TV station with some serious dead presidents in my back pocket, you're gonna be staring at a full-court press."

"Two hours, that's all I'm asking," Jules pleaded. "I'll make something happen. I promise." The muscular musician put his hands up defensively, apparently afraid I was going to punch him.

"Fine," I said. "I'm going to a funeral. I'll swing by later." I tugged the sleeves of my suit coat, flattening my silk tie. "But I'm warning you: funerals put me in a really bad mood."

At the posh downtown mortuary, I dutifully stood before the casket of my seventy-eight-year-old client, Myron Thurlingate Sr., wondering if they'd ding me for parking in the chaplain's space. I needed to get my head in the ballgame, make it look like I actually cared. This was my biggest advertising account after all—well, my *former* biggest account.

Everyone knew Myron, the "Sultan of Super Scorching Car Buys," the "Prince of the Avenue of Majestic Savings." His popularity was well established, having bought a ton of advertising on our TV station. The "Guru of Slashed Prices and Ridiculous Rate Reductions" had a passion for selling cars and a penchant for playing to the masses. He had a longstanding relationship with the factory in Detroit, was able to run the competition ragged, and made the whole thing work for decades.

And now he was dead.

Sighing quietly—or should I say discreetly—I studied his tastefully powdered face. I hated funerals—or wakes, or memorial services, whatever you want to call them. It wasn't so much the finality as it was the fragility. Standing across the way was Myron Jr. with his longsuffering wife, Doris, and their three kids. Talk about pressure. The entire weight of the dealership had suddenly fallen on his broad, incompetent shoulders.

Lady Luck was smiling down on me the other day when the old man finally got his ticket punched. It could have been me sparring with the fiery auto trader over price points on one ad package or another. Instead, Myron was lambasting his sales manager over financial improprieties in the service department.

Wasn't that how it always rolled with the car tycoon? Didn't it always come down to money? The sales manager had apparently promised a free oil change and lube to a customer whose warranty had already expired. That set off Myron's notorious temper which, according to reports, reached epic proportions. Excoriating the sales manager with a profanity-laced barrage, he coded in a heap atop the imported terrazzo tiles.

Weird things flooded my mind as I studied the play of light across the burnished profile of the luxurious coffin. *Did the old man take the casket for a test drive before deciding to purchase it? Was it a pre-owned? Do they measure usage in terms of mileage or millennia? What kind of warranty comes with it? Was sticker shock what finally sent him over the edge?*

A muffled cough wrested my attention. I drew away from the opulent casket realizing I had overstayed my visit.

"May I ask everyone to please begin finding their seats?" The slender man in the dark suit ushered us toward the neat rows of white chairs on the other side of the ornate funeral parlor. He could only be described as a pleasant-looking vulture. His pastel tie reminded me of Miami, where I'd been a few months back interviewing for a job.

As I padded across the plush, burgundy carpet in my Marco Vittorio loafers, I was suddenly overcome by a great sense of choking emptiness. It wasn't the funeral that was sucking the life out of the room, it was my own feeling of . . . of what? Total abject despondency? What was the point of life anyway? What did it all add up to other than acquiring wealth, status, and power? What was the purpose of constantly chasing rainbows over the next horizon and never being satisfied with what you had? And what did it all mean when, no matter how successful you were, you always ended up like Myron Sr.?

It wasn't the first time in my adult life I'd experienced these feelings—maybe not to the extent that it was happening right now—but it was the first time in memory I couldn't shake the depression by promising myself an imminent round of golf.

My mind raced and took me to dark places. I felt weak and detached, on the verge of passing out.

I had to find a seat. Fast.

Settling into an end chair fairly near the front, I admired the floral arrangement our TV station had sent: a large, showy spray of blue delphinium and white lilies. Was it understated? Not really. But that's what I wanted—something that would stand out in a crowd. Mission accomplished.

I nearly gagged in the stuffy confines and wondered if a little air conditioning was asking too much. Peeling back the starched cuff of my pinpoint Oxford shirt, I checked my Tag Heuer watch. It was already going on two o'clock. Talk about a day shot to low tide. Sighing deeply, I powered down my Nokia 1610 cellular phone while noting the date on the little screen: Tuesday, April 22, 1997.

Adjacent to the dais, a frail spinster slid her bony frame onto a mahogany piano bench. She switched on the light that illuminated a crinkled sheaf of music and struck the first chords of some long-forgotten dirge.

I would never tire of this sight: Belle Murphy, the customer service manager, strutted down the center aisle in all her glory. My eyes locked on her and I was unable to pry them away. There was no other way to put it: this chick was tighter than a hairpin turn. I'd buy a lemon and then file a complaint every day just to be able to speak with her. Somewhere in her forties, fresh from the tanning bed, her frosted blonde hair fell halfway down her bare, sculpted back, and it just got better and better the farther south you went. How she ever poured herself into that scalding little black number was beyond me.

Don't worry, the deal killer himself, her husband Murph, brought up the rear. I didn't even know his full name—just

Murph. The bearded dude was built like a freight train, a stack of ripped body parts jammed into a tailored black suit. A successful repo guy, he had a string of field offices across the Mid-Atlantic region. I would never understand what she saw in him. So what if he was a great father to their four kids? So what if he could bench press a two-car garage? So what if he treated her like a queen? I ask again: what did she see in him?

Once the piano recital ended, things got a little sketchy. One of the family members, Arnie "Crusher" Thurlingate, swooped to the lectern and put on his game face. I knew Arnie from the dealership, where he was in charge of fleet sales. A bruising, prototypical outside linebacker in college, his fierce nickname embodied the tough love he dished out to running backs and tight ends during his illustrious Big Ten career. Word had it he contemplated becoming a preacher after an abbreviated stint in the Canadian Football League, but then switched gears when he realized he could make more money selling cars at the family dealership.

"You know, this is going to be you one day." Arnie laid it on thick. At six-foot-two, he wore black-dyed crocodile boots accented with bright yellow stitching. The immaculate coat sleeves of his hand-tailored Italian suit snapped stiffly and his monogrammed, diamond-studded cufflinks glinted in the overhead lights.

"We don't know the hour or the day when it's all going to end. My dear departed uncle proved that point." In his relentless fervor, Arnie was apparently atoning for all the missed opportunities to preach up a storm in his own church because he had chosen to go for the Benjamins in the car biz instead. "So I want each of you to take stock now. Look deep down inside your souls and ask: what is the current condition of your relationship with the Lord?"

Yeah, yeah . . . *whatever. La-de-da-de-da.* I shut it all out. It was a knee-jerk reaction to such blathering, but one that had served me well over the years. Whenever I encountered someone who started . . . whatchamacallit—proselytizing?; yeah, right: proselytizing—laying their unsolicited spiritual guilt trip on me, I instinctively shut down. Refusing to play into it, I would exercise a heavy dose of plausible deniability. The way I figured, when the gig was up and I went to meet my Maker, the less I knew about this religious bunk the better. If I could convince the Man Upstairs I didn't know the score because I didn't have all the facts in front of me, he would surely understand and give me a pass. This was a busy life; it took a lot of time, energy, and effort to stay on top of things. What was more important? To be a good, upstanding, overworked, debt-ridden corporate citizen, or to be all caught up in spiritual things you couldn't even see? The answer was clear to me: being a workaholic was a far nobler pursuit.

Anyway, why did I want some killjoy raining on my parade? Didn't I deserve everything I worked so hard for? And what did all those do-gooder Christian folk really know about me? They had no right telling me what to believe and not to believe. It was my life and I was going to live it exactly as I saw fit. That was the way God made me, right?

Glancing down at my handout, I realized that Crusher wasn't even on the agenda. So, were you telling me this guy wormed his way into the proceedings to offer up his own two cents—and for exactly what purpose? To traumatize us? To torment us with a backwater Bible rant? Not on your life! And I didn't give a flying you-know-what if he did play Big Ten football.

How much of a delay is this going to cause? Didn't Crush realize I had other clients to service, other places to be, other people to see? Sure, this car dealership was important, but it wasn't the whole nine. I had to get back to the salt mines. The way things were going, I'd probably be at the office until midnight tonight. That was, of course, if this service ever got underway.

I sighed from the depths of my anxiety. Clinging to my sanity, I asked what it all meant and whether any of it really mattered. Where was I headed in such a hurry?

Palms sweating, I shifted in my seat. This pathetic exercise in futility was killing me—but that was the least of my problems.

I didn't know it at the time, but in the next few minutes my life was going to inexplicably, inexorably, and unalterably change.

CHAPTER TWO

And Now a Word from Our Sponsor

Arnie, the "Crusher," turned solemnly to the attendees. "Does everyone know what a cat-o'-nine-tails is?" Breathing heavily, he scanned the room. "Show of hands. Don't stand on ceremony. Get 'em up for all to see."

Dutifully, hands were raised—including, reluctantly, mine. My intrigue grew with each passing second. Inching forward, I studied the hulking man pacing the carpeted platform.

Arnie raked thick fingers through his blond hair. "Cat-o'-nine-tails. I'm talking one mean, sick weapon. Three-foot leather strips knotted into a handle built to wreak havoc on a victim's body." He pretended to wield an implement in vicious slow-motion blows. "But I'll go one step further: the ones used by the Romans had bits of shells and metal scraps and sharp rocks and other lethal stuff tied to the ends of the straps. Do you know what happened when they struck flesh? Can you even begin to comprehend the brutality when those debilitating atrocities rained down on the defenseless peasant man, Jesus Christ?"

I blinked, breathing slowly. Admittedly, Arnie was a formidable pitchman. A charismatic force, he held the audience spellbound while taking advantage of every moment of borrowed pulpit time.

"Do you know the pain, the horror, of a savage beating like this? Do you know how much blood you lose and the shock you go into at the hands of these maniacal executioners?" Head down, face twisted, Crusher slowly paced the altar.

I didn't know if I should even be looking at the former football star. He appeared in so much private agony, as if I were somehow intruding in his gut-wrenching introspection.

Arnie gestured painfully, his face ashen, his knuckles white as he gripped the microphone. "So I want you to see, I want you to feel what this meek, mild-mannered man put himself through for me and you. The ends of the whip cut through him like hooks, slicing his skin all the way to the bone. Arteries, veins, nerves—you name it—were ripped out, exposed to the air, along with muscle and sinew. This poor man was literally torn inside out on the flogging post. Two Roman soldiers, one on each side of him—and oh, by the way, these weren't your typical garden-variety shrinking violets. These were battle-hardened warriors trained to kill. It excited them to no end when they were splattered with the victim's blood."

I swallowed thickly. The whole episode of Christ's death was being brought home like never before. What if Crush was right? What if this was how it had actually gone down?

"They marched him up a mountain and splayed him face up on the cross, then prepared to drive the nails home." Crusher breathed heavily, extending an arm. "Do you know what it feels like to have nine-inch spikes driven into your wrists? You think these were trained surgeons mindful of his nerve endings? You think they gave him anything to deaden the pain? You think there were dutiful nurses taking his pulse every five minutes to make sure he was maintaining? Yeah, right. Dream on."

I studied Arnie's sweaty face. He was fired up enough to start a fight.

Struggling to maintain his composure, Arnie continued. "You have brutal mongrels whose sole purpose in life was inflicting pain on their fellow man. Only this was not their fellow man. He was a whole lot more. This was the God of the universe who was now reduced to a sack of hamburger meat. You think those paintings of Christ losing only a couple drops of blood are accurate? Huh? Think again. Those are gross distortions. We're talking about a bloody heap of mutilated flesh basting in its own sweat and blistered arteries, mocked by the splinters of the jagged cross digging into the gaping lacerations inflicted by the bloodlust of a totally lost, depraved, and craven generation!"

I glanced around. People were riveted to the gruesome reality of Crusher's haunting, heartfelt oratory.

Arnie leaned forward at the podium. "And to think . . . he subjected himself to all this knowing what was coming. It was like walking through a tunnel toward a blinding light, only the blinding light was attached to a freight train. Jesus knew it all along, but it was his mission to save humanity. And I ask you, how many people—don't forget, he came for all of us . . . how many people really know what he did? Or worse, how many even care? Do I have a witness?"

"Amen!" shouted someone from the parts department.

I thought about all the paintings I'd seen of Christ. I didn't remember many. But I had to admit, I'd never, to my recollection, seen a painting of the Messiah as messed up as Crusher made him out to be. In fact, I didn't even know about this scourging thing. I just thought Jesus ended up on the cross as a political dissident, a nice enough guy unfortunately on the wrong side of the law. And that was the end of it. But if there was more to this story, and there apparently was, why did he subject himself to all that torture?

Arnie closed his eyes. "And as Jesus . . . Son of God . . . Lord of lords and King of kings, the most important person to walk the face of the earth . . . as his lungs filled with fluids on that cross, as his mother looked on in abject terror, as our Lord and Savior gasped for air, as soldiers cast lots for his clothes in fulfillment of prophecy . . . he took on the sins of the world now and forever-more." Crusher nodded stoically. "Jesus Christ, the perfect man, born in a cattle trough to a virgin, teenage peasant girl, raised as a Jewish carpenter, died as a hero for me and you, and rose from the grave to defeat disease and death for all eternity. As God's precious Son, he sacrificed his life and bore the world's sin on his back so we would be spared."

It was too much to process. If they ever taught this in Sunday school, I must not have been paying attention.

"On the unrelenting cross, Jesus became a thief, an adulterer, a murderer, a liar, a cheat, a womanizer—and worse!" Crusher counted on his fingers. "He took the hit for us—so me and you wouldn't have to suffer the eternal consequences of our sins."

The chaplain in charge paused along the far aisle on his way toward the dais.

Arnie turned up the heat. "Do you know what that brutal act on the cross signified?" He zeroed in on me with hawklike eyes. "Love. Pure, unadulterated love." He reared back. "God is love, friends. He loves us with an unfiltered, unconditional, unbiased, undying love that is so matchless and so powerful we are incapa-ble of fully comprehending its dimensions." He gestured grandly. "The purest form of gold, the most rarified silver, the clearest cut of a diamond can't compare with the potency of the love God has for us. Psalm 136:26 says this: 'Give thanks to the God of Heaven; his love endures forever.'"

I didn't exactly tune Arnie out, but that didn't mean I agreed with him. I had definitely never felt the all-encompassing love he raved about. I was a normal guy who fought for what was mine; sometimes I got it right, sometimes I didn't. Love had no place in the equation.

Arnie squared his shoulders. "Here's the whole enchilada: John 3:16 says—you know, the one you always see at sporting events—'For God so loved the world that he gave his one and only Son, that whoever believes in him shall not perish but have eternal life.'" Nodding reverently, he scanned the room.

I glanced around. Most in attendance were attentive if not mesmerized.

Arnie continued to passionately quote Scripture. "First John 4:7: 'Dear friends, let us love one another, for love comes from God. Everyone who loves has been born of God and knows God.' Psalm 36:7: 'How priceless is your unifying love, O God! People take refuge in the shadow of your wings.' Jude 1:21: 'Keep yourselves in God's love, as you wait for the true mercy of our Lord Jesus Christ to bring you to eternal life.'" Arnie leaned forward with barely a whisper. "The question is, do we love God back with the same level of intensity as he loves us?"

All this talk about love made me uncomfortable. Quite possibly, I was incapable of loving others—and that included loving myself. Maybe that's why I had never married. I tried shutting out the rhetoric, but the message kept seeping through the cracks.

Crusher massaged the burnished edge of the mahogany pulpit. As he switched the microphone to his left hand, I realized he was staring at me again. Was this his twisted version of a Las Vegas floor show? Was he going to call me up to the stage as a willing—or unwilling—shill? I slumped in my seat wondering how many eyes were on me and just wishing this would all go away.

"We share the same human condition, you know." Arnie gripped the mic and turned his attention elsewhere. He continued in a measured tone. "Blaise Pascal, the Greek physicist, claimed we all have a vacuum in our souls that only God can fill. The theologian Saint Augustine said our hearts will always be restless until we find our rest in God. The biggest minds throughout history talk about a torment, a sorrow that rules our lives no matter how upbeat we try to appear on the outside."

Crush just scored a direct hit: that restless, empty feeling he spoke about was exactly what I had experienced a few minutes earlier. I felt anxious and alone, inadequate and disconnected. I glanced around, wondering if others were feeling it too.

I grew more attentive as Arnie continued: "We all feel guilt for things we've done in the past. Another word for guilt is sin. None of us is without sin. I don't care who you think you are, how good you think you are, none of us is blameless, including Mother Teresa. None of us—except Jesus Christ. Have you thanked him today for dying on the cross and rising from the dead so you can have everlasting life? He's here right now, just waiting for you to cry out to him."

Arnie dabbed his forehead. "Saints, listen up. Do you think you can secure your own eternal salvation? Congratulations, by the way, if you can. It would be the same thing as creating a hydrogen atom from scratch or manufacturing a cherry blossom from a tree branch. How's that working out for you?"

I muffled a vexed sigh. Of course that stuff was impossible. What was he driving at?

Arnie shifted into full preacher mode: "We can't engineer our own salvation no matter how hard we try. There's only one solution: the answer supplied by Jesus Christ on the cross. He came out of Heaven, assumed the form of a lowly peasant man, and proceeded to take the weight of the world's sins—yes, my sins and your sins—on his pulverized back. He bore the brunt of

God's hatred of sin so that we will be spared. Three days later, he shattered death by rising from the grave."

The imposing speaker piled it on. "But if you don't need Jesus, if you really believe you can do it on your own . . . then I'm here to tell you, meeting God will be like stumbling into the Supreme Court without a lawyer, like digging a pit two miles deep with a teaspoon. Oh sure, you say, you're a good person. But no matter how much we give to charity, no matter how many generous deeds we do, unless our hearts are right with God, we are not prepared to go to Heaven. And the only way we can get right with God is to confess our sins, genuinely work at repenting of what is offensive to him, and welcome Jesus into our lives as the one—the only one—who will bridge the chasm that sin has created between God and us."

I started shutting down. Crush had managed to sweep me off my feet for a few provocative minutes, but now he'd exposed himself as a fraud. The bookends of his specious argument had just collapsed, as was always the case with these self-righteous Bible-bangers. What gave him the right to think that the faith he professed somehow provided a monopoly on getting into Heaven?

Crusher lowered his voice. "God gave us the blueprint for life with the Ten Commandments. Most people say, 'These don't apply to me. I'm not a murderer.' But what does your heart say? That's what God is interested in, the condition of your heart. What if you're cut off in traffic and swear you're going to kill the person who did it? Haven't you become a murderer in God's eyes? The thought is certainly there. The only reason you don't follow through is because you don't want to get caught and have to pay the penalty."

I thought about all the times people had cut me off in traffic. As much as I tried to deny it, I had to admit: I'd fantasized about yanking dudes—even old farts—out of their cars and whupping their butts until they figured out how to drive better. And yes, I'd thought about doing even worse things. I wondered what people thought about me when I unknowingly cut them off in traffic.

Beads of sweat glistened on Crusher's sculpted forehead. "Let's talk about death. It's going to happen to everyone. It's only a matter of time. So I ask you: are you ready to meet God? You're one heartbeat away from eternity. What will you have to say for yourself? I'm telling you: don't miss Heaven by eighteen inches—the eighteen inches between your head and your heart. You can have all the book knowledge in the world, but that doesn't amount to a hill of beans. What counts is your heart. You can donate millions to charity, but it's totally for nothing if you snub God in the process. He wants you, he wants all of you. He doesn't care one iota about your money. All he wants is your love and adoration."

"Preach, Crush!" squealed a petite blonde from Accounts Receivable.

Crusher glanced my way again. I tried hiding my resentment, but I'm sure he saw right through me. He took a deep breath. "If you're sitting there thinking you've got it made in the shade, think again: Are you arrogant? Are you quick to anger? Have you failed to forgive someone who did you wrong? Are you prone to greed? Are you jealous, lustful, or deceitful? Are you a gossip, a slanderer? Are you an idolater? Are you judgmental? Are you one or more of the above or a little of everything? Any one of them can jump out and bite you when you least expect it. Are you proud? Are you proud of all your accomplishments? Are you too comfortable with your bank account? How will you explain yourself once all is said and done? As we all know . . . you're not such a bad person. Of course not. None of us are. Sure, we all have our faults. But for the most part, we're not armed robbers. And even if we were, God can forgive that—if we repent and put it all at the base of the cross. Remember, Jesus died for armed robbers the same as he died for me and you."

Why did he have to keep staring at me? Did I look like an armed robber? Surely that's what everyone was thinking now. I glanced away, hoping he would follow suit.

"God is perfect. He doesn't make mistakes. There's a reason you are who you are—God has a plan for you, whether you're willing to admit it or not." Arnie paced with his head down. "But you say: 'I am lonely, out of sorts, fatigued, stressed, suffering from a broken relationship, experiencing darkness from within.' Maybe you're into drugs, alcohol, pornography. None of that is impossible for God to overcome. God can wipe all that out of your life faster than you can spit. He can replace all of that debauchery with the peace of still, living waters."

I wanted to break out in applause when the regular pastor signaled a wrap to Arnie's segment. *Good.* It appeared the cavalry was ready to take over. Crusher's freewheeling ruminations were gratefully coming to a close.

Crusher switched on the afterburners. "Do you think you're in the clear just because you don't openly hate and despise God? You think that gives you some kind of golden hall pass? Think again. Maybe you don't reject God outright, but instead you just ignore him and refuse to make him part of your life. In other words, you just wish he'd go away. Millions of people are okay with that. But I'm here to tell you, it doesn't work that way. God demands a yes or no answer; there's no middle ground. You're either all the way with him or all the way against him. So please, don't think you're scoring points in the court of public opinion by disavowing Christ as your Lord and Savior. Don't kick God to the curb in the name of tolerance. No matter how upstanding your intentions, your actions speak volumes. God will honor your desire to be apart from him and give you exactly what you want—for all eternity. And that, dear friends, by any other name, is Hell."

Arnie moved forward as the chaplain stepped to the dais behind him. "But it doesn't have to be that way. We are all going to have a meeting with God, face to face, even those who have rejected him. Don't be left standing on the dock as the doors of the ark close. You feel the first raindrops and something in the back of your mind wonders if you made the right choice staying behind—and you don't even have an umbrella." Crusher nodded with intensity. "Don't let that happen to you. You can change the course of your life for all eternity this very instant. All you need is to confess your sins to the Almighty. That's why he gave us free will to begin with."

On that merry note I peeked at my watch. This agonizing affair had run its course. Arnie had been entertaining while it lasted, but it was now time to start thinking about the real world. I just hoped the minister in charge didn't run long. I wondered about crosstown traffic at this hour and whether I should take surface streets to reach the mayor's office on time.

But Crusher wasn't finished. And I guess, when it came right down to it, neither was God. In the next breath, the muscle-bound orator shattered my apathy, exposed the coldness of my heart, and buzz-sawed my cynicism.

I realized my life would never be the same from this moment on.

"We're leaving this existence with only one thing: our relationship with God, Creator of the universe, Maker of Heaven and Earth. And when we go to stand before him, naked to the heavenly host, our souls stripped to the bare essence—then, at that seminal point in our eternal history, what are we going to say for ourselves? It doesn't matter that you were born into a loving Christian household. It doesn't matter that you go to church twice a year. It all comes down to your heart. Where's your heart?

This is a heart condition. God knows your heart—but wants to hear it from *you.*"

And then it happened.

For the first time in my life, I realized I hadn't been very nice to God. In fact, I'd been a miserable SOB, a selfish, self-serving, narrow-minded, arrogant boob. What had God ever done to deserve my lousy attitude? I was suddenly confronted with the prospect of life after death. Was I really that confident about what will happen the second after I die?

"How is the spiritual condition of your heart today?" Crusher nodded toward the back of the room. "Do you mock God and shake your fist at him? Do you ignore him and hope he goes away? It doesn't matter if you hate God with a passion or you just don't acknowledge him. Either way, you show you want nothing to do with him. And being a loving God, he will give you everything you want. So I ask you. Would you prefer to spend an eternity *with* God, or one apart from him? Do you want all the love, hope, and infinite peace of a life everlasting with the Creator of Heaven and Earth, the Maker of an ever-expanding universe? Or do you want an eternity of constant mayhem, disease, and destruction apart from him? It's the same as enjoying the best day of your life forever and ever—or spending the rest of eternity in a never-ending day that gets worse and worse with each passing minute. And by the way: forget about sleep in Hell. It doesn't exist."

Gasping, I didn't know what was happening. I broke into a cold sweat. The world began spinning in slow motion. Crusher was speaking directly to me. I was a captive audience of one.

The capper came when I saw Belle Murphy's subtle gesture. She was definitely into this, but not making a big show of it. It was like this whole scene was second nature to her, like she'd been at it a long time. I realized if this stuff was good enough for Belle, it was good enough for me.

Whatever "it" was, I wanted to know more about it. And I wasn't going to stop until I'd found it.

Arnie spoke in a rasp, barely more than a whisper. "So I ask you. If your heart stops beating this very instant and you are released into eternity . . . and you're standing before God and he asks, 'Why should I let you into my perfect Heaven?' what will you say? That you're a good person who can stand on your own without Christ? Or will you admit to being a broken sinner, totally irredeemable without the precious blood of Jesus, blood shed freely on the cross for me and you? Remember, Jesus died for our sins and rose from the grave to bridge the chasm between God and our fallen state. Are you walking that bridge with Jesus? Or will you face God in the court of justice without the greatest lawyer in all creation by your side?"

I remained perfectly still.

When Crusher zoned in on me, he saw mind-numbing confusion.

My first instinct was to run.

But a deeper instinct said it was too late for that.

CHAPTER THREE

But Wait, There's More

Bam! I burst through the double doors in back of the funeral parlor. It was like breaking out of the stadium tunnel for the biggest game of my career, like heading out of high school for the very last time. I was on a mission: to get my head screwed back on right following Arnie's nutzoid sermon.

I made a beeline for the imposing bruiser. He stood beside the open trunk of his mint condition 1964 Lincoln Continental, waiting to queue up with the rest of the procession headed to the midtown cemetery. "Crush, I need a word with you, man!"

Arnie flashed that trademark frat smile. As a straight-up stud coming out of the defensive trenches of the Big Ten, he could hold court just about anywhere. "Brother Vance Chelan! Glad to see you were in attendance today, and that you made yourself so . . . visible." He wiped the back of his sweaty neck with a small white golf towel. "It was a fitting sendoff for the 'Prince of Price Gougers,' don't you think?"

I switched gears in deference to the prone guest of honor and regurgitated the canned speech I had rehearsed in the event cameras were present: "Myron Thurlingate Sr. was a proud man. He was true to the American dream, building his business out of literally nothing. We all can learn a thing or two about marketing one's product and promoting one's ideals from this icon of the community."

"Well said," Arnie observed. "Interesting you would laud him for being a proud man."

"So much for the sound bite." I moved closer, looking over my shoulder to make sure we wouldn't be interrupted. "I've got a question."

"And I have an answer." He dabbed his tanned, chiseled face, then tossed the towel beside his expensive tour golf bag. Crusher played to a three handicap, way out of my league.

"Did you lay a spell or something on me back there?" I asked.

"A spell?" He looked at me rather oddly, like he'd just tasted week-old sushi. "What the Sam Hill are you talking about?"

"I don't know. Ever since you said we're all gonna die one day, I've started feeling kind of weird, like I'm not myself, like I got something running around inside of me." I was frustrated that I couldn't articulate my feelings. "It's like I need a drink, you know? But realize it would only make things worse."

He closed the trunk and drew a pair of sunglasses from the vest pocket of his expensive suit coat. Obnoxiously aloof, he inspected the eyewear at arm's length. "Yeah, it was pretty intense in there, wasn't it?" He scraped lint and blew on the lens. "It's no wonder you feel that way. You're still basking in the glow of the Holy Spirit." He broke into a huge grin. "I know I still am. Praise God!"

"There you go, Crush, talking in circles again." Exasperated, I put hands on my hips. "It all sounds like hocus-pocus to me. Are you sure you didn't do something to me in there? Hypnotize me maybe?"

I was ill-prepared for Arnie's reaction. He stopped messing with his shades and focused on me like a laser. "Vance, level with me. When I tell you the Holy Spirit is present, you know what I'm talking about, right?" His green, searching eyes locked on mine, his passion at a fever pitch.

"Dude, I don't know. It sounds to me like you're talking about ghost stuff."

"Of course I'm talking about ghost stuff! The *Holy Ghost*, to be precise." His eyes drilled mine with that hawklike intensity. "So let's take this from the top. You're a believer, right? I mean, you certainly gave that impression back there."

Arnie was calling me out in a big way, but he wasn't trying to purposely belittle me. I gave him a blank stare, a regular deer-in-the-headlights look. I swallowed thickly, fighting for equal footing. "Sure I am." My mind raced; I was totally out of my element. I took a wild guess, throwing out anything that might stick. "I've been a Christian all my life."

"That's not what I asked." He grew more adamant, his eyes seeming to drill deeper. "I asked if you were a believer."

I looked at him dumbly. "What's the difference?"

He eased up on the throttle. "Listen, bud. I'm going to need a little more to go on. What exactly happened to make you think I hypnotized you?"

"Well." I drew up and looked around. "Like I was saying, it began when you brought up the bit about everyone kicking the bucket."

Perplexed, Arnie narrowed his gaze. "I'm not getting this. We just got done with a funeral. Are you implying that you never considered the fact you are going to die one day? I know people don't like thinking about it, but it's not like you're being confronted with the prospect for the very first time." He bobbed his neck. "Am I right?"

"Yeah, yeah. I'm cool with all that. It's what happens afterwards." I gestured feebly. "You know—the meeting you were talking about. The one with, uh, you know . . . God."

"I see," Arnie said. "I take it you never gave much thought to what happens when the lights go out." He nodded. "It's the most important meeting of this life—or any life." He grew solemn. "Praise the Lord we're talking like this while there's still time left on the shot clock."

"Yeah." I chuckled nervously. "I guess that's what it all comes down to. I've gone my entire life knowing there was a God, but not wanting anything to do with him."

"And all that's about to change." Crusher smiled exuberantly. "He's just waiting to welcome you into the kingdom with open arms."

"Not so fast," I said. "Why would he want anything to do with me?"

"Because he loves you! He loves you with a love beyond belief."

"Well, I want to give him more credit than that," I said. "You told us back inside that God knows everything. If that's true, and I don't have a reason to doubt you, then he knows what a complete jerk I am and will steer clear of me—from now 'til the cows come home."

"Whoa, whoa, whoa, partner. Let's back up the truck a minute." Arnie stiffened, spreading his legs to emphasize the point. "The takeaway is this: yes, God loves us all with an incredible love beyond all reason and rationale. But, being a just God, he hates our sins with the same intensity. So we're at loggerheads—literally at the crossroads. What are we going to do with this reality? That's why he sent Jesus. So we can have a Savior. The Son of God performed the perfect sacrifice on the cross to atone for our sins so we wouldn't have to incur the wrath of the Father which, needless to say, none of us would walk away from."

"Is that supposed to make me feel better?" I asked, squinting at him. "I'm sure that God, knowing what he knows about me, can't wait to get his hands on me."

"Don't buy into those lies, Vance." Arnie made a pained face. "It's the evil one trying to tear you down."

"What's the big deal?" I took a deep breath. "See, I never looked at God the way you describe him. I always thought he was an ogre. Not quite a monster . . . but someone who was standing around waiting to blowtorch me for the slightest mistake." I shrugged. "He's impossible to please. So why even bother?"

Arnie brightened. "Brother, don't you see? You've been blinded all these years as to the true nature of God. But now the scales are falling away. Do you know how exciting this is? Do you know how your life is about to change—for the better? And, may I add, for all eternity?" Arnie put his hand firmly on my shoulder.

I hit the brakes before Crush drove me over the edge of the ecumenical cliff. "Whoa, pal. Who said anything about wanting to change?"

"What are you saying?" Crusher bowed his neck. "You want to maintain the status quo? You want to continue cozying up to emptiness, loneliness . . . despair—not to mention mediocrity?"

I ignored the fact Crusher had just called me mediocre. "How can I relate to somebody—or something—that doesn't understand me?" I asked.

"What do you mean? *Who* doesn't understand you?" Arnie's eyes darted. "Are you talking about God?"

"Of course. God. He's . . . no offense. He doesn't have it together. He's a simpleton."

"A simpleton, huh?" Arnie mulled the concept with a degree of amusement. "I see. I may need some convincing of that."

I waved him off. "Come on, man. Are you kidding me? God doesn't understand what I go through in a normal day. How could he? The contracts, the stuff I gotta deal with on a min-

ute-by-minute basis. I gotta babysit the FCC for crying out loud."
I gestured. "You know the score, Crush. It's the same with you
in fleets. All the regulations you gotta wade through, plus the
numbers crunching. How do you expect God to keep up with all
that? And you know he doesn't have a clue about the women in
my life. So I just have to give him his space and try to keep him
from stepping on my toes. Just so long as he stays in his box with
all the church people, everything's copacetic."

Arnie nodded and straightened up. "Is that it? Are you
finished?"

"Yeah, pretty much." I ran through a quick checklist in my
head. "I could go on probably a couple more minutes, but that's—
you know, that's pretty much the gist of it."

"Okay, I think I see." Crusher took a big breath. "Let me address a couple of your firmly held beliefs." He leaned into me
heatedly. "First, the clueless guy you're talking about is the God
of the universe. He is the God of order, whose perfect mathemat-
ical equation for life equals infinity. He doesn't need a wristwatch
because he's figured a way to make this whole thing work outside of time. The doddering fool you're talking about built every
last cell belonging to you in your mama's womb billions of years
before you were born. He knows your deepest, most intimate
needs. And he hungers for the day you will acknowledge him and
tell him you love him. That's all he's waiting for. And by the way,
if you think God doesn't fully understand the women you run
with, then answer me this: who built them all in the first place?"

Crusher turned to watch the coffin being loaded into the
hearse. "Even though our life as we know it is temporary . . . "
He paused as the rear door to the long, shiny vehicle was closed.
" . . . God still built us to have eternal fellowship with him long
after we're gone from this earth. And it can start right now if we
let it."

"Are you all set, Mr. Thurlingate?" One of the dark-suited associates called from across the parking lot as cars began rolling into position behind the hearse.

Arnie waved to the man. "All set." He turned to me. "Are you coming to the gravesite?"

"Nah, that's okay. I need to hit it."

"Okay. But before you go, let's say the Sinner's Prayer. Let's get you headed in the right direction. You know. Confess your sins and give your life over to Jesus."

I stepped back. "That's okay. I think you've given me enough to chew on for one day."

"Nice try, Vance." The big man applied more pressure, crowding me against the side of the Lincoln. "You're gonna say the Sinner's Prayer and confess your sins."

I wondered if these were the same tactics he employed when closing a fleet buy. Glancing around, I saw more people filing into the parking lot, heading for their cars. "Easy, man," I said. "I don't want anyone to hear."

"Who cares? This is a celebration!"

"A celebration?" I gagged. "It's a *funeral!*"

"Let the dead bury the dead." Crusher seethed. "Read about it. It's all in the Bible. This is about you coming alive!"

"Coming alive? What are you talking about?"

"It's about you accepting his invitation. You know, Jesus knocks, but there's no handle on the outside of the door. We all have to open the door from the inside—just like *you're* getting ready to do right now. And once you do it, brother, once you do it, your life will never be the same. You'll be living it for all eternity instead of living for the cheap thrills of the moment. You're about to enter into the adventure of a lifetime that will last throughout all eternity. Hallelujah, Vance!"

"But in the meantime," I blurted, "I've got a meeting at the mayor's office." My eyes darted as I scoped out an escape route.

"A meeting at the mayor's office, is that so?" Crusher chided. "You've got a meeting at *God's* office!" He stood me up straighter, smoothing my lapels. "Tell me something. Between God and the mayor, who's more powerful?"

"Well, since the mayor's a woman, I'd probably say her."

"Hah hah hah. Very funny." Crusher's chuckle was dangerously disingenuous. "So you incorporate blasphemy into your little standup routine. Does that make you feel like the biggest squirrel on the nut pile? Huh?"

I recoiled in horror. *Is this guy crazy? Or is it me going insane?*

In the raw silence I felt a majestic presence. Turning slowly, I looked into the raging beauty of Belle Murphy. I thought my heart was going to dislodge its moorings and plunge into my gut. My knees shook harder than the prospect of a four-foot putt. When she tenderly put her hand on my arm I was packing my bags for Heaven.

"Hey, Vance."

I swallowed. "Belle—I . . . I'm so sorry about the loss here. The loss of your boss, I mean." I glanced at Arnie. "Listen to me. I'm a rhyming fool."

Arnie shook his head. "No, you're just a fool."

Belle continued, oblivious. "We will all miss our dear, beloved leader, that's for certain." She flashed one of the sweetest smiles I'd ever seen. "I just wanted to make sure you knew how much he looked up to you."

"What?" I drew a total blank. "Who looked up to me?"

"Myron Sr., of course," Crusher interjected.

"Myron Sr.?" I said. "I always thought me and him were mortal enemies. At least when it came to negotiating ad buys."

"Oh no, you misread it altogether," Belle said, nodding eagerly. "In fact, he used you as a role model. During sales meetings he would tell us we needed to be more like you, willing to stand up for what we believed in and refusing to back down."

"What?" I couldn't believe what I was hearing. "Myron Sr.?"

"He always claimed that, in the end, you wanted what was best for the dealership," Belle said, her smile radiating with reassurance.

I was suddenly bursting with so much pride I could barely contain myself. Belle Murphy was giving me the time of day—wonder of wonders—and even the intimidating Crusher was regarding me with a modicum of respect.

Crusher sighed. "Don't get a swelled head. But some of what he said about you sank in. It made us more attuned to the customer's needs—though we still wanted to kill you."

"Man, who knew? I never woulda guessed it in a million years." I shook my head slowly.

"Well, don't be a stranger around the dealership," Belle said. "Little Myron will need you more than he can ever imagine. I know you'll play a major part in this new season of his life."

"Oh, you bet I will. You got it!" I had rarely been so hyped. When Belle hugged me I thought I was going to melt into the steamy pavement.

Crusher and I watched Belle's sensuous departure. "You know what kind of shape that woman was in before she accepted Christ in her life?" The muscular man nodded respectfully.

"No." I flashed a totally blank stare.

"The difference between night and day." Crusher spoke admiringly. "Murph's the one who brought her to the doorstep. He presented the Gospel and got her off that one-way party train to Hell."

"Do you really have to go there with Hell?" I stopped gazing at Belle and turned back to Arnie. "Everyone knows there's no Hell."

"You want to separate yourself from God's love for six seconds and see if you're whistling the same tune?" He dug keys out of

wrap your head around the Bible. It's the most important play-book of all. Let the Word of God seep into your every pore. It's the most powerful tool of transformation in existence." His grip tightened. "Plus you'll need a study guide to fill in the blanks. And prayer! I want you down on your knees tonight. You hear me?"

I had to keep up with the car because Crush had started rolling forward and he wasn't letting go of me. "Whatever!" I gasped.

"Agreed?" he shouted. "And make sure the Word is preached at your house of worship on Sunday! Make it worth your while!"

"Okay, okay!" As he let go of me, I barely missed caterwauling into a Honda Civic. I righted myself, blinking, checking my suit coat for rips and tears, amazed all the buttons were still intact.

What was happening to me? If this was the onramp to Heaven, maybe I needed a set of training wheels first.

Crusher rolled on, honking the horn, his gold Rolex glistening in the late afternoon sun. He jerked his hand out the window and pointed to the blue sky that was framed by the towering corridor of downtown buildings.

"Glory be to God in the highest!" he shouted. "All glory be to God!"

CHAPTER FOUR

POTHOLES IN PARADISE

I stopped at the light at the intersection of Fourth and Water. Eighty-five feet above, smiling down pristinely from one of the region's premium billboard sites, was the fabulous "Tax Angel" herself, Verona Shrevesworth. All she lacked was an airbrushed halo.

This was Exhibit A for why you should not become romantically involved with your tax accountant—or I guess with anyone, for that matter. After Arnie's admonition only a little while earlier, I was now painfully aware that God did not smile on sexual escapades with the same degree of felicity that was shown by the Tax Angel from her billboard perch. This was not some fling from the past, either. To put it in perspective, today's date was April 22. Her time of the year ended on April 15. You do the math.

Hey, take it easy on me! How did I know she was going to explode out of the 1040 gate like a Triple Crown hotfoot?

It was no secret: Verona was not discriminating about those with whom she shared the elation of post-filing hoopla. I just didn't see how she turned it on and off like that. We'd met at a party last Halloween. She was big into astrology, fascinated with numerology, which kind of fit her profession; I learned early on not to make light of her avocation.

Until now she had been my ace out of the bullpen on those nights when the starting lineup grew thin. Verona had no expectations of ever rising above second string status, which was fine with both of us and made her rather refreshing. There was something to be said for spending time with someone when the pressure cooker was turned low.

Everything had been fine until right before the holidays. Then, as the weather started getting colder and December seeped into January, she started getting more and more . . . how should I say? *Frigid.* Maybe our relationship had run its course; so be it. Maybe she had found another guy. More power to her. Be it bizarre reclusiveness or damnable depression, she grew more and more inward until just before Valentine's Day, when I stopped hearing from her altogether. Then fast-forward to last week. Tax season was over and the spigots had been unleashed like nobody's business.

But things were going to have to change mightily with Verona following Arnie's fire and brimstone sermon. According to Arnie, Verona and her tax loopholes would be hitting the bricks. I was still smoldering over the word he'd used: *fornication.* He made it sound like a clinical aberration or a punishable offense. Good luck with enforcing that. Nobody was going to change my ways. But why did I have this feeling? Was it guilt? When had I ever felt guilty about anything?

I gripped the steering wheel, ready to blow through the red light just so I wouldn't be under Verona's spell anymore. Why had I gone to that stupid funeral anyway, and why had Crusher inserted himself so aggressively in promoting his sick, twisted beliefs?

That wasn't the worst of it: there was a glaring issue of accountability. According to Crusher, we were supposed to refrain from being deceitful. Cue the elephant in the room. I had unknowingly become a tax cheat. Okay, okay . . . so maybe it wasn't unknowingly—but it hadn't started out that way. Honest!

For the last two years, during my spare time and weekends, I'd been running a broadcast consulting business on the side. I had a rather impressive clientele of television stations coast to coast. My specialties included new business development, political ad spending, and killer promos.

A lot of my compensation came in the way of travel perks and other stuff they could pawn off on me via trade incentives. Lately, though, there was a growing number of straight cash deals. I neglected to report any of these activities when tax time rolled around, even though my ancillary revenue had been rising steadily year over year. If Verona got even the slightest whiff I was underreporting income, she'd march me straight to Treasury.

Under this new set of guidelines, I had to know where God stood every step of the way. If Verona would pitch a fit over my withholding shortfall, how would God react? According to Arnie, Verona—being a mere mortal—had no knowledge of my end around with the IRS, whereas God knew . . . well, *everything*!

My palms were sweaty on the steering wheel. Horns honked as motorists let me know it was time to get a move on. What happened; did I pass out at the light? Maybe it was the two junior bison burgers I pounded down on my way to the funeral. Maybe this was all a bad dream.

If this wasn't a bad dream, it sure was turning into a scary day. It was about to get worse.

I arrived at City Hall five minutes early, which was totally out of character. In the past I would have driven around another ten minutes yammering on the phone just so I could come in late and make myself look important. Today I was so disoriented and out of sorts I found myself looking to the company of others for solace and support even though they were members of competing media and not at all disposed to providing warm and fuzzy shoulders to cry on.

The fifteen-person committee was handpicked by Mayor Myrna Klawzer. We met once a month to advise on issues facing the community and how we in the media could champion a climate of solidarity and civic pride. This had been going on the better part of three years, and I couldn't really comment on its effectiveness. I just looked at it as one more way to elevate me and my TV station above the competition.

I usually sat beside Kenzie Cayman, who represented half the morning drive team at the city's number one FM rocker. The game plan was to worm my way into her heart and score a date. It had been a long time coming, and I had always been told that good things took time. But unlike fine wine, this relationship didn't seem to be improving with age.

Instead of sitting beside Kenzie this afternoon, I took a seat next to Teddy Grearson, a reporter for the local newspaper who had written an article criticizing my decision to air sitcoms instead of local newscasts. That had been a well thought-out plan on my part; it was working in other markets and already paying dividends for us. My main job was turning a profit for ownership. But you really didn't want to highlight significant paydays in the paper, particularly when it came to an emotional flashpoint like the local news. Teddy had escalated the rhetoric, wildly misquoting me and portraying me as a money-grubbing buffoon.

I got a rise out of Teddy—and everyone else—when I slid in beside him. This suddenly became the hot topic of the meeting. Even Mayor Klawzer warmed to the prospects of a fight.

"Teddy, how goes it?" I said coldly.

The slender young man with the bushy black beard and thick-framed eyeglasses stiffened. "Vance . . . " He metered me as you would a deadly snake—with good reason.

I didn't even know why I had gravitated to the empty seat. It must have had something to do with Crusher's afternoon oratory. Everything revolved around that cork-bending sermon. My whole life had changed because of it. He had spoken about the ills of harboring bad thoughts and storing up anger. If I was nice to Teddy, maybe he'd go easy on me next time. So I gave it a try.

"I saw your article on the drawbacks of redistricting," I said as politely as possible, even though it was killing me. "It was obviously well researched. You made a lot of good points."

"Really? You actually read?" He seemed genuinely impressed. "I mean, I thought you guys in TV were . . . uh . . . not that big on literacy, being on the electronic side of things."

"Well, we still have to read the instruction manuals that come with all those fancy gadgets, you know." I listened to myself speak. I was trying to make a joke but came off sounding serious. This wasn't even my usual inflection. If this were a normal day I would have sat across the table from Teddy and stared daggers at him the whole meeting. *What is with this encouragement I'm giving him? Don't I know he's the enemy?*

"Let's get started, shall we?" Myrna said. "Vance, I'm glad you made it on time today."

No one paid attention to the mayor singling me out. They were so used to me getting the lion's share of attention that it just came off as business as usual. Across the way, Kenzie made goo-goo eyes at me. *What is that all about? The one afternoon I don't sit beside her, and* now *she's coming onto me? Chicks!* Who in their right mind can figure them out? Not me, that was for sure. After Arnie's no-nonsense talk this afternoon, count me out. A certified *fornicator*, I no longer had the energy to pursue this endless herd of sex kittens.

"I think the mayor likes you," Teddy whispered, eyeing the petite speaker.

"No comment," I said. Anything other than that was fraught with peril. I trusted Teddy about as far as I could heave his bony butt cheeks. I sighed and leaned back. Why had he planted that thought in my mind about the mayor? Didn't he know I was a depraved sinner? Then I found myself wondering if there could be anything between me and Myrna. But from everything I gathered, she was a confirmed bachelorette. Maybe the right person just hadn't come along—yet.

"Vance, do you want to fill us in on your progress with the hurricane evacuation promos?" Myrna asked from her seat at the head of the table in the ultra-modern conference room.

I stiffened, realizing all eyes were on me. What was I going to report? *How about coming clean and telling the truth?* But . . . wouldn't it make me look better if I just provided the usual song and dance? Not with the sudden need for wall-to-wall accountability—thank you very much, Arnie "Crusher" Thurlingate. "Here's the thing," I began. "Those are all public service announcements, and we're producing them gratis. Consequently, I've moved them down the production queue. With any luck, I'll have them cut by July."

The collective gasp in the room was palpable. People were in disbelief I had so freely made such an admission. It even amazed me. But I was only following Arnie's guidelines: I was no longer in the business of falsifying timelines and embellishing delivery dates.

The whole ordeal left me spent and listless. Feeling isolated, I just stopped talking the rest of the way. It actually helped make the meeting more productive. Without me hogging the agenda, other people responded with useful comments and suggestions covering the topics of public safety and emergency preparedness. I realized I didn't need to be the center of attention all the time. It also clarified how expendable I was. It was quite humbling—and liberating.

Sitting quietly at the table, a jumble of disconcerting thoughts clattered through my head. The clumsy transformation to a "new me" would take some getting used to. It was like learning a different language under the most stressful of immersion conditions. This most radical of makeovers was akin to changing the head gasket while the engine was running. I detested what it did to my self-confidence and just hoped the whole thing blew over by morning.

As the meeting adjourned, Teddy tried ensnaring me again. "The mayor's economic plan is not exactly taking off the way she envisioned. Could I get your feelings on that?"

I shuddered at stepping into that politically toxic quagmire. "You have an active mind," I said. "I'll grant you that."

"Just keeping it real," he murmured.

I nodded and smiled. Teddy wasn't such a bad guy. He had a job to do just like the rest of us. There was no point in viewing him as the enemy. I felt a sudden sort of affinity to the hard-charging reporter, a modicum of respect. Before Arnie's sermonizing at the funeral this afternoon, it would have been a totally different story: I would have been at odds with Teddy and ready to show him up every chance I got. But now, instead of meting out retribution, I was feeling sorry for him. I hoped he had more going on in his life than just stirring up bad feelings with an endless string of salacious innuendos and accusations.

As we were leaving, Kenzie hustled beside me, squeezing others out of the way. "What happened back there? I thought you were the king of overpromising and under-delivering. You of all people are actually admitting to being overbooked!"

"What else was I going to say?" I gave a weak shrug. "I didn't have much of a choice."

"I mean, that took a lot of guts," she said, nodding eagerly. "Admitting that you're incapable of making deadlines—*and* blowing off the mayor like that."

"I'm not blowing off the mayor," I said. "It's more a function of prioritizing."

"She's right, Vance," Teddy said, inserting himself in the conversation. "You definitely blew her off."

I saw a flash of excitement in Kenzie's eyes. I stopped walking. What was this all about? Did Kenzie find the scrawny reporter attractive?

Had she been making goo-goo eyes at *him* the whole time instead of me?

CHAPTER FIVE

THE POOPED PAYSAN

The Dijon rabbit was stupendous. Having been torn between it and the prune-studded meatloaf, by all rights I made the right choice. Telbrina Flourenden, who had unwittingly become my enduring lifeline over the course of the last couple of hours, polished off a white wine soup and an apricot quiche made with free-range eggs. I hoped her vegetarian leanings would not be a sticking point in our budding relationship. Possibly it meant giving the heave-ho to my beloved beef and hopping on the vegan express. Well, I'm sure bigger sacrifices have been made throughout the annals of time in the name of love.

I watched the play of light on Telbrina's pretty face as she sipped red Bordeaux from an oversized goblet. Tall and lean, she wore a simple dark suit with a smartly tailored black leather jacket and spiked heels. Enjoying herself to the hilt, she tossed back her long, dark hair and lustily partook of the garlic-encrusted artichoke hearts I had ordered as an appetizer.

We had joined up around 7:30 following the meeting at the mayor's office. Afterward I had swung by the construction site to collect from Jules, the wayward "Rock 'n Roll Plumber." Thankfully I hadn't needed the ladder as a stealth tactic this time; Jules had amicably come out to meet me with an envelope containing his overdue payment.

The restaurant Telbrina had chosen was a new favorite of hers specializing in rustic French cuisine. She told me the name of the place, loosely translated, meant "French backwater peasant." It definitely had the word *paysan* in it. I gave up on the pronunciation and just let the food do the talking. The establishment, located on Folsom Street in Mid-City, featured reclaimed beams and plank floors salvaged from a cattle ranch in the western region of Anjou. The tables and chairs were rough-hewn; thankfully, I didn't get any splinters when I sat down.

I'd only known Telbrina a little more than a week, having met her at the media mixer kicking off this year's flower show. She was a landscape architect for the city, specializing in environmental remediation and stormwater management. We'd hit it off from the start. I don't know what it was. Animal magnetism? Love at first sight? Call it what you want, I was anxious to scale the heights to reach the next level.

However, I hoped I hadn't blown it already. Last Saturday night had been our first official date and we decided on a movie. I wanted to see the new one that was really being hyped, *Grosse Pointe Blank,* with John Cusack and Dan Aykroyd, but she wanted to see—who woulda thunk it?—the screen adaptation of Tolstoy's *Anna Karenina.* Guess which one we saw? I spent the whole flick drifting in and out of sleep while hoping Telbrina appreciated my abiding sacrifice.

We had coffee afterward and things started going sideways. Overcome by the residual angst of the movie, I rambled a little too much about my struggles as a commitment-phobe. Before I knew it, I was spewing a veritable who's who of former girlfriends.

The prospect of a relationship with Telbrina was so refreshing because it was one of those rare times when I actually felt I had met my match. You didn't come across a woman of substance like her very often, and it made me all the more remorseful that I'd vented the other night about my previous flameouts. But nothing, I told myself, was insurmountable.

I had gone into tonight's dinner with all good intentions of putting Telbrina's needs and desires ahead of mine. Moving forward with our relationship, I felt it necessary to establish goals and manage expectations on a fair and equitable basis. In deference to Arnie's lecture this afternoon, I was looking at future relationships in a whole new light. That meant focusing on a monogamous game plan. Even though we'd technically only been on two dates now, I was already thinking about the possibility of marriage—after a long courtship, of course. I wasn't going to just jump into anything. Telbrina, being a consummate environmental custodian, would help with my commitment issues. What could possibly go wrong?

"Would anyone care for dessert?" The blonde waitress cleared plates dispassionately. She was definitely not part of the French motif. "Tonight's special is pumpkin curd with plums." She smiled tiredly. "Yum."

Telbrina flashed a playful grin. "One order of the curd, two spoons—and coffee. Two steaming mugs of your robust, organic French roast."

"Very well," the waitress said, half bowing. She wasn't in the best of moods, and serving a couple of lovebirds wasn't helping. It was the end of her shift; she didn't need the aggravation.

"You look a little tired. Worn out." Telbrina smiled demurely, ensnaring me in her mysterious slate-blue eyes. "Rough day?"

"Yeah, I guess you could say that." I kept things purposefully vague. Talking about the religious aspects of my angst might throw water on an otherwise promising night. I had to tread lightly. "I was at a funeral this afternoon. There was this guy. My biggest client, actually. I thought he was a friend, but then he turned on me. He started criticizing me—you know, really getting in my face. And on top of it he got all judgmental, making it way too personal."

"Jerk." Telbrina brushed it aside. "Nothing that a good massage wouldn't cure, I'm sure."

My ears pricked up. "Massage?" I couldn't believe she'd just said that. "You know where I could get one—at this hour?"

"I'm sure that could be arranged." She smiled mischievously and lowered her gaze.

This was getting better and better. I realized why my day had been such a blowout; I was being prepared for the prize at the end of the trolley line.

She nodded for me to pull my chair closer. That was all the invitation I needed. Over the years I was a pretty fair judge of character; I had become adept at reading "tell" signs. You acquired that from dealing with clients, determining when to close a deal.

And all the signs were lining up like clockwork. This was it; I could feel it. This was going to be the start of the most meaningful relationship of my life.

"So tell me, Vance . . . what was so bad to get you all tied up in knots?" Telbrina's presence was intoxicating. She leaned into me and lightly touched my kneecap.

I tried to control my breathing. There was no point holding back anymore. If Telbrina and I were truly soul mates, we'd be spending the rest of our lives talking about intimate stuff, so I may as well start unloading now. After dancing around the topic, I soon struck solid ground.

"I guess you could say it was all pretty enlightening," I said. "The whole funeral and what happened afterward." I gauged her beguiling eyes. Admiring her staggering beauty, I was more and more mesmerized by the minute.

"Enlightening, huh?" She smiled, genuinely amused. "Enlightenment is good."

"In small doses, I guess." I tilted my head. "Why? What do you know about it?"

"I'm starting to really get into Buddhism, now that you ask." As the topic turned more serious, she lost her playful edge.

I nodded, suitably impressed. "Buddhism. Wow. How 'bout that?"

"Do you have a problem with that?"

"No. Of course not." I quickly drained my remaining burgundy.

"I'm still pretty much new to the concept," she said. "You know, it takes years of devotion and sacrifice to make significant inroads."

"I'll bet."

"Hey, I just thought of something." She pressed her face very near mine. "Maybe me and you can start meditating together."

My concentration was totally shot. I was driven up the rustic walls by her exotic scent and the warmth of her breath on my cheek. "Sure," I half-gasped.

"Really?" She drew back casually, seemingly impressed. "You're not just saying that?"

"Not a problem," I said. "What do Buddhists believe in, anyway?"

"Tell me how much you know and I'll fill in the blanks."

I stretched out my hands. "Next to nothing, I guess. Sorry to say . . ."

"No problem. At least you're being honest." Telbrina made a sweeping gesture. "It basically provides the framework for spiritual growth by offering meaningful and abiding insight into the basic essence and significance of life."

"So far, so good." All I was really thinking about was what I had to do or say to make her pull closer again.

"We study things like the Four Noble Truths—those are the ones that deal with suffering—and the Eightfold Path. Does any of that sound familiar?"

"No, not really. Does it have anything to do with reincarnation?"

"Well, to some extent." She nodded enthusiastically. "We live in an impermanent world, and we are constantly reincarnated in past and future lives."

"So the next panda bear you see might be your wayward uncle," I observed.

"Or your highly exalted uncle," she corrected. She slumped her shoulders. "Look, I don't exactly know where animals fall into the equation. It's past my pay grade at this stage." She nodded. "But I'm sure I'll get the answers eventually."

"So where does karma fit into all this?"

She bit her lip. "Why don't we leave that for another time?"

I smartly resisted the urge to blurt out the hackneyed bumper sticker quote: "My Karma Ran Over Your Dogma." I was glad I kept quiet. She had probably heard it anyway.

She brushed against my arm. "If you want, feel free to join me Wednesday evenings at the Burnt Willows Zen Center. We're right now in a series on the Five Precepts. This month we're talking about not taking things that don't belong to you unless they're freely given."

Electricity was flowing. It was a challenge keeping the topic in perspective. "Wednesday evenings. I'll definitely keep it in mind," I said.

"It's B-Y-O-M," Telbrina said.

"B-Y-O-M? What's that?"

"Bring your own mat." She smiled, pleased with herself.

I looked at her quizzically, and she burst out laughing.

"Don't get all paranoid. It's just a joke," she said.

Laughing weakly, I shrugged. I was in so far over my head. I didn't know the Dalai Lama from a Himalayan haberdasher.

The waitress clattered two plates on the table and hastily poured coffee. The pumpkin curd laced with plums was a nice distraction from the heaviness of the talk.

"So I'm curious," I said. "Where does accountability fit in with Buddhism?"

She paused before taking a spoonful. "Well, that's sort of an abstract concept. We need to be accountable to a lot of different areas in life. For instance, the environment. That deserves a disproportionate share of care and concern. We also believe in accountability to each other, if that's what you're driving at." She brought the spoon to her moist, inviting lips. "We cannot overemphasize the need to be kind and considerate to absolutely everyone."

"So . . . is God in the overall game plan?"

"God? Oh please." She made a face and pretended to drop the spoon. "That's where all the world's problems stem from."

"Huh?" I squinted. "What do you mean?"

"Who do you think starts all the wars?" She jammed another heaping load of curd into her mouth so she wouldn't have to talk.

Transfixed by the subtle sucking sound she made, I dove in further. "Okay, so who watches out for you? Who's the higher power in the Buddhist equation?"

She took her time savoring the delicacy before swallowing. "Well, Guatama Buddha, who we call the Awakened One . . . he pretty much got the ball rolling. But it's really more about the Eternal Now," she said, nodding. "And we get our inspiration and direction from each other, of course, as well as from nature and animals. It's kind of an immersive concept." She brushed hair from her alluring face. "Why do you ask? Where do you come down spiritually?"

"Well, my parents were—are—Christians. That's how I was brought up."

"Ugh. Spare me the details. So are mine." She pointed at herself. "I was a dutiful churchgoer right up 'til I left for college. Then I saw the truth for what it was."

"What is the truth?"

"Well, for one, that Christianity is basically part of the problem. Definitely not the solution." She grew more animated. "But more than that, it's the sum total of the destination of our lives. Each of us must shoulder the responsibility to explore the world around us and arrive at those truths that will elevate self and community to a higher purpose. Don't ask me what that higher purpose looks like. For some, including me, it's just a feeling. You know: a *feeling* that allows you to know when you're doing things right."

"I can really relate to what you're saying," I said. "Just today I was made to feel like some sort of lowlife, a regular second-class citizen, just because I don't march in lockstep with the common mind-set." I nodded and found myself growing more confident by the minute. "So I guess my question is: what gives anyone the right to think they have the market cornered on a certain belief system? Isn't it more closely aligned with the truth that we're all in this together?"

"Nice." She nodded, licking the spoon extravagantly. "I like the way you think."

I couldn't believe it. Instead of ripping us apart, our little talk on religion had knit us closer together. I just knew tonight was the night.

As the table was being cleared, Telbrina ladled a heaping teaspoon of raw sugar into a kiln-fired mug. I studied her easy smile. I was feeling closer to her, possibly, than I had felt to any woman before.

Once the sugar was stirred, the first satisfying sip consumed, and the mug perfectly placed on the rugged tabletop, Telbrina, a gleam in her eye, leaned into me. "Baby, what if I were to tell you I'm bi?"

I blinked.

"You do understand what I'm saying?" She tilted her striking face. "You can think of me as polyamorous with a bent toward multilateral, nonexclusive network tendencies." She appraised me rather critically. "Does that make sense?"

I swallowed hard trying to take it all in. I nodded choppily, disjointedly. "Yeah, yeah. No sweat. I'm with you all the way."

She peered at me curiously. "So where do you stand on it?"

"Hey, who am I to judge?" I shrugged. "It's all good, right?"

"Is it really, Vance? Is it really all good for . . . *us?*"

"Uh . . . " I could only stall for so long. "It's just that now . . . it's all hitting at once. It's something I have to process."

"I don't understand your use of the word 'process.' What exactly needs processing in your regressive vernacular?" It appeared she was restraining herself from coming across the table at me. "Are you comparing me to a reengineered Cuisinart?"

"Huh? Where'd *that* come from?" My eyes wandered toward the swinging kitchen door across the way.

"You can't help yourself, can you? Your judgmental streak is clearly evidenced in the overt passivity of your sickening moral orientation. On the outside, you're this 'whatever goes' kind of guy, but inside you're nothing but a prude. A closet *vlakódis* prude!"

"Me . . . a closet prude?" I flashed a pathetic expression.

"No, a closet *vlakódis* prude. There's a quantifiable difference. A closet prude is a big joke, but a closet *vlakódis* prude is an uncontested moron!"

My eyes widened. "Is this how you treat a customer who wants a pear tree in their backyard instead of a dogwood?"

"Don't go there with the dogwoods. I'm warning you." She clenched her jaw, whispering savagely. "And leave my precious clients out of this. They've got more class in their toenails than you have in your entire body."

I sat numbly as her meltdown raged. To the best of my knowledge, I had never dated a bisexual. Coming on the heels of Arnie's "Fornicators-R-Us" lecture, I was unsure how this was going to jibe with the new call for pared-down love interests. This, it seemed to me, would create a more crowded field than not.

"Don't bother calling. You're beyond hope." Telbrina bolted to her feet, slamming her napkin atop the splintered table.

I kept staring at the front door long after she'd departed. Stunned by the confrontation, I was left with the fallout—and the check.

Then I came to my senses.

Man. Rabbit sure is expensive.

CHAPTER SIX

FEELING AROUND
IN THE DARK

"Four . . . three . . . two—and action!" shouted Jeremy Prinzen, the punishing director, as the overworked clapboard registered yet another take.

It was almost 10:00 PM, and the workday was still going strong. But this was the only way I'd have it. Television was in my blood. As a kid growing up in the western suburbs of Chicago, I tracked story arcs for reruns like *The Beverly Hillbillies* and *Gilligan's Island*. I stayed up late writing treatments for game shows and went to sleep reciting ad copy for local commercials. As my career progressed, late nights became commonplace. These days, I would not feel right unless things were happening pretty much around the clock.

Having just returned from the emotional beatdown with Telbrina, I fumbled through the first aid cabinet in the shadows of Studio B. Clawing open the Advil, I chased a couple tablets with scalding, industrial grade coffee.

Tonight's commercial shoot was taking place in a production facility I had designed and built four years ago when I first started working for A.G. Spagway & Company. The Spagway Trust owned an East Coast heating oil conglomerate, and the principals knew virtually nothing about operating a TV station. The estate had acquired the property as part of a settlement package from a third-party bankruptcy restructuring. They might as well have won the sucker in a poker game.

It helped that I had vision. When I took control of this facility, it was a classic underperformer. In less than a year I transformed it into a regional powerhouse. Through aggressive program buys of first-run and off-net syndicated shows, plus acquisition of premium movie packages, our ratings skyrocketed across all dayparts. I vowed that someday we would start producing our own original programming for worldwide distribution.

My all-around go-to person was the freewheeling patriarch Reginald Spagway III. To an increasing extent, Reggie preferred the natural heat of St. Croix and obsessed over his faltering golf game. The further he distanced himself from day-to-day operations the more his daughter, Regina, was forced to pick up the slack. Regina was not nearly the industry dynamo she fashioned herself to be. In maintaining a seamless operation, I had to work with her—and around her—and this required a finely honed set of diplomatic skills. Most of the time I was able to navigate the challenge, giving deferential treatment, and a wide berth, to her supercharged ego.

"Strut your stuff, man," Prinzen barked. "Show some attitude!"

The object of Jeremy's overheated exhortations was Felix Fenton, the "Slip-and-Fall Ninja." The rotund litigator, in his early fifties, cavorted in bright yellow leotards, an electric green jersey, and a crimson satin cape. Bathed in lights, he stabbed the air with a wooden Kung Fu sword and snapped nunchucks overhead. After nearly a hundred commercials, it was a wonder there hadn't been more injuries, self-inflicted or otherwise.

"Cut! Somebody fix his mask." Jeremy slid the headset around his neck and attacked a bottle of water, chugalugging lustily.

A production assistant bolted from the shadows and tugged Felix's purple eye mask then flounced the scalloped hem of his shiny red cape. Large photos adorned the set depicting people in mid-spill, or "full ninja mode," their legs flying out from under them and their eyes clamped shut as they braced for a bumpy landing. *Ouch!*

Talk about bumpy landings . . . it had been quite a day—or should I say, quite a decade, which is what this day felt like. I couldn't begin to enumerate the emotional gyrations that had overtaken me since Arnie's fireside chat at the funeral parlor this afternoon. My world had been rocked to its tectonic plates and the wheels were still off the wagon. I kept telling myself it was all my imagination and everything would return to normal after a good night's sleep, but things only seemed to grow weirder by the minute. This feeling refused to leave me alone.

And it only got worse. I spotted the "Stooge Trio" as they entered the control room. What a waste of perfectly good breathing air. The jaunty threesome was probably just returning from a late dinner at the country club and decided to hang out here to lord it over us. If this evening wasn't distressing enough, now I had to deal with *them!*

I avoided eye contact with the exalted members of the pompous posse. They were all former classmates from Regina's elite alma mater in Vermont. The bland-looking guy with the medium build and mustache was Bryce Whittington, Regina's husband of ten years.

"Cabana" Clarence Harkridge was the short one with the open shirt and hairy chest. An overly enthusiastic tech specialist, he was responsible for implementing the company's digital mandate. The "Cabana" moniker alluded to a bit part he once had in a college musical about a vegetarian pirate who eschewed cannibalism in favor of a less confrontational plant-based diet.

At six-foot-six, Bennett Fellingston stood tall among them. A power forward on the school's conference champion basketball squad, he was handsome, gregarious—and generally worthless. His overriding ambition in life was to produce a weekly car show. In the interim, I used him as a national pitchman for an over-the-counter rash cream.

I jiggled the remaining capsules in the plastic container while staring vacantly off in space. I couldn't take this any longer. I had to scram.

"So you're the one hogging all the Advil. Why don't you leave some for the rest of us how 'bout?" Anastasia Scanlon, my worst nightmare, pried the pill bottle from my clutches. She washed down two tablets with Mountain Dew and stared at me quizzically. "You look a fright. That suit qualifies for the summer line of Skid Row Casual." She winced. "Don't you own an iron?"

"It must have happened after the memorial service." I made a weak attempt at brushing a crumpled sleeve. "I was outside in all that humidity."

"Memorial service?" She blinked.

"Yeah. You know, Myron Thurlingate?"

"Vance, do you think it's in the best interest of time management to attend funerals in the middle of the workday?"

"Excuse me? He was only our biggest client." I stopped myself before crushing my Styrofoam cup. *Easy, easy, easy! Just keep it together. Keep everything in check.*

Anastasia was a pencil-neck geek, gangly and pale. She was a nice enough girl—or at least had been until Fellingston made her his number-one love interest. His influence was evident not only in her artificially induced confidence, but also in her choice of apparel. "Bring It On Ben" was both coaching her up and dressing her up, and the results were bizarrely off-putting. Imagine a country girl who harbored hidden aspirations as a streetwalker: typical motifs consisted of floral print peasant dresses and stiletto heels.

Soon after Anastasia and Bennett became an item—albeit an under-the-radar item—she began shoving her stork-like frame around in what I called "bantam tantrums," because she was a lightweight in every sense of the word. In an overnight transformation, she had gone from being an enthusiastic go-getter, though probably a little too anal, to being a first-class twit. She figured as long as she was riding the range with the former hoops star she could call all the shots. Had her level of incompetence not been so pronounced, she might have pulled it off. But Regina needed to put a damper on Anastasia's pathetic, power-grabbing antics before more egos were rankled—including mine.

"Here's last quarter's payment from Jules." I pulled the unopened envelope containing the Rock 'n Roll Plumber's check from the vest pocket of my suit coat.

Fingering the envelope, Anastasia appeared disappointed I had coaxed a payment from the wayward tradesperson. She envisioned a collection agency rushing to the rescue, a move that would make me look totally ineffective. Any fool could see Anastasia was gunning for my job, meaning I had to be especially guarded whenever I was around her. The Spagway brass would immediately hear about any improprieties. If you wanted to look good in the eyes of the family, you had to really be creative in outflanking her.

Removing the check from the envelope, she laughed at the ceiling. "What a joke! You gotta be kidding me!" She was back in control again. "He owes more than this measly amount—a ton more." She was delirious with joy. "This doesn't even cover interest!"

"What?" The bottom dropped out. I grabbed the check in shaking hands. It was barely legible, but I think the amount was $143.68. "What's this?"

"You tell me. You're the one who collected." She smiled snidely. "Or tried to."

I closed my eyes to shut it all out. I couldn't believe it. It was worse than I imagined. Jules stiffed me because I had trusted him, not bothering to look inside the envelope when I'd picked it up. When was the last time I trusted anyone?

I had listened to Crusher and tried heaping on love and patience, treating Jules with respect instead of browbeating him. I realized that piling on like *WWE Monday Night Raw* was not the best way to move forward. By stopping to listen and build a relationship—and that was key, building a relationship—I hoped to develop a whole new level of understanding and compassion for the man.

It wasn't easy being a celebrity plumber.

"Look, here's the deal." I fought to regain my composure. "He's going to Nashville next week to cut some new material. I'll make good on what he owes in the interim."

Her neck snapped back. "You? Where are you going to get that kind of scratch?"

My mind raced. *Is she sniffing out my consulting fees?* Clearly, this wafer-thin piranha was my shadow. I was now more certain than ever the company was using her to spy on me. She could torpedo me on any number of counts, starting with my burgeoning nationwide consulting business. But I also had exposure in other areas: an alleged affair with the mayor, dysfunctional time management, ineffective client relations, and let us not forget my biggest shortfall of all . . . holding back dear Bennett from his own syndicated automotive show.

We engaged in an uneasy standoff. She sucked Mountain Dew noisily from the can. "I don't know if the Spagway Trust will be agreeable to this," she sighed in a cheesy, theatrical way. "How should I phrase the memo: that our derelict plumber is getting flush in Tennessee with a new album?" She laughed at her pun. Only yesterday that response would have propelled me to the moon. *Who the so-and-so does she think she is?* But not now. After Arnie's sermon today, I was working hard at trying to see things through a different filter: instead of animosity, I tried feeling empathy for this lanky neophyte. She was using her relationship with Bennett as a springboard to get over on the rest of us. Imagine what would happen if her beau decided to pull the plug on the liaison. Where would that leave her? For starters, she'd lose her identity. And if I understood correctly from my wake-up call this afternoon, there was only one identity in life that really mattered: the one we have—or don't have—with God.

"Seeing is believing," Anastasia said. "We'll see if you can salvage the plunger-pusher's bacon." She lowered her voice. "I hope you know what you're doing."

My ears pricked up. We had a problem across the studio.

"So if you want to make chopped liver out of the mofo prosecution, hitch your wagon to the backside of the Ninja!"

I peeled away from Anastasia and squinted at the set. What had the sawed-off attorney just said? After years of sorting out studio cross-talk and scrambled control room chatter, I could discern just about anything amiss with an audio feed.

"With feeling this time!" Jeremy yelled.

The Slip-and-Fall Ninja folded his arms and blurted, louder: "So if you want to make chopped liver out of the mofo prosecution, hitch your wagon to the backside of the Ninja!"

"Again!" Jeremy shot.

Felix reared back. "So if you want to make chopped liver out of the mofo prosecution, hitch your wagon to the backside of THE NINJA!"

"What the . . . ?" I tossed my coffee cup in the trash and hustled across the studio. "Whoa, whoa, whoa! Time out!" I made the requisite "T" sign while dodging camera cables and audio cords. It was a wonder I didn't become a slip-and-fall client myself. I got right into the shot and waved off the cameras. "What did you just say?"

Everyone was totally ticked that I had stopped production. "You just killed the best take of the night!" Jeremy screamed.

As crew members started losing it, even I was amazed at what I'd done. "'Mofo prosecutor'? Did I hear that right?" I browbeat Felix, intimidating the combative attorney with my six-foot, 185-pound frame.

"Yeah. 'Mofo prosecutor,'" Felix muttered. "What's the big deal, chief? Don't get your panties in a wad."

Jeremy tugged the headset from his ears and batted his clipboard on a jeaned thigh. "If you ask me, boss, it's one terrific tagline."

"Oh, I'm sure it ranks right up there with the all-time classics," I said, looking around. "Which one of you mental giants came up with it?"

"It was a mistake," Jeremy said. "You know how mistakes become the mothers of invention, so to speak."

"Well, this is one mama that ain't gonna fly, I'm sorry to say." I stared everyone down. "So to speak." I pivoted in a tense semicircle. "How was it a mistake for crying out loud?"

"The original copy said, 'Let the Slip-and-Fall Ninja get his *mojo* on for you,'" Jeremy said. "Okay?"

"Great." I blinked. "So how did we go from mojo to *mofo*?"

"Felix misread the copy," said Yolanda, a production assistant in her mid-twenties.

"You misread the copy?" I stared at the runt barrister. "You represent people in a court of law and you can't *read*?"

"Lighten up, boss," Jeremy said. "He didn't have his specs on, okay?"

"Yeah, do you know what glasses do to the overall effect of my eye wrap?" Felix asked. The diminutive attorney was growing more ill-tempered by the second.

"Well, do you know what putting the word *mofo* on the airwaves does to the overall longevity of this TV station?" My general demeanor lightened only slightly. "It's a good thing I nipped this sucker in the bud before it went into the commercial rotation is all I can say."

"I don't get it," Felix said. "What's wrong with mofo?"

"Are you nuts? That sort of language could get us a fine from the FCC—or worse. Do you want to put the Spagways' TV license in jeopardy because you came up with a bodacious tagline?" I was gaining momentum. "Let's see. Does anyone have a spare eighty-five million dollars laying around? That should just about cover the loss."

"Come on, dude. You're overreacting," Jeremy chided me. "You're usually all in when it comes to pushing the envelope."

Jeremy was right. Before today, I would have been yukking it up, finagling a way to bend the rules. "Mofo" would have still needed to come out; I just wouldn't have made such a scene. But now it was all about responsibility and accountability. Was I becoming one of those boring "by the book" types on top of everything else?

"Less pushing the envelope, and more concentration on the delivery," I said. "Don't make me have to bust somebody's stones over this."

"Let's call the FCC lawyers," Jeremy challenged. "They'll set the record straight."

"Are you crazy? You want to run up our bill with something I've already ruled on?" I squared up Jeremy. "Who's in charge around here?"

"They won't run up the bill . . . " Jeremy sloughed it off. He wasn't used to pushback. "I'm sure they have the answer at their fingertips."

"Yeah, right," I said. "An attorney who doesn't run up the bill. When have you known an attorney to not run up the bill?" I turned to Felix, who was melting under the lights in his gaudy tights. "Tell me, Felix. Do you ever run up a client's bill?"

"Well, that all depends." Felix wiped his brow with the sleeve of his sweat-stained green jersey. "Exactly what do you mean by 'running up a client's bill'? Are you using 'running up' the same way you would refer to a person 'running something up the flagpole'? In that case, you need to examine the issue from all sides depending on the prism you're looking through."

"Prism. I see . . . " I said slowly. "And we all know what you can do with that . . . prism."

My cell phone rang. I pried it from my coat pocket and squinted at the display. Verona Shrevesworth. My heart sank. I was suddenly plunged back to reality. What was I going to tell her? Not tonight, that was for sure.

I let it go to voicemail. I had to get away from this nonsense and start strategizing the rest of my life. "I'm outta here." I waved vacantly with the hand that held the phone.

Everyone looked around. Jeremy threw up his hands. "What are we gonna do?"

"Fix the spot!" I yelled, walking from the studio with my back to the crew. I held the phone to my ear to check Verona's message.

"Fix the spot!"

CHAPTER SEVEN

THE GARGANTUAN
MYSTERY OF GOD

The padded studio doors closed behind me as I trudged up the carpeted stairway to my third-floor office. Squares and rectangles on the faded walls represented places where paintings and plaques once hung.

It had been nearly a year since the A-team vacated the premises and relocated to the ritzy new district just outside of town. Regina Whittleson was all agog over the brand new Country Club Corporate Center, also known as the "Four Cs." The zip code elevated the posse's stature. They had access to a host of upscale shops and restaurants, including the golf complex that was attracting the praise of tour professionals the world over. It gave Spagway management a swank platform to impress traveling dignitaries whose ranks included producers, syndicators, communications attorneys, and broadband lobbyists.

The threadbare appearance of the former headquarters grew more pronounced as I turned into the rotunda. A depression in the middle of the common area revealed the vacated position of the reception desk where Anastasia Scanlon's angular figure had first caught the hyperactive eye of Bennett Fellingston. Though Anastasia had not yet made the trek to the new digs, everyone figured it was only a matter of time before her business cards reflected the posh address—and a promotion to boot. Whether that promotion took the form of my current job title was yet to be seen.

The place reminded me of someone's political headquarters the morning after losing a big election. Wires and severed cables exploded from junction boxes with conduit unceremoniously yanked from the walls. Telltale signs of plasterboard powder on the forest green carpet were like lines of poor man's cocaine. I kept forgetting to remind the cleaning crew that there was still business being conducted on this level, such as it was.

I unlocked the French doors and hit the lights. Yellow Post-it notes were plastered across the chipped walls. My desk and credenza exhibited controlled chaos with papers and documents stacked high. *Okay, it was an unmitigated disaster area. So what?*

A red light blinked on my phone. I could not imagine the number of messages I'd received during the day. I wondered how many were from Verona. The one she'd left on my cell phone made me think twice about ducking her. It was obvious she wanted to see me. But tonight was out of the question. I was totally spent—"rode hard and put away wet," as they said in the Old West.

I paused at the large window just to the left of my desk. It looked down on Studio B where the ninja spot was being shot. I fell back in my chair and hastily loosened my tie. Anastasia had been right about one thing: my clothes were a fright. The rain squalls and humidity had really done a number.

But this was the least of my concerns. Something had taken a toll on my psyche this afternoon. The way I saw it, Crusher had broken a cardinal rule: he had failed to close me. He had lit me up, convinced me, cajoled me, and sold me on the glaring need to get right with God—but then he'd totally dropped the ball. He had led me to the water cooler but couldn't get me to drink from the little paper cup. I thought he was a better closer than that. After all, that Crusher moniker did not just apply to his football prowess.

The more I thought about it, the more I took exception to his unsolicited rant. He'd brought God into the equation and held a mirror to my face. I resented feeling like I had to make amends for every last thing I'd done wrong in my life before sunup tomorrow.

Until a few hours ago, my spirituality was pretty much a given. Embodying the thinking man's approach, I borrowed a little bit from this worldview, a little bit from that. I added a dash of my own cosmic seasoning with a healthy dose of common sense.

I had a hundred different ideas about who God was and what the afterlife entailed. Whenever God became inconvenient to my lifestyle, which was nearly always, I kept him at arm's length. I called on him only in times of urgent need, like summoning a talisman, all the while questioning him severely to the point of mocking him. I delighted in demeaning Christians, especially those who were outspoken in their beliefs, routinely labeling them bigots, hypocrites, and intolerant boobs.

My fallback position was the heady world of reincarnation. Welcome to the land of many happy returns, where the words "If at first you don't succeed, try, try again" rang eternal. It was so comforting to know we had unlimited chances to hit heavenly pay dirt. It just took some of us longer than others to get it right. But like the burnouts of the family tree showing up late for Thanksgiving dinner, us lovable ne'er-do-wells would one day be welcomed into Paradise with open arms.

I was going to be a cosmic cutup in the afterlife, the eternal class clown with coeds draped all over me as I strode triumphantly up the endless high school hallway. We all knew those characters were desperately needed in Heaven, right?

Right.

Wincing, I leaned on my cluttered desk while rubbing my temples. Today's events felt like a board of directors meeting inside my head with all the corporate officers pounding on the conference table at once. It had all given me a raging headache that only intensified throughout the day. Fighting off sleep, I tried convincing myself I was still in control. The memory of Telbrina storming from the restaurant continued to sting. I played the botched night over and over in my head, focusing on her unprovoked hostility. *Where did it all go so wrong? What had she called me on her way out? A "vodka-esque prude"? What is that supposed to mean?*

Exhausted, I was on the verge of passing out. Ringing erupted in the pocket of my suit coat. Clawing at the cell phone, I regained my senses. My pulse quickened, hoping it was Verona. I needed her right then. I needed her badly.

My heart sank when Arnie Thurlingate's name popped up on the display screen—Crusher, my new best friend. *Get off my stinking back!* My fingers tensed around the phone. I couldn't blow him off. He still represented a ton of business as a major client.

"Yo." I leaned back and closed my eyes, wondering if there was any Tylenol nearby.

"Are you down on your knees in prayer?" His booming voice made my headache worse.

"Very funny," I said. "I'm still at work."

"What for? You know what time it is?"

"Newsflash, Crush. This is the TV biz. It never stops. I've got satellite feeds filtering down from the West Coast and operators in four time zones." Stiffening in my chair, I nodded. "And I'm the bridge between all the moving parts."

Arnie mulled it over. "Interesting you should mention bridges. Jesus was a bridge, you know. The bridge between our sins and God, the bridge from eternal death to eternal life."

"Can we save the Sunday school talk for another night?" I took a deep breath and closed my eyes. "I'm sorry, man. No offense. I'm just really beat."

"Sure, no problem," Arnie said. "But since you brought up Sunday school, tell me something. Do you ever work on Sundays?"

I dug in my heels and rocked forward. Sundays were primetime for my freelance consulting gig. "You bet I work Sundays." I flung papers to make it sound like I was working right then. "I get a lot of work done too. You wouldn't believe how productive I am with no one underfoot."

"The Ten Commandments have something to say about that." Crusher sounded distant. "Check out what the Bible says about keeping the Sabbath sacred."

"I thought we were putting a lid on the holy-roller chatter."

"If you have a problem shutting down, you probably consider yourself a workaholic. Is that a fair assessment? Are you a workaholic on top of everything else?"

"You bet I am. And proud of it!" I slapped the desk. "I'm on call around the clock, solving problems when others don't have a clue. I swear, if they ever put a shower in this joint I'd never leave. So, yeah, I'm a workaholic, and that's my calling card. And if that makes me a lesser human or a bad guy in your book, so be it."

"Wow, you're right. You're a straight-up workaholic."

Battling rage, I flexed my fingers. I was a straight-up workaholic, all right—as well as a straight-up closet prude. Next!

"Brother Vance, the main reason I called was to apologize for this afternoon."

"Well . . . " I leaned back in utter disbelief. Finally we could have a sane conversation. "Now that you bring it up, you *were* a little oppressive. Not to mention judgmental. Don't get me wrong, Crush. I know you meant well. But this arcane viewpoint on sex—you really need to walk it back. We're at the doorstep of the twenty-first century for crying out loud. It's a whole new ballgame. It's time to jettison the old-fashioned beliefs and start living in the present. The old rules just don't apply anymore."

"The old rules don't apply. I see . . . " Crusher grew quiet before turning up the heat. "Here's why I need to apologize. I apologize for not being harder on you this afternoon."

"*Harder* on me?" I bolted forward. "What are you talking about? Are you nuts?"

"You listen to me and listen good. You're skating so close to the edge it's not even funny. And on top of it I find out you're trampling on the Sabbath and worshiping false gods by being a workaholic—neither of which, by the way, was the reason I called." Crusher caught his breath. "The reason I called was to let you know you're messing with your eternal destiny and it's my job to head you off at the pass. So I'm asking you: have you found a church yet? Have you been down on your knees in prayer? And are you sleeping alone tonight?"

"No! No! And . . . no!" I wrenched from my chair and kicked papers across the floor. "Are you happy? You're ruining my life! If you don't back off, I'm coming over there to . . . to . . . " I was on the verge of hysterics, like I was going to beat him up or something. "Oh, just forget it." I raked fingers across my face. I needed a drink. *Man, did I ever need a drink!*

"All right, Brother Vance. Maybe you've had enough for one day. Just realize that I'll be praying for you. And I'll be joined by many, many others including my wife's international prayer chain and all of Belle Murphy's folks. Even though you may not be sold on the power of prayer yet, there will be people from all over the world interceding on your behalf."

"Whoa, whoa, whoa! I never signed on for that!" A whole new wave of anxiety swept over me. "What gives me the right to ask for prayer? They don't have to do that."

"I know they don't. But they want to."

I was feeling more distraught than ever. "I'm telling you, man. It's not gonna do any good. Everyone's just spinning their wheels. I'd feel so much better if they focused on world peace or animal rights—something that has a more doable risk-rewards ratio."

Crush kept his voice calm. "Get some sleep. And remember: God loves you with a love that never stops burning. He loves you so much that he sent his one and only Son to rescue you from the stinging bonds of death so you can have a place at the eternal feast in Heaven—if you put your hope and trust and faith in Jesus."

"Yeah, yeah. Good night." I squeezed the kill button until all life was drained from the handheld device. "Screwball!" I threw the phone across the littered desk and it skipped against the wall. I slumped in my chair.

The intercom buzzed. Jeremy's voice sounded tinny from the studio below. "We nailed it, boss. We're heading out."

"Okay, man." I was barely able to speak.

"Thanks for all the input, chief. See you tomorrow."

"*Ciao*, baby." I watched the studio lights go dark, one grid after another.

I was more spent than I could ever recall. It was a weird sensation too. More than just fatigue, it felt like part of me was being ripped away. I was undergoing a remodeling I hadn't contracted for and hoping the carpenters weren't tearing down any load-bearing walls. If I had the power to stop it, I would have done so hours ago. But like a heavy snowfall, I figured I'd just let it all come down at once and then worry about shoveling out later.

I needed to leave the office myself, but not until I kept my pledge to Arnie about finding a church for Sunday. I may have had numerous shortcomings, but failing to keep a promise was not one of them.

Attending church on Sunday, though, was going to entail some real sacrifice: no sleeping in, no lollygagging over ESPN updates, no mid-morning trip to the gym, no thoughts whatsoever about a round of golf. And what was Arnie talking about when he said "the Word" needed to be spoken? What exactly did that mean?

I'd spent a lifetime demeaning people who went to church regularly. That, I guess, would have to change, at least for this limited engagement. It's easy to call people narrow-minded, hypocritical, and sociopathic when you didn't know them. Since the day I walked away from Sunday school I wanted nothing to do with organized church and the nitwits who populated the pews. I now wondered, for the first time, where God stood on that viewpoint.

I thought about my parents, living out their retirement in Arizona. They would be thrilled to hear I was going to church this Sunday. Certainly they could answer some of my basic questions. But even I wasn't that cruel. Let's not kid anyone; this church appearance was a one-time-only affair, a novelty act. What gave me the right to get my parents' hopes up only to wash my hands of the proceedings once I had fulfilled my obligation?

I leaned back. How was I going to choose the right venue for my little spiritual charade? Did this make me a "closet Christian" on top of everything else? No, at its core, this was a business deal, an attempt to placate a major client. My main goal was locating a place where no one knew me, and where there would be absolutely no level of expectation.

With my eternal salvation on the line, I reached for the definitive source, the most trusted name in decision-making generation after generation.

The Yellow Pages.

Back home, I poured a stiff Tanqueray and tonic with extra squeezes of lime. Barefoot, wearing plaid golf shorts and a polo shirt, I padded through the sliding glass doors onto the deck. The open-air veranda of my eighth-floor penthouse apartment provided a spectacular view of shore-based casinos and hillside mansions lining the river.

I slid atop the chaise lounge beside a miniature pond. It was not quite midnight and the bars and bistros were still going strong. Jovial voices and laughter wafted up from patios and outdoor terraces. Had this been any other night, I would have headed down for a nightcap at one of the hopping establishments. This was not a normal night, though. I wasn't interested in happy banter and mindless giggles. I wasn't even interested in the heavy-handed libation beside me.

I looked up at the brilliant heavens. How many stars were up there? Thousands? Millions? The planets had been spinning in perfect harmony for all these millennia. I knew God was up there calling the shots. My overriding question was where I fit in with his game plan—or whether I even wanted to.

But it was the next part of the equation that really puzzled me. Right up until that day—April 22, 1997—I had always considered my place in Heaven a given, a birthright. I had never spent much time thinking about my qualifications much less my vulnerability. I was this great guy, after all. Not perfect by any stretch, but just the kind of person Heaven was looking for.

But what did I really know about the hereafter? According to Arnie, we will all live forever in either of two places. Apparently one option, Heaven, is infinitely more palatable than Plan B. I still maintained there was no such thing as Hell. But if you choose to live apart from God, I guess eternity could be a very long and lonely time.

When I got to Heaven—*if* I got to Heaven—would God be glad to see me? *Would I be glad to see him?*

I fell asleep under all the stars . . . amid all the confusion of this most baffling of days.

CHAPTER EIGHT

VIXENS YOU MEET AT CHURCH

The following Sunday morning, I pulled into the manicured parking lot at Chorus Lake Holy Covenant Church. The objective was simple: serve my self-imposed one-hour sentence to satisfy Arnie's high-minded ultimatum. Since enduring the fallout of his biblical tirade at the funeral last Tuesday, I had come to view his judgmental browbeating as nothing more than an acrimonious guilt trip. Still, I had promised to attend church today and was going to follow through come hell or high holy water.

I hadn't done half bad choosing this house of worship from the Yellow Pages. The immediate goal was to preserve my anonymity. It was here that no one would know my name—the opposite effect of the *Cheers* theme song.

The imposing establishment sat on the eastern shore of spectacular Chorus Lake, an expansive body of water that rivaled an inland sea. Though I was familiar with the general layout of the lakeside district, tucked along the leeward side of the coastal range, I was unaware that a church of this size existed. The distinctive design, blending steel and glass, catered to the eco-minded sensibilities of the forward-thinking residents of the waterfront community. What would Telbrina Flourenden, a self-professed architecture buff, have to say about the award-winning aesthetics? Who cared what Telbrina thought?

I rolled my 1996 company-leased Lexus LS400 into a space on the north side of the church that faced the lake. It was surely one of the most breathtaking parking spaces in America. I kept the engine idling in a last-ditch appeal to my defiant streak. Did I really want to go through with this? I was amazed I'd come this far. On the way over I had almost convinced myself that a trip to the gym would be far more beneficial than sitting in a pew collecting dust.

On the plus side, though, I could certainly use additional shut-eye. I had even started some mental horse trading: if I attended church this morning, did that mean I could forego the mandatory Christmas Eve service next December? Easter was in the books already as I had attended that service last month. But a Christmas Eve swap-a-roo was very much in the picture. I'd wager there would even be a football game on the tube that night.

My reverie waned as a van pulled up on my immediate right. Of all the spaces in this sprawling parking lot, they had to jockey into the one right beside me. Of course they did; they were Christians, weren't they? I figured they would target me for proselytizing on their way inside, banging on my hood, pressing their nostrils against my windshield. *Hey, folks: don't pass up a good chance to badger a bad sinner!* Would another vehicle squeeze me on the left, effectively parking me in? And they'd better get my license plate number because if I even *thought* about skipping out early they would track me down with a herd of organically raised bloodhounds.

A family of four piled from the van. I was amazed no doors or body parts banged into my side panel. No one looked at me or even remotely acknowledged my presence. They all appeared lost in the swirling haze of their own little worlds. The dowdy woman strode past sucking dispassionately on a tall latte. I could see right from the jump I was overdressed. Every time I went to church, Christmas Eve or Easter, everyone was pretty much dressed to the nines. But this crew could have just come from a landscaping job. Who knew? Maybe after the service there was a hoedown at the preacher's boat launch.

I shut off the engine. Tired of stalling, I had to get a grip and put this sorry episode in perspective. I wasn't signing my life away. So what if I was showing up for a "regular" service? This constituted a one-time affair, a fulfillment of my pledge to Arnie. Already I was thinking about calling Verona for brunch once this ruse was over.

During the last few days I was finally realizing that she was the "one," my proverbial soul mate. I had given a lot of thought to how much we had in common. We were closer to an ideal match than probably ninety percent of the couples out there. I intended to propose that we start spending more time together on the way to marriage. I wasn't going to breathe a word to her about my church attendance this morning. If she asked, I'd tell her I was fulfilling a business obligation. Verona would go berserk if she got so much as a whiff I was in church. There was no sense getting her all out of sorts when we really should be celebrating our new life together.

There was only one glitch—but it could be a potential deal-killer. I had to come clean with her about the unreported income from my side consulting business. If I'd learned anything lately, it was the need for accountability. There could be no secrets between us. I would tell her what I'd done, beg her forgiveness, promise not to do it again, and work to right my previous wrongs. Whether she'd buy it was an entirely different story.

I slid from behind the wheel and stretched. The spring air was fierce with a commanding sense of life. Birds chirped amid the scented brilliance of flowering magnolia trees. Just below, deep blue waves crested robustly across the craggy shoreline.

Pulling on my suit coat and adjusting my tie, I finger-combed my hair and headed off to meet the warden of Holy Covenant Federal Penitentiary. I was still ticked at being overdressed. The last thing I needed was to stand out in the crowd. I wondered if the preacher would call me onstage as an example of someone all messed up in the sin department who didn't even know what to wear for a typical Sunday morning service.

I paused at the massive glass-encased front doors and squared my shoulders. Taking a deep breath, I tried to shake this feeling of raw despair, of being trapped. Butterflies pounded in my gut like I was heading into the most dreaded shareholders meeting of all time. I kept reminding myself it would be over soon. It all depended on keeping a razor-sharp focus. Job number one was no conversing, no fraternizing, no acknowledging anyone. In and out was the game plan. This was going to be a stealth effort in every sense of the word.

As I pulled open the big glass door, the luxurious crispness of the climate-controlled paradise engulfed me. I glanced up at the steel-trussed ceiling that seemingly arched into the clouds. The whole package was incredibly impressive, but I didn't feel intimidated. A striking aura of calm came over me, one providing a sense of confidence and belonging. Maybe this wasn't going to be such a bad experience after all.

"Welcome to Chorus Lake, where the waves sing continuously to the glory of our heavenly Father." A surfer dude in his early twenties handed me a program containing a schedule of events.

I removed my sunglasses and looked around, nodding with overly enthusiastic appreciation. "Nice."

"Is this your first time here?" The pleasant young man wore a faded button-down shirt, cargo shorts, and flip-flops. His tanned face sported a light scruff of beard, and it was debatable whether he had ever shaved before.

I didn't want him thinking I was fresh meat, ripe for the spiritual slaughter. "I don't know," I said with a shrug. "What's it to you?"

He leaned into me with a thin, all-knowing smile. "Church shopping, maybe?"

"Church shopping, huh?" I recoiled. "Does that mean if you hear something you don't like you can take it back for a refund?"

Either my comment went right over his head or he wasn't agile enough to deviate from the script. "We have other visitors who are shopping around as well." He nodded pleasantly though robotically. "I hope everything turns out for you in a very blessed way."

"Hey, thanks. I really appreciate it." All I could think of was my date with Verona later on when I got sprung from this asylum. I could barely contain my hungry-wolf smile. Yeah, that was the game plan, all right: for everything to turn out in a very . . . "blessed way."

I strode diagonally across the back of the sanctuary, my Italian loafers striking the green slate tiles. I was reminded again how cool and clean the air seemed inside the hushed confines, as if scented with jasmine. The dramatic seating area sloped toward the front and must have accommodated a few hundred attendees. As I angled toward the aisle on the far right, I was amazed at how empty the place was—and hoped it would stay that way. Maybe this was typical for a non-strategic Sunday.

I was highly pleased with the seating. I could get in and out like a phantom, come and go as I pleased, and stretch out just like in first class. This would be ideal for catching up on my sleep. Who knew? They might even have a fax connection back here.

What was not to love? The only downside would be if the preacher asked everyone to fill in the pews by moving up front. If he did that I'd point-blank refuse. I'd get up and walk out, case closed.

I slid into the end position of the eighth or ninth pew from the back. I sat there like I owned the place, a regular immovable object. I soaked in some of the ambiance. Here and there were eager helpers, volunteers and ushers communicating in hushed voices. Behind the stage area was a glass expanse affording a spectacular view of the lake. The place would make a great nightclub, or maybe an upscale furniture store, if they ever got tired of operating it as a church.

The first measurable sign of life appeared through a bank of doors up front. As if a classroom had just adjourned, about twenty or thirty people of various ages and ethnicities, some toting Bibles and coffee cups, moseyed into the sanctuary. Seeming relaxed, easygoing, and way too confident, they leisurely found their seats. Didn't they realize they were about to be carved up like so much spiritual roadkill?

Trying to look important, I flipped past the first page of the program to a little thing called the Prayer of Confession. My eyes glazed over as I realized things were already off to a rocky start: "We confess we have gone astray, O Lord; we confess we have not loved you with all our hearts, minds, and souls; we confess we have little passion for your majestic presence; we confess to being held in bondage by the past, holding grudges and hanging onto bad habits . . . " *Blah-blah-blah.* Wasn't this swell? You couldn't get past the second page without being buried in guilt. Why didn't they spell it out that way on Christmas Eve and Easter?

"Vance Chelan—is that you?"

"Huh?" I jerked up and stared at 110 pounds of sky-high maintenance. Alarm bells exploded in my head as I staggered to my feet. *Who is this woman?* I recognized her from somewhere. A freelancer? No. Maybe a director. Uh-uh. Possibly talent. Yeah, right. That was it: talent. She did that spot for the Carpet Rodeo last quarter. Oh, man, what a piece of work. I vowed I would never, *ever* work with her again. And now, front and center, here she was, poised to make my life miserable all over again. *What is her name? What-what-what . . . is her name!* I smiled tersely and stuck out my hand. "Well, imagine meeting you here. On a Sunday morning, no less."

"Go figure." She froze me with her mesmerizing emerald eyes. I wilted in her presence. An airbrushed beauty, possibly of Italian or Greek descent, her long brunette hair fell luxuriantly past her sculpted shoulders. She wore an immaculate cream-colored silk blouse, gold cufflinks, and a wide bracelet made of hammered silver. Her long, wraparound skirt was a Southwest-inspired weave that locked in her shapely figure all the way to her well-defined ankles. Her fingernails bore an understated, burnished red polish, and her toenails, visible through the opening of her platform sandals, were of the same mysterious shade.

"So tell me, Vance. Do you attend this church regularly?" Her acute interest in me made hardboiled detective work seem tame.

"No." I shook my head. I didn't know what else to say. I just wobbled in the aisle succumbing to her thick, full lips, her expressive eyes, and sensuous neck. Inside, I screamed at myself. *Buck up, Sonny Boy! You gotta recover!*

I frantically processed bits and pieces of information. There was one thing I remembered from the shoot: she may be long on physical attributes, but the old elevator didn't travel at warp speed to the penthouse. And she tried to cover up her deficiency with bluster. *Yeah*, now I remembered. I'd never seen anyone flub their lines so routinely and blame so many others. She was a regular excuse factory. She was chief cook and bottle washer of the Heaving Hemorrhoids Club.

"So what brings you here today?" She seemed genuinely curious if not outright amused. "I'm church shopping."

"Yeah, well . . . " I piled high the attitude. "I'm church hopping. Is that the same thing?"

"Church hopping. Hah!" Her haughty catcall echoed in the vaulted rafters. Toning it down, she leaned closer. "From what I remember, that's not the only form of hopping you engage in."

I grated my jaw, having already reached my limit. "What's that supposed to mean?"

"You're the last person I figured for church." Her demeanor was now suddenly snide and overbearing. "Forgive me for saying this. I mean, don't take this the wrong way. But . . . aren't you being a little hypocritical?"

"Hypocritical? Me?" I'd been called many things over the years, but never a hypocrite. Who was this jerk and what gave her the right? "I think you're mistaken. Maybe you have me confused with some other guy." I was on the verge of losing it.

"Well . . . your reputation, for one. I mean . . . come on, Vance. Really."

"What about my reputation? I'm one of the hardest-working people in my business. I study the industry inside and out and capitalize on every trend. I'm known for being resourceful, hard-nosed, and probably most of all, innovative."

"Come on. You know what I'm talking about."

I stared at her, grinding my jaw. *That's it. Keep piling on, baby! Let's get it on!*

"And your temper . . . " She made a fanning motion like she'd just eaten something hot. Those thick, glossy lips were driving me up the wall.

I sighed in defeat. "Okay, maybe so. But none of it was directed at you."

"Hah! Right!" She tossed back her lustrous brunette mane.

"Honey . . . " A lean, well-proportioned guy called to her from a doorway up front. He could have been a marathoner or a cycling enthusiast, maybe a triathlete. He pointed to his watch. "Tea and coffee in the parlor with the associate pastor." He sounded like a Brit.

"Coming, dear." She waved lovingly, ladling on the schmaltz. Then she turned back to me with a sneer. "That's Laird, my fiancé. We're looking for a church where we can get married and raise a family."

I nodded, grateful that I was far removed from that dysfunctional game plan.

"Laird is from Sydney," she announced for no particular reason. She looked at me oddly, like she'd lost her train of thought. "That's in Australia."

"Dang," I said. "And here I thought it was Alabama."

"Very funny. He's a big-deal programmer on the Eastside. You know . . . stuff dealing with assembly language."

My eyes turned into overwrought slits. "I'm sure he's a rock star."

She was preoccupied with her watch and didn't catch my sarcasm. "Gotta run!"

"Wait, before you go . . . " I looked deeply into her eyes. "What's your name?"

"I figured as much." She narrowed her gaze. "Collette. Collette Mankershim."

"Collette . . . right!" I smacked my forehead. "Coletta's Closet."

She bowed her neck, incredulous. "*What?*"

I snapped my fingers. "Sure! It's that new Italian place on the way to the mountains."

"Excuse me?"

"You know, specializing in northern cuisine? The veal smothered in ham and fontina cheese is to die for."

"That sounds positively *gross.*"

"So, do you run the place? Maybe you're part owner?" I gestured with upturned palms. "Collette . . . Coletta's Place? Gotta admit. It's close."

"That's the stupidest thing I've ever heard." She screwed fists into her waist. "You just proved you're as dense as you are obnoxious."

"He's waiting, hon." Laird called louder from up front.

"Coming, dear."

As I reeled in abject humility she flashed a wilting, over-the-shoulder smile that said a million things corkscrewed into three simple words: *Don't you wish*. She blew an exaggerated kiss supposedly designed to make me heartsick for having allowed this scintillating ode to womanhood to elude my hypocritical clutches.

As she gaily sauntered up the aisle I slumped back in the pew. Overcome with guilt, remorse, and shame, I had seldom, if ever, received a hosing down like that. Who did she think she was? She had put me in such a foul mood, I had half a mind to get up and leave. And now on top of it I was salivating for the ham-smothered veal.

So much for picking a place where no one knew me; this was precisely why it was so critical to go undercover with this little caper. Where had it gotten me? The whole thing had blown up in my face. Talk about dumb luck. Now I wouldn't be able to get Collette out of my mind for weeks—or months. Why did her name have to be so close to that of the five-star restaurant? If I could pick one person on the entire planet I would not want to deal with it was her. And there she was, all up in my grill. How could she have come out of left field like that? Drooling like a lunatic, I suddenly had the overpowering urge for pumpkin-filled ravioli.

On cue, the place started filling up. People of every nature, persuasion, and physical description poured through the doorways. It was similar to being inside a movie theater when everyone piles in at the last second right after the final trailer. But this was worse, a lot worse. People were crawling all over each other, scraping bodies, and stepping on toes even in the back pews. It made Easter Sunday look like a hassle-free walk in the park.

Jostled and pummeled, I stoically looked straight ahead. I wondered if I was as bad a person as Collette made me out to be, a vile hypocrite no less. And I wondered if all these fine, up-standing Christians were sizing me up, just hankering to get their pure-as-the-driven-snow meat hooks on my sin-infested body in order to drag me kicking and screaming to the other side.

I made a snap decision: *I'm outta here. I don't have to put up with this drivel for one more second.* But just as I stood to leave, a family muscled into the pew, effectively blocking my egress. The man of the house wasn't budging an inch and just kept pressing onward, pushing me farther and farther backward. He reminded me of a gassed halfback looking to plant his butt on the bench next to the oxygen tank, and everyone in his way had best steer clear.

Herded into the center part of the pew, I ended up wedged against a tall angular woman with long, jet-black hair wearing a tie-dyed bandana and pearl earrings. She nodded at me with an all-knowing smile.

And then I smelled it: she had the worst breath in all creation.

CHAPTER NINE

Hunkered Down in Halitosis Hell

The rest of the service went downhill from there. I was one hundred percent trapped; I couldn't break free if the future of the Federal Reserve depended on it. Heaven forbid if I needed to take a leak. We sang a hymn that may as well have contained the lyrics "*. . . sweating bodies marching forth to the beat of horrifically foul and rancid breath . . .* " because I was knee-deep in malodorous bodily malfunctions.

Peering past the hymnal, I spotted the premium seat at the end of the pew I'd been forced to vacate. It was now occupied by a teenage girl who didn't look like she even wanted to be there. So that was the thanks I got: I'd given up my seat for some ingrate who didn't know how good she had it.

Oh, this woman's breath—was it ever going to end? The hymn was really taking a toll. Whenever she reached for a high note, it was like the barn doors blew off and farm stench was regurgitated, only it was recycled through a corrugated curtain of hard-boiled eggs. You've heard of dog's breath? I don't know who had it in for dogs. Never in my life had I smelled dog's breath that bad. It was like the woman had just licked the coat off a sweating skunk!

Glancing over my left shoulder, I nearly lost it. What the hey! There was hardly anyone sitting in the back section across the way. Why had everyone flocked over here? Did I have a sign on me? "First-timer at a non-holiday service: knock him to the floor with bad body smells and roast him on a hellfire spit while he's still kicking!" This was stupid. We were all packed in like sweat-soaked sardines while elsewhere you could stretch out across the pew and go to sleep if you were so inclined.

Thankfully, the hymn concluded and the woman's "Highway to the Halitosis Hellhole" took a powder. As I sat down I swore the guy sitting directly behind me was drilling holes into the back of my head. It was apparent I was sitting in his regular Sunday morning seat. *Gimme a break. Engrave your name on a gold plaque next time, okay?* I wanted to whip around and smack him. Instead, I glanced at my watch and observed the slowest passage of seconds ever in recorded history: *tick . . . tick . . . tick . . .*

I nearly passed out when the preacher asked us to bow our heads in prayer. Overcome with claustrophobia, I felt an anxiety attack bearing down. I experienced a choking feeling, like part of my life was ending, as if a piece of me was slipping away. I should be at Starbucks right now, or maybe even still in bed. And was my temper as bad as Collette made it out to be? Was I such an irascible, contemptible person? *Well hey, sister. If you can't take the heat, get out of the hot tub!*

I was nearly asleep by the time the silver-tongued preacher finally proclaimed "Amen." Someone up front yelped, "Hallelujah!" Hallelujah indeed. I dragged my sorry chin off my chest and unleashed a monumental yawn.

Connelly Caslett, the senior pastor at Chorus Lake Holy Covenant Church, glanced one last time at his notes. Firmly grasping both sides of the pulpit, he prepared to deliver his sermon for Sunday, April 27, 1997. He was one suave, polished act and had the blistering esteem to back it up. Eschewing the typical robe and raiment, he wore a well-tailored suit. Though probably pushing fifty, he was incredibly well-preserved and didn't look a day over thirty-five. His frosted blond hair was short-cropped on his classically regal forehead. At six-foot-two and luxuriantly tanned, he had a commanding presence that was punctuated by a strong and expressive voice.

"Now I'm going to talk to you about a number of despicable people today," he began. He stood at the lectern like a sentinel, like a bird of prey scouring the landscape for timid, unsuspecting rodents. "Your job is to see if you're one of them."

My heart sank: more of the despicable types. *I'm guilty. Guilty as charged. Just let me out of here!* I wondered if Collette had caught his ear, telling him to go especially hard on a certain visiting guest this morning—a certain *first-and-last-time-visiting guest.*

The debonair pastor continued his introduction: "We will focus our study today on a timeless gem from the Book of Luke, This is one of the most recognizable passages in all Scripture, the Parable of the Prodigal Son."

Members of the congregation murmured in anxious anticipation. Bibles were opened and pages hungrily flipped.

Pastor Caslett made a sweeping, theatrical gesture. "In fact, none other than the great English author Charles Dickens hailed the Prodigal Son as the greatest story ever told."

A cloud of horrendous halitosis floated about my shoulders as the woman next to me whispered. "He was a tennis star in college."

"Who? Charles Dickens?" I gagged.

"No, silly. The pastor." She nodded proudly at the pulpit. "He played at one of the Arizona schools before they joined the

Pac-10." She nudged me. "You know, when they were still in the Western Athletic Conference."

"Yeah, sure," I whispered. I realized I had to breathe through my mouth if I was going to carry on a conversation with this woman; either that or risk being carried out of the sanctuary feet first.

The pastor checked the battery pack of his wireless mic and stepped away from the lectern. "Before we get into the meat of the actual passage, you need to know a few things about the people we're dealing with. I need to set the stage for you. And you must think in terms of Middle Eastern culture. Things were a little different back then. For instance, the tax collectors, also called publicans, were the scourge of the earth. They were born Jewish but served the Romans by collecting taxes for their empire. The Jews positively hated paying taxes to the Romans, but they hated the tax collectors more. And don't forget, the tax collectors lined their pockets by charging exorbitant fees above and beyond the standard rates. It was no wonder that they were viewed in a worse light than traitors. And they hung with one of the most unsavory crews on earth. Imagine, if you will, walking into a biker bar— and this wasn't like the sanitized version you see on TV. This was a roomful of outcasts and desperados whose sole job in life was to protect the tax collector. They'd slit your throat in a second if you looked at one of them the wrong way. And the women who ran with these posses? I don't have to talk about the services they performed . . . "

Was I losing my mind? He was talking about people who hated to pay taxes. He was talking about me! Forget the loose women! I felt the heat ratcheting up. *Okay, okay! I'm going to come clean with Verona over brunch today. I promise!*

"And straight up in the middle of all that murderous mayhem came none other than Jesus Christ, eating with those raunchy, scurrilous people, sharing table fellowship with them, seemingly at ease and enjoying himself in their company."

There was a collective gasp from the congregation. My ears pricked up.

Pastor Caslett nodded in understanding. "Well, you can imagine what the high-and-mighty people of the day thought. And by that I'm referring to the quintessential holy rollers known as the Pharisees. They took one look at Jesus at the table with these filthy miscreants and were ready to scuttle his seemingly sacrilegious act right on the spot."

"Preach!" shouted a man up front.

"So against that seedy backdrop, Jesus tells the first parable, this one about a lost sheep. Basically, you have ninety-nine sheep and one goes astray. Back in the day, sheep were used to describe the human plight. So the shepherd puts it in high gear when he realizes that one of the ninety-nine has wandered off. He goes out looking for it—big-time. Meanwhile, the ninety-nine are left on the hillside in the middle of the night unattended. Anything could have happened to them, right? A pack of wolves could have cut a bloody swath through the defenseless flock. All ninety-nine could have run off in different directions. But not to worry, because the next thing you know, the shepherd returns triumphantly carrying the single lost sheep, and great rejoicing erupts. Nobody wants even one sheep to go astray, certainly not the diligent, loving shepherd."

Pastor Caslett paused, drawing himself up dramatically. "And the point of this is what? We all know when one of us goes astray and is rescued there is great rejoicing in Heaven. But what about the ninety-nine left behind, the ones who haven't gone astray? Does the parable suggest that these sheep are already 'in the fold,' so to speak, and not in need of the shepherd's rescue? Or possibly the ninety-nine merely *think* they are righteous and obedient, when in truth they are in just as bad a shape as the lost sheep—if not worse—but are too arrogant and self-righteous to realize it. This, of course, was embodied by the holier-than-thou Pharisees, who thought none of it applied to them."

I sighed in resignation. As much as I was now wanting to follow along, this was getting a little too deep for me.

The pastor gazed intently at the congregation. "It's the same reason Jesus was hanging out with the tax collectors, the prostitutes, and dregs of society: because the Father loved them and Jesus was there to save them . . . " Connelly Caslett paused dramatically. "*If* they realized they needed to be saved, and if they repented of their sins. It is no different today, ladies and gentlemen. Absolutely no different today."

I closed my eyes, shutting out this whole sorry episode. I wondered if my life was going to flash before me in twenty seconds or less. What had I done to myself? What had I done to deserve this? I so desperately wanted things to return to normal, the way they were before that debacle of a funeral last Tuesday. Something told me, though . . . that train had already left the station. And it was never coming back.

It was all Arnie's fault, the lousy jerk! He was the one who started all this. Why had I snatched the bait and co-opted this need for a spiritual makeover? In the grand scheme of things, what was it really all about? And what was with my new outlook on life? Why was I so hurt by what Collette had just revealed to me about my abrasive behavior? Only days before I would have dusted myself off and been done with her. But . . . *what if she was right?* What if I was as lousy a person as she made me out to be? What if I was worse as a person than the woman's breath next to me? Hold it. Was I suddenly beginning to care about how others perceived me? *Where did that come from?*

I was trapped—not just in the pew but in my whole sorry existence. I couldn't go back to my old way of doing things, and I couldn't figure out what was expected of me moving forward. I'd heard of people reinventing themselves, but that hardly applied here. People who reinvented themselves were somehow in control. That definitely was not the case with me. I was just out there flip-flopping around like a beached fish in the midday sun.

Pastor Caslett rapped the podium twice with his knuckles; obviously, a practiced move. "Now that I've laid the foundation, please turn with me to Luke chapter 15, verses 11-32, the Parable of the Lost Son, one of the most endearing tales of all time."

Yeah, yeah . . . *blah, blah, and more blah* . . .

I closed my eyes, trying to shut it all out. My mind drifted aimlessly to sports. What schools were in the Western Athletic Conference?

Let's see, we've got San Diego State, Utah, BYU, Colorado State, New Mexico, Air Force, Fresno State . . . how about Wyo . . . Wyooooo . . . Wyoooooooooo . . .

I jerked awake, a searing pain in my side. "What?"

"You were snoring."

Bandana Lady's nasty halitosis worked better than smelling salts. Jolted back to reality, it was obvious she'd sucker-punched my ribs with an overzealous elbow. Though she'd really laid the lumber to me, I couldn't show how much it hurt.

Pastor Caslett was now getting wild, banging the pulpit mercilessly. "And that profligate, ingrate of a son hung out with prostitutes and harlots all the days of his ruinous life!"

"Bring it, baby!" shouted a man from the left side.

The preacher now was on fire; I'd awakened just in time. "And when he returned home, do you know the reception his father gave him? Do you know how overjoyed his father was? His father broke with all tradition and humbled himself every way imaginable. He girded his robe around his waist and sprinted from the porch, showering his wayward son with kisses before the villagers could stone the young man." In the echoes, Pastor Caslett nodded. "And that same Father—God Almighty—is bursting with love to do the exact same for you. Will you let him into your life?"

As the sermon ended we all bowed our heads in prayer. I could barely keep my wits about me. I was afraid of falling asleep again, so I didn't close my eyes and kept staring down, trying to analyze the bevel on the slate floor. When the prayer concluded we stood to sing the last hymn. My rib cage still smarted from where Halitosis Hazel had thrown her flying elbow.

"Isn't it the most beautiful thing you can imagine?" she said.

"What's that?" I winced.

"We are loved by God to such an extent . . . " She sighed blissfully and glanced up at the towering glass ceiling. "We just need to show the same love back to him."

I pondered that a moment. I also pondered how long before I could breathe through my nose again. And I wondered if the stale remnant of her runaway halitosis was somehow going to linger in the fabric of my clothes.

Mercifully, the service wound down to an uneventful ending. If you want to talk about joy, this was pure, unadulterated ecstasy. I couldn't recall a time when I was so glad to be cut loose from something as when the forehand-smashing preacher announced that this mind-numbing ordeal was in the books. And, may I add, never to be repeated again. Yessir, this was a limited engagement, a one-time-only run. I was outta town! *Sayonara!*

Now the only pressing goal was to get out of this place unscathed, totally void of conversation and commitments. Once in the parking lot, I'd call Verona and our new life together could start for real. I'd gone over how I wanted to broach the tax issue with her; we were both grown-ups, this could be worked out in a caring, sensible way.

"Coffee and pastry in the parlor up front," the tall, stately bandana lady said, motioning to me, adjusting the wide brim of her hat. "Sounds scrumptious, yes?"

"Sounds like a winner." I had absolutely no desire to partake of any of that frivolity. I nodded politely as we parted ways. She headed to the front of the church, and I turned toward the rear. I focused my energy on making a swift exit, but this was easier said than done. We were all being herded, like cattle—dare I say, *like sheep?*—toward the entryway, where the celebrity pastor was greeting the fawning members of his flock.

"Hello there." Someone tapped me on the shoulder.

I turned around slowly, warily. "Hey."

A tall, dignified man wearing an expensive Western-cut suit, powder blue shirt, and bolo tie smiled warmly. Longish white hair was scooped back from his tanned, handsome face. I figured he was a big-time rancher from east of the mountains. "Chuck Simmonson," he said, sticking out a thick, friendly hand.

"Hi, Chuck. I'm Vance." We shook firmly. I realized he was the guy boring holes into the back of my head. "Hey, I'm sorry if I was sitting in your seat today."

He studied me intently. "What are you talking about?"

"Do you have assigned seats on a normal Sunday?" It seemed like a fair enough question.

He stifled a guffaw. "Not exactly, son. What constitutes 'a normal Sunday' in your vernacular?"

This was becoming too much like a conversation. "Uh . . . nothing. Forget it."

"I take it we'll see you next week, then? Same time, same station?"

"Well, I'm church shopping, see. Other fish in the pond, if you know what I mean."

"Do those other . . . fish . . . preach the Word like this one?"

"Sure, they're all in English."

"That's nice to hear," Chuck said. "It would be a real shame if any of them were in French." He gave me the once-over, rather amused. "So maybe when you go to your next church you'll get a little sleep the night before."

"Yeah, heh-heh. I guess I nodded off awhile. Sorry about that." *Wait a minute. Why am I apologizing for being bored out of my mind?*

Chuck clasped a warm, comforting hand on my shoulder. "Have a blessed week."

"Yeah." I nodded. "Likewise, Chuck. Same to you."

He ambled toward the parlor while I considered any and all options to escape this nuthouse. I tried to keep from getting distracted. As the door to the parlor constantly banged open I got more than my fill of that babbling coffee klatch on steroids. The incessant chatter and giggling ricocheted off the steel-and-glass ceiling and reverberated squarely atop my overtaxed head. Could someone please enlighten me on something: if you've just been subjected to being called a filthy, miserable wretch and an abject, reprobate sinner for the last sixty-five minutes, how can you then go into a coffee bar and laugh your head off?

I was jostled this way and that as we, members of the Sunday Morning Sinners Club, were herded toward the front door. There appeared to be an exit on the far side, but who knew where it led? Knowing my luck, Collette would be standing at that door, tapping her toe, and saying that only despicable people took that way out.

Then things started clearing out and the front doors were dead ahead. I decided to stick with the tried and true, just keep it light with Reverend Backhand Volley. Hopefully I'd be on my way in short order. As I approached Don Juan, I finally got the full measure of his presence: indeed, he had it all going on. Even I was impressed. Having dealt with a host of entertainment industry types over the years, he was the real deal.

As I approached him I wondered why he chose this gig over the clay court. But who was I to question another's motives? "Hey, man, nice service," I chuckled, leaning into him. "Or should I just say . . . nice serve."

He was all over me like cheap cologne, radiating mirth with his broad, toothy smile. "Why, I don't believe we've met." Confidence oozed from his tanned pores.

"I'm Vance. Vance Chelan."

"Connelly Caslett." He extended his hand and we shook.

I don't think I'd ever been subjected to a vice grip like that. The man's fabled power serve was no joke. I was nearly reduced to tears. "ASU, right?" Wincing in pain, I took a guess on his college. The stinky possum breath lady had told me it was one of the Arizona schools. So I had a fifty-fifty shot at being right. I must have hit the jackpot, because he positively beamed.

"You've got the correct state!" He nodded enthusiastically. "But it's actually Arizona Wesleyan-Copper Valley." His teeth sparkled in the bank of overhead marquee lights. "I appreciate the try, though. Not many people get as far as you."

"Gotcha. No sweat." I made a note to strike Halitosis Hazel from my source list.

"So what about you, Vance? To what do we owe the honor of this visit? Are you traveling from out of town?"

I paused, trying to be vague while remaining cordial. "I live in South Point."

He lost none of his charismatic luster. "So you're quasi-local."

"Quasi. Yes."

"Great. So we'll see you again." He stared me down with those steely blue eyes. I don't think I'd ever been locked and loaded like that before. It must have been a tactic held over from his tennis days. He said, in barely a whisper, "Just remember: once God starts a work in you, he doesn't stop until he's finished." Connelly

Caslett drew away and broke into a championship smile. "Don't be a stranger now, Brother Vance!"

I nodded feebly, wilting in the preacher's commanding presence.

Then he slapped my shoulder.

Hard.

Really, really hard.

CHAPTER TEN

DOUBLING DOWN
FOR JESUS

Bam! I barged through the double glass doors leading to the parking lot, my hand still throbbing from Pastor Caslett's steely handshake. It seemed like decades since I'd left my car. At least I was free from the backbreaking oppressiveness of that spiritual circus. I'd fulfilled my obligation to Arnie and thus reclaimed Sunday mornings for my own. In fact, I had the rest of my life to myself. I never had to attend church again—ever, and that included Christmas Eve and Easter. I vowed to keep on walking and never look back.

The day became alive as I strode past parked cars savoring my newfound freedom. Vibrantly colored birds flitted about the towering trees, punctuating the shadows with a chirping cantata. Technicolor waves rolled against the shoreline, amplified in bold rhythms. Man, did that fresh air feel good!

I powered up my phone. Angling toward my car, I punched Verona's number and waited three rings. When she answered, I had never been so glad to hear another person's voice. I knew, right then, that she was the one for me. "Hey Rona!"

"Vance! Finally!" she gushed. "You don't know how hard I've been trying to reach you!"

"Yeah, honey. I know, I know. I've had a lot going on lately." I loosened my tie. "Just trying to sort it all out, get a handle on things. You know how it goes."

"Sure, baby. I know how it goes . . . " Her voice trailed off precipitously.

I plowed forward, imbued with the heady prospects of spending the rest of my life with this woman. "Not to worry, though. I've just about worked everything out."

"That's good to hear. I'm glad." It sounded like she was nodding on the other end, reaffirming her side of the conversation. "I'm real glad, Vance."

This developing terseness in her voice made me wonder if she was going to banish me to the penalty box for ignoring her. Not a problem. I'd make it up to her in ways she could not even begin to imagine. I might even spring for that boxed set of vintage tarot cards I'd seen last month at the antique bookstore in Manhattan.

Donning my sunglasses, I was pleased there were no fingerprints smudging my sunny view of the world. "So what are you doing in say . . . an hour or so?"

"An hour or so. Well, uh, that's about the time Owen will be picking me up." Rarely, if ever, did anyone sound so uncomfortable with a mere statement of fact.

But that uncomfortable feeling soon grew tentacles as I felt the first flash of nausea. "Owen." My mind raced. "The airline pilot?"

"Yeah, him and me—well, I've never been real good at this, Vance. See, me and him . . . I don't quite know how to say this." She paused once more. "We're getting married."

"*What?*" The freight elevator was hurtling straight for the mezzanine level of Hell—with me on the underside.

"That's why I've been trying to get ahold of you." Now that the cat was out of the bag, she suddenly turned jubilant. "Can you believe it? Right out of the blue! Of course, what can you expect from a pilot! Out of the blue, get it?"

As the world cratered around me, I experienced the raw agony of a thousand ferrets clawing my eyes out. "Wow," was all I could manage. Who could have seen it coming?

"Are you happy for me?" she squealed.

"Oh, yeah . . . " I was gasping, gagging, dying. "Happy? Happy's not the word."

"Oh, Vance, that's so great! And here I thought you might take it the wrong way and want to rip him a new one."

I gripped the phone. *Don't give me any ideas, sister. Don't give me any ideas.*

"Not a word of this to anyone though, okay? I haven't even told my parents yet."

"Whatever." Fighting to maintain my sanity, I was processing things rapid-fire. I thought she'd dumped that arrogant boob of a flyboy months ago. Maybe if I had returned her calls on a timely basis, things would have turned out differently.

"Wait 'til you see the ring," she purred. "He really shouldn't have. But I'm glad he did!"

I held the phone away from my ear as she incessantly blathered. I couldn't believe the utter devastation. This was the king of crotch kicks.

"Look, I gotta run. Watch for the invitation in the mail." She was breathless. "*Ciao!*"

I listened to the click. My knees knocked as I melted into a puddle of despair. Talk about a bad dream; I didn't know whether to cry or scream. I hurled the phone at my Lexus.

The flying device missed the car, proving once again why I never made it past Babe Ruth League; I could never hit the cut-off man. The phone banged into a trellis and lodged in a bed of flowering bougainvilleas.

I leaned against the car roof, cradling my head. All the chickens had come home to roost. I'd been outmaneuvered by a pilot who flew for the airline that regularly lost my luggage!

I wandered off to the vacant field in back of the church and found a patch of high weeds where I laid myself down hoping to fall asleep and never wake up. Waves washed against the nearby craggy shoreline making me realize just how much my life was on the rocks. I was on the verge of tears as I squinted up at the steel-blue sky. I envisioned a miniature skywriter high above spelling the words "loser" and "jerk face." The pilot may have been Owen himself. Whoever it was had picture-perfect penmanship.

Sappy banter invaded my pity party. I cocked my head sideways and squinted through the weeds. A young couple, apparently giddy with love, strolled hand in hand along a nearby path. Charming. I tried shutting them out, but to no avail.

"Oh my gosh!" The petite blonde pointed frantically. "Over there! A body!"

"What the . . . " The ripped guy hustled over to where I was laying in the weeds. Breathless, he dropped to a knee. "Dude, are you okay?"

"Oh man, Billy! Does he have a pulse?" The slender woman bunched the hem of her cowgirl skirt and feverishly knelt beside me. "Should I call nine-one-one?"

I cocked an eye. The chick had short blonde hair and a terminally cute face. She effectively blocked the sun as she frantically patted my forehead.

"Who are you?" I asked.

The two exchanged a relieved glance.

"Praise God, he's alive!" gushed the woman, smiling gratefully.

"More to the point, who are you?" asked the man.

"Vance Chelan," I said.

"Vance Chelan." The big dude glanced at his counterpart. "Are we supposed to know that name?"

"I don't know," she whispered. "It doesn't ring a bell."

"So who are you?" I grew more adamant.

The chiseled man in the plaid shirt nodded. "I'm Billy Whatcom, associate pastor at Chorus Lake Holy Covenant." He nodded proudly at the woman. "And this is my fiancée, Josie Grandelear. She teaches elementary school and helps out Sundays in the nursery."

"It's a pleasure to meet you," I muttered. "So what do you guys want?"

The two members of the makeshift rescue crew appeared startled at first, then quickly became hacked off.

"What do *we* want?" Billy gave Josie an exasperated nod. "We just want to make sure you're okay." He narrowed his gaze. "If that's not asking too much."

"Well, do I look okay?" I started doing a slow burn myself. After all, my reverie had just been obliterated by these fresh-scrubbed church mice.

"You tell us." Josie seemed to suspect I was playing them. "Is this like . . . normal behavior?"

"Yeah," the associate pastor said. "Forgive us if we disturbed your little commune with nature there, bud."

"No sweat." I closed my eyes, effectively shutting them out. "Catch you later."

Billy knotted his thick fists, quickly losing patience. "I wish it were that simple, Hoss. But you're on church property, which makes you kind of my responsibility. Sorry."

"Do you want me to leave?"

Josie nodded at Billy. "That would probably be best." She tried looking at me dispassionately but couldn't hide the fact that she genuinely cared. "If you're sure you're okay, that is."

I nodded. "You guys haven't seen God, have you?"

Billy jerked his head around. "What kind of loaded question is that?" His frustration now turned to confusion.

I studied the cloudless blue sky—the territory where that louse Owen plied his trade. "I thought I had him. Now I don't." I made a face. "God, I mean."

"That's crazy talk," Billy said. "And do you have to be stretched out like that? Tell me you didn't OD on something."

"No," I sighed from the absolute pit of anguish. "It's not that."

"What's your struggle, darlin'?" Josie's tone was now softening substantially. "Do I understand you correctly? Are you searching for God?"

"Ever since last Tuesday my life has been upside down." I grabbed clumps of grass, kneading the moist clots. "That's the day I went to a funeral." I hastily relived the chaotic event, including Arnie's rant. "For the first time I heard about God in terms I'd never considered before." I glanced at Billy, then Josie, who both listened intently. "Now everything's gone haywire. I don't know what God wants from me. I don't know how to act or what to say. I'm more confused than ever." As emotion washed over me, I couldn't believe it. I was close to tears. "It feels like I'm in a box, trapped, without a clue, unsure of which way to turn." I breathed deeply. "I'm in stinking limbo, and I hate it."

"Man, you're light years ahead of a lot of people!" Billy squeezed my bicep reassuringly. "You acknowledge God, right?"

"Yeah, sure. I mean, for the most part. This is all his show, right?" I gestured vacantly to the heavens. "I never had a problem admitting God's existence. What I think about God's character is another story."

"No sweat," Billy said. "You're on the right track now. None of that other stuff matters at this point."

"Have you been to our church before?" Josie asked.

"No, this was my first time." I studied the fancy stitches of her monogrammed boots.

"So what brought you here in the first place?" Billy inquired.

"The Yellow Pages," I said. Watching the confusion on their young and impressionable faces, I relayed how Arnie had threatened to beat me up if I didn't promise to attend church this morning. For good measure I threw in the bit about Satan hunting me down if I didn't make good on my pledge. I further explained that I didn't want to aggravate Crusher because the car dealership was a big client. "So I found this place in the phone book by taking a literal stab in the dark."

Billy was warming to me. "Well, you're right about Satan. The enemy does his best work discouraging people just new to the faith."

"At least I fulfilled my end of the bargain." I nodded with satisfaction. "I showed up for a church service and it wasn't even Christmas Eve or Easter."

"Congratulations," Billy said, then stifled a chuckle. "Did you get your free toaster?"

"Free toaster?"

"We give them to newcomers who make it through the whole service."

"Knock it off, Billy!" Josie giggled and pretended to smack her muscular fiancé. "He's just havin' a little fun," she said for my benefit, then glanced up. "Not funny, Billy!" She leaned curiously into me. "So once church ended, why didn't you just drive away like a normal person?"

"I would have, but an airline pilot ruined everything." I countered their blank stares with a brief explanation of Owen wresting away my would-be bride—not quite in midair, though it might as well have been. That apparently tugged at their heartstrings. With everyone's guard down, they seemed particularly keen on learning more personal stuff about me.

Billy dissected the finer points of my spiritual angst. "Vance, tell me again what happened at that memorial service last Tuesday."

"Well, Arnie—or Crusher, as a lot of people call him, the guy I was telling you about who handles fleet sales for the dealership—talked about the meeting we're all going to have with God once we die, and for some of us, the meeting will turn out better than for others. He also said there's nothing more important than building a rock-solid relationship with God."

"Do you understand what he's talking about?" Billy locked on my eyes.

"I think so. But if I'm such a jerk, what does God want with me?"

"No, Vance," Josie cried. "You've got it all wrong!"

"She's right," Billy said. "In fact it's just the opposite. God loves you in a majestic, monumental way."

"Correct," Josie declared. "We're all sinners who have fallen short of the mark. We're all in the same boat on that score. But he loves us unconditionally in spite of all that."

"But because we're all sinners," Billy said quietly, "there's only one way to be rescued from the brink."

"Jesus," Josie said. "He's the way, the truth, and the life. He died for you. The most horrific death you could ever imagine."

"Have you asked Jesus into your life as your Lord and Savior?" Billy asked.

Their shadows eclipsed me; I was being attacked by the Killer Kumbaya Kids! Billy and Josie touched me gently and prayed over me fervently. I didn't know how much time had elapsed, but the whole thing was making me more anxious than ever. Finally, Billy asked if I wanted to say the Sinner's Prayer. My guard went up; that was what Crusher wanted me to pray the other day. "What is it with you people and that prayer? Is it some kind of anthem?"

"It's simple, man." Billy now suggested I go to my knees, as he did. "We'll get it done before you know what hit you, and you'll be on your way."

Who was I to resist throwing another log on the sinner's bonfire? "Okay, as long as you do it quick," I said. "I'm all for painless."

Billy knelt beside me, draped a muscular arm over my shoulder, and clenched shut his eyes. Everything grew quiet except for the lapping waves and chirping birds.

Josie crowded in. She bent her head, closed her eyes, and lightly touched my back.

Billy whispered, "Okay, Vance, repeat after me." He began to pray somberly: "Dear God, I come before you a humble, broken sinner . . . "

I repeated the words dutifully just to get Billy and Josie off my back—literally. "Dear God, I come before you a humble, broken sinner . . . "

"I have strayed from you, Father, and violated every one of your laws."

I wished there was a forum for rebuttal because I didn't agree with this, but I gamely forged ahead: "I have strayed from you, Father, and violated every one of your laws."

Billy went on. "Father, help me turn from my sins and accept your Son, Jesus Christ, into my life as my Lord and personal Savior."

I tried to remember what he'd just said. "Father, help me turn from my sins and accept your Son, Jesus Christ, into my life as my Lord and personal Savior."

Billy tightened his grip on my triceps. "I pray this in the name of your holy Son, Jesus Christ. Amen."

I was grateful to be done with this exercise. "I pray this in the name of your holy Son, Jesus Christ. Amen."

"Whoo-hoo!" Josie shouted, thrusting her arms upward and whistling exuberantly.

Billy banged my back. "Congratulations, brother! Welcome aboard!" He extended his hand triumphantly and I responded with a less-than-enthusiastic handshake.

Billy read my mind. "Don't worry. Sometimes you just have to let it sink in. There's a lot of emotion swirling around inside of you right now. You just have to give it a little time."

"Well, I'm not very good at waiting around." Amid all the hoopla, I scrambled to my feet. Feverishly, I ripped off my tie and started unbuttoning my shirt.

Josie and Billy blanched. "What are you doing, man?" Billy gasped. "Turning this into a pagan nudist festival?"

"We're gonna double down," I said eagerly, yanking off my Italian slip-ons.

Billy went on heightened alert. The script was veering wildly off course. "What do you mean, 'double down'? You think this is a table game or something?"

I ripped off my shirt. "Dunk me."

"Dunk you? *What?*" Billy gestured. "You mean like the Salem witch trials?"

"I've seen it on TV. You know what I mean."

Billy most certainly did know what I meant. "I'm sorry, brother, but if it's baptism you're talking about, it's not something we take lightly here. There's a six-week course to make sure you're up to speed on the significance of the sacrament."

"Six-week course?" I mumbled. "I could learn how to operate a forklift in less time." I gestured. "Can't you make an exception?"

"No exceptions," Billy announced. "This is not a throwaway exercise."

"Oh. Okay, then." I stopped pulling off my right sock. Figuring this was probably a dumb idea to begin with, I plucked my shirt from the weeds.

"Billy, are you nuts?" Josie was suddenly spitting nails. "Dunk him, for Pete's sake! If that's what it's going to take for him to come to faith!"

Billy nodded. "Okay, right. I guess it couldn't hurt just this once." He undid the first two buttons of his plaid shirt then stopped abruptly. "I could get a reprimand if they saw me doing this on church property."

"You're going to deny him on those grounds? How do you suppose that would sit with the Lord?" Josie wrenched off one of her turquoise-trimmed boots. "I'll do it!"

"Oh no you don't! *I'll* do it!" Billy tore off his shirt.

Wearing only our trousers, Billy and I approached the craggy rocks piled atop the shoreline. Suddenly, inspiration hit me. "Here's how we're going to let this play out," I said, backhanding his muscular arm. "If this makes me feel any different, I'll give God another look-see."

Billy stiffened. "Let's get something straight. The only one who's going to let this 'play out' is God himself." The muscular man glared at me. "And no funny business."

Billy's eyes darted back and forth as though trying to read me. It seemed it was slowly dawning on him that he may have made a mistake by entertaining this caper in the first place.

But by then it was too late.

CHAPTER ELEVEN

JESUS, AM I REALLY THAT FULL OF MYSELF?

Tips of switchgrass scraped my knees as Billy and I approached the rock outcropping above the shoreline. The lake stretched into the horizon, spectacular yet mysterious, enticing and foreboding. Below, waves crackled, clinging like white veins against the black rocks.

Scared out of my mind, I was close to hyperventilating. I gauged Billy's resolve, hoping he'd come to his senses and back down. Behind us, Josie grabbed her boot and clomped through the scrub, none too happy. "Watch those rocks under the surface," she warned. "They can get awfully slippery with moss."

Billy ignored her. Monitoring the roiling expanse, he turned to me. "Last chance to bail."

"No man," I answered. "It's go time." I tried to conjure up some mind-over-matter propaganda from a corporate retreat, but to no avail.

"It's your call." Those were his words, but Billy did not look pleased.

We descended, picking our way through a cleft in the rocks before pausing at the water's edge. The surface temperature must have been five degrees cooler, aided by an intermittent breeze. A lone cloud passed by the sun, momentarily casting us in shadows and making things even cooler.

Billy turned to me. "We'll both walk in to about waist level. I'll carry you from there, and we'll seal the deal." He slapped my back. "Sound like a plan?"

Nodding, I grabbed a jagged ledge and clenched my eyes. "Sounds like a plan." The first wave washing over my feet sent me into hypothermic shock. I jumped back like it was fire, tightening my grip on the outcropping.

"I don't know about this, boys . . . " The proximity of Josie's voice startled me. She hovered like an angel.

"Move." Billy pried my handhold off the ledge.

Nearly passing out with fear, I let go of the rock. Billy trudged in ahead of me, stoic and focused. He was up to his waist in no time.

I closed my eyes and took a deep breath. I refused to fail with Josie watching. I thought back to my youth when I'd gone swimming in lakes. Once the initial shock subsided, it got better. I gamely plowed forward, but something was wrong: the shock wasn't wearing off, and I was shivering uncontrollably.

"Let's get this over with," I stammered. If I shook any worse I'd start throwing off body parts.

"You asked for this, Einstein." Billy appeared in total control, not in the least bit fazed. It's likely he felt much better when he saw what a mess I'd become. "Kick yourself up," he said. "I'll carry you."

Gasping, I wrapped an arm around his neck and hopped up. His bulging forearms caught me behind the calves and supported the small of my back. I may have been going out of my mind, but I was in business.

"Let me get a better grip," Billy said. "You're shaking so bad you might flip away." He took each step gingerly, making sure he still had good footing.

"Careful," Josie called warily from above. Her voice now sounded distant, even a little haunting.

We stopped so Billy could adjust me in his arms. "Here's the deal. I'm going to basically give you up to the Lord, then down you go." He smiled as I forced a shivery nod. "And once you're in, you're coming right back up."

Just then . . . Billy lost his grip. I kicked up to get better balance but couldn't lock in. Billy was so eager to get this over with he ignored my struggling and raced forward with the proclamation: "Having confessed your sins and been forgiven, I now baptize you in the name of the Father, the Son, and the Holy Spirit . . . "

It was a breath-stopping jolt to my system when Billy put me under. The frosty water crashed across my face in claustrophobic waves. Burning pain seared my senses as water rushed up my nostrils. I didn't pinch my nose, which was what I should have done, because I wanted to look cool in front of God. When I saw the sky disappear—possibly for good—I knew I had a problem. And God didn't care one way or the other whether I was pinching my nostrils.

Next mistake: I didn't draw a deep enough breath. I was gasping so hard in the cold it never occurred to me to do a better job of expanding my lungs. Too late now; what little air I had in reserve was rapidly vanishing.

So now I was somewhere beneath the surface, running out of oxygen, sucking ice-congealed mucus, ravaged by shock, probably hypothermic, and then . . .

Billy?

I was in sudden free fall. He had apparently lost his footing as I broke from his clutches. *Where'd he go? Which way is up?* I was running out of time—and hope. *Billy, where are you? Billy!*

I kicked hard against the roaring spring-fed undercurrents. I lost my bearings: what I thought was up was sideways, and down was . . . I had no clue.

Was this it? Was this all there was? I closed my eyes as darkness enveloped me . . .

The back of my head burned like a hot poker, jolting me from my stupor. I wanted to cry out, but I was still underwater! My lungs nearly burst as I refused to breathe. Then an incredible thrust exploded me through the surface of the frigid lake.

"Satan! Release him!" Billy screamed, clutching the hair on the back of my head.

Gagging and heaving, I gasped for breath.

"Billy!" Josie cried, ready to rush in herself.

I coughed and choked, spitting up water while sucking in gaping gulps of succulent spring air.

"Don't fight me or I'll coldcock you!" Billy heaved through gritted teeth, encircling my torso with his right arm while paddling powerfully with his left. "Thank God I was a lifeguard at youth camp." He spat water, plowing toward the shore.

"I told you to watch the moss or you'd lose your footing!" Bunching the hem of her western dress, Josie slid along the rocky buttress.

Billy carried me on his broad shoulders. Water sloshed as he trudged to the base of the rock formation. He pushed me part of the way up on the craggy surface. Josie grabbed my armpits and struggled to tug me along. Water flowed from my pants, steaming atop the hot surface of the dark rocks.

"This is what happens when you go against your better judgment," Billy said, scraping water from his beet-red face and helping Josie haul me the rest of the way up.

Gassed, I lay on my stomach in the tall grass, heaving in the early spring air. Josie patted my shoulder. "That's it, Vance," she whispered lovingly. "It's all over. Everything's going to be okay from here on out."

Billy grabbed the waist of my trousers with one hand and cleanly flipped me onto my back. He didn't appear very pleased. "Okay, Mr. Double-or-Nothing. A bet's a bet and you lost."

"Bet?" Wincing, I raised my neck. "I didn't make a bet."

"Oh yeah. You went all in at the Pearly Gates—and hurled your lunch." Billy straddled me. "I don't know what you're fuller of: anger, rage, self-loathing. Or if you're just plain full of yourself. But it's all coming to a close."

"What'd I bet?"

"Sunday morning attendance for six months. That's what this stupid stunt cost you." Billy glanced at Josie. "Or should I make it a year?" He didn't wait for her to reply. "Six months it is." He nodded with conviction. "And since you're into full immersion, we'll enter you into a full immersion crash course so you can learn all about the Lord Jesus Christ."

"Good luck with that. I never agreed to any such thing."

"Keep it up and we'll make it a year."

"Who are you, the Sheriff of Nottingham?"

"We'll see you next Sunday."

"Ha! You'll see me on the seventh tee." I crawled onto my knees and clumsily stood. I was sore and stiff in joints I didn't even know I had.

Billy narrowed his gaze as he sized me up. I had apparently really ticked him off. "I don't care where I'll see you. And truth be told, I don't care if I ever see you again. But I want you to take away one thing from this sad, sorry episode."

I blinked, wondering if he was going to haul off and hit me.

He pointed with a shaking finger, barely able to contain his impassioned ire. "Don't you ever, and I mean . . . ever, drag the Lord into a cheap parlor game like this again. You hear me?"

This guy was serious. I'd rarely, if ever, seen anyone react so strongly in defense of a person or ideal. If he felt this convicted, it must be important. I agreed with him out of respect—and straight-up fear. "Yeah, man. Sure thing. Whatever."

"All right." Billy ripped his shirt off the ground. "May the peace of Christ be with you now and all the rest of your days." He could no longer hide his disdain. "Don't cause a scene as you leave the premises."

Staring at Billy, I was impressed by his staunch, otherworldly loyalty to the faith. I couldn't get over his dogged determination. It was a thing of beauty in its genuineness, powerful in its conviction. It made me realize there was some unfinished business on my end.

Billy and Josie stared suspiciously at me as I stood before them, half-naked, unmoving.

"What are you waiting for?" Billy asked, buttoning his shirt. "Hell to freeze over?"

Josie shielded her eyes from the sun. "Hold up, Billy. I think there's something stirring in him." Still minus her boot, she strode unevenly toward me. "What is it, dumplin'?"

"I think I missed something the first time around." I glanced at Josie, then Billy. "When we said the prayer, something didn't compute. I lost something in the translation."

All of Billy's frustration and disappointment—and yes, even anger—melted away. He was now filled with compassion. He looked at me with genuine warmth and concern. "You'll be fine, Vance. It's a lot to digest all at once."

"I guess what I'm saying is: can I have a do-over?"

"You bet, darlin'!" Josie laughed. "The Lord specializes in do-overs."

Overcome with emotion, I dropped to all fours. I barely felt it as Billy and Josie slipped to their knees on either side and laid hands on me.

"Okay," Billy said quietly. "These five words will change your life forever." He waited for me to nod. "Repeat after me: Jesus, come into my life . . ."

I choked back the words. I wanted to say it but something was holding me back. "Jesus . . . c-come . . . come into my life."

"That's it," Billy whispered. "Now say it again—with meaning."

Closing my eyes, I summoned every ounce of strength. Each fiber of my being bristled as my current life, as I knew it, seemingly drained from me. "Jesus, please come into my life."

Billy patted my back appreciatively. "Praise God, brother!" He laughed joyfully, close to tears.

"Praise God!" Josie squealed. She whistled shrilly. "Praise God everybody!"

Celebratory hoots, whistles, and cheers rose in the distance. Squinting past the tall grass, I saw about twenty people on the lanai in back of the church. I grew anxious as they started walking toward us. "Man, I don't know if I'm really feeling this," I sighed.

"No sweat, bro. Just give it some time to sink in." Billy pulled me up and handed me my shirt. He called to the advance party, "Meet Brother Vance, a new creation in Christ!"

Collette, lacking any sign of jubilation, led the contingent. She testily squared me up. "That lousy stunt you just pulled better not have been a ploy to grab attention." She gestured crazily to the sky. "The Lord is watching. And he is not amused!"

I shook my head, buttoning my shirt. "Don't worry, this was no PR stunt."

Someone lovingly offered a beach towel for my wet hair. Another person meticulously picked up all my belongings including my watch and wallet.

"Here's your phone." A kind, elderly man handed me the device, fully intact. "I pulled it from the vines in the parking lot. It doesn't seem to be any the worse for wear."

"Thank you, sir." Cradling the phone, I was reminded of my painful last call to Verona. But it didn't matter anymore. Nodding with gratitude, I didn't care if I was totally undone in front of all of these strangers.

It all seemed perfectly right.

"Here." Billy handed me a Bible.

"What's this?" I finished the orange tea from a Styrofoam cup. I sat in a wing chair in Billy's immaculate office adjacent to the parlor. The sweatpants I wore were a size too large; my white, button-down dress shirt was draped over my bare shoulders. Through the glass panels framing the closed door, I saw the last of the stragglers preparing to leave.

Billy wore jeans, flip-flops, and a faded polo shirt that was a size too small, accentuating his impressive build. "I've got to close up, but we'll go over the passage when I get back."

"John, chapter fourteen." I nodded at him.

"You know where to find it, right?" Billy smiled encouragingly. "Matthew, Mark, Luke, John . . . " He ticked off the names of the Gospels. "John is the fourth book, located in the New Testament, roughly three-quarters of the way through the Bible." After observing my blank stare, he took a different tack. "Vance, tell me something. Don't take this the wrong way. Do you even own a Bible?"

I sighed, greatly relieved. "Oh sure. You bet." I wished every question regarding my fledgling faith was that easy.

He nodded patiently and leaned down. "So what version do you have?"

"I–uh . . . " I made a big, sweeping motion. "The version. . . um, the one everyone is most familiar with." My eyes tracked Billy's, but I couldn't read him. We'd both been through an awful lot today, and I didn't want to strain the relationship before it got a head of steam. "Don't worry, it's in one of my boxes. It won't take me long to find it."

Billy shrugged. "All in good time." He turned for the door. "See if you can plow through that chapter before I get back. Believe me, it's doable."

As Billy closed the door, I watched Collette through the glass panels. Laird was hanging all over her. So be it; more power to him. They looked happy enough as they prepared to leave. I sighed, thinking about the good-bye I'd just experienced with Verona Shrevesworth. How long would it take to get over her?

I glanced at the framed photograph on the credenza behind Billy's desk. It was taken during the finals of the state high school wrestling championship. The guy had lost very little muscle mass from his glory days, to be sure. No wonder he was able to heft me out of the water like he did.

I confronted the inevitable. It was time for the Gospel of John. Pleased with the fact I could locate it in the table of contents, I was amazed there were even page numbers. This was way too easy. I wondered why they called these things "books" when some of them were only a few pages long. As soon as I zeroed in on the fourteenth chapter of the Book of John, I did what came naturally whenever I encountered tedious material: my eyes rolled into the back of my head and I passed out.

Bam! Bam! Bam! I didn't know how long I'd been asleep. Chuck Simmonson hammered on the door, then ducked his head inside. "We'll see you next Sunday then?"

Shaking myself awake, I was caught in the crosshairs. "Well, I uh . . . " It was the moment of truth. I had no intention of gracing these doors ever again. Yet Chuck seemed a nice enough guy, and I didn't want to hurt his feelings. I just sat there with glassy eyes and a glazed smile.

"I'll take that as an affirmative. Have a great week, Vance!" He nodded enthusiastically and backed out of the doorway.

I quickly regained my senses. In all the excitement this morning, my initial game plan had been blown sky-high. My goal in coming here was to remain anonymous, to steer clear of any connections. Now I had become the church mascot.

It was time to shove off, time to blow this pop stand. I was gassed and out of sorts and didn't know where I'd go from here but, believe me, I'd figure something out. I slid the Bible atop Billy's clean desk and pulled my shirt back on. I didn't know what I'd do about returning the sweats; probably just stick them in the mail.

Billy breezed back into the office having finished his security check. He glanced at the unopened Bible on the desk and then to me buttoning my shirt. "Did you finish the chapter?"

I saw the way he looked at me. It was very subtle, but you could sense his disappointment. He knew he had caught me in the act of trying to slip out.

I clumsily tried to cover up. "I guess I dozed off."

"Oh." He nodded. "That can happen."

"Look." I felt miserable. "I know I owe you. But that six-month plan . . ."

"Don't worry." He waved me off. "It was heat of the moment stuff. Just some crazy dare." He squared me up, looked deeply into my eyes. "I get a little hyper when people come so close to accepting Christ. You don't want to lose any of them." He held out his hand. "You're a great guy, Vance. Different, yes, but it's been a pleasure meeting you. I wish it could work out differently, but I understand where you're coming from. In the end, it's all up to God anyway."

As we shook hands firmly, I realized something deeper was going on. Billy was demonstrating an intense compassion, as though he cared for me—really and truly cared for me. Possibly like no one else before.

Time stood still. Words tumbled from my mouth. "Count me in," I heard myself say. "I might not be able to make every Sunday, but I'll try." Reeling in confusion, I couldn't believe what I'd just uttered.

Billy smiled at me warmly. "That's nice, man. But people say that all the time. Bottom line: the proof's in the pudding. It all comes down to what you and God work out among yourselves."

I reached for the Bible. "You don't mind?"

"By all means, have at it. It's all yours." Billy scribbled on a blank piece of notepaper. "Here are my numbers. Call me twenty-four/seven." He chuckled. "You can even fax me."

"Thanks." I folded the sheet and stuck it in the Bible.

We hugged—now like true brothers.

When I walked out of that building, I didn't feel the same as when I'd pulled into the parking lot earlier. The sting of losing Verona did not grip me as fiercely as it could have.

There was something at work in me.

And like the preacher had said, the work wasn't going to stop. For anything.

CHAPTER TWELVE

WHOREMONGERING
IN HOG HEAVEN

The following Wednesday afternoon I swerved into the shadows of the vendor lot at the Thurlingate car dealership. The landmark neon sign, visible for miles around, flashed: "Your Platinum Price Savings Difference."

My lungs still burned from the rumble in the lake last Sunday afternoon. Whatever had possessed me to demand to be baptized? *What had I been trying to prove?* And who was I trying to impress? *Possibly God?* As these questions kept pounding inside my rattled psyche, I struggled to get my old life back. But ever since the funeral, things had been headed downhill at supersonic speed. I needed to slam on the brakes—but couldn't find the pedal.

In a lot of ways, walking through the dealership was like returning to the scene of the crime. Amid the bustle of activity, I saw people in the service department and on the sales floor I had seen at Myron's funeral. Were all of them on board with the spiritual game plan Arnie had so passionately spelled out from the lectern? Or were they feeling glum as ever, unmoved by his fiery admonition, thankful to be left alone to lead their lives however they chose?

I felt trapped somewhere in the middle. Something had undeniably touched me. I didn't know what, but I didn't like the direction things were headed. *And where, by the way, is Belle Murphy?*

Myron had just parted ways with a factory rep and didn't seem particularly pleased to see me. Trying to be as upbeat as possible, I did not extend my hand, figuring that a handshake would only aggravate him further. "Hey, man, I know I don't have an appointment."

"I know." He looked at his watch with agitation.

Well, this was awkward. I couldn't blame Myron for feeling a little exposed these days, a little vulnerable. In the past, you could always count on a battle royal when he and I and the old man got together. Now that Myron Sr. was gone, so was Junior's firewall. It meant the two of us would be squaring off and there would be no one to run interference—with the possible exception of mama— and I didn't think Junior especially relished that proposition.

"What's up?" He straightened his tie and finger-combed his thinning brown hair.

"Nothing major." I made a mental note to come bearing swag next time. "I was just on my way to the mixer in Mid-City and thought I'd swing by. Are you going?"

"Right, Vance. Like I've got time for mixers." Junior brushed the sleeve of his suit coat, a slight tremble in his left hand. "My four o'clock should have been here by now."

"Look, I don't want to keep you. I'll make an appointment next time. I promise."

Distracted, Junior stared past my shoulder into the front parking lot. "I can't stand it when people are late without calling."

"Okay, man. I'm outta here. You enjoy your day." I figured I'd better cut and run before Junior found a reason to really get hacked at me.

I hustled back to fleets, hoping that Arnie didn't have a customer. The door was open but his office was empty. He could have been anywhere. Too bad. I really wanted to know whether that spell he'd put on me at the funeral had an expiration date.

I resisted the urge to look for Belle Murphy and headed outside. It was hot and particularly humid for this early in the season. Sliding behind the wheel, I checked my phone messages. Millie Deckerton from our graphics department had left a playful addendum to a question about a special effects issue. *Is she hinting at the possibility of something between us?* Millie and I always got along at company functions, though our taste in art was wildly divergent. I was far more traditional—in keeping with my "closet prude" persona, I guess—while she championed the avant-garde. Maybe it was time we went to dinner and checked out some of the galleries in my end of town.

I backed from the space and rolled through the auxiliary lot behind the dealership. Picking up speed, I reached for the phone to call Millie back. I wondered if I really had a shot with her or whether my romantic imagination was playing tricks on me . . . again.

A ghost bolted from the base of the neon sign and into the path of my car. "Nooooo!" Tires screeched as I slammed the brakes.

Arnie banged the hood with a wicked forearm like he was fending off a pulling guard.

I laid on the horn. "Get a grip, Crush!"

Hustling around the front bumper, he draped himself across the driver's side window. "You didn't return my call last night."

I clutched my phone, thankful I hadn't just dialed Millie back. "Are you nuts?"

He straightened up, squinting into the last burst of daylight. "Let's grab a cup. I don't have all day."

I parked where I'd been before and followed Arnie into the employee break room. Jubilant, he turned over his shoulder as we headed toward the coffeemaker. "I just hit it out of the park with Highfeld Gas and Electric. We're talking everything from light-duty to freight boxes, cargo vans to cutaways, and everything in between. That's not even counting the office fleet."

"Good for you," I said. "It sounds like you do more than preach."

"All glory to God." Crusher was immaculately attired in creased khaki slacks, a navy blazer, a powder blue pinpoint Oxford shirt, and a red, white, and gold-striped tie. He pulled up at the coffeemaker. "Now to the real business at hand: tell me all about the church you went to."

I thought about everything that transpired on Sunday, including the ill-advised lake dousing. I figured keeping it vague was better at this point. "It went okay. No complaints."

"What's the name?" Arnie's hand engulfed a Styrofoam cup. He poured from a pot that was thoroughly stained.

"A place over in Chorus Lake."

"Chorus Lake?" He cocked his head. "That's a little far from home, isn't it?"

"It was important to keep my anonymity."

"Does that include your anonymity from God?" He handed me the pot.

"Chorus Lake Coven . . . no. Chorus Lake Holy Covenant." I poured coffee into my cup.

"Holy Covenant. Hmm. I guess you can't go wrong with that." Arnie shook out sugar and creamer, stirring lustily with a skinny red stick. "Do you know what the word 'covenant' means?"

I shrugged. "You hear it in legal parlance, like a binding agreement made between two parties. You also hear it when it comes to marriage, which, I guess, stands to reason."

"Okay, so tell me something." Arnie licked the end of his stir stick then dropped it in the trash. "What's the common denominator in all those examples?"

I glanced away. "I don't know. You got me."

"Relationships, Vance. It's all about relationships."

"Oh." I reestablished eye contact. "Okay."

"But when we're talking about God's covenant, it's a whole different story. God's covenant is stronger than titanium, more powerful than a cat-five hurricane. It is a relationship that was fused before time itself began, a relationship that knows no bounds and is perfect in its infiniteness. God desperately wants this relationship with each and every one of us, sealing us in a bond that cannot be broken or voided by anyone or anything."

"I guess the word 'holy' doesn't hurt either then, right?"

"God is holy, that's the long and short of it, meaning he's set apart," Arnie said. "Tell me, did they preach the Word there?"

I nodded, having learned to just go with the flow whenever this issue came up. "Sure thing." My eyes followed the muscular salesman over to a round table draped with a copy of the dealership's four-color, double-page newspaper advertisement.

Arnie's chair squealed when he settled his girth into its too-small steel frame. "Have you been down on your knees in prayer? And do you have your hands on a good Bible?"

"They gave me a Bible Sunday. I was supposed to read John chapter . . . chapter . . . " I snapped my fingers. "I don't know. The guy—Billy—wrote it down somewhere."

Arnie stared at me with his piercing green eyes. "So you haven't read it yet?"

I made it look like I felt badly. "Just haven't had the time."

"You gotta make the time, man." Arnie bowed his thick neck. "You can't let the SOB get the better of you."

"SOB?"

"Satan, of course. He wants to run your butt outta town on a rail." Arnie leaned into me. "And he will, if you let him."

I averted my eyes. "Yeah, well . . ."

Arnie leaned closer. "So what'd they preach on?"

"Uh, let's see." I exhaled, mulling it over. "One dude went after a lost sheep, leaving the other ninety-nine to fend for themselves. And the other was about a kid who demanded his inheritance, then blew it on hookers and ended up on a pig farm. It all turned out okay when he was welcomed back home with open arms by his old man." I purposefully left out the part about me dozing off then being awakened by the flying elbow of a woman with the worst breath I'd ever smelled.

"That's good, Vance. Those are two of the most famous parables in the Bible." The beaming Crusher nodded. "So far, so good. You understand the significance of those stories, right? You understand they aren't about the lost sheep or the lost son, but instead apply to the bigger picture."

"No, man," I shrugged, chuckling lightly. "I don't have a clue."

"It's simple: take the Prodigal Son. You know who that parable was really about? The son? The father?" Arnie nodded, intent on keeping my attention. "For sure, it was about those two. But there was also an older brother in the mix. That cat never broke any of the rules; he was a real straight arrow. Do you know how ticked he was when the old man gutted the trust fund to pay off Sonny Boy's early inheritance? Elder bro was entitled to his share of the dough too, you know."

"Bummer." I checked my watch. I had to hit the road soon or risk losing out on fresh hors d'oeuvres at the Mid-City gabfest.

"He probably wanted to *kill* the old fart for caving in like that." Arnie batted my arm. "So the younger son limps home stinking of pig manure—he was Jewish, don't forget—and the old man runs out to embrace him. Do you know how *wrong* that is in Middle Eastern culture? But that's what relationship building is all about. It's called unconditional love, and it's what God gives us every minute of the day." Crusher nodded. "It's also what he wants from all of us in return."

Mention of the pig farm got me thinking about delicacies wrapped in bacon. My mouth watered, anticipating the savory fare at the mixer. "Well, if you ask me . . . I mean, if I were the other son, I'd be righteously hacked off too."

Arnie was pleased I was keeping up. "Yeah, especially since all the brat wanted was Daddy's shekels—the total opposite of what a healthy relationship is built on." He shifted his weight in the small chair.

"You mean one that's give and take," I said. "It can't be all one-sided."

"Right. But the older brother doesn't get it and thinks he's somehow superior to the father. He doesn't understand the concept of forgiveness and redemption." Arnie leaned back. "And if we start playing those games with God, trying to elevate ourselves above him, that is definitely a recipe for disaster."

I caught myself glancing at the wall clock. "I'm sure we've all been there before."

"Bottom line: the older brother doesn't have a relationship with the Lord because he doesn't think he needs one. He thinks that rigidly adhering to the rules and laws is all that counts. That becomes his idol. When it becomes a source of pride, you are on very dangerous ground."

A light suddenly went off. "So if I'm the older brother, and let's say . . . my younger brother is addicted to something, and he tries desperately to get help, I'm the one standing around in judgment, looking down my nose at the situation, questioning God about what's fair and not fair."

"You nailed it!" Arnie slapped the table and leaned back. "The addict looks to his father—in other words, God—for forgiveness and help kicking the habit . . . while you, the older brother, stand around on the sidelines not giving a rip about your brother's addiction. Instead, you're only worried about your own sorry self. After all, you've played by the rules all along, right? You deserve to be taken care of."

"Generally," I said with a quick nod, trying to mentally assume the role of the older brother. "I've done my best."

"Relationship-building gets past all that legalistic dreck," Crusher continued. "It's no different with God than people. Do you want someone coming on to you as a friend because they think they can get something from you, or do you want them as a friend because they genuinely care about you and enjoy your company?"

"Yeah, I hear you." I thought about the supercilious claptrap I'd endured over the years in my industry, a lot of it laughingly disingenuous. "Definitely the latter."

"And believe me, God sees through all that hooey like nobody's business—like the world's most powerful laser." Arnie paused. "Don't forget. The only thing we're leaving earth with is our relationship with God. And that cuts both ways."

"So what are you saying? That I need to start blowing it to get in his good graces?" I couldn't believe I was actually taking an active part in this conversation.

"God wants our love, devotion . . . adoration—call it what you want. He's done his part, sacrificing Jesus on the cross for our redemption. Now it's up to us to respond to the invitation." Arnie tapped the bottom of his cup on the table. "Do you know how we do that? By confessing our sins to our heavenly Father and asking him to help us repent. Have you done that yet?"

A flood of memories from last Sunday overwhelmed me. There I was all over again, waterlogged on the shoreline as Billy and Josie desperately tried to coax a confession of faith out of me. I shrugged. "Yes and no."

"What the Sam Hill is that supposed to mean?" Typical Arnie. Straight to the point.

"Yes, I verbalized I was a sinner. And no, I don't think I actually meant it."

"Well, that's no good." Arnie stiffened in his chair. I could tell he was frustrated, but still unbowed. "Anytime you talk to the Almighty you've got to mean it. He's got all the time in the world for you, and desperately wants to hear from you, but you've got to hold up your end of the bargain or else it's nothing more than a busted play. If you're gonna pray it, bro, you gotta mean it. Otherwise you're just wasting your breath—not to mention stepping all over God's holy timetable."

"That's the whole point," I said. "How can I make any connection when I can't see him or touch him? I feel stupid talking to someone I can't see."

"The big thing is realizing who Jesus is and what he means to you. He is our Lord and Savior. A lot of people want a savior but not a lord. They treat Jesus like a rabbit's foot, leaning on him when things get tough, turning their back on him when times are good. But to have a true relationship, to have a true identity in Christ, you need to put all of your faith, hope, love, and trust in him."

"Yeah, man, easy for you to say." It was all I could muster.

"Don't sweat it. It'll come in time." Arnie smiled reassuringly. "For now, just know there are people all over the world praying for you. And believe me, no one is worried about praying to someone they can't see. God is more real than anything you're going to encounter in this life—and you can stake all of eternity on it."

I thought about people praying for me. "Didn't I tell you to call off the dogs on the prayer front?"

"It doesn't work that way. Once the request is made, it's like live meat to the warriors. No one knows the full extent of the power of prayer."

"So what are they praying about? Are they casting a spell on me? 'Cause over the last few days I've been feeling kinda . . . I don't know—kinda off. I'm wondering if those warriors, as you call them, are witch doctors after my soul."

"Knock it off with the voodoo stuff." Arnie made an offhanded gesture. "Mixing that up with prayer is blasphemous, if you want to get technical about it."

"Okay. But does all this make you act and think differently? It's really weird, some of the things happening to me. For instance, the women in my life are dropping like flies—and I don't even really care."

"That's God at work in you, pure and simple. It's the Holy Spirit taking control of your life." Arnie read my confusion and forged ahead. "He's alive in you, brother. Whether you want to admit it or not, he's come to live in you." Arnie grabbed my shoulder. "It's up to you to welcome Jesus Christ into your life as Lord and Savior."

"It sounds like what the preacher said to me Sunday as I was leaving," I murmured. "'Once God starts a work in you, he doesn't stop until he's finished.'"

"There you go." Arnie drained the last of his coffee. "Like they say, 'God loves you too much to leave you alone.' He's going to make you a new person from the inside out."

"Well, it's getting old in a hurry," I said, turning brutally honest. "I'm pretty much used to getting my own way in life, and if that means being combative or confrontational, so be it. But now I'm more interested in being compassionate. It's like I've lost my competitive edge." I flattened my hands on the table. "It's the same with accountability. All of a sudden I feel the need to shine a light into every corner of my life, like I want to come clean on everything and tell the whole world about my faults."

"Totally understandable." Crusher grinned. "It's a transitional phase. You're in the biggest life-altering transformation you'll ever experience. It's not always pretty going from point A to point B, but in the long run it's worth every uncomfortable, inconvenient minute of it."

"Well, I'm not giving in to this new way of thinking. I'm going to fight it with everything I've got." I nodded. "I'm going to personally will myself back to the way things used to be."

Crusher chuckled, though his demeanor was now completely void of humor. "Well, if you're talking about duking it out with God, good luck with that."

He stood slowly in deference to the arthritis in his knees. "Good luck with that, Vance."

CHAPTER THIRTEEN

CHRISTIAN SEX ON THE FM DIAL

Crosstown traffic was building in a sea of taillights. I clutched my phone, having retrieved messages and returned the last of the time-sensitive calls.

Angling into the middle lane, I laid out the schedule for the rest of the evening: the Bulls and Bullets tipped off at 8:00 on TNT. This meant I had to be well clear of the meet-and-greet by 7:30. A group of us would probably end up at the Golden Lawns Bar and Grill for a widescreen orgy featuring another Bulls play-off victory.

Growing up around Chicago, I had followed the Bulls since their days playing in the fabled Stadium, an arena gone to seed that probably ended up with a larger rat population than fan base. How times had changed: the sleek United Center was now home to Michael Jordan and the Bulls, a prodigious brand on the world stage, winning multiple NBA championships. But I would never forget the DNA of the franchise and its inauspicious beginnings.

I flashed back to the Bulls' satisfying home win last Sunday against the Washington Bullets. The breakup between me and Verona had not been the only fireworks that day. Hundreds of miles away in Chicago, MJ had gone off at the United Center for fifty-five points in a 109-104 Bulls victory in Game Two of the Eastern Conference playoffs. Tonight they were down in Washington to finish off the Bullets before moving on to their next foe, probably Atlanta.

I finally convinced myself to invite Millie Deckerton to join us at the Lawns tonight. Adrenaline kicked in as I punched up her callback number and breathlessly counted each ring. When her phone kicked to voicemail, I was disappointed but left a heartfelt message. As I killed the connection I realized it was short notice and that she'd probably blow me off. But if she did show, that would say volumes. Something told me Millie could be a lot of fun.

I fiddled with the FM dial, tuning in the new sports-talk station. I wanted to deliver a favorable report to the owner when I saw him at the agency function. In a great marketing ploy, he had retained the old dial position on the AM band and then added the combo punch of an FM behemoth. It allowed the station to expand its program offerings by adding play-by-play packages and much more in-depth coverage of a wide range of sports topics. It also provided opportunities for time-shifting and repurposing, meaning the outlet could reach a boatload more listeners throughout the metro with double the ratings.

But there was a slight glitch on my way to the new dial position, a little unexpected static on the road to easy listening: I landed on the local Christian station that resided on the adjacent frequency. Wasn't that just swell? How could a Christian radio station "just so happen" to be jammed up against the new FM home of my favorite sports-talk station?

I soon realized this was not your run-of-the-mill Christian format. The scathing drawl of a man possessed suddenly pounded through the speakers like a runaway jackhammer.

" . . . And I ask you, was having sex with that hot li'l doxy you met in the produce section of the supermarket the other night worth eternal damnation?"

"Say *what*?" I gripped the wheel as my eyes bugged.

The fire-breathing radio preacher had a riveting voice driven by a raspy, southern twang. "I'm not going to relive it for you. You're doing a pretty good job of that, I'm sure. You convinced yourself it was a one-time-only deal. What the old-time country crooners call a one-night stand. You know the drill. And you both said it will never happen again. Yet one of you is just one step away from picking up the phone and dialing. Two steps away from plunging yourselves that much further into the un-quenchable fires of eternal damnation!"

"Hey pal, not so fast!" I shouted at the radio while signaling for a left turn. "If you're talking about the supermarket the other night, I only *thought* about it. I never actually went through with it. Big difference, okay?"

Hold up a sec. Am I actually shouting at the radio?

The ramrod preacher continued to blister the airwaves. "What was the point of the tryst to begin with? Or what the young bloods call a hookup. You can say you were attracted to each other all you want. It's all a lie, perpetrated by the Grand Schemer, the Big Liar, the Pants-On-Fire Prince himself, old Beelzebub. You know who I'm talking about? I'm talking about Sledgehammer Louie, the one ready to bust your life apart at the seams, the guy who whispers in your ear at two in the morning and says it's okay to take that dolly home. Besides, who's going to care? What harm are you doing to anyone? You're both consenting adults, right? Well, you are, aren't you? Isn't it so?"

"Hey, man, it never stopped me before!" I was now fully on-board with having this one-sided conversation with the very strident voice on the radio.

"And there you go, rustling in the satin sheets, clinging to each other, sweating on each other, not giving the slightest thought to the stink you're leaving in Heaven. Not the slightest thought to the streak of excrement you're painting the halls of Heaven with! No, you don't care about any of that! All you care about is pleasuring each other, just losing each other in the dark, dense lusting world of forbidden passion."

"Lighten up, man." I glanced in the rearview mirror. "You're killing me."

"What do you do in the light of day, waking up beside her?"

"Punt!" I slammed the steering wheel.

"Just think of it: God's beautiful, impenetrable, unbelievable light of day, the gift of absolute life he has so lovingly bestowed upon us—squandered by a couple of hedonistic sinners enjoying the company of each other's flesh, wrapped tighter than a sausage melt at the Waffle House."

"Nooooo!" I banged the steering wheel, drooling maniacally. "Not the Waffle House!"

"And as long as we're talking about the gift of God, what about that long, supple frame of the girl in the slippery satins beside you? She ain't bad, is she?"

I gritted my teeth. "I don't know, Pops. You tell me."

"Did it ever occur to you, genius, that she may be the handiwork of God? That God Almighty knitted her lovingly in her mama's womb and that, quite possibly, she's *his* and not *yours*? You know what that means, fireball? It means you're stepping all over God's personal property. You just strode over the fence, college boy, and trampled the flowers in the front yard. And those flowers wilted and died. And it's your fault for letting your lust get the better of you and being disobedient to the will and way of the heavenly Father."

"Hold it, man." I balled a fist. "God may own the property, but she's the one renting the joint—and she said the coast was clear."

"Why you slimy, rationalizing sack of toasted razor clams, you think that one is going to fly with the Exalted Captain, the Number One Skipper? You think that will score points in the pearly boulevards of Heaven? Huh? The bottom line is this, you mealy manure-slinger: you took advantage of the opportunity. You were opportunistic on the Hedonistic Highway. Do you hear what I'm saying, you unwashed heathen? You took not one woman, but how many? *How many?* You took them all down the drain with you, all flushed with the moment, all feeling good about themselves, and you spat on the lilies of the valley. So you'll go to the Seat of Judgment and have to explain why all these women have so much discomfort right about now because they're not exactly cleaned up all nice and tidy for the big event. And it's all your fault for making them feel that way."

"All right! Enough already. I'm sorry!" I did my best to sound sincere . . . speaking to a radio.

"You dog! You parasitic mongrel! I'll bet you treat sex as a commodity, don't you? You may not pay for it, in fact you may be all proud and haughty that you've never paid for it—according to your twisted standards—yet you *do* pay for it. You pay for it in the everlasting fires of your rapidly perishing soul. You treat it like something you can just buy, sell, and trade. I'll bet you even use it to hold over someone's head to get your way. Huh? Ever done that? Don't lie to me, son. Sure you have. I know you have."

"Not that I recall," I cried. "Not in the last five days!"

"Do you know the ultimate slap in the face? Do you know how to rip a woman's heart out, tear her self-esteem to shreds? It's when some Lace Panty Romeo—and that would be you, sugar nuts—whispers highfalutin lies in her ear while he hauls her into the sack with his sorry, lust-filled lines. That's the World Series of disrespect for a woman. Here you go out on a date with her, and all night you've been holding the door open and bowing and scraping, making her feel like there ain't none other like her in all the world, treating her like the queen of the car wash—and then you get the lights down low and all of a sudden all that respect goes out the window. Oh yeah, it's suddenly all about you, ain't it? All about you getting exactly what you want. No time for her. She's nothing more than a slippery satin sheet princess, the deflowered object of your numb-knuckled passion. And all the while you're proving to the Almighty you're quite content to lead the life of a heathen pig destined for the flaming slop mill of eternal cloven-hoof devastation."

Gasping for air, it was all I could do to turn left at the light. I tapped the dashboard above the radio. "I'm getting near the garage now, Pops. Your time is running very, very short."

"You think you're going to put me in a box, flypaper boy, is that your deal? Well then, punk tart, answer me this: did you know that sex is a drug?"

I slammed the brakes before entering the garage.

"I thought so. Do you know something, gunslinger? If they bottled sex and put it on the shelf with the other hedonistic make-me-happy-with-a-swallow pills, it would be *three hundred times* more potent than heroin. You got that? And you think you're gonna treat it like a spin in Daddy's car? Huh, ferret breath? Is that the game plan? You gonna put sex on the same level as heroin, you cheese-eating skirt clinger? How 'bout crack, croak, and crank, you mealy centerfold-drooler. Because I'm here to tell you, sex ain't a drug for lightweights."

"I'm not buying it, Grandpa. Not for a second." I checked my rearview mirror to make sure no one was behind me.

"And you wanna know who made it all possible? God. That's who. He gave us a drug that can burn moth holes in your underwear from your ankles to your sweaty crotch. Oh yeah, it's more powerful than a speeding locomotive into kingdom come. You know what a bottle of sex would do for you, maverick? Huh? Your toenails would grow two inches every five minutes, your pit hair would fall to your ankles, and your teeth would explode through your cheeks! You'd be a babbling fiend, eating your cufflinks and washing windows with your fevered tongue. Do you understand, highflier? The Supreme Commander gave us sex as a birthday present all wrapped up in a box with a ribbon. Not as some crazed, perverted romp around Nasty Acres with naked, bowlegged songstresses. You like that, Leotard Lou? You like bringing down them fine dollies with your craven-hoofed happy prancing? Huh, Peaches? You feelin' good about that? Well just wait until Judgment Day. We'll see how all that's working out for you, you gilt-edged whore, you maggot-licking loser."

"Later, pal!" I hit the gas and ran hard into the parking garage.

"Are you a merchant of the skin trade, Mr. Bubbly Cheeks Knuckleballer?"

"I'm going under steel and concrete now," I announced to the radio. "I'll be losing you. Buh bye!" I cruised the aisles, but there were no spaces. As I descended to the next level and the next level after that, the pounding voice on the radio grew . . . somehow louder and stronger. I glanced at the car windows, seemingly bulging out in response to the fury of the apoplectic preacher's hellfire rant.

"Tell me something, Giddy Gonads. On Judgment Day, what are you going to be driving? A VW bug, a minivan, or a Greyhound bus?" The rasping clergyman snapped his fingers violently. "Come on, come on. I ain't got all day!"

"A VW bug, a minivan, or a Greyhound bus? What are you *talking about?*" I gripped the wheel, slowly patrolling the aisle for any sign of a vacant space.

"For all the women you're taking down with you, you free-range turkey gizzard. Could they all fit in a VW bug? A minivan? Or a Greyhound bus? Answer me. Or are you gonna tell me a Boeing 747? Gimme a head count, Hedonist Herbert. I wanna know everyone you're taking with you on that Grand Canyon Tour of No Returns."

"How am I supposed to remember them all?"

"You orgiastic miscreant! You're gonna tell me you can't remember every last nubile creature you've ever frolicked in the mud with? All the women you've ever deflowered outside the sacred institution of marriage? Is that how little they mean to you?"

"Okay, okay! I guess I could come close. Should I start now?"

"Not now, you overheated nut bucket! Instead I want you to picture yourself on Judgment Day. Picture all the trumpets and angels and the heavenly hosts and the gold-lined streets. But realize something: you're looking at it through a window. Don't forget, you're still at the Hot Seat Table, Bruiser Cheeks, and you have a couple more questions to answer. You're watching those angels licking their lips, thinking they're about to blow their trumpets for you. Well, think again, you unholy quagmire of rotting hog muffins. They're getting ready to herald in the cat before you. And you wanna know why? Because he could control himself between the sheets. Sure, he made mistakes. He wasn't perfect. Who is? But he had it enough under wraps that he finished the race strong. He confessed his sins when he messed up and did his best to repent, always talking with his heavenly Father about where things stood. So how 'bout you, Son? What's it gonna be like for you at the Big Table? Are you gonna be partaking of the Feast of Feasts or grabbing week-old fast food at the old Damnation Drive-Thru? Ain't it about time you knotted your jockstrap and got right with God? You never know when it's gonna end—and when it does, it's gonna be too late."

I swung into the last space on the lowest level. I was in the pit of Parking Lot Hell. I'd never seen it this full—*ever*.

The voice on the radio kept booming. "This has been Reverend Rory Psalter coming to you from somewhere high in the Smokies saying have a blessed day, y'all. But before I go, here's the good news. There is a way to fix things. No matter how bad you may have run afoul of God our Father, there's still a way to make it right. All you have to do is accept Jesus Christ into your life as your Lord and Savior." Rory's voice hung eerily in the air. It sounded like he was sitting in the front seat beside me. "Can I pray with you, Son?" It startled me. He had crossed the line and was getting way too personal.

"Thanks but no thanks, man." I came to my senses. "Game over, dude." I flipped the dial to the FM sports station. All I got was static—exceedingly loud static. "Go figure." I wrenched the key from the ignition and climbed outside. Slamming the door, I pretended that everything was normal.

But I knew everything was far from normal.

CHAPTER FOURTEEN

KEEP YOUR JUMBO PRAWNS TO YOURSELF

As I exited the elevator I paused to straighten my tie in the reflection of a plate glass window. Trying to look composed, I strode toward the broadcast center, wrestling with the question: why had I talked back to my radio like a raving nutcase? It was weird, though. That preacher sounded like he was squatting inside my dashboard, screaming at me through the air conditioner duct. I made a note to tone down my act. Maybe I'd been dining too much at the Beef Penguin of late.

Entering the main complex, I was overpowered by a tidal wave of sound. Acoustics apparently had not weighed heavily in renovation plans with no consideration given for baffles, diffusers, or bass traps. So a couple thousand screaming, laughing voices funneled maniacally down a flight of steel stairs, struck a massive concrete floor, and bounced straight up into my eardrums. But let me not forget: I was a closet prude and a blatant hypocrite—which meant I had it coming to me.

Aesthetically, I loved what the architects had done. The one-time garment factory, located in a formerly rundown part of Mid-City, had been gutted to make way for this spectacular broadcast facility. It was one of those rehab jobs where they left the brick in place and redid the hardwood floors while leaving the ductwork exposed. The engineers and designers had done a masterful job of putting it all under one roof: two powerful AMs and three FMs, including the region's top-rated alternative rock station. In addition there was a full range of audio and video production facilities and a host of ancillary support services.

I signed in at the reception desk at the foot of the stairs. Scribbling "Vance C" on a chintzy label, I stuck it on the pocket of my suit coat and wondered how long before it curled up and fell off. The shindig was being hosted by the Kresslane Media Group; I hoped that the CEO, Horst Kresslane, was upstairs making the rounds.

As I ascended each stair the decibel level rose until I could barely hear myself think. The thing about these schmooze-paloozas was this: if you didn't want to deal with the details of someone's job, life, or business, you needed to be a moving target. If you were nimble enough you could get your name out to a good number of prospective clients and still have time for the most important aspect of all: gorging yourself so you didn't have to worry about dinner.

I paused on the last stair, momentarily frozen in time. I thought back to what the tennis-playing preacher said to me last Sunday as I left church: "Once God starts a work in you he doesn't stop until he's finished." *What's that supposed to mean?* And more importantly, why was I thinking about it now?

I opened my eyes and stepped into the ribald, blathering sea of hotshots, hard-chargers, up-and-comers, wannabes, and has-beens. The event was an amalgamation of the Mid-City Enterprise Zone, downtown Arts Council, the Ad Club, and the regional broadcasters association—meaning there were a lot of people at this mixer I knew. Like being caught up in the swirling vortex of a pinball machine, I kept veering toward the inimitable Horst Kresslane, who ran a stable of some of the most cutting edge radio stations in the country.

Horst was wrapping up with a couple of reps from a local ad agency. A tall, elderly gentleman, he appeared to have serious indigestion—until he saw me. "Vance, you sly dog. Have you poached any more of my air personalities for your nightly newscasts?"

"Horst, we've been through this how many times before? It wasn't me." The dude Horst referred to was the news director at a smoking-hot affiliate the next market over. "You're thinking of, you know . . . old what's-his-name."

"Oh, right." Horst lost his bluster and became more interested in a refill of his wine.

"Don't worry," I interjected. "I hate the putz as much as you."

"Come on now. We don't *hate* anyone." Horst flagged a waitperson wielding a tray artfully brimming with grapes and an impressive cheese selection. "We just leave them in our rearview mirror and move on."

"You're a lot kinder than me."

"Have you tried the smoked salmon yet?" The congenial host plucked a bunch of grapes from the tray and pondered the cheese selection. "It's from British Columbia."

"No, but I will." I nodded. "Hey, by the way, congratulations on your new signal."

"Thanks!" He turned from the cheese tray and snapped to attention. "How do we sound?"

"Man, you're . . . " I didn't have the heart to tell him he was being decimated by a perverted southern preacher on an adjacent frequency. Ordinarily I would have just blurted it out and ruined his day. But somehow I didn't feel like bringing Horst down just to rub it in. "Your station sounds phenomenal! Booming signal, clear as a bell. You're bringing down the house."

"Oh, that's a relief!" Tension drained from Horst's lanky body. "Coming from you, you don't know what that means."

"No sweat." I glanced over my shoulder. A growing number of agency pros was queueing up to pay their respects to the iconic host. It was time to let someone else have the limelight. "I'm going to grab some of that salmon before it runs out."

"Please do," Horst said. "And let's have lunch before things get crazy with summer."

"By all means. I'll be in touch."

"You know, Vance . . . I want to crack some top ten markets. And I'm told you're the one to spearhead it."

"Anytime, Horst. Happy to be of service." As we parted ways I happily waded through the body press in search of that succulent Canadian smoked salmon. I grabbed an iced-down Heineken from a galvanized tub and waved to a group of agency colleagues in the atrium.

The aroma of roast beef assaulted my senses and I paused to sniff the bovine-perfumed air. Then I saw her: *Collette*. She wore a knee-length skirt with cowboy boots and one of her trademark silk blouses. She was flapping her gums with a mid-level marketing type, free as a bird and oblivious to my imminent presence. I figured it was only a matter of time before our paths crossed at one of these industry hoedowns, but I sure didn't think it would happen this quickly.

So there we were. Time to get it on. I had her on my turf now; we were no longer in the cozy confines of church. I was going to jab back with some of those blow darts she'd peppered me with Sunday and let her see how it felt. If she fought back then we might have a full-blown scene on our hands. Who knew what was going to happen? Surely it was something that needed to play out. Even if I got tossed, I'd make sure it was an epic performance worthy of my local legacy.

"Vance, am I glad to see you. It's about time you showed!" Barry Tammers, a muscular, balding man, grabbed my arm and whisked me into a side conference room. "They got a special stash of smoked salmon in the production department." He lustily munched a jumbo prawn.

"Barry, you're killing me, man." Quickly deflating, I wondered if I could rekindle my ire for Collette before this shindig ended. Now all that mattered was the carving station at the head of the conference table. I grabbed a plate and motioned with the hand throttling the green neck of the beer bottle. "Just keep piling it on," I told the young guy wearing the chef's hat.

"So, did you hear about Lorna Bongles?" Barry asked heatedly. He was a little on the disheveled side, sporting a three-day beard growth, but he had talent to burn. Barry's video production company was no joke; he bagged clients from a five hundred-mile radius.

"Where'd you get that?" I gestured to the fat prawn Barry was gnawing on, thicker than a lineman's Super Bowl ring finger. He vaguely pointed to another room as I spooned creamy sauce onto the meat then cut up a soft roll into a flimsy excuse for a sandwich. I stood at the credenza behind the conference table chewing noisily, realizing I hadn't stopped for lunch today. "Now, what about Lorna?" Yammering with a full mouth—and not caring—I took a lusty swig of beer.

Barry leaned into me like it was a guarded secret. "Hot off the press. She's being kicked upstairs to a TV group in Texas." He nudged me. "Does that frost your lemons or what?"

I didn't know if Barry was looking for me to crawl out of my skin and start throwing things. Clearly, Lorna and I had a history, and it definitely had its colorful moments. A first-class piece of work, she'd caused me more headaches than I could count, outmaneuvering me with questionable backdoor programming deals and pitting her station, a well-financed network affiliate, against mine. Why should I lament not having to compete with her anymore? I didn't have the heart to tell Barry she called me yesterday to say good-bye. "I wish her well," was all I said. Nodding quickly, I dove in for another bite.

"Come on, Vance." Barry gestured with his half-eaten prawn. "We were taking bets on whether you'd hop the first flight to DFW and head up the Welcome Wagon committee."

"I don't want you to . . . " I swallowed as I watched Collette and her associates stroll past the conference room window. As they disappeared down the stairs, I realized the dustup would have to wait for another day. I paused to collect my thoughts. What was the big problem? Was I jealous of her relationship with Laird? Or was it the relationship she had with God?

"Hey, are you okay?" Barry batted my arm. "What were you going to say about Lorna?"

I took another bite, returning to the business at hand. Deep down, I was happy for Lorna. I saw no reason not to be. This new spirit of heartfelt camaraderie I seemed to have acquired was totally unexpected—and actually quite refreshing. For once, I didn't have to prove anything.

Barry frantically pushed buttons, looking to ignite my ire. "She's a serial backstabber. You know it, I know it, the whole town knows it."

Nodding, I took another bite. "You mentioned lemons earlier."

He blinked. *"Lemons?"* It looked like he'd just bitten into one. "What about them?"

I took a lazy sip of beer and stared into space. "I wonder where the United States ranks in terms of lemon production. Worldwide, I mean."

"Who cares?" He tried modulating his voice. "I thought you were gonna blow a gasket, and all you want to do is talk about citrus stats? My aching back, it was just a figure of speech!" He slapped the table and started choking on his prawn.

People standing around the sumptuous conference room stopped conversing and stared at us with varying degrees of curiosity.

"Easy." I grabbed his collar and leaned into him. "She's a flaming moron, okay? Is that what you want me to say? Let's just get past it."

Barry swigged chardonnay from a clear plastic cup and wiped his mouth with the back of a hairy hand. "Whatever."

As I straightened up, it occurred to me I owed Barry. He'd saved me from a potentially embarrassing meltdown with Collette when he intercepted me earlier. "So tell me. How's your wife's bed and breakfast coming?"

"You're really on a roll today, aren't you?" Growing pale, the stout man mopped his cringing forehead with a greasy napkin. "I take it you haven't heard. It's bad juju." He exhaled anxiously. "Belinda blew chunks on the location and we're losing dough hand over fist."

"No, man. That's news to me." I couldn't believe how badly I felt for him.

"I've got two daughters to put through college, you know. I don't need this aggravation."

My next utterance was such an uncharacteristic part of my lexicon, it didn't even sound right coming from my mouth. Days before I might have possibly mentioned it as a joke, but never in the context of a serious solution to a pressing need. I patted Barry's back and said, "I'll be praying for you."

Barry's eyes bugged. He spit-sprayed me, then began violently hacking and coughing. I slapped his back, which only made things worse. "*Praying* for me?" he gagged, flicking wine off his fingers. "Are you *insane*? What's gotten into you?"

"You're right," I gulped. "I'm sorry. I must have misspoken." I stood back brushing the front of my suit, struggling to make sense of what I'd just said. Barry was correct: *where had I come up with that one?* Talk about left field—this was getting scary. I leaned forward, tried to calm the waters. "Are you all right? I didn't mean to set you off like that."

All eyes in the conference room were now squarely on us.

Calming slightly, Barry wiped his chin with the now-tattered napkin. "Man, you sure know how to keep it real. I will never accuse you of being predictable."

"Right. No sweat, man." I looked up and saw the bemused specter of Iris Halfontaine. I was attracted to those dancing octogenarian eyes like a kamikaze moth to an ultraviolet porch light. "I'll catch up with you, Bar." I patted his back and approached Iris. She was the elder statesperson of the media scene in this town and had no reservations letting you know it. She had come from money and continued to make it—by the gobs.

"What did you do to Barry?" Her boney hands cradled a plastic wine cup. She dressed like something out of the fifties; her leathery skin suggested one too many afternoons on the French Riviera, or maybe in her home tanning bed. "Are you tormenting that poor man again?"

"One of those prawns must have gone down the wrong pipe," I suggested. "But what do you expect? They're the size of small hyenas." We slowly moved to another part of the conference room. "So how are you doing?"

"How am I doing?" Her eyes darted. "That's a rather odd question coming from you."

"Why?"

"You're always concerned only about yourself. You never ask about the other person." Iris narrowed her gaze. "I get it. You want something from me. That's it, isn't it?"

"No, that's not it at all." I innocently swigged beer. "In fact, I was just thinking about you the other day."

"You were?" She grew wary. "How do you mean?"

"That trip to Nepal you were talking about a while ago. Are you still planning on going?"

"Now you really have gone too far." She shifted her weight, grinding her heel into the hardwood floor. "There is no absolute rationale for you remembering that facet of my itinerary. I made a passing remark at the Ad Club a few weeks ago, but that was the extent of it. For you to recall that precise detail is highly unlike you and, may I add, rather suspect."

Uncertain if Iris was joking or serious, I let it roll off my back. "You're involved with the charity group. And you're bringing over the water purification system. Am I right?"

Iris dropped her guard. "So you actually *do* pay attention."

"I guess. When I put my mind to it." I gestured with the beer bottle. "Of course, it helped when I saw a poster for the same purification system at church last Sunday."

"Church?" It was like someone just slammed her in the gut with a four iron.

"Yeah, they're sending a mission team to Uganda with the same device."

"Church," she hissed, her brown eyes becoming angry slits. "Where did *that* come from? What possible reason could you have for being in church?" The skinny woman started to shake.

I was unprepared for her reaction. I frantically tried plugging the dam. "Forget it. It's not important."

"Oh no. I'm not letting you off the hook that easily. Obviously it is very important." She appraised me hypercritically. "And let me add one thing while we're on the subject of church. My project has nothing to do with religion, do you understand? Nothing! There is no way my beautiful vision will be tainted by religious zealots." She drew up, ramrod straight. "Now, I don't know what has come over you with this church thing. Hopefully it's a temporary condition. But unless you can prove to me it was a one-time fluke or a bout with momentary whimsy, I don't think we have much more to discuss." She stared me down like I was the Devil incarnate.

I'd been in a lot of confrontations in my day, but nothing like this. I didn't think I'd ever seen such a look of disdain bubbling just beneath the surface of someone's countenance. And she was supposedly a trusted friend. "Man, I'm sorry, Iris. I didn't mean to light you up like that."

"If you knew, would you have refrained from telling me?"

"Of course."

"Nice try, Vance. I know people of your ilk. Once they get religion they can't keep it to themselves. It behooves them to make everyone's life miserable with that 'good news' crap—whatever that means." Her gnarled hand shook as she drained the wine in her cup. "Now, if you'll excuse me, it's been nice knowing you."

"Iris, dial it back a notch. Please!"

"Shove it, buster!" She leaned into me like a spindly mobster. "Listen to me and listen good." She ground her frail shoulder into my ribcage. "Don't you dare think about calling me until you have shed this detestable folly. It will take *months* for you to detox." She punched me with her empty cup on the way out the door.

I did a slow burn in the wake of Iris's stormy exit. I looked for a place to put the cup. Where did Barry say they were hiding the salmon—the production department?

"You play much baseball?" Tina Jabberts sidled up to me with an ill-concealed smirk. An on-air host and budding sales pro, she had played college hoops in the Missouri Valley Conference. She was a majestic five-ten without heels, a regal beauty. "Between Iris and Barry, you got two strikes against you."

It was obvious people had taken notice of my dustups.

"So what will you be?" I decided to ask. "Called third strike or a grand slam?"

"Right. As if you already have someone on base. You're stirring the pot more than usual today. Did you have two bowls of Wheaties instead of one this morning?"

"I'm doing nothing differently . . . that I'm aware of."

"Let me guess." She drew close and whispered. "You're leaving the Spagways to start a media empire of your own."

"No. Not bad, though. I kinda like it." I nodded approvingly. "I'm sorry if you were angling for one of the VP positions."

"Then what?" She narrowed her gaze. "I'm not leaving 'til you tell me."

Feeling like a schmuck, I stood there still clutching Iris's empty cup. No way was I going to tell Tina about last Sunday. I didn't know where she stood on religion, but my track record so far was less than stellar. I wanted to leave this function with at least one friendship intact. "Got it." I snapped my fingers. "It's gotta be the Bulls!"

"The Bulls?" she said. "What about them?"

"They tip at eight tonight. A bunch of us are meeting at the GL." I nodded. "It's your front row seat to another playoff victory."

"Thanks." Tina finished her Dos Equis. "My flight leaves at six in the morning for the all-star volleyball tournament in Tulsa."

"You're putting volleyball over the Bulls?" I feigned indignation. "What would MJ say?"

"You tell MJ that TJ will deny him that storied fadeaway eight times out of ten."

"Come on. Your flight's not 'til six. You can sleep on the plane."

"I'll be up half the night watching tape."

"*Tape?*" I winced. "Of *volleyball?*"

"It's called commitment." She tossed her beer bottle into the nearest receptacle and called over a shoulder. "You knew what that was at one time, right?"

As I watched Tina head gracefully for the exit, I realized something was digging into my hand. It was the empty cup Iris had given me, and I had it in a death grip. People were really starting to clear out now. Feeling more and more alone, it gave me renewed impetus to find out where they were hiding the smoked salmon.

CHAPTER FIFTEEN

PUTTING THE "SIN" IN SINCERE

I stepped from the elevator into the parking lot at sub-level three. It was a ghost town compared to a couple of hours ago. My footsteps echoed on the low concrete ceiling as I hustled to my car, anxious to flip on the radio and find out what that crazy Christian sex station was up to next.

Sliding behind the wheel, I paused before starting the engine. I was still haunted by Iris's meltdown over the water purification device. Her reaction to my mere mention of church had been way out of line. As long as I'd known her, she'd kept things pretty close to the vest. Following that blistering reaction, it was like part of her soul had been exposed, and the sight was not pretty. Brutally chilling was more accurate.

Then I thought back to Sunday afternoon and the lakeside debacle with Billy Whatcom. He'd nearly come out of his skin defending the faith while accusing me of engaging in "parlor games"—whatever that meant. His conviction was undeniable—

as ferocious as Iris's had been—only they were coming at it from opposite ends of the spectrum.

I stared through the windshield at the starkly lit concrete wall and contemplated a really big question: if I had to choose between Iris Halfontaine and Billy Whatcom, with whom would I ultimately cast my lot? When all the chips were down, all the masks were off, push came to shove . . . when every cliché had been thoroughly exhausted, when all the trappings were gone, all the awards, careers, cars, houses, vacations, and boats, when everyone in the world was essentially naked in front of the Almighty . . . which side did I want to come down on: Iris's or Billy's?

I'd known Iris for years and now it was like I didn't know her at all. I'd known Billy for a few days and it was like I'd known him my whole life. What did that say about building strong, motivated, intentional relationships?

I started the engine and fiddled with the radio dial. Thick, heavy static filled the airwaves across the AM and FM bands, except—

"Hi, I'm Wallace!"

"And I'm Wanda!"

"And you're listening to another installment of . . . *The Sinners for Beginners Show!*"

I jerked back. The grating voices screamed from the speakers like amplified fingernails on a blackboard seasoned with cat urine. Sappy theme music made me want to gag; were the off-key voices those of the hosts singing along with the opening track? I backed from the stall and rolled slowly up the ramp, glad there was no line at the payment booth. Small consolation in the face of this raging insanity.

Wanda's voice grew even louder once I exited the garage. "Reach us toll-free at 1-888-400-7700 if you want to be a part of the program. Once again that's 1-888-400-7700."

Her chirpiness made me want to put my fist through the dashboard, but what the hey. I guess that just meant I needed a crash course in self-restraint.

"Wanda, I've got a letter here from one of our listeners. Before we get to the callers, let's see if I can unpackage it, shall we?"

"You mean . . . unpack it. Don't you, dear?"

"That's what I said." Wallace amateurishly crinkled a sheet of copy into the mic and cleared his throat. "Inez writes: 'Wallace and Wanda, I'm feeling pretty satisfied with myself these days. I'm not a murderer, an adulterer, or a fornicator. The way I see it, I'm pretty much good to go in the eyes of God.'"

"Good to go where, Inez?" Wanda mused. "Straight to Hell? I'm kind of offended you didn't put buttered popcorn on your exalted list. You know, that's one of the biggest sins mankind perpetrates—putting too much butter on their popcorn. Think about that the next time you go to the Saturday matinee!"

"I think what my esteemed colleague is trying to say, Inez, is that we sin more times in a minute than we fart during an entire day." Wallace chuckled at his cheesy observation. "And it doesn't have to be one of the 'majors' that you so cavalierly listed. Consider all the other junk that gets under our fingernails: arrogance, avarice, greed, vanity, bullying, anger, gluttony, lust, jealousy . . . it just goes on and on."

I gripped the steering wheel while wondering if I was going to make it to the Lawns in time for the Bulls tipoff. If not, it meant switching to the radio station that was carrying the game. Such a loss that I would have to tune these two losers out!

"I think," Wallace continued, "you should look at sin like an iceberg. The sensational, glamorous ones—the majors—are the ones you see sticking up above the waterline. But the deadly sins, the supposedly less significant ones, stretch well beneath the surface. Those are the ones you never see, yet those are the ones that can take you down. And believe me. They will pull you under every time because you don't even know they're there."

"Or how about the one you didn't mention, Wallace: pride? You think you may have a little of that, Inez? Is it possible you are proud of the fact that you live such a lily-white, Teflon-coated life because you haven't committed any of the majors—*yet?*"

I took a left at the next light. Now these yahoos had gone too far. There was nothing wrong with pride. Without taking pride in everything we did, where would we be? Right?

"Inez, let me ask you a question," Wanda continued. "Have you ever *thought* about killing someone? You can level with us, because you will surely have to level with God. Have you ever wanted to put rat poison in a coworker's coffee because they showed you up on an important project? Or did someone cut in front of you at the supermarket checkout line and you wanted to carve them up with a straight razor? Don't you think either of those is tantamount to murder?"

"Wanda's right, Inez. Having those thoughts is just as bad as going through with the act itself. And the situation is on you so fast you don't even have time to react. Your true feelings come out whether you want them to or not. God is reading your heart the whole time. There's no hiding from him." Wallace lowered his voice. "And here's the capper: God loves the person who supposedly did you wrong to the same extent he loves you. So you'd better figure out a way to forgive your neighbor and show your love, because God surely loves them—through and through."

"Yes, dear," Wanda offered. "And remember who is puttering around behind the scenes: that deceitful wretch Satan. He wants to make your life a pile of dog doo. And he'll gladly set up shop inside of you to accomplish his ruinous purpose. That's why we need to be strong, vigilant, and on guard at all times. We need to put on the full armor of God."

"And that starts with reading the Bible," Wallace intoned. "Regularly."

"Amen to that, Wallace. That's the most important thing any of us can do."

My pulse rate surged as I tried to process this garbage. Forget the Bible; I was still caught up with all the so-called "major" sins. These happy-go-lucky lunatics made it sound like going to the penalty box in a hockey game.

"Let's give that toll-free number again, shall we?" Wallace said. "To be a part of the program dial 1-888-400-7700. That's 1-888-400-7700!"

"Well what do you know?" Wanda trilled. "We have the first caller of the night." The convivial host executed the phone patch. "Welcome to *The Sinners for Beginners Show*. Kindly state your name and where you're calling from."

"This is Inez."

There was a prolonged silence over the airwaves.

Wallace finally cleared his throat. "Would this be the same Inez who wrote to us about her sinless life?"

"I don't know what's up with you clowns. I'm trying to lead my life the best I can, and then I run into a two-person wrecking crew."

"Wanda, who's she talking about?"

"I don't know," Wanda whispered.

"There you go!" Inez shouted. "You're a couple of jerks who probably got religion before you could walk. And you sit up there all high-and-mighty on your perch and take it out on the rest of us."

I pulled to a stop at the red light. This was good radio; they were really getting into it. Who thought I'd ever find something as provocative and entertaining as this on a Christian radio station?

I squinted into my rearview mirror as a pickup truck barreled to a stop behind me. Headlights bathed the interior of my

Lexus. Did the dude have his high beams on? If so, they were on steroids. The intensity of the situation was quickly shifting from annoyance to anger. I wondered if I should just whip around and offer up the old one-finger salute, or possibly storm from behind the wheel and make a big scene.

"I don't think you're being entirely fair here." It was Wanda, back on the radio. "If you knew either of our testimonies—Wallace's and mine—you would know how wrong you are in your assessment."

"Yes," Wallace said authoritatively. "I was hardly fresh from the womb when I gave my life to Christ. I was a salty twelve years old, if you really want to know."

"Twelve years old. Am I supposed to be impressed?" Inez asked.

"And I was seven when I got saved," Wanda said.

"Whoop-de-do!" Inez snapped. "What a couple of boobs! Are we keeping score now?"

Mesmerized by the shtick on the radio, I sat for a second after the light turned green. The driver behind me started laying on the horn.

"Give me a break!" I shouted into the rearview mirror. I was already hot enough under the collar to start a rumble. But something suddenly caught my attention. I heard honking on the radio. It matched what I heard behind me. Was the driver of the pickup truck . . . Inez?

"Move!" Inez barked across the radio. This was followed by more incessant horn honking. "Can't you see I'm late for work?"

It took everything I had to restrain myself. Begrudgingly, I took my foot off the brake and started rolling from the light.

"Who are you talking to?" Wanda gasped.

"The jerk in front of me!" Inez kept squeezing the horn.

"Whoops! It appears we have another caller," Wallace announced.

There was mild confusion on the radio as the air personalities fumbled around. "I don't want to lose Inez," Wanda whispered. "Patch the next caller in to the conversation."

"I'll see what I can do." Wallace cleared his throat as he opened the second line. "Good evening, and welcome to *The Sinners for Beginners Show*. To whom do we have the pleasure of speaking?"

"This is Vance from South Point. And you'd better stop riding my tail, honey!"

"Who's riding whose tail?" Wanda cried.

"Is that you, moron?" Inez screeched. "You know what that pedal on the right is for?" The honking grew more intense. "Move it!"

"Would you both kindly turn down your radios?" Wallace pleaded. "We're being bombarded with interference here."

"Interference? I'll show you interference!" Inez spat.

We were rolling down the Ballard Falls Causeway. The speed limit was fifty-five, but I was barely doing forty. "If you'd listen to me for a minute, I can explain," I said to Inez.

"You can't explain squat!" She violently wrenched her F-150 around me, tires squealing, and sped off.

"You're gonna regret it, Inez." I watched her taillights disappear over a rise.

"In your dreams!" Inez spat. "Eat my soggy corn flakes, all you losers!" The line went dead.

"What's going on?" Wanda gushed. "Do we have our first documented instance of road rage in real time?"

"Inez, you just blew your sinless veneer with that furious outburst," Wallace scolded.

"Let her go," I said. "She's gonna get what's coming to her."

Seconds later, blue and red lights exploded from a tree grove as she blew through a notorious speed trap.

"Vance from South Point, what's your involvement here?" Wanda asked. "Are you somehow related to Inez?"

"If she had only listened to me, I could have saved her from a speeding ticket." I actually felt sorry for the young woman as I rolled past her. She was slumped behind the wheel, probably in tears, as the officer approached the late-model pickup.

"I think we've really witnessed something here," Wallace said quietly. "Something really remarkable."

"What's that?" Wanda asked.

"Vance from South Point was trying to save her from a ticket, but she didn't listen to him. How much is that like what we do? We ignore God and go our own way. And look where it gets us."

"I'd say that's pretty spot on," Wanda offered. "Congratulations, Vance. You really distinguished yourself."

"No sweat," I said.

"And you didn't crack under the pressure. You didn't give in to her rage," Wallace agreed. "Great work, chap."

"Just keeping it real."

"So why did you call?" Wanda asked. "There must be something on your mind."

I had to think fast. How was I going to ditch these knuckleheads and end the call gracefully? "Yeah, well . . . " I watched the flashing lights recede in the distance. "What do you mean by being saved?"

"Wow, you sure know how to get to the heart of the matter," Wanda said quietly. "Wallace, do you want to take a stab at this?"

"It would be my honor," Wallace said. "'Being saved' literally means being saved from eternal damnation, which amounts to separation from God for all eternity."

"So much for sugarcoating the issue," I mused.

"It's by the grace of God," Wanda said. "We'd all be lost if God did not shower us with his grace—otherwise known as unmerited favor—which none of us deserves, nor none of us can do anything on our own to earn."

"So here's the dilemma," Wallace continued. "The whole enchilada, as people are fond of saying. God desperately wants a relationship with each and every one of us. It doesn't matter who we are and what we've done. And that relationship will last for all eternity. But our sins, otherwise known as disobedience and rebellion, create a barrier that cannot be overcome without a crisis intervention. And leading the charge is none other than Jesus Christ."

"He rushed out of Heaven to rescue us," Wanda said. "He led a sinless, blameless life, incurred the wrath of God on the cross on our behalf, and created a path for us to achieve eternal peace with our Heavenly Father."

"He died for our sins and transgressions, then rose from the tomb three days later," Wallace said. "Once and for all, he defeated sin, death, disease, and suffering. Anyone who believes in Jesus—who puts their faith, love, hope, and trust in him—will enter into the relationship of a lifetime with God."

"And that relationship will last forever and ever, for all eternity," Wanda added. "And it can start right now, whenever you proclaim Jesus as your Lord and Savior."

"Have you done that yet?" Wallace asked.

"Done what?"

There was a pause on my end as I contemplated where I stood in the process. This constituted dead air; if it persisted much longer, people would start tuning out.

"Have you asked Jesus Christ into your life as Lord and Savior?" Wanda prompted.

"Yeah, yeah, yeah, yeah," I stammered. "It's not about me. I'm calling for a friend."

"Okay, I get it." Wanda didn't miss a beat. "Here's how it works: you, me, your friend—the whole world—we all need to recognize our sins. We need to confess them to God our Father, then roll up our sleeves and start repenting of those offenses. I'm not saying it's easy. I'm not saying it's all going to happen overnight, nor am I saying it's always going to appear a nice, tidy package. But what I am saying, with one hundred percent certainty, is none of us can do it on our own. That, again, is where grace comes in."

"Wanda's right," Wallace added. "Pick your sin. You want to go with anger, no problem. You own that sin as it presently stands. You need to turn it over to God and let the Holy Spirit work on your heart to purge you of that toxic emotion."

"Right," I said. "Turn it over to God. You make it sound so easy, like running errands. I'm gonna leave my clothes with the dry cleaners, then drop my anger off with God."

"Let's not get caught up in semantics," Wanda said, suddenly a bit testy. "By turning our sins over to God we recognize their existence and admit we are not happy with them and vow to purge ourselves of their effects."

"Exactly," Wallace said. "And here's where the big stumbling block comes, especially for a lot of new Christians—and even people who have been in the faith a long time: you've got to give it up to God before you can start defeating the demons in your life. And once you do that, God will fill every void with the peace and purpose of his heavenly being. He loves you beyond measure and wants only the very best for you."

"The very best . . . I see." I was having a problem computing; none of this made a whole lot of sense.

"Let's cut to the chase, sweetheart," Wanda said. "Has your friend ever prayed to Jesus to come into his life?"

I had to think fast. It wasn't a trick question, but I was perilously close to exposing myself. "I don't know. I think so."

"Well," Wallace said. "Let me ask you a question directly. If that's okay, of course."

"Shoot."

"Have you *personally* given your life to Jesus Christ as your Lord and Savior, Vance?"

Now the curveball was coming in big. I laughed nervously, buying time. "Come on. I wouldn't be calling you guys if I hadn't, right?"

"Well, we'd like to think that," Wanda said coolly. "Of course, we all know it isn't always the case."

"Of course not." I scrambled for a way to kill the call.

"You sound like you're on a little shaky ground there, friend," Wallace said. "So tell me, have you confessed your sins to God? Have you told him you're sorry for everything you've done and prayed for him to take those sins out of your life?"

"No comment," I said in a knee-jerk reaction.

"No comment?" Wallace squawked. "What kind of response is that?"

I pulled into the crowded parking lot of the Golden Lawns Bar and Grill, illuminated by a massive wall of yellow neon. "Just a fallback position. No big deal," I said as an afterthought.

I cruised the aisles looking for an open space. Bigger fish awaited inside at the Bulls playoff bash. I really hoped Millie showed up so our budding relationship could begin for real. Pulling into a slot, I realized I was still on the air; they hadn't pulled the plug on me yet.

"I think that's your starting point before you go to sleep tonight," Wanda said.

"What's that?" Having lost my train of thought, I had to give these crackpots the slip and get on with life.

"Well, I recommend confessing your sins, asking God for forgiveness and for him to scrub the slate clean through the shed blood of our holy Savior, Jesus Christ. It doesn't get any better than that." Wanda's voice rose. "Does that sound like a plan?"

"Okay, then. I guess that should do it," I said.

"Stand by. I see we have a hard break coming up," Wallace said.

"Thanks, Vance. And praise God! You call us back anytime," Wanda warbled.

I ended the call then turned the radio back up in time to hear Wallace proclaim, "Just remember, folks. Sin is a three-letter word with 'I' in the middle."

"Be blessed now," Wanda said. "And we'll all meet up on the other side right after these words from our precious sponsors."

I doused the engine and stared out the windshield. Laughter, loud voices, music, and the amplified broadcast audio of the pregame announcers cascaded from the open windows of the sprawling sports bar. I tried to digest what I had just done: I had actually been speaking with the hosts of a Christian radio talk show—not to complain or mock, but to seek answers.

What possessed me to do such a thing?

I pocketed the phone. Weird. Apparently, I wasn't dreaming this.

CHAPTER SIXTEEN

THE BIGGEST, BADDEST BEST SELLER IN ALL CREATION

Stripped to a pair of striped boxer shorts, I stepped onto the back deck of my penthouse apartment puffing a limited edition Naranja Steel Crown cigar. Cradling a stiff Tanqueray and tonic with extra lime slices, I clutched my Nokia phone along with the Bible. As I slid onto the chaise lounge, boisterous voices and laughter welled up from the overheated club district eight stories below. A recap of Game Three of the Eastern Conference playoff round between the Bulls and Bullets blared on ESPN from inside my living room. It was going on midnight.

I got everything situated and looked up at the cloudless heavens stretching into eternity. I blew a prolonged column of satisfying, medium-bodied cigar smoke. Closing my eyes, I tried to shut out the debacle that this evening had become, but it was no use. I couldn't shake it.

The night at the Golden Lawns, by any sane definition, had been a disaster. I didn't think I'd ever live down the embarrassment. Millie had strutted through the door just before tipoff, and she was hot—smoking hot: leather jacket, short skirt, spike heels, and long brunette hair. She was loaded for bear and I thought I was the biggest grizzly in the woods. Instead, it turned out I was Boo-Boo Bear's long lost cousin with a thumb up his rear.

I was just about to give her a royal Golden Lawns welcome when "Cabana" Clarence Harkridge, the bumbling tech-head at our station, strolled through the door after parking the car. What was he doing there? Did these two polar opposites have a thing? If so, how long had it been going on right under my transom?

Curbing my shock, I sprang into "High Oscar Mode," putting on the performance of a lifetime. I dialed my bulging eyes back into their sockets and threw on a big PR smile. I had to make the whole thing look like I didn't care. Millie probably saw through my sorry charade, but if she was going to hitch her wagon to that techie-tyke, I wasn't sure I gave a flying turkey leg what she thought.

Then Clarence—being a geek and unable to help himself— commandeered the place with talk of a new PDA. Everything stopped and the Bulls game even took a back seat to his nerdy show-and-tell. I didn't know what he was talking about, and I didn't give two hoots about that newfangled stuff, but apparently others did, and they were fixated on his every word. My mind went into overdrive as I visualized my plum contacts starting to pop up on his Rolodex; the next thing you knew, I'd be out in the cold, jangling my loose change at the corner laundromat.

To be perfectly clear about this, if I were going to invite Cabana Clarence to a function, I'd be sure the party favors included fruit punch, balloons, a ventriloquist, a polka guy, and at least a half dozen clowns. And to rub even more salt in the proverbial wound, his "Cabana" shtick reminded me so much of the song "The Girl from Ipanema" that it was now nearly impossible for me to get the tune out of my head!

It got so bad I had to leave early. Clarence's incessant tech chatter and Millie falling all over him totally ruined it for me. What a waste of a hot babe. I made some lame excuse about having a client meeting early the next morning and said my good-byes. I was so hacked I didn't even make it over to the Takoda Steak House for cards and cigars, the usual late Wednesday night custom.

Outside in the parking lot, bathed in blushing yellow neon, I fiddled for the game on the car radio. Flipping between two of the monster sports outlets on the AM side, I caught the live play-by-play. Then, much to my consternation, I realized what I was missing.

In my petty desire to hightail it from the Lawns, I deprived myself from witnessing one of the greatest chapters in Bulls play-off history. With seconds winding down, Scottie Pippin grabbed the rebound off a missed Jordan jumper. Charging the baseline, he fiercely jammed it home with both hands. One-point lead, Bulls over the Bullets, with just over seven seconds remaining.

But Scottie, taking one for his teammates and all of Chicago, got twisted up and landed wrong and hard, flat on his back in the paint. With his heroics-assuring victory, it was one of those great Bulls moments you love to cherish. And I missed it because I was upstaged by a loquacious geek and a hot graphics chick—who, at the beginning of the evening, was supposed to be mine.

Sighing deeply, I turned my attention to the assignment Billy had given me last Sunday. I had dreaded this moment long enough: it was time to roll up my sleeves and crack the old "Good Book." I may have been brand new to this game, but everywhere I turned people were freaking out if you didn't know the Bible. I always thought the book was a big head-scratcher, a front row seat aboard the "Enigmatic Express," but now they were telling me it's worth its weight in gold, a direct line of communication with God. More and more I realized that unless you were big-time into the study of Scripture, you were shortchanging your relationship with the Almighty.

Whenever I got involved in something, I did it all the way. I certainly proved it playing football. Unless you played hard all the time, somewhere along the line you were going to get pulverized. The broadcast industry was no different: unless you were well-versed in a host of disciplines and knew all the laws and statutes, you were going to be less than effective in certain regulatory areas, exposing you and your shareholders to potential liabilities.

So why was my spiritual involvement different? If in-the-know people said the Bible was the real deal—even though all my previous experience shouted otherwise—then I had to give it a fair shot. But why did it have to be so confusing? If any other document had so frustrated me, I would have heaved it across the room long ago. Something told me it was better not to do that with the Bible.

Checking the table of contents, I flipped to John, chapter fourteen. After trying to digest the first two verses, my eyelids turned to lead-plated shutters. Before nodding off, I grabbed Billy's home number off the notepaper.

The phone rang six times, then the handset clattered off the hook. "Yo," Billy whispered hoarsely. "What's up?"

"Billy, man, it's Vance. Vance Chelan. Remember me from last Sunday? Uh . . . did you catch any of the Bulls game tonight?" I relit my cigar and blew a plume of smoke. "I'm telling you, there's no keeping them down. I don't see anyone stopping them from going all the way again."

After a painful pause, Billy said, "You know what time it is? I'll catch the highlights in the morning."

I checked my watch. "Forgive the intrusion." I batted ashes and nodded skyward. "And I know everyone in your camp is into forgiveness. So just bear with me: this Bible thing has me tripping over my jockstrap, and I need a little help sorting through the jargon."

"I'm glad you have a burning desire to dig deeper, but . . . *tonight*? At this hour?" It sounded like Billy was getting hacked. "And what's with the music? Are you at a club?"

I didn't think a man of the cloth was supposed to cop an attitude. Then again, I had only been to his church once. I was hardly a preferred customer. "No, it's just spillover from the neighborhood joints." I held up the phone. "We call it ambient sound in the production biz."

"That's just great . . . ambient sound." There was a long pause, like Billy didn't know what to say or do. "I'm going back to sleep. Good night, Vance."

"Okay, but before you sign off, I just need you to coach me up a little on the Bible."

"What on God's green earth are you talking about? 'Coach you up'?" It sounded like Billy wanted to come through the phone at me. "What are you looking for, a pep talk or a flat-out diagram of plays? I'm sure at this hour everything will make a world of sense. And I still think you might be at some bar."

"Just help me get the ball rolling," I pleaded. When it came to the Bible, I didn't have a clue. With so many mysteries and nuances, I figured I would never get a handle on things without a serious jump start. "I figure there's a ton of stuff I'm missing because I don't have all the stats—all the inside dope, if you follow my drift. With your training, you could kind of walk me through it. Give me all the salient points. Not the whole play-by-play, mind you. Just what I'll need to run with it on my own."

Billy had either fully awakened or just ingested a chill pill because he was suddenly a different person. "Vance, I think you might have hit on something. There's a group of you guys pretty much in the same boat who would really benefit from something like this. I propose we start a Bible study that meets once a week—something you rookies can wrap your heads around. I'll bet Laird Plechard will really be up for it."

"Laird Plechard?" I felt a sucker punch to my gut. "Collette's guy?"

"You bet. If I can get five or six of you together, you can all go at the same speed and kind of tackle it on your own terms." Billy brightened. "This is great. You've identified a real need. I'll get back to you with dates as soon as I set it up."

"Super. Only problem is, I can't wait. I want to get started tonight."

"Tonight?" Billy asked. "Why tonight—after spending your entire life ignoring it?"

I was amazed that the pussycat had exploded out of the blocks like a tiger. "Okay, if we're gonna go there, what's the point of even reading it in the first place?"

"You're in the media, right?" Billy asked. "What if you had an important guest on your TV show tomorrow? Would you be reading every book he or she ever wrote? Would you be doing research to the nth degree? Of course you would. And why? So you could carry on a halfway coherent conversation with the other party. Do you think it's any different with God? When you're all alone at the Seat of Judgment, what will you talk about with the Almighty? The championship run the Bulls hope to have this season?"

I had to agree with the feisty clergyman: if I had a big guest on tomorrow I'd be cramming my brains out right now. I batted ashes onto the deck. "That's assuming, of course, I'd actually be able to see my guest on the set tomorrow. Not so with God."

"We're going around in circles. That's why the Bible's there in the first place, so you can meet God where he lives and see who he really is."

"Come on, man. Who's buying into any of that these days? Outside of church people, everyone I know is trashing it."

"And you think that's anything new?" Billy shot back. "You don't think people haven't been doing the same thing for generations? For hundreds—no, *thousands*—of years? It all boils down to choice. You can choose to believe it or choose not to. You can choose to mock it. That's your right, your prerogative. Just remember, everything you do has eternal consequences. So you always have to ask yourself which side you want to come down on when the lights go off for good."

"Okay, so maybe it's not all a crock. Maybe some of it is true."

"It's either all true or none of it is true. There's no middle ground with the Bible. That's because there's no middle ground with God."

I vacantly jangled the ice cubes in my glass. "Come on, man. They talk about some bad stuff in there. Not the kinds of things you'd bring up at a dinner party, if you know what I mean."

"On whose authority? You said you never read it."

"Yeah, I know. But anytime I hear someone on one of the talk shows, they're bashing it pretty good."

"No offense, but that's what most in your beloved media do. They don't tell you the Bible is the building block of life, the DNA on which everything hinges. Without it, you're shooting blanks. So get used to having it as your constant companion."

"Not with something so outdated."

"Outdated?" Billy said. "You're gonna dredge up that one too?"

"Come on. Those guys were tooling around on camels and living in caves. What did they know about homeowners associations, cell phones, and cussing people out in rush hour traffic?"

"So it's still all about you, right? You're always bringing it back to your station in life."

"Well, yeah. You gotta have a frame of reference, right?" I felt pretty good about myself, like I'd won the argument.

"Does love ever go out of style?" Billy asked. "Because that's what this is all about. God hasn't changed one iota since time began. In fact, he exists outside of time so none of the rules apply. Yet God loves you to no end and yearns for a close, intimate relationship with you throughout eternity. And that never grows old or goes out of fashion."

Realizing I was in over my head, I nonetheless shambled into even deeper waters. "You hear things about plucking your eye out if it causes you to sin and other assorted gross gems. What kind of nonsense is that?"

"Sure, if you take it out of context," Billy said, "that's what you'll get. But if you study it and apply it to the culture and the times, you would understand the true meaning of the passage."

"And turning the other cheek? Let's not forget that one."

Billy paused to come up for air. "Look, we can go all night taking uneducated potshots at the text. It will get us nowhere. Let's just call it for what it is: the most life-changing, transformative book on the planet. It's the key to knowing God, which is our whole reason for living. God gave us his Word so we can immerse ourselves in the center of his kingdom. It's a supercharged, supernatural blueprint for living."

"Supernatural? Here we go again . . . "

"Let me ask you a question, Vance. If you read a best-selling book, is the author in the room with you? Does the author know what chapter or even what page you're on?"

"Come on, man. That's crazy."

"Right," Billy said. "It's impossible. The author may generally know how many copies of his or her book were purchased and the type of people reading them. But needless to say, he or she is not in the same room as every person who has a copy. God, on the other hand, *is* in the room with you. If one hundred million people are reading the Bible in 156 different languages, he's with each and every person, sitting beside them, urging them on. That's the supernatural aspect of this."

"Right, I'm supposed to believe that. It's like playing badminton on the back lot with rejects from the *Twilight Zone*."

"Don't doubt the power of God." Billy seemed to suddenly grow cold. "Do you know the meaning of the word history? It's actually 'H-I-S story,' which translates to *His* story. You see where I'm going? That's the whole point for us being on Earth. We're all part of *His* story."

I thought I recognized a woman's voice from the bistro below. I shook myself awake. "Okay, man. We'll be in touch." I yawned extravagantly. "*Ciao.*" Dumping the call, I tamped out my cigar and settled back in the chaise.

It was then I realized that, like everything else in life, if I was going to make any headway with Scripture, it was up to me to take the initiative. As I prepared to dive in, laughter and voices from the neighboring establishments rattled my concentration. In what amounted to an insane display of discipline, I ignored the temptation to head downstairs.

Cracking open the Bible, I did what any respectable truth-seeker would do: I started at the top, Genesis 1:1, and commenced reading out loud: "In the beginning God created the heavens and the Earth. Now the Earth was formless and empty, darkness was . . . over the surface of the deep . . . of the deep . . . of the . . ."

As the words blurred together, I felt myself drifting off. I wondered if the Bible would be a sticking point in my newfound journey of faith. If I was ill-prepared—or just didn't feel inclined to go the extra mile—then what was the point? Why was I even pretending? Maybe this foray into all things spiritual was not my cup of tea after all.

Billy Whatcom sighed in resignation. "Kind of funny. Out of all you guys, Laird was the most gung ho when I initially presented this." The muscular associate pastor raised his hands defensively. "Don't get me wrong. This is by no means a criticism. And I'm not standing in judgment. I'm just observing human nature."

It might have been "kind of funny" to Billy, but I wasn't laughing. Laird had cunningly commandeered the de facto leadership of this little group. By dint of his absence, he was always the elephant in the room. In most things in life up to now, I was the one who elicited this kind of deference; I was the one who called the shots. If I chose not to attend a particular function, I was still in charge because my absence had infiltrated the minds of those who had chosen to come. People would experience a nagging doubt, wondering why I wasn't there and what I was doing instead. They would ultimately question their own motives and wonder if I had something better going on.

Did Laird have something better than the Bible occupying his time? Well, really, who cared? I was nearing the end of my rope—not just with this Bible study, with this Christianity thing altogether. It just wasn't doing it for me. Maybe I'd been kidding myself all along.

Topping it off was my sense of personal stagnation. It didn't seem as though I was moving the ball forward. I was no longer growing, no longer getting anything out of this.

During the last few weeks I'd been merely going through the motions. The return on investment—the all-important ROI—was not registering. I had expended buckets of sweat equity trying to define and reshape my life as a good practicing Christian. For my misguided efforts I had only received sarcasm and cynicism from skeptical colleagues. And here I thought I was the only one allowed to be sarcastic and cynical.

It had just become too much of an effort. My social life was in the toilet. I had walled myself off from women, not wanting to start something I couldn't finish. I had forfeited a big advertising contract by not showing up for a client golf outing last Sunday morning. Someone I thought was a friend told me my new Christian faith was a mental disorder. And making everything worse, I was really beginning to resent God's ambivalence. I was down here slugging it out, giving it all up for the Almighty, and I got the distinct impression that either he expected me to endure all this pain and suffering—or he just didn't care.

As my newfound faith began to wane, I cut down on my trips to visit Arnie at the dealership. When everything was brand new and shiny, I used to love getting Crusher's take on things, like the meaning of sermons and how current events impacted the Christian worldview. Now I went out of my way to avoid him. I didn't even relish doing business with the dealership anymore, and I certainly didn't want his wife and her international friends praying for me—I didn't even want Belle praying for me. *Hold it. Did I just say that?* Yes, this even applied to Belle. If it were up to me, I'd just tell them all to shove off and mind their own business.

Sunday mornings in church had devolved into nothing more than my personal think tank. I loved planting myself in one of the back pews where no one would bother me and strategize at will. It was a glorious undercover ploy. You couldn't pick a better hideout; no one would think of looking for you in church. It was akin to locking yourself in the bathroom for hours on end.

But there was a word other than hideout that also began with h: *hypocrite*. I realized I was headed there faster than a runaway freight train. And that's where I drew the line. I had to. We all have to live with ourselves. I couldn't go on pretending any longer. I had to shed this duplicitous lifestyle and start living for me again. The way I figured, it was probably going to get messy before it got better. I hoped, at least, that it would all be over quickly.

"Does anyone know the best way to get to Boston these days?" Fred Bannett asked. He was a structural engineer, very analytical, with thick glasses and an angular face. "We're going up for Fred Jr.'s graduation, and I really want to avoid all that stuff around the Tappan Zee."

I could have easily advised Fred on the best route, but I was so hacked about Laird's absence that I just shut down.

"If it were me, I'd just take the New York Thruway, then cut across the Mass Pike," said Clay Hanson, a county commissioner. Clay was a familiar figure in local politics, always sure to get his face in front of the cameras. I had gotten to know him better during the last few weeks; he didn't seem such a bad guy.

"I'd stick with the tried-and-true I-95," Drake Sheridan said.

"Not me." Clay made a pained face. "That can take hours with congestion."

"Righto, you might want to recalibrate that a tad," Fred said.

"What do I know?" Drake chuckled. "I'm unemployed."

Everyone appeared uncomfortable with the awkwardness of Drake's statement. Other than me, the cheerful dude was the only one wearing a suit. Having just come from a job fair, it looked like he'd spent a full day at the office.

I couldn't deal with this anymore. "Why don't you just fly up there instead, Fred?" The minute I said it I knew the guys would take it the wrong way. The tone of my voice was way too agitated.

Clay sneered at me. "You're just feeling your oats because the Bulls made it to the Finals. Again."

"What can I say?" I shrugged. "And I'm really liking the matchups with the Jazz."

"When's the first game?" Fred asked.

"Sunday night."

"That's the first of June," Clay said. "They'll be playing 'til the Fourth of July."

"How's the job hunting going?" Billy asked Drake, attempting to make the younger one feel a part of the group.

"Ah . . . you know." Drake made a sketchy gesture. "I'd be working yesterday if I was willing to compromise."

Compromise: that was an interesting choice of words. I felt as though I was being compromised by Laird. *There I was going again with Laird.* I obsessed about what he was doing right now.

Gordon Plintock returned from the bathroom. He picked up the Bible and study guide on the chair beside me. I liked Gordon a lot. He was an HVAC guy, totally down to earth. And best of all, he knew Jules, the Rock 'n Roll Plumber.

"We'd better start," Billy said. "I'll open with prayer."

I stared at the floor of our little classroom, not paying one lick of attention to the prayer.

Tonight was so typical of my nosediving Christian experience. I had given up a dinner meeting with Tammy Holver from Garden Rapids Pictures in LA. She had a hot new portfolio of movies that was going to smoke the competition. But no, I had to drop everything and hightail it out to Chorus Lake so Laird could traumatize me with his leering, in-your-face absence.

It meant that I was going to have to meet Tammy at the office tomorrow, just like every other program director schmo in stations across this great land. It meant I probably couldn't swing the concessions I would normally get from contracts negotiated over a protracted dinner. And I didn't care anymore that some of the titles had racy content. I couldn't let all this faith stuff stand in the way of what audiences really wanted. Business was business.

Billy's prayer droned on and on and on . . .

My eyes traveled from the bowed heads in the little circle out the expansive windows to the setting sun on Chorus Lake.

Then I made a decision.

I was outta there.

I didn't mean just this Bible study; I was done with the whole church scene. Period. I wasn't going to storm out of the room. I didn't know if I was even going to tell Billy that something had come up. I was just going to vanish, becoming a wisp of vapor, a permanent no-show.

Just like Laird.

But was that really a swift move? Even I realized that it may not be pleasing to God. But there was no hiding the fact I was just going through the motions. And if anything was definitely not pleasing to God, it was that.

"Amen," Billy said, finishing the prayer.

"Amen," I said with a satisfied smile. It felt like the weight of the world had been lifted.

"Okay," Billy said, "let's open our Bibles to Luke chapter 10, verses 25-37."

The sound of pages being hungrily flipped filled the small room. I hadn't studied for the lesson, but I had kept a bookmark in Luke from last week, so at least I was in the right neighborhood when we began.

"This is one of the most famous, enduring passages in all Scripture, the Parable of the Good Samaritan." Billy glanced up from his Bible. "Who knows what a parable is and why they were so effective in Jesus' teachings?"

"They're stories," Gordon said.

"Stories. That's good," Billy said. "What kind of stories?"

"Stories with a spiritual significance," Clay said.

"Great," Billy said. "And why did he use them so liberally?"

"For a number of reasons," Fred offered. "First, it was the language of the people. From the highest and mightiest to the lowest on the totem pole, people were going to relate to what was taught. So it was a way of personalizing these heavy-duty spiritual truths, distilling them into bite-size morsels that people from all walks of life were able to understand."

"Very good," Billy said. He turned to me. "Vance, do you have anything to add?"

"No."

Nobody looked at me. I knew I was making the place tense. *Tough. Maybe this will teach Billy not to call on me again.*

"So, Vance, who is the individual who asks Jesus how to inherit eternal life?"

Okay, Billy was really pushing his luck. I sucked the last of my coffee and crumpled the Styrofoam cup. "I didn't get his name." It was a good thing I didn't grab my things and storm out the door right then and there. *Sayonara!*

"He didn't have a name," Billy said.

"He was a lawyer," Fred said, hoping to stave off a confrontation.

"Well, if not a lawyer per se, at least someone very familiar with the law," Clay quickly added.

I glared at the floor, wondering if Clay had been a lawyer before becoming a county commissioner. The thought struck me: maybe I should get a lawyer to sue Jules. Then I wondered if anyone was hiring a lawyer to sue *me*—like my current employer, for instance, claiming that I was running a side business right under his nose. Or what if I got sued by one of my client stations for disseminating bad information? What then? How could I ever survive a lawsuit like that?

The Bible study forged on, with or without me. "Drake, can you tell us what made the road between Jerusalem and Jericho so treacherous?" Billy asked.

As Drake answered circuitously, I glanced at Gordon, sitting on my immediate right. Gordon, being in the building trades, might be a real help to me down the road. I had never gotten over Jules stiffing me on his invoice and then taking advantage of my short-lived kindness—or was it my weakness?—letting *me* bankroll his little trip to Nashville. I would never forget that he'd gotten over on me. Well, those days were done for!

I wondered if I could convince Gordon to take out a hit on Jules. I thought about ways we could eliminate him: the most sensible solution I came up with involved a supercharged bidet. It would be outfitted with a fire hose. The celebrity plumber would be strapped to the contraption with a five-point belt system like they used in NASCAR, including mounting hardware for a restraint assembly. Then . . . *let 'er rip!* I'd be anxious to hear him sing a ballad about *that!*

"So, the whole point of this parable," Billy went on, "is the recognition of your neighbor being in need. And your duty is not to judge, but to come to their aid with unconditional love and assistance. That's what it means to love your neighbor as yourself."

What a crock. I leaned back in my chair, realizing this was the reason I didn't fit in with these yokels and their chintzy game plan. Didn't they realize this was a dog-eat-dog world? There was no such thing as loving your neighbor—unless your neighbor was good for something. Unless your neighbor was Raquel Welch or Marilyn Monroe. Otherwise, it was like everything else. You couldn't trust your neighbor any further than you could throw him or her—and you could bet they were trying to get over on you the first chance they got.

I sighed deeply as the study began to wrap up. Billy asked Clay to close us in prayer; again, I didn't pay attention to any of the petitions. I was just glad to be cut loose—and filled with the joyous knowledge I was never coming back.

"Okay, before we leave, I have an announcement to make." Billy leaned forward. "I might have told a couple of you—I definitely told Laird over the phone. I'm not going to be your leader anymore. I'll be your support system and you can come to me with questions whenever you feel burdened, but the best way to get you up to speed is to hand over the reins to one of you. Besides, I'm a member of clergy. Who wants to listen to my blather, right?" He smiled good-naturedly.

"Don't look at me," I quickly said. "I'll be in and out of town the next few weeks." I was relieved that I didn't even have to lie to get out of the commitment. My busy travel schedule peaked in July, when the TV industry staged its annual blowout in Las Vegas. I couldn't wait to get out there and start mixing it up in the real world again.

"Nobody was . . . looking at you, Vance," Billy said. "Are you okay?"

Right, like I was going to get into it with him now. The whole thing was caving in on me. I was so done with all of this. "No. Everything's fine." I didn't even look at Billy. "Why don't we just appoint Laird," I said. "Maybe that's what it'll take to get him to come to one of these."

Everyone in the group was too polite to acknowledge my mini meltdown.

"I'll take it," Drake said. He raised his hand dutifully. "It's the least I can do seeing how the rest of you gents might be a little busy."

I sighed. Drake volunteered his services because he was unemployed and available—two really good reasons to underscore one's lack of competency. Well, this was no longer my problem. Drake was a nice enough guy. I'm sure the group would thrive under his tutelage.

Everyone was appreciative that the unemployed cat fell on his sword to accommodate us. I didn't say anything, but he would have one less person to prepare for because, after tonight, I was history.

When the affair had mercilessly concluded, I remained seated for a minute. While the boys gassed about the baseball standings, I congratulated myself on my decision to leave the faith. It felt good, really good, liberating. I couldn't wait to start putting my life back together again on my own terms.

Drake was all over Billy, asking if he really should be leading the group. As Billy assured Drake he'd do fine, I saw Billy look at me out of the corner of his eye. I was sure, after all Billy had done for me, I at least owed him a civil goodbye.

But civility was for losers.

I was back in the saddle again, and I had a wide range to ride.

I stopped at the Golden Lawns for a quick dinner. I was so confused and out of sorts I wasn't even into watching the baseball game. I went home and poured a stiff drink. I leaned back in the chaise lounge and looked up at the constellations, sipping mechanically, deep in thought. I couldn't say I was totally excited about getting my old life back, but I could tell you this: I hadn't felt this normal since the funeral. Whatever had overtaken me seemed to have moseyed on out of my soul. It was now back to business as usual.

Who was I trying to kid with this religious caper anyway? I was so far out of my league it wasn't even funny. It was a delusional joke thinking I could measure up to God's exacting standards. And you know something? That was okay. Sure, I had met some nice people who viewed the world in a different—even a bit refreshing—way. But my dalliance into religion had hit a serious snag and was now DOA. It had been a nice ride while it lasted, one that amounted to a curious diversion that ultimately resulted in an inconclusive experiment. At this point, a dead-end street offered more promise than my flailing, faltering Christian walk of faith.

I couldn't believe I was actually validating what I'd learned at the tender age of ten. I had walked away from Sunday school because I didn't feel a connection; the excitement level was lacking. To me, it was a fruitless pursuit that bore no discernible benefits.

Decades later, what had changed? My recent foray into organized religion only substantiated what I'd gleaned as a preteen: it wasn't for me, just wasn't my thing. I just didn't feel this one-on-one relationship everyone was talking about. God seemed content playing hide-and-seek with me, and if that's how it was all going to end, so be it.

I viewed it this way: whenever I took on a new project or responsibility, I literally threw myself into the fray, attacking from all angles. Everything was fair game including research papers, instruction manuals, personal interviews, and playbooks. Critical to my success was an overriding passion bordering on obsession. My pride was always in the lead; no one was going to outdo me. That was why my generally blasé approach to finding God was . . . unacceptable. Though something had admittedly piqued my interest for a short, intense burst of time, the sense of urgency had now subsided, slipping from my radar screen as quickly as it had materialized.

Though I never did anything halfway, I'd learned enough about God the last few weeks to know that he didn't do stuff halfway either. So, starting right now, he and I had an agreement: he knew where I was coming from, and I knew where he was coming from, and never the twain shall meet.

Or something like that.

I wondered how all that was going to work out for me.

CHAPTER EIGHTEEN

THANK GOD JESUS
WASN'T LIKE ME

The late-model cab screeched to a stop beneath the covered valet stand in front of my apartment building. The driver laid on the horn even though I was only a few feet away.

"Easy, easy," I said, not too subtly. "Keep your shirt on."

It was a little before 7:00 PM on Wednesday, July 16, 1997. I was heading to Las Vegas for the Federation of Affiliated Broadcasters convention, the annual conference that attracted more than 125,000 radio and TV executives, as well as regulators, on-air personalities, and equipment vendors from around the world.

"Airport?" The sprightly driver stole my breath as she swung from behind the wheel. Somewhere in her twenties, standing five-foot-five in boot heels, she had long brown hair with cascading curls, topped by a smart-looking newsboy cap made of Italian tweed. Faded denims, a large cowboy belt buckle, and a complement of hammered silver and turquoise jewelry completed her ensemble. Tugging on a pair of black leather driving gloves, she deftly popped the trunk.

"Airport. That's me." I lowered the handle on my green-and-sage roller bag and watched her hoist the case containing my Callaway golf clubs into the trunk.

"Anything else?" She nestled my garment bag beside the golf clubs.

"No, that's okay. I'll keep the rest with me." I hefted my Toshiba laptop along with my Kenneth Cole black leather flip-over briefcase.

"Your call." She closed the trunk lid.

I piled into the back seat as she slid behind the wheel. My eyes locked on the certificate beneath the dashboard where her name, Jess Genes, was prominently displayed. I tried not to stare at the laminated placard, but couldn't help wondering: was that her real name? And where had I seen her before?

The hat was first to go. She dropped it on the seat beside her and made a big thing of shaking out her luxuriant hair, running her slender gloved fingers through the rich, dark brown field of shapely curls. Her riveting brown eyes blinked at me in the rear-view mirror and she stopped preening after realizing she'd been caught in the act.

"What are you looking at?" she questioned.

"Nothing. Not a thing." I wondered if this squirrel sled had an escape hatch.

"This is my first run of the night and I want it to go smoothly, okay? No upper air turbulence, if you know what I mean." She nodded once in the rearview mirror. "So what little smiley-face airline are we leaving on tonight?"

"Delta."

"Delta Dawn it is." She tried to act civil, as though it were killing her.

Glancing at my watch, I tried to quell my anxiety but knew this was cutting it way too close. I never should have taken that last call from Curtis Fellkins in Toledo.

As we rolled from the curb, something on the radio attracted my attention. The audio was barely detectable, but I swore I heard the grating voices of Wallace and Wanda, the sappy hosts of the schmaltz-fest, *The Sinners for Beginners Show.* I was happy the audio was tamped down and preferred it stayed that way.

I hadn't listened to these fruitcakes in weeks, ever since my decision to bail from all this religious bunk. Spirituality was definitely not my bag. Since coming to grips with that reality, my life was back to firing on all six. Totally in charge, I was once again calling my own shots, living for the moment. With no one to answer to, and with no damnable accountability partners, I was loving every minute of my glorious, unfettered freedom.

Though my short-lived interest in religion had cratered, I retained one essential tenet: I would never be critical of Christians again. I respected them for holding fast to their beliefs, to the point of incurring societal wrath. I admired their convictions. And I realized they did a lot of good in the world. It wasn't their fault that the church scene hadn't worked out for me.

Billy was going to be righteously indignant when he found out I had pulled the plug. Billy was the one casualty of this ruse I sincerely felt badly for: I had never known anyone quite like him, and I considered our relationship special. I knew he cared for me like few others had; that care extended even to today, when he'd left a concerned message on my voicemail. After I dropped off the face of the earth, he was worried for my safety. I showed my appreciation by dodging his call.

Oh well, hopefully he'd give up on me soon. Surely there were bigger fish in the ocean he could work to fix.

During the last few weeks I'd returned to previous form and rediscovered my true nature. Spending Sunday mornings on the golf course or at the gym, I found I was able to clear my head a lot more effectively than merely taking up pew space.

The one area that hadn't received much attention was my love life. For whatever reason, it seemed like I couldn't buy a date. I swore, women were sniffing something out. Was I being ambivalent? Was I projecting negativity? Were my commitment issues more evident than usual? It seemed like women were going out of their way to avoid me. I vowed to rectify the matter just as soon as I could get a handle on it.

As we passed the turnoff for the Golden Lawns sports bar, I couldn't believe it: the NFL preseason was just around the corner. That meant fall wasn't far behind, then winter. Once you got past the Fourth of July, it all seemed to go downhill from there. Well, at least the Bulls had another championship under their belt. And all was well with the world.

"Can you please find me the baseball game?" I called up front. I was back to my old ways in terms of media consumption, more concerned with sports-talk radio than religious nutjobs on the Christian airwaves. It felt good being free of all that pent-up pressure.

"It's gonna cost you." She glanced sternly in the mirror. When she saw my confusion, she made a goofy face. "Relax. What station?"

"Five-seventy." I suddenly felt a lot better about her. Maybe since I was her first fare of the night, she was just off to a rocky start.

She turned up the audio on the Christian station. "Is it AM or FM?"

"AM," I said.

"I'll find it at the next light."

The curdling voices of Wallace and Wanda now filled the cab. In the ensuing interval Wanda announced, "Wallace, we have a caller from the west side, the Chorus Lake district. But she doesn't want to give a name."

"I'm sure we can deal with that," Wallace said. "What seems to be the issue?"

"It's a sticky wicket, I'm afraid," Wanda sighed. "Her live-in boyfriend slash fiancé wants to jump the gun in a certain area of the holy matrimony equation, if you catch my drift."

"I do catch your drift," mused Wallace. "It's a dangerous drifting that can lead to ultimate sorrow."

"We'd better get her on the line posthaste." Wanda patched in the caller. "Hi, honey. This is Wanda and Wallace. Welcome to *The Sinners for Beginners Show.*"

"Thank you for making this time available to me." The subdued caller spoke in a measured tone that sounded almost apologetic.

My heart leapt into my throat.

It was Collette.

After stopping at the light, the cabbie dutifully punched up the AM station.

I had a technicolor canary. "Whoa! Whoa! Whoa!" I clawed the back of the front seat. "Go back to where you had it!" I was half out of my mind, not wanting to miss a single word. "Now," I moaned. "Please!"

"Make up your mind!" Jess screeched. She shook her head and punched it back to the FM band.

"Thanks." Releasing tension, I eased into the back seat and focused on what was being said on the radio.

Jess sighed as the light turned green and we started moving again.

"So when did you start noticing this change in your boyfriend's—excuse me, your . . . *fiancé's*—attitude?" Wallace asked.

"Oh, nothing out of the ordinary. Just kind of gradual," Collette confided. "A few weeks ago he started hinting around.

You know, using other couples we mutually know as an example. Then, it started getting . . . uh . . . getting a little more personal."

"That's okay, honey. You don't have to tell us any more if you don't want to," Wanda said.

"Yeah, I think we're getting the picture just fine," Wallace agreed.

"Laird, you're messing up, pal," I whispered. "Big time."

"Have you always articulated your stance?" Wallace probed. "Has he always known where you stood on the issue of abstinence?"

"Yes," Collette said softly. "And here's the crazy part: it was him pushing for it even more than me at the start."

"Where does he stand in his faith?" Wanda asked.

"I don't know. I guess it's strong enough." There was skepticism in Collette's voice. "Actually, in all honesty, I'm beginning to wonder."

"Red flags at dawn," Wanda said.

"When do you plan to get married?" Wallace asked.

"Unsure. No firm date has been set yet."

"Is that part of the problem?" Wanda asked. "Is he playing hard to get?"

"I don't know." Collette seemed at wit's end. "Whenever I want to talk about setting a date, he can't change the subject fast enough."

"Oh brother," Wallace said. "Run—don't walk—from this relationship."

"Not so fast," Wanda cautioned her cohost. "Honey, do you love him?"

"I . . . uh . . . " Collette sounded on the verge of hyperventilating.

"Come on," Wallace hooted. "This isn't a multiple choice question. You've got to do better than that."

Ratcheting forward in the back seat, I felt my heart pounding.

"Do you love him?" Wanda asked again.

Jess screamed at the radio. "Come on, nimrod! Answer the question!"

"If this were a game show, the buzzer would have already sounded," Wallace lamented.

"What do you want from me?" Collette whined. "I'm going through with it. I'm definitely going to marry him, and there's nothing anyone can do to stop me."

"*What?*" Wanda squealed. "You just got through saying you don't love him."

"But it'll be different once we're married." Collette's voice cracked with the onset of tears. "I'm convinced of it."

"Oh, that's profoundly true. Yes indeed, it will be different," Wallace howled. "Then you'll be legally bound to your misery."

"This is a half-baked plan from the start. You're fully aware of that, aren't you?" Wanda's vexation now seemed to be turning to anger.

"Everything would be coming up roses if he wasn't pushing the sex issue," Collette interjected. "It's plain as day. That's where I'll have to dig my heels in."

"And while she's digging her heels in, we'll go to break," Wallace declared.

"You dumb bunny!" Jess shouted at the radio.

Emotionally cratered, a million thoughts collided in me simultaneously. *Do I actually care for Collette more than I thought? Am I insanely attracted to her and just refusing to admit it? And what right do I have to feel this way?* Out of her own mouth she said she was getting married—against all rational odds. So that was it. Case closed.

As the commercial break wound down, Jess lightened up and caught my attention in the rearview mirror. "Ready for the game now?"

"Naw, keep it where it's at." I didn't have the heart to ask her to change. If she'd been listening to the Christian station before picking me up, she obviously needed this ersatz brand of preaching more than I did. She may actually be learning something about God from these Bible-spouting nutjobs.

"If you're sure." She nodded, absorbed in her driving chores.

Coming out of the break, the next caller broke from the gate before the bumper music had even ended. "You people are charlatans of the highest order. You talk about the concept of Hell so cavalierly, but we all know a loving God would never . . . *ever* send a soul to such a place. You two should be ashamed of yourselves!"

"My stars, what a ringing endorsement," Wallace said. "Do you suppose our dear caller is on to something? Should we be ashamed?"

"That all depends," Wanda huffed. "What's your name, and where are you calling from?"

"This is Polly from Marina Heights."

"Nice neighborhood, Polly," Wallace offered.

"Which neighborhood are we talking about?" Wanda asked. "Marina Heights, or Hell?"

"Come on, Wanda," Polly snapped. "Me and you both know it doesn't exist."

"What doesn't exist? Hell?" Wanda laughed. "I wonder what the Bible says about that."

"It's the separation of your soul from your body," Wallace declared. "Can you even begin to visualize what that process entails? But the good news is . . . there is a way out."

"The fact is, God built us all with eternal souls," Wanda said. "You, me, and everyone else who's ever lived. Meaning we're all going to exist forever, whether we like it or not."

"So true," Wallace said. "And how we choose to live the rest of forever—which, by the way, is a very, very long time—is contingent on how we exercise our free will."

"Yeah, right," Polly muttered. "That's just your opinion."

"I think the Bible would beg to differ," Wallace said.

hen I cringed with shame for not being more forthright with
n speaking up for my faith.

also realized that maybe, just maybe, God wasn't done with
fter all.

hen again, my next stop was Las Vegas.

"Do you understand the pure, unmitigated horror of Hell, Polly?" Wanda asked. "God does not want that for anyone. But if you spend your life rejecting God, he will give you exactly what you want. In other words, he won't force you to spend another second with him once you depart from earth."

"Let's get one thing straight before anyone hangs up," Wallace said. "The entire crux of your eternal salvation, your deliverance from the ravages of Hell, depends on the triumphant work done on the cross by our humble and loving Savior, Jesus Christ. As sinners, we deserve every ounce of God's wrath, but Jesus endured the punishment on our behalf so we could avoid it. Have you put your faith and trust in him today?"

"Jesus is our best friend, yes," Wanda said. "And when we meet him on Judgment Day, which we're all going to do, what are we going to say to him?"

I swallowed hard. It all came flooding back. The same notion that had been dogging me for the last few weeks returned with a vengeance. What was I going to say for myself at the end of the line when I stood naked before the Lord?

"I can't take this anymore!" Jess slammed her fist into the radio, cracking the face of the dial. The cab fell silent.

"Wow," I murmured. This chick really was crazy.

"Are you happy now?" Jess drilled her boot heel into the gas pedal. The cab exploded in the express lane, pounding serious Gs, jolting us along the magic carpet ride from hell.

We blew past cars like they were standing still. As I rocked in the back seat, I figured this might work out fine: if we didn't get pulled over, we'd make it to the airport with time to spare.

"What didn't you like?" I shouted up front. "I thought you were listening to that station when you picked me up."

"Guess again!" Jess's hair blew in the open window like angry wings. She shouted above the squealing tires, weaving in and out of traffic. "That was the driver before me. He plays this garbage all day long. I just hadn't gotten around to changing it yet."

"Well, it didn't kill you to listen." I took a deep breath, hoping Jess would keep it together long enough to get me to the terminal.

It was right then that it hit me, where I'd seen her before: her airbrushed photo was on the reader board in front of the local gentlemen's club on my way to work—only in the photo she had spiked blonde hair. Why was she driving a cab instead of strutting the runway? Was exotic dancing not paying the rent? Was it time for a career change? But the biggest question of all . . . where was the *snake*?

We hit airport property at gale force speeds. Careening off a cargo exit, we shot the backdoor transit corridor. The toll booth at the livery exchange screamed in the windshield. I braced for the collision as we blew through the portal gate.

"And the horse you rode in on!" Jess shouted at the stunned attendant.

A minute later, she blasted past another checkpoint. Barreling into the departure lane, she squealed to a stop at Delta. Whipping around, she laid into me. "It's all your fault, slack jaw! Now I gotta go back to dancing!"

"Me? What'd I do?"

"Get outta my cab!"

I rolled from the back seat, amazed there were no flashing lights—yet.

She popped the trunk and heaved my Pullman bag and golf clubs onto the curb. Spitting on her gloves, she glared at me. "I wanna hear it straight from you, straight from the horse's patoot. Do you really buy into all that happy religious hooey?"

The world stopped spinning. It was another moment of truth: where did I stand in my faith? My answer would resonate for all eternity.

"Generally," I said stoically.

"Generally? What kind of gutless answer is man, you hear me? Weak!" She kicked my Pu pointy toe of her fancy boot. "At least with d real when you're showcasing in the pit. You k coming from." She wrenched around. "I'm boyfriend happy with a normal job. Stick a f on the planks tomorrow night!"

Dumbfounded, I paid the flat fare and tip She stared at the bill like it was festering flank how much I get for a typical lap dance?"

My forehead twitched as I fought to block do you want from me?" I'd suffered about as laundry-dropping lunatic as I could handle.

"Be real," she said. "Stand up for what you you're asked."

I couldn't deal with the abuse. More probler that she was right! I did need to do a better job faith next time I was asked—if there was a next

I tipped her an extra fifty.

"You can't buy me." She stuffed the bill into along with the twenty. "Get a life." She slamm squealed tires.

Just like that she was gone.

In the disquieting aftermath, I realized how I never did anything halfway, yet there I was, d tionship with Jesus. I felt like the dude who had and a foot on the curb. Everything was copace started moving. Then what were you going to d

As I stood in line to check my luggage, I Collette and the fact that she'd almost sounded radio. Once again, I resisted the urge to admit feelings for her.

DO PEOPLE HAVE SEX IN LAS VEGAS?

David's manhood was always a big hit in Vegas. Shutterbugs from all over the world crammed Appian Way in Caesars Palace, enamored with the nine-ton, eighteen-foot-tall replica of Michelangelo's masterpiece.

"What's Knoxville's projected growth rate over the next decade?" I asked Brad Trokerson, a broker buddy, as we navigated a busload of international photo hounds.

"Hang on a sec." Brad stuck a finger in his ear as he listened to a message on his cell phone.

I glanced at my watch. It was 9:25 PM Pacific Daylight Time, and there were still items on my agenda for the evening.

Welcome to the annual Federation of Affiliated Broadcasters convention. Measured in square acres instead of square feet, the massive confab showcased anything and everything broadcast-related—from soundboards to cameras to helicopters to production trucks.

Broadcast professionals from around the world came to bone up on all facets affecting the radio and TV industry: briefings on regulatory matters; engineering concerns with the crossover to digital; developments in the way news was delivered; advances in the latest studio equipment; and, most important of all, the opportunity to interact with peers.

It was the place where ideas converged, or in some cases collided, where players become very visible—and very vocal. If your company's key executives did not view the broadcast bacchanal as an all-hands-on-deck proposition, something was seriously wrong with your corporate org chart.

Brad and I had just wrapped up a quiet dinner at The Palm Restaurant and were heading from the Forum Shops to the cab-stand in front of Caesars. I had been in Las Vegas barely twenty-four hours and it already seemed like an eternity. Every year grew more hectic as the convention marched onward into the digital age.

"Change of plans." Brad pocketed his mobile phone. "It looks like I'll be meeting the radio group here instead."

"Lucky you," I said. "Then I'll head back to the Hilton solo."

We strode diagonally across the carpeted casino past the sports book. Banks of slots clanged and jangled in a mind-numbing, nonstop clamor. A barrage of cover tunes pumped out by mid-level bands blared from themed lounges. To the left, well-dressed couples queued up at the velvet rope in front of one of the Strip's more popular nightclubs.

"Do you really need to go back down there tonight?" Brad shifted his briefcase to the other hand. "There's something to be said for pacing yourself."

"It's all about my clients." I referred to my growing list of side accounts. "El Paso needs a new transmitter and Boston is ready for a retrofit. I want to talk with the manufacturer tonight before they hit the floor in the morning." I felt the adrenaline kick in as the pressure mounted. With the digital era bearing down on the industry, the demand for new RF equipment and ancillary components was monumental. I needed as many vendors in my hip pocket as possible to remain competitive.

"I'll wait to hear back on Knoxville, then," Brad said, glancing at his watch.

"Don't worry. It's a perfect fit for my client in Buffalo."

"Whatever," Brad said. "Just so you keep it all straight."

"Not a problem. I can do this stuff in my sleep," I told him.

"Here's where I get off." Brad thumbed to a busy watering hole. "Be safe."

As we shook hands, I pulled him closer. "Brad, you know how important this property is to me, right? With Knoxville in the fold, I'll really rack up the points."

"I have no doubt."

I looked him squarely in the eye. "I just want to make sure it's still available when I pull the trigger."

"No sweat, Vance. Have I ever let you down?"

"Right." I drew back. "No, of course not. I'm sorry."

"You feeling okay?" Brad looked at me curiously. "I've never heard you apologize before. Maybe this place has finally gotten to you."

I smiled wearily. "Forget it. Let's just get it done." After parting ways, I waded through the maze of slot machines serenaded by bass-thumping lounge acts. I didn't relish going back to the convention center tonight, but it was critical to the long-range plans of my clients.

And as everyone knew, my clients came first.

Outside, I waited at the cabstand, glad the line was relatively short. The warm desert air enveloped me in an ethereal cacophony of aromas: the natural southwest scents of mariposa and verbena comingling with cigar smoke, exhaust fumes, and vintage road-tested cologne. I reached in the vest pocket of my suit coat to retrieve my mobile phone to check for messages.

The comparative calm was shattered when a group of female news anchors and reporters spilled into the covered waiting area. It was a glorious caterwauling of laughter, friendly chatter, and high-spirited camaraderie. How did I know who they were? Well, for starters, this wasn't my first rodeo. It didn't take a genius to figure out these were special women: focused, ambitious, and talented. Women who commanded positions of high visibility in markets large and small across the country, who possibly had gone to school together, who possibly had worked together, who possibly had been at each other's throats at one time or another.

And then . . . *wham!* I recoiled in shock. Tentacles of fire shot up my arm from where it had been punched. Fighting the urge to grimace, I refused to grab the sore spot. This sucker was going to burn for a week, but you know what? That was okay. Based on the source, it was worth every searing, throbbing second of it.

"Vance Chelan, you inveterate cactus licker! Are your fingers broken? You can't dial?" Ronni Westerley stood toe-to-toe. A sly smile crept across her ravishing face. A light breeze picked at her immaculately coiffed dark brown hair. I was fixated on her riveting steel-blue eyes.

As I tried to keep from trembling, I might as well have jumped into one of the massive, ornate fountains across the way that Evel Knievel had attempted to clear years ago. And we all know how that had turned out.

"You're on my call list. Believe me," was all I could sputter.

"Yeah, right. Let's go." She grabbed my elbow and spun me around. In one of the slickest moves on record, she peeled me out of the cab line and away from her colleagues, none of them the wiser. Before I knew it we were back inside Caesars ordering

"Do you understand the pure, unmitigated horror of Hell, Polly?" Wanda asked. "God does not want that for anyone. But if you spend your life rejecting God, he will give you exactly what you want. In other words, he won't force you to spend another second with him once you depart from earth."

"Let's get one thing straight before anyone hangs up," Wallace said. "The entire crux of your eternal salvation, your deliverance from the ravages of Hell, depends on the triumphant work done on the cross by our humble and loving Savior, Jesus Christ. As sinners, we deserve every ounce of God's wrath, but Jesus endured the punishment on our behalf so we could avoid it. Have you put your faith and trust in him today?"

"Jesus is our best friend, yes," Wanda said. "And when we meet him on Judgment Day, which we're all going to do, what are we going to say to him?"

I swallowed hard. It all came flooding back. The same notion that had been dogging me for the last few weeks returned with a vengeance. What was I going to say for myself at the end of the line when I stood naked before the Lord?

"I can't take this anymore!" Jess slammed her fist into the radio, cracking the face of the dial. The cab fell silent.

"Wow," I murmured. This chick really was crazy.

"Are you happy now?" Jess drilled her boot heel into the gas pedal. The cab exploded in the express lane, pounding serious Gs, jolting us along the magic carpet ride from hell.

We blew past cars like they were standing still. As I rocked in the back seat, I figured this might work out fine: if we didn't get pulled over, we'd make it to the airport with time to spare.

"What didn't you like?" I shouted up front. "I thought you were listening to that station when you picked me up."

"Guess again!" Jess's hair blew in the open window like angry wings. She shouted above the squealing tires, weaving in and out of traffic. "That was the driver before me. He plays this garbage all day long. I just hadn't gotten around to changing it yet."

"Well, it didn't kill you to listen." I took a deep breath, hoping Jess would keep it together long enough to get me to the terminal.

It was right then that it hit me, where I'd seen her before: her airbrushed photo was on the reader board in front of the local gentlemen's club on my way to work—only in the photo she had spiked blonde hair. Why was she driving a cab instead of strutting the runway? Was exotic dancing not paying the rent? Was it time for a career change? But the biggest question of all . . . where was the *snake*?

We hit airport property at gale force speeds. Careening off a cargo exit, we shot the backdoor transit corridor. The toll booth at the livery exchange screamed in the windshield. I braced for the collision as we blew through the portal gate.

"And the horse you rode in on!" Jess shouted at the stunned attendant.

A minute later, she blasted past another checkpoint. Barreling into the departure lane, she squealed to a stop at Delta. Whipping around, she laid into me. "It's all your fault, slack jaw! Now I gotta go back to dancing!"

"Me? What'd I do?"

"Get outta my cab!"

I rolled from the back seat, amazed there were no flashing lights—yet.

She popped the trunk and heaved my Pullman bag and golf clubs onto the curb. Spitting on her gloves, she glared at me. "I wanna hear it straight from you, straight from the horse's patoot. Do you really buy into all that happy religious hooey?"

The world stopped spinning. It was another moment of truth: where did I stand in my faith? My answer would resonate for all eternity.

"Generally," I said stoically.

"Generally? What kind of gutless answer is that? You're weak, man, you hear me? Weak!" She kicked my Pullman bag with the pointy toe of her fancy boot. "At least with dancing, people are real when you're showcasing in the pit. You know where they're coming from." She wrenched around. "I'm done keeping my boyfriend happy with a normal job. Stick a fork in it! I'm back on the planks tomorrow night!"

Dumbfounded, I paid the flat fare and tipped her a twenty. She stared at the bill like it was festering flank steak. "You know how much I get for a typical lap dance?"

My forehead twitched as I fought to block the image. "What do you want from me?" I'd suffered about as much from this laundry-dropping lunatic as I could handle.

"Be real," she said. "Stand up for what you believe next time you're asked."

I couldn't deal with the abuse. More problematic was the fact that she was right! I did need to do a better job of defending the faith next time I was asked—if there was a next time.

I tipped her an extra fifty.

"You can't buy me." She stuffed the bill into her breast pocket along with the twenty. "Get a life." She slammed the door and squealed tires.

Just like that she was gone.

In the disquieting aftermath, I realized how messed up I was. I never did anything halfway, yet there I was, dogging my relationship with Jesus. I felt like the dude who had a foot on the bus and a foot on the curb. Everything was copacetic until the bus started moving. Then what were you going to do?

As I stood in line to check my luggage, I thought about Collette and the fact that she'd almost sounded human on the radio. Once again, I resisted the urge to admit that I may have feelings for her.

Then I cringed with shame for not being more forthright with Jess in speaking up for my faith.

I also realized that maybe, just maybe, God wasn't done with me after all.

Then again, my next stop was Las Vegas.

CHAPTER NINETEEN

Do People Have Sex
in Las Vegas?

David's manhood was always a big hit in Vegas. Shutterbugs from all over the world crammed Appian Way in Caesars Palace, enamored with the nine-ton, eighteen-foot-tall replica of Michelangelo's masterpiece.

"What's Knoxville's projected growth rate over the next decade?" I asked Brad Trokerson, a broker buddy, as we navigated a busload of international photo hounds.

"Hang on a sec." Brad stuck a finger in his ear as he listened to a message on his cell phone.

I glanced at my watch. It was 9:25 PM Pacific Daylight Time, and there were still items on my agenda for the evening.

Welcome to the annual Federation of Affiliated Broadcasters convention. Measured in square acres instead of square feet, the massive confab showcased anything and everything broadcast-related—from soundboards to cameras to helicopters to production trucks.

Broadcast professionals from around the world came to bone up on all facets affecting the radio and TV industry: briefings on regulatory matters; engineering concerns with the crossover to digital; developments in the way news was delivered; advances in the latest studio equipment; and, most important of all, the opportunity to interact with peers.

It was the place where ideas converged, or in some cases collided, where players become very visible—and very vocal. If your company's key executives did not view the broadcast bacchanal as an all-hands-on-deck proposition, something was seriously wrong with your corporate org chart.

Brad and I had just wrapped up a quiet dinner at The Palm Restaurant and were heading from the Forum Shops to the cabstand in front of Caesars. I had been in Las Vegas barely twenty-four hours and it already seemed like an eternity. Every year grew more hectic as the convention marched onward into the digital age.

"Change of plans." Brad pocketed his mobile phone. "It looks like I'll be meeting the radio group here instead."

"Lucky you," I said. "Then I'll head back to the Hilton solo."

We strode diagonally across the carpeted casino past the sports book. Banks of slots clanged and jangled in a mind-numbing, nonstop clamor. A barrage of cover tunes pumped out by mid-level bands blared from themed lounges. To the left, well-dressed couples queued up at the velvet rope in front of one of the Strip's more popular nightclubs.

"Do you really need to go back down there tonight?" Brad shifted his briefcase to the other hand. "There's something to be said for pacing yourself."

"It's all about my clients." I referred to my growing list of side accounts. "El Paso needs a new transmitter and Boston is ready for a retrofit. I want to talk with the manufacturer tonight before they hit the floor in the morning." I felt the adrenaline kick in as the pressure mounted. With the digital era bearing down on the industry, the demand for new RF equipment and ancillary components was monumental. I needed as many vendors in my hip pocket as possible to remain competitive.

"I'll wait to hear back on Knoxville, then," Brad said, glancing at his watch.

"Don't worry. It's a perfect fit for my client in Buffalo."

"Whatever," Brad said. "Just so you keep it all straight."

"Not a problem. I can do this stuff in my sleep," I told him.

"Here's where I get off." Brad thumbed to a busy watering hole. "Be safe."

As we shook hands, I pulled him closer. "Brad, you know how important this property is to me, right? With Knoxville in the fold, I'll really rack up the points."

"I have no doubt."

I looked him squarely in the eye. "I just want to make sure it's still available when I pull the trigger."

"No sweat, Vance. Have I ever let you down?"

"Right." I drew back. "No, of course not. I'm sorry."

"You feeling okay?" Brad looked at me curiously. "I've never heard you apologize before. Maybe this place has finally gotten to you."

I smiled wearily. "Forget it. Let's just get it done." After parting ways, I waded through the maze of slot machines serenaded by bass-thumping lounge acts. I didn't relish going back to the convention center tonight, but it was critical to the long-range plans of my clients.

And as everyone knew, my clients came first.

Outside, I waited at the cabstand, glad the line was relatively short. The warm desert air enveloped me in an ethereal cacophony of aromas: the natural southwest scents of mariposa and verbena comingling with cigar smoke, exhaust fumes, and vintage road-tested cologne. I reached in the vest pocket of my suit coat to retrieve my mobile phone to check for messages.

The comparative calm was shattered when a group of female news anchors and reporters spilled into the covered waiting area. It was a glorious caterwauling of laughter, friendly chatter, and high-spirited camaraderie. How did I know who they were? Well, for starters, this wasn't my first rodeo. It didn't take a genius to figure out these were special women: focused, ambitious, and talented. Women who commanded positions of high visibility in markets large and small across the country, who possibly had gone to school together, who possibly had worked together, who possibly had been at each other's throats at one time or another.

And then . . . *wham!* I recoiled in shock. Tentacles of fire shot up my arm from where it had been punched. Fighting the urge to grimace, I refused to grab the sore spot. This sucker was going to burn for a week, but you know what? That was okay. Based on the source, it was worth every searing, throbbing second of it.

"Vance Chelan, you inveterate cactus licker! Are your fingers broken? You can't dial?" Ronni Westerley stood toe-to-toe. A sly smile crept across her ravishing face. A light breeze picked at her immaculately coiffed dark brown hair. I was fixated on her riveting steel-blue eyes.

As I tried to keep from trembling, I might as well have jumped into one of the massive, ornate fountains across the way that Evel Knievel had attempted to clear years ago. And we all know how that had turned out.

"You're on my call list. Believe me," was all I could sputter.

"Yeah, right. Let's go." She grabbed my elbow and spun me around. In one of the slickest moves on record, she peeled me out of the cab line and away from her colleagues, none of them the wiser. Before I knew it we were back inside Caesars ordering drinks at a dark corner bar that was smaller than the bellhop closet.

"So how've you been lately?" I asked without really wanting to know.

Ronni and I first met years ago while I was building a TV station in LA. The transmitter facility was located atop a mountain on the way to Palm Springs outside a small desert community that was Ronni's hometown. A recent grad from a college up north, she was trying to make it as a freelance reporter at a local radio station. I ran into her at a sparsely attended chamber mixer and half-jokingly hinted that I needed on-camera talent to read the news at the top of the hour between off-net sitcoms.

She showed up the next morning with her own makeup kit and two changes of wardrobe. Though her innate talent was impressive, it paled in comparison to her driving passion. I took an immediate interest in her, though I kept it strictly professional. Ronni was a good five years younger than me, and, at that juncture in our respective careers, five years was an awful lot.

It was soon obvious she was destined for a bigger stage. I made calls to buddies around the country and got her hooked up at an indie in a backwater Idaho break-in market. That started her on a really good track because from there she went to Monterey-Salinas, then Omaha, and most recently—I thought—Louisville. This was a well-balanced, well-choreographed upward progression, all top-flight stations, all plum assignments. She had done incredibly well for herself, battling hard every step of the way.

More than anything else, though, I guess it came down to mutual respect. Even though we'd fallen out of touch, the trust and regard we had for each other would never die.

"Do you remember the time we were driving up to the transmitter and that sidewinder popped your front tire?" She broke out laughing. "You could see the fang holes." Ronni made hooks of two fingers and hissed. "I'll never forget the look on your face!"

"It was a good thing Verizon came along right after us." I shook my head incredulously, as if it was only yesterday. "And then when the window jammed and wouldn't close—what a mess. I thought it was going to jump in with us!"

"Remember my mother's snake repellant?"

"That homemade brew?" I closed my eyes. "How could I forget?"

"Ever figure out what the main ingredient was?"

"No."

"Good."

"How's she doing these days?"

"Same as always. She remarried again." Ronni tilted her head, her hair shimmering in the muted light. "So what's on your schedule this week?" She downshifted like silk, showing off her polished journalist chops.

"Keeping busy." I purposely kept it vague. No way did I want her knowing about my side action. "Trying to keep it together at my station back east. I've got a couple new programming deals that will get done early next year."

"I'm sure I'll read about it in the trades," she said. "I like it when they quote you. When you mix visionary stuff with philosophical insight."

"Like I know what I'm talking about."

She pushed away her wine glass and leaned into the table. "So here's the deal . . . "

This was it, the moment of truth. The electricity that had built between us all these years was about to be released. All we needed was a game plan.

"Do you think I should jump markets to Indy?"

The question caught me off guard. Had I grossly misread her intentions? Was she interested in corralling me in this little hole-in-the-wall bar at this precise juncture of the convention for no other reason than picking my brain about her next career move—as though I were some run-of-the-mill consultant?

Unwilling to let her see my disappointment, I realized this was for the best. Keeping the relationship platonic ensured its longevity, preserved its purity. Nothing would interfere with the virtue of our sweet friendship. Her mother would be proud—though I still wondered about the secret ingredient of that snake repellant.

Relieved and relaxed, I sighed extravagantly. It was the first time I'd genuinely smiled since seeing Ronni at the cabstand. Out from under this self-inflicted "rite of passage" malaise, I was thrilled to be able to concentrate again. "Okay, you're in Louisville now, right?"

"Dayton," she said with a wince. "But who's counting?"

"Sorry. Either way, Indy would be a logical bump."

"I'll anchor both the 5 o'clock and the 11, plus host a weekend magazine."

I nodded. "Not bad. Are they committed to promotions?"

"Big time. With way better lead-ins."

"Sounds like you hit pay dirt. When do you start?"

"Fourth quarter. They'll hammer out the contract next week." She brought her wine glass closer and seductively traced the lip with an exquisitely sculpted fingernail. "I don't come cheap, you know."

"No. I'm sure you don't."

Before I knew it, we were on dangerous ground again. Like a fruit fly dive-bombing a frozen daiquiri, my mind rushed headlong to a place it had no business going.

"Where are you staying?" she asked way too matter-of-factly. She was on the scent of live meat, and it was open season.

"Here in Vegas?" I stammered. "You mean . . . now?"

"No, two weeks from now. When hell freezes over." She squinted and made an irked gesture. "Of course now."

Things started spinning. I barely remembered my hotel. "The uh . . . the Mirage."

"I'm at the Luxor. We'll go there."

"The Luxor?"

"You make it sound like a foreign country."

I fidgeted with my hands, scratching my jaw when there was no itch.

"I don't have any meetings 'til noon tomorrow," she said. "How about you?"

"A breakfast meeting with our lead FCC attorney."

"Like that's going to happen. Next?"

I drummed fingers on the bamboo tabletop. "I'm supposed to meet with transmitter people back at the Hilton tonight."

"Are you putting hardware above me?"

"No." I was going hoarse with nerves. "Of course not."

"What's the problem then?" She leaned in to me like a seasoned reporter. "Did you get married on me?"

"No."

"Good. Neither did I," she declared. "Well, in the interest of full disclosure, I've been divorced a year and a half now."

"Divorced?" I said. "I didn't even know you were married."

"It happened when I was working in Nebraska. It's very rare to find a man with a good job willing to jump markets at the drop of a hat."

I blinked.

"So what about you?" she asked. "Are you seeing anyone?"

"No."

She stood up, brushing the front of her black trousers. "Then what's your problem?"

"I don't have a problem." I remained riveted to my seat. "Who said I had a problem?"

"I'm not buying it, Vance. As long as I've known you, you've never been hesitant or tentative about anything." She narrowed her gaze. "So why tonight?"

I stood from the table, yanking out my wallet. I was scared. Scared I'd lose her as a friend. Nothing was going to be the same after tonight whether I went through with it or not. I was in over my head and felt myself shutting down. I didn't care anymore.

"That's better." She nodded, pleased we were on terra firma again.

I dumped more money on the table than the drinks and tip would ever be worth, even by Las Vegas standards. "Let's go." I touched her elbow and headed for the exit.

I wanted to get this show on the road before I changed my mind.

Billions of flashing lights flooded the back seat of the cab as we rolled south on the crowded Strip toward the Luxor.

Everything was falling down on me like a rickety roof of slate tiles. Intrinsically, I knew this was wrong. It wasn't her age; she was a consenting adult. In truth, Ronni had better instincts about most things than I did. Rarely, though, had I been so conflicted. I was on the verge of an experience with this woman I'd dreamed about for years, yet something was throwing up more red flags than the front end of a bridge washout.

And then, lest we forget . . . there was God. According to my eclectic roster of spiritual advisors, this little lash-up was not exactly going to please our heavenly Father. And if I really forced myself to admit it, I guess it was beginning to bother me as well.

Ronni narrowed her gaze. "What's the problem? You're shaking like a leaf."

"No I'm not."

"Don't worry. We're almost there." Her cold pronouncement offered no reassurance.

I closed my eyes.

And then the voices started raging inside my head.

"Hellfire holy pants on fire!" Rory Psalter screamed. *"You weak-kneed, spineless slop bucket of day-old heifer dung! Old Satan's gotcha, don't he, boy? Gotcha right where he wants you, right in his old hip pocket. Enjoy the show, fancy pants, because you ain't fast-talkin' your way outta this one with the Almighty!"*

"You weak-kneed, spineless slop bucket of day-old heifer dung," sang the chorus from the night shift at the Waffle House.

"Why . . . Vance from South Point," Wanda huffed. *"You should be ashamed of yourself!"*

"Yes, Vance," Wallace intoned. *"Are we contemplating a little spiritual suicide here?"*

"Brother, I told you that when God started a work in you, he wasn't going to stop until he was finished." Connelly Caslett, the tennis star pastor, chuckled amiably. *"Well, I guess he just got through hanging that big old 'Gone Fishin'' sign on his storefront window, didn't he?"*

"Hah! I should have known!" Collette cackled. *"You're nothing but a two-bit whore!"*

"Vance from South Point, you're such a mess," Wanda scolded. *"Taking this once sweet, impressionable girl into your own sordid clutches!"*

"She's right," Wallace opined. *"You're her mentor, for crying out loud. Can't you give a better account of yourself than this? Come on lad, buck up!"*

"Mr. Fast and Easy," Wanda cautioned. *"Ripping out this poor woman's heart and positively trampling it. For what reason? For what gain?"*

"Old boy, you will never be able to look at her the same way again," Wallace said. *"What a tragic waste."*

"*Hey, bro,*" Billy Whatcom drawled in disappointment. "*We got a name for guys like you: carnal Christians.*"

"*He's Mr. Carnal Christian!*" sang the backup chorus from the Waffle House.

I felt like screaming. Clearly, I was not supposed to go through with this. But how could I slam on the brakes at this late juncture? Where was I going to come up with the stones to shut this down? If only I had a pair half as big as those on the David statue back at Caesars.

Ronni sighed, reaching for my hand. I turned to liquid; I sensed every wondrous ounce of her forbidden energy fusing with my body. I was sorry to let down my boisterous back seat contingent, but the die was cast: I was unable to extricate myself from this prickly jam, this undeniable date with paradise. I closed my eyes, trying to feel bad about this. But it was useless. This was going to be the night to end all nights.

In a hackneyed attempt to make peace with my invisible entourage, I offered up a silent prayer to God: *I know you've been trying to help me and now look at what I've gone and done. I'm sorry, and I hope you understand that I didn't see this coming. I'm going through with this, and I'm probably going to ignore the fact I'm not making you very happy. I am sorry and can't even guarantee I will do better in the future. Thank you for listening to this and for putting up with me.*

As I opened my eyes, Ronni's phone rang. She riffled through her designer handbag. Straightening up, she was all business, glancing at the call screen and answering on the third ring. "Ronni Westerley." There was not a trace of huskiness in her voice.

I watched the play of lights on her stoic face as we rode through the canyon of neon.

Ronni stiffened. She listened intently, staring dutifully out the window, fixing herself in the reflection of the glass. "Really?" She nodded in a very controlled, self-assured way.

I was starting to sense something was up.

"Okay, okay. Yes, I'm very interested. Hold on a sec." Ronni clamped the mouthpiece and leaned into me. "Vance," she whispered. "It's my agent. New York wants to meet with me in half an hour. You understand, right?" She nodded that, well, I had no choice in the matter.

I put on the gamest face I could muster. "Oh yeah. Sure, sure." I nodded robotically, gesturing for her to go ahead and take care of biz.

She leaned forward and jabbed the cabbie's shoulder. "Let him off at the corner."

The next thing I knew I was in a dark alley between two hulking resort properties, the Monte Carlo and the New York, New York. Somehow, I didn't think this was the "New York" Ronnie had just referred to. As the cab sped off, I sighed deeply.

And then, just like that, the world changed forever.

My disappointment vanished when I realized what had just happened: God had shown up in the back of that taxicab. He had invaded my life like a highballing train, like a roaring thunderclap, barreling out of nowhere to rescue me.

This was not about voodoo spells, lucky charms, superstitions, or talismans. This was the embodiment of the most meaningful, dynamic, and powerful relationship you will ever have—now throughout eternity.

Exhilaration pounded through every pore and nerve fiber. I was more alive than ever. I was soaring on the wings of a singular, all-powerful reality: the most important commitment a person could ever have—the one that had always eluded me—was now mine.

I finally had God in my life.

As I joined the sea of pedestrians on the wide sidewalk heading north along the Strip, I was not alone: the God of the Universe knew my every step, my every thought, my every desire. He loved me with a love beyond measure and wanted only the very best for me—even though I didn't always want it for myself. Most of all, I was filled with an overwhelming sense of purpose. I knew, beyond any shred of reasonable doubt, that I was going to meet Jesus one day and we were going to have a conversation that would last an eternity. Jesus, my best big brother of all time, was waiting for me with a beautiful smile and outstretched arms. And God would receive all the glory in his vast, infinite regality, with places reserved for all who should choose to trust him, forever and ever.

Perfection would reign supreme. No more doubts or self-recrimination.

Peace.

I still tingled with the afterglow of what had just happened. The true meaning of the word *relationship* had just played out before my eyes. I had actually had a conversation with God—crude as it was—in which I acknowledged him and endeavored to include him in my current predicament. He had responded in a totally unprecedented, unpredictable, unexpected way.

As only he could.

God knew I was in over my head with Ronni. I had spoken to him in the bluntest of terms, in a more brutally honest way than I would address most humans. I put it all on the line, admitting to the Creator of Heaven and Earth that I had messed up and wasn't really interested in fixing it. Yet he knew my heart; he knew my intentions and motivations. He turned an evening headed for disaster into the most amazing experience of my life.

Now I saw firsthand what Arnie Thurlingate and Billy Whatcom had been talking about: it really was a relationship. God was just waiting for me to cry out to him, and it didn't matter the hour of the day or night. Or the location. Or the situation. It was all about acknowledging his sovereign, unchangeable, inscrutable essence. And realizing what he'd done for me.

Would it always be easy? Would it always make sense? I didn't know; it was too early to tell. Would it pay off in the long run when I died and came face-to-face with Jesus?

Yes.

It was a long trek back to the Mirage, but what did I care? I suddenly had all the time in the world.

I had all of eternity.

I didn't know how long or far I'd been walking. People passed in the night beneath the brightest neon backdrop known to man, serenaded by a diversity of music escaping from stage doors and car interiors, the air punctuated with catcalls, whistles, and ambulance sirens. It was all a blur. I paused to watch workmen under the lights building the Bellagio, a massive new luxury resort rumored to boast a spectacular water feature across the front of its colossal property.

By the time I reached the iconic volcano at the entrance to the Mirage I was laughing. God knew I was too weak to turn Ronni down on my own so he'd extended a helping hand in the form of a job offer from the Big Apple. It all became blatantly clear: I couldn't figure a way out, so he grabbed me before I fell. What did they say? "The truth will set you free." After all these decades, I finally understood what that meant.

When I entered the tower suite overlooking the Strip, I fell to my knees at the side of the bed and loudly poured out my heart to God: "I get it now. You heard me. You listened to me. You did what I didn't have the guts to do myself. I don't know why you'd want anything to do with me. I kick you in the teeth every chance

I get. Oh God, forgive me, please, for every hurtful thing I've ever said or done. You are the greatest. I will never dispute that. And I will never say I don't measure up. I know you love me unconditionally, beyond all comprehension.

"And even though I can't see you or touch you, I know you're more a part of me than anyone else. Thank you for never, ever giving up on me, and thank you for Jesus, who died horrifically on the cross to bear my sins so I can have eternal life. I will never forget this night as long as I live."

As I stood, a little wobbly, I remembered I hadn't said Amen. So I knelt again and proclaimed it with feeling. It was 11:47 PM PDT on Thursday, July 17, 1997. I rose to my feet, a changed person. I had just been resuscitated by the greatest first responder in all of creation. I didn't look any different on the outside, but inside I was the epicenter of an explosion of hope.

All eternity hinged on what I did from now on. I had officially begun preparation for my meeting with Jesus Christ.

I had just died to my old self and was alive unlike ever before.

CHAPTER TWENTY

GROUND LEVEL EUPHORIA

The prospect of a clandestine meeting at the airport was doing a number on my nerves. At least Reggie Spagway hadn't given me much time to stew about it. For one thing, I didn't even know he was in town. And then calling me after hours and telling me to get down here as fast as I could—without breathing a word of it to anyone else—did not bode well. I was filled not so much with intrigue as downright trepidation.

The airport was nearly deserted at this late hour. You could fire a cannonball down Concourse B and not hit a single roller bag. All the storefronts and kiosks were dark and shuttered. Every once in a while there were pockets of travelers, like schools of fish darting through the cavernous terminal on their way to baggage claim.

"Flight 752 to New Orleans, now boarding at Gate L-28."

I glanced at my watch and picked up the pace. I rode the escalator to the mezzanine level of the main terminal. It had been three weeks since my triumphant trip to Las Vegas. Now I was back in an airport, though this excursion was far more cryptic than my trip out west. There was nothing about this meeting that gave me any hope. Instead, could this be the long-awaited slamming of the door on my employment with the Spagway Trust?

"God, thank you for watching out for me." I bowed my head and prayed quietly. "I don't know what's going on here, but if there's any unresolved stuff I need to address, please give me a clue. Thanks." In the back of my mind I had the nagging suspicion that God wanted me to come clean with Reggie about the consulting business. But I really didn't want to broach the subject unless it was the absolute, total last resort. The one thing I knew for certain: if God wanted it on the table, he'd find a way to get it there.

Only a couple of months ago, my little prayer would have been unthinkable. Back then I questioned prayer to the extent of mocking and ridiculing it. Friends would have been aghast to hear me even entertain the need for prayer, much less say one. Now it meant everything to me. Ever since the episode in Las Vegas, narrowly missing the "night of all nights" with hard-charging news anchor Ronni Westerly, I knew God was with me at all times in everything I did—the good, the bad, and the stupid—and it only made me want to try harder to be a better person even though I continued to blow it every chance I got.

When the escalator reached the mezzanine level, I headed across the tiled floor to the Skyview Club. The automatic doors silently opened into a sumptuous reception area. I stepped into the hushed confines and angled toward an attractive middle-aged concierge sitting at a cherrywood desk. She stopped scrutinizing her computer screen long enough to acknowledge me. "Good evening, sir. How may I assist you?"

"I'm supposed to meet one of your members here. A Mr. Reginald Spagway."

She brightened. "Of course. He should still be in the lounge. Keep going down the corridor until you reach the last bend.

Then it's straight ahead." She gave the two-finger point, the same gesture used by flight attendants indicating the placement of emergency exits.

"Thank you." I walked through the lavish confines, past vacant workstations. Across a marble-lined portico I saw the lounge. Reggie appeared to be the only customer.

I took a deep breath to keep from hyperventilating. Why on earth had Reggie called this impromptu meeting? It was killing me to find out. People had meetings at these airport clubs for a variety of reasons, primarily for the sake of convenience. But what if the meeting went sideways? Would it provide Reggie the opportunity to make a quick getaway?

I hoped this would not be the case tonight. But I couldn't help being apprehensive. Was he going to nail me on the supposed fling I was having with the mayor? Was it going to center around my less-than-stellar collection efforts with a certain celebrity plumber? Or was I going to get rung up for stalling production of the PSAs for the emergency preparedness committee? So many entrapments, so few escape hatches.

I strode into the lounge and sought to be as upbeat as possible. "Reggie, how goes the battle?"

"Vance, great to see you!" Reginald Aaronson Spagway stepped from his bar stool with an engaging smile and twinkle in his blue eyes. In his late sixties, he was slender, tanned, and fit, modestly attired in a button-down dress shirt and navy blazer. "Thanks for swinging by."

"No sweat. I know how travel schedules are." We shook hands warmly with a sincere air of mutual respect. "I don't get it," I said, looking around. "Why are we in the main terminal? Where's Claudius?" I was referring to the pet name for his ten-seat private jet.

"Don't ask." He gestured for me to sit. "The old boy was in for routine maintenance and they discovered some corrosion in one of the wheel wells." He leaned back with deep sigh. "So while they do repairs, I'm reduced to flying commercial."

I settled atop the adjacent barstool wondering if that last crack warranted a comeback. I held my tongue. As the muscular bartender approached, I glanced at Reggie for a cue.

Reggie nodded. "What'll you have?"

I spied his trademark Chivas rocks and ordered a Heineken.

Reggie folded the sports section of the *New York Times* on the onyx bar and pushed it toward the rail, nodding to the bartender that he was finished with the box scores.

My mind raced: *What is this meeting all about?* Surely it was more than me keeping the multimillionaire company at this late hour. Was he onto me about my freelance consulting business? If so, what should I do, fall on my sword and pledge I'll never take a side job again? I shot up a silent prayer: *Lord, help me out. What am I going to do?*

Reggie grabbed a fistful of peanuts and started methodically popping them into his mouth, chewing thoughtfully. His eyes traveled to the TV screen above the bar where the Golf Channel aired. "Who's going to win the PGA next week? You think Tiger has another major in him this year?"

"Tough to say." I fought to keep my emotions in check. I surely hadn't been summoned here by one of the wealthiest men on the East Coast to talk about golf.

"I mean it." Reggie stared with consternation at the monitor. "How many majors you think he has in him?"

"This year?" I fished a couple peanuts from the crystal bowl.

"No, for his whole career," Reggie said. "If he builds on what he did at the Masters, he'll eclipse Nicklaus, no sweat." He turned to me. "That is, of course, if Jack doesn't win another one himself."

"How long's it been since Nicklaus won a major?" I nodded vacantly. "Ten years?"

"That's about right." Reggie leaned closer. "So take a guess. Let your mind run wild. How many majors do you think Tiger will win before calling it a day?"

"Wild guess?" I said.

"Sky's the limit."

"Then I'll go out on a limb and say nineteen."

"Nineteen. That's very interesting." Reggie mulled it over. "Do you realize if you stick to that number, you'll have him winning exactly one more than the Golden Bear?"

"Right," I said. "Who plays for a tie?"

"Vance, I always knew there was something about you." He smiled wryly.

I didn't know if that was a compliment—or a veiled threat.

Reggie tapped the edge of the crystal bowl and smiled at the barkeep. "Can we have another installment of these addictive nuggets, please?"

The bartender nodded and reached for a new bowl from beneath the bar.

"Thank you." Reggie greedily filched peanuts from the fresh stock. "Now, tell me about the current state of your game. Have you done anything about that slice?"

I hid my frustration. My golf game was the *last* thing I wanted to talk about.

"When we spoke in the winter, you weren't playing a lot of golf," he said. "Has that changed?"

"Not substantially," I said. "I'm still trying to play at least twice a month."

"Nice try, Vance, but twice a month won't cut it," Reggie said. "Me and you both know you need to devote more time than that."

"I know, man, you're a hundred and ten percent correct." I picked at the peanuts. "But with all I got going on, where am I going to find the time?"

"What do you have going on? I thought everything was under control at the station?"

I froze. Was the tycoon lulling me into submission as a ploy to interrogate me about my side enterprise? Had I just unwittingly stumbled into a slick game of cat and mouse? Was he baiting me in hopes I'd spill my guts and admit to everything? I refused to give him the satisfaction. "That station commands a lot of my attention." I nodded. "To do it right, I mean."

"Of course," Reggie said. "And we all know you do it . . . right."

What was that supposed to mean? I was now more on edge than ever.

"So what are you shooting now?" the tycoon asked. "What's your handicap currently?"

I tried to read him. Was he playing with me, trying to catch me off guard and pump me for answers? Or was he genuinely interested in my golf game? "Seventeen," I said weakly. "I'm right now playing to a seventeen handicap. The highest in years."

Reggie nodded. "No worries. You can do something about that." He took his eyes off the television, suddenly deep in thought. What followed was an excruciating pause. He finally spoke: "Did you play any in Vegas?"

I refrained from answering quickly. This was too much like a legal deposition, where you had to ponder the consequences of an answer from all angles. "I took my clubs, but as it turned out only had time for one round."

"That's tough," he said. "There was a lot going on at the convention, I take it."

My heart pounded. He was definitely sniffing around; I had to head him off at the pass. "What can I say? It's the annual showcase, the absolute essential marketplace for broadcast stakeholders, the worldwide destination for everyone remotely connected."

"Bennett Fellingston says you cut quite the figure out there." Reggie chewed more slowly, narrowing his gaze. "He says you know a lot of people, you know a lot about the industry. You seemed to be getting a lot accomplished." He swallowed dispassionately.

"Bennett?" Alarm bells thundered in my head. I scrambled into overdrive. "I don't get it. Are you telling me he was out there?" Cornered like a caged beast, I beat back the urge to lash out. *So they sent Bennett to Vegas to spy on me!* He was my shadow, reporting my every move. How long did he tail me? How many of my confidential contacts did he see me with? Was he taking notes? Did he have field glasses? A camera? This was unacceptable!

What was I going to do? How was I going to respond? Was I going to berate Reggie for not trusting me? Or should I just storm out? I did the unthinkable and said another silent prayer: *Oh God, keep me from doing something I'll regret in the morning.* I opened my eyes, waiting for a sign. Nothing. More ticked than ever, I reared up on my hackles, ready to blowtorch the mega-millionaire.

"Hallelujah! We've got a winner!" The woman from the concierge desk triumphantly slapped a computer printout on the bar just to the left of Reggie.

"Finally!" Reggie brightened, whipping around to the woman. "What do you have?"

Jubilant, she leaned into him. "Not the most hospitable, but at the eleventh hour it's about all we can do." She traced the itinerary with a bright red fingernail. "It goes from here to Pittsburgh to Miami, where you'll connect with a nonstop flight to Christiansted."

Reggie exhaled, leaning back. "I'll be flying all week," he murmured.

"It's not as bad as it looks," she said. "Barring weather and anything unforeseen, you'll be home in St. Croix before noon."

"Are you saying noon, as in noon tomorrow?" he asked.

"Believe it or not," she said, "the connections all just seemed to open up and fall into place." She nodded exuberantly. "It's a miracle."

Reggie turned to me. "Nadine is involved in a fundraiser for the restoration of the boundary reef." He referred to his wife, who had taken an active interest in local causes in and around their second home. "I'm in charge of the golf mixer. The first foursome tees off at one in the afternoon tomorrow."

I looked away, not wanting Reggie to see the pure rage in my eyes.

He turned back to the woman. "Book it."

"Already done," she smiled.

"I like your style. Get me the name of your CEO before I leave. I'm putting in a good word for you." Reggie checked his watch. Sipping Chivas, he swam happily in triumph.

"Bennett," I whispered. Seething, I reared on my stool, coming out of my skin.

Rooted from his euphoria, Reggie made a pained face. "Yeah, right. What's with him, anyway?" He leaned back with a perplexed sigh. "I barely know the guy. Apparently Regina met him at school. He was a pretty good shot blocker back in the day, but now he's somewhat of a hanger-on, so far as I can tell." Reggie turned helplessly to me. "What's his deal? They said he was in Vegas to pitch a car show. You know anything about that?"

His question stunned me. I instantly backed down. "Car show," I said slowly. Shaking my head, I stifled a chuckle, pouring the rest of the beer into my glass. I took a deep, satisfied swig, relieved that the endgame of Bennett's Vegas spy mission was that stupid car show. "I've spent a lot of time with him on the preliminaries. But he's never come back to me with a workable treatment. I'm going to want to know his intended audience, segment lengths, and breakdowns, and who he's going after for co-op advertising. That all happens before a pilot gets shot."

"That explains it, then," Reggie said. "He's trying to ramrod this project down our throats, obviously behind everyone's back—most notably yours." He drew up sternly. "I'll put the kibosh on it first thing in the morning."

Suddenly, I felt sorry for Bennett. "Look, I'm not trying to torpedo the show," I offered. "I'm just saying to do it right. You have to follow protocol."

"I'm with you all the way." He glanced at his watch. "That's the reason I'm meeting with you tonight."

"To discuss Bennett Fellingston?" I bristled.

"No. To discuss the future of this company," Reggie said. "I just came from a special meeting of the board of directors. Do you know anything about that?"

"No. I'm totally in the dark," I said.

"And so is everyone else. Not a word of this to Regina, right?" He set his glass down. "The only person who knows I'm here is Nadine, and we need to keep it that way."

"Not a word. I promise." My heart raced. What could he be telling me that was so sensitive that not even his own daughter could know?

"Here's the deal." He nodded at me coolly. "We're diversifying."

"Diversifying?" Somehow that did not sound as sexy as I'd hoped.

"We're not going to make our nut in heating oil forever." He took a long sip of Chivas. "There are a lot of alternatives for the consumer on the horizon. It's only a matter of time."

"Okay," I said. I was no authority on heating oil—and wanted to keep it that way.

"You've opened our eyes to the prospect of broadcast. To that end, a couple of our directors researched the industry. It's no secret, there's money to be made in ownership of properties. And no one is denying that you are the one to lead us forward."

I was in a state of shock; I couldn't believe I was hearing this. "Right. You've totally nailed it: the future is now in broadcast." I could barely contain my zeal. "How big are we talking?"

"That's up to you as far as market size and cash flow multiples. We would either fold them into a loose network or group ownership scenario. We will spin it off into a subsidiary of the Trust. You will have total control of all phases of decision-making, including programming, content development, acquisition, operations, and distribution."

I swallowed, unable to digest what I was hearing. This couldn't be actually happening. There had to be a catch. I had to be dreaming this. Right?

Something didn't seem right; something wasn't adding up. How was he able to tick off my job duties, almost by rote? These were the same services I offered my national clients on a freelance basis. How would he know what they were unless he'd got his hands on one of my rate cards? And I held those very, very close to the vest. Definitely, he knew more than he was letting on. I realized right then: this was either an elaborate trick to expose my side ventures or the cruelest of jokes.

Reggie was aloof as our game of high-stakes poker played out. "Of course, you will be well compensated." He gauged my reaction. "I must apologize for what they were paying you up until now. I recently saw the books." He squinted painfully. "Why didn't you say something to me? I would have made it right."

I shrugged. "I didn't want to rock the boat." My mind couldn't process all of this fast enough. *Is he on the level? Is he toying with me, ready to spring the trap at any minute?* I walked a fine line, not wanting to doom this if, indeed, it was a legitimate job offer. "I was biding my time, keeping my powder dry, as they say."

"Those days are numbered if you accept our terms," Reggie said. "The package I'm proposing includes a competitive salary, performance bonuses, and stock options. For once, your talent and acumen will be accorded what they're due."

I stared numbly ahead. This had to be a dream. Nothing in life ever fell together like this. Somewhere in this rosy equation, there had to be a deep, dark underbelly.

"Vance?"

Metering the wealthy man, I was suddenly burdened with the overwhelming need to come clean about my consulting business. If my life was indeed transformed, if I truly was a changed person, then it was time to tell Reggie about my side ventures. If he fired me, so be it. If I lost out on all the perks he was offering as part of the promotion, then it wasn't meant to be. But I was finished with all the chicanery and deceit. "I have a confession to make."

"We all have confessions, they're dime-a-dozen." He slowly worked his jaw, giving me a glimpse of that fabled "Killer Eel" look. "The only thing that matters right now is this: do we have ourselves a deal . . . or not?"

Okay, forget the confession. He was clearly about to lose his cool. I had strung him out far enough. Everything from now on would be scorched earth unless I showed a sign of life. I became guardedly upbeat. "I knew there was a reason I never gave up on this property," I said with a slow nod.

Reggie couldn't hide his relief. "All in the timing," he said.

I backed off to indulge my fantasy. What if this were all true, all on the up-and-up? If so, I should be walking on air. Was this how Heaven felt? Or was Heaven even better?

"So, do we have ourselves a deal?" Reggie smiled, nodding expectantly.

I couldn't contain myself any longer. If all this were an elaborate hoax, then so be it; I had never felt so good about being deceived.

"Yeah, Reggie, you bet." I smiled broadly, my enthusiasm building. "We've got ourselves a deal."

"Superb!" He stuck out his hand and we shook firmly, with conviction. "I'll have Legal draw up the papers."

The whole thing suddenly hit me. I couldn't believe what had just happened. "When do I start?" I asked numbly, almost an afterthought.

"Hold off until we make it official in the trades. And first I'll have to break it to Regina. Talk about the sales job of the century."

"I gather I'm not answering to her after this."

Reggie stood. "Hopefully she'll come around." He paid the bar tab, drained the last of his drink, and collected his things.

As we headed toward the exit, I knew my life was never going to be the same. I realized God was present and totally behind this. I realized nothing had transpired for which I could claim any of the credit. That alone was a major reboot in my new way of thinking.

Sauntering down the paneled corridor, Reggie nodded at me with an easy smile. "Just think. You won't need to moonlight any more in order to make ends meet."

I didn't react. Did that mean he was on to my rogue consulting business after all?

At that point, what did I care?

CHAPTER TWENTY-ONE

SUNDAY SCHOOL
FOR SINNERS

"**I** want you to picture this." Connelly Caslett, the dashing pastor with the wicked tennis serve, was belting out his sermon from Matthew 14:22-33. "A bad storm on the Sea of Galilee roiled in the predawn hours." He gripped both sides of the pulpit. "Things were going from bad to worse in the boat, the disciples were being tossed and turned and thrown about. I'm sure most thought they were going to capsize—and die."

I sat erect in the second-to-last pew, trying to keep my mind in the ballgame. While the Word of the Lord endures forever and God remains immutable and unchangeable, the rest of the world kept spinning, transitioning, and morphing at a prodigious clip.

In the two months since being promoted to CEO of the Spagway Broadcast Group, I quickly became a sought-after figure in the TV management business, a regular industry insider. My workload and responsibilities had increased exponentially, but I let God shoulder the burden. It was such a relief knowing I didn't have to do everything alone.

During that hectic time frame, I had targeted six broadcast properties to purchase. Two of the TV stations were located in the plum markets of LA and Chicago. We were poised to close on both deals shortly, just as soon as the financial gurus pulled the trigger. It couldn't happen fast enough. Timing, as they always said, was everything. As soon as we purchased the first tier of stations and got up to speed with the operational aspects, I had another six properties waiting in the wings

The documentation required by these new acquisitions was formidable. I was knee-deep in due diligence, feasibility studies, pro forma income statements, tower negotiations, financing, sales, staffing, distribution, operations, production, and promotions.

Thankfully, I had the nucleus of a loyal, hardworking staff that included Regina, Bryce, Bennett, Clarence, and, yes, even Anastasia Scanlon. Reggie had done a masterful job convincing them that ownership of multiple stations coast to coast was far superior to owning one fledgling station in the Mid-Atlantic region. Considering the magnitude of the logistics, overnight we went from playing tiddlywinks to backgammon. If anybody wasn't fully onboard with what all that entailed, they were going to be left choking in the digital dust.

"The storm reached epic proportions, as often happens on the Sea of Galilee. You can only imagine the fright as the boat started breaching." At the pulpit, Pastor Caslett continued expounding on the Matthew passage. "Then, suddenly, through the howling winds and thrashing waves, a figure was seen. Some said it was a ghost, an apparition. In reality it was Jesus Christ, the full embodiment of his miraculous presence, walking across the water to calm the seas and bring safety to the occupants of the boat."

"Amen!" shouted a man up front.

Connelly Caslett gestured to the congregation. "What must they have been thinking in the boat when they saw the drenched figure of Jesus? Were they scrambling to find a lifeline to throw him? Maybe not. Most likely they were all in shock."

I was spellbound. I always pictured Jesus walking across water as smooth as a swimming pool. My preconceived notion was nothing at all like the description of this raging storm.

The preacher squared his shoulders. "As it turns out, Jesus used this as a lesson in faith-building. He invited Peter to join him on the liquid stage, offering his hand for the disciple to leave the safety of the boat."

Members of the congregation sat in rapt attention. Not even a soft "Amen" was being uttered.

Pastor Caslett continued. "We can only imagine what was going through Peter's mind at this point. But he showed true obedience and took Jesus up on his challenge. Of course, we all love Peter because he's often impetuous and, in a lot of ways, so much like us. So here he goes, climbing out of the boat into the swirling vortex—literally going from the frying pan into the fire—with Jesus patiently standing by."

I found myself locked into this passage. It consisted of such strong imagery. Would I have had enough faith to get out of the boat? Not on your life!

Pastor Caslett nodded resolutely. "At first it goes okay. Peter is fully aware of the Lord's presence keeping him upright. But does anyone know what happens next? Peter takes his eyes off the prize. That's right, he takes his eyes off Jesus. He listens to people in the boat possibly telling him he's insane; he listens to the voices in his own head telling him this is physically not possible. Then, just like that, all is lost and down he goes. Of course, Jesus plucks him to safety before he sinks to the depths."

Relieved that Peter was okay, I lost focus. The cares and concerns of the world crowded in on me like a gathering storm.

I checked my watch, needing to get to the office. I was in the middle of compiling an exhaustive equipment rundown for one of the stations on our initial purchase list, a property in Portland, Oregon that I had visited last month. The report was getting the better of me. It probably meant staying up most of the night tying together the finer points before close of business tomorrow.

This posed the question: why had I even bothered coming to church today? Because whenever I was in town, I made it a habit to attend. And habits—even relatively new ones—die hard.

Pastor Caslett gripped the pulpit as he prepared to close. "So if you don't remember anything else, just get one thing straight: Peter, by leaving the safety of the boat to pursue a relationship with Jesus, encountered incredible doubt, risk, and hardship. At the same time he experienced a great period of growth. And God encourages each one of us to follow Peter's courageous example so we can experience that same opportunity for growth ourselves."

A hush fell across the sanctuary as people let the meaning of the sermon sink in. Pastor Caslett said a closing prayer about pursuing Jesus at all costs.

When the last hymn was finished I made a beeline for the door.

God, I prayed silently, *I know you don't like people working Sundays, but I'm not doing this by choice. I really hope you understand where I'm coming from . . .*

I knew this prayer was cheesy and disingenuous, but at least I was acknowledging God, inviting him into my business. I was trying, sometimes unsuccessfully, sometimes misguidedly, to include him in every facet of my life, elevating him above all else. As I had been told over and over, and as I slowly came to realize, our relationship with God is the most vital element we take from our time on earth. It is the catalyst that will fuel all of eternity after we die. And Jesus was the One who made it all possible.

As the sanctuary emptied, I focused on Pastor Caslett bidding people farewell at the front door. As I waited in line to exit,

I geared up for another domineering handshake from the clay court preacher. Job number one was making a clean break and hustling back to the office; this meant forgoing nearly all forms of serious conversation and pleasantries.

Then I felt a tug on my arm. "Vance, we need to get you into adult education."

I flinched, ready to jump out of my skin. *What is this all about?* I composed myself and turned. "Hey, Chuck. What's up?"

Chuck Simmonson, the dignified cowboy, looked particularly solemn. "We're starting a new study on Luke today. I need you to join in."

"Sorry, man. I'd love to, but no can do today." I tried to make the burden look really onerous. "Big project back at work. The deadline's tomorrow."

"That's nice to hear, but it's Sunday. Your project can wait." He nodded stiffly. "I've been observing you lately. It seems you've hit the wall."

"Huh? I don't get it." I winced. "What are you talking about?"

"You've stopped making discernible progress. It's time to step it up a notch."

This was news to me. By all rights, my Christian life was progressing swimmingly. "I don't understand, man. I've been trying to get here as often as possible."

"I can say the same about the field mice that come in from the cold at night." Chuck frowned at the floor. "Do you want to take their spiritual temperature?"

I stared at him with equal parts frustration and vexation. Why did I win ninety-five percent of my arguments in the real world but get hosed down every time out of the gate with church people? Were they just that much more persistent—or flat-out pigheaded? I sighed heavily, making this look like the biggest imposition of all time. "Whatever . . . "

"Go through those doors to get to the classroom." Chuck pointed toward the head of the sanctuary. "Look for the signs for Luke."

"But that's the parlor," I whined.

"See you in ten minutes." Chuck clapped my back. "Grab some coffee on the way."

Trudging to the head of the church, looking for any excuse to bolt, I pushed through the parlor doors into a cacophony of voices and laughter. It was like a tidal wave of insanity rolling over me. Here we were together: all of us sinners having a riotous old time.

I moseyed toward the bank of coffeemakers hoping no one would collar me and ask about all the sins I'd committed the previous week.

"Lookee-lookee at what the cat dragged in!" Billy Whatcom batted my arm.

I turned from the formidable selection of spigots and gave the beaming associate pastor a half-baked hug. "You need earplugs around here," was all I could muster.

Over the last few months, Billy had been a constant encouragement in my walk of faith, suggesting events like men's retreats, singles conferences, and Christian concerts. Though I always turned him down, we both knew it was only a matter of time before something would click. It was a testimony to his genuineness and compassion that he never stopped trying. I conceded that God did not design us to handle the business of life alone. Billy never let me forget that.

"So what's up? Why the cameo?" Smiling broadly, Billy draped a ripped arm over my shoulder and made a sweeping gesture around the packed, boisterous room.

"Chuck Simmonson wants me in his class." I took a deep breath as I poured rich Colombian coffee into a floral print paper cup.

"Good for Chuck. I'm glad he lassoed you."

I turned to Billy. "Where's it being held?"

"Down the hallway. They'll have a sign on it. I think it's the Perennial Room."

"Swell." I slipped a collar bearing the church logo around the steaming cup. "I didn't really plan on any interruptions today. I have documents to compile back at work for a new property in Oregon."

"Oh wow. That sounds important." Billy pretended to be impressed. "So you consider the study of Scripture a detriment to your plans to work on the Lord's Day."

"No, I didn't say detriment. I said interruption. There's a difference."

"Of course," Billy chortled. "God is more than capable of making that distinction. But when you go to meet him, how will you explain the fact that paperwork was apparently more important than studying the Bible?"

"It's not paperwork, man. There's millions of dollars at stake here."

"Do you know how far a million dollars will go in Heaven?" Billy narrowed his eyes, a sure sign he was about to lower the hammer. "Or a few billion, for that matter?"

"I've never given it any thought." I sipped contemplatively. "Do you think they're even on the gold standard up there?"

"Gold can't compete with the infinite perfection of Heaven," Billy said. "Don't even try putting human values on what God has promised us in the afterlife."

"Right," I nodded, staring down at my cup. How was I going to offer a comeback to that? I realized that, once again, I had been shut down by one of the faithful.

Billy gave me a conciliatory one-armed hug. "I know it's still a little hard for you." He drew away. "Just remember to focus on what—and more important, who—really counts."

"No sweat, man. No need to remind me." I sucked coffee noisily.

"Oh yes, there is." Billy's jaw tensed. "We need to remind ourselves of that every waking minute."

"Got it." I always grew nervous when Billy turned dead serious about something. I knew it was time to stop joking and buckle the chinstrap.

As we parted ways I glanced at the roomful of gregarious sheep gone astray. I caught my breath when I spied Collette across the parlor. She was smartly dressed in a white silk blouse and navy slacks. Gabbing with Josie Grandelear, her eyes wandered my way. She snapped her attention back to Josie after making eye contact with me. Busted. She couldn't deal with it.

I closed my eyes and turned away, trying to purge her from my mind. I thought back on that night in the cab, listening to her on the radio. Were it the "old me" in the heady, bygone days, I would have been blabbing my head off about her spilling the beans on the airwaves. That wasn't the case now. I realized gossip was not viewed by God in the most favorable light.

Then the thought struck me: what if that wasn't Collette on the radio? The person hadn't given her name. She may have sounded like Collette, but that didn't mean she actually was Collette. Maybe it was just wishful thinking on my part that she and Laird were having problems. Maybe everything was patched up now. All hunky-dory.

"Let's go." Chuck patted my back.

As we ambled through the parlor, Collette glanced up and made no effort to hide the fact she was staring at us. It was like I was being led to the principal's office after acting out in class. When we hit the comparative quiet of the hallway, Chuck leaned into me. "It's a good thing she finally dumped that creep."

"Huh?" I briefly stopped walking. "What are you talking about?"

"It's been a few weeks now. Haven't you heard?" Chuck smiled smugly. "Interesting what you pick up when you stick around for class." He patted my back. "Come on. We don't want to be late."

I started moving again, but it was like walking on air. *Is this a dream? Did I hear Chuck correctly just now?* The news was just starting to sink in. I was breathless and speechless as things involving me and Collette zoomed through my head.

Chuck made a face, wondering if I was okay. "You know who I'm talking about, right? The whack-job she was dating. Laird Big Pants what's-his-name."

"Yeah, yeah. Sure." I nodded, my mind racing. "The dude from Australia, right?" I veered to avoid a woman coming up the hallway in the opposite direction.

"Ha! You mean the con man from Alberta," Chuck said.

"I thought he was some big-wheel programmer."

"Yeah, he programmed his own résumé and burned a lot of good people along the way." Chuck nudged my shoulder. "Including Collette."

"I'm sorry to hear that." Slowing down, I turned to Chuck. "So what are you saying? Is she . . . available?"

"What do I look like? A dating service?" Chuck stiffened as we stopped at the door of the classroom. He straightened his bolo tie, totally focused on the business at hand. "It's showtime."

"Yeah," I mumbled, visions of Collette dancing wildly in my head. "It's showtime."

I let Chuck lead the way. I had never been in this room; the setting was breathtaking. Two walls, completely glass, afforded a striking view of the sparkling blue lake. The morning was gloriously sunny with most of the marine layer already burned off. Framing the waterfront and hillsides were trees resplendent with vibrant oranges and reds.

A strange peace came over me, as if everything in life was fitting together: the phenomenal fall colors that only God could paint—and now the prospect of Collette.

The classroom was half full. About forty people, representing every tier of the social strata, were interspersed among rows of desks.

Chuck grabbed my elbow so I couldn't peel away. "You're sitting up front."

"Why?"

"One, I need you for moral support. And two, I don't want you dozing off."

"Okay, you're the boss." I smiled weakly and slid into a desk at the head of the class.

"Here." An elderly woman handed me a Bible and a two-page outline. "We're starting in the Book of Luke."

"Thanks." Sighing, I leafed through the pages of the Bible trying not to look completely lost. I ended up sneaking a peak at the table of contents. Realizing people were drilling holes into the back of my head, I resented being front and center all the more.

Chuck cleared his throat nervously and clung to the lectern. I strained my neck, seemingly looking up his nostrils. The guy appeared a little uneasy—but why? He struck me as a CEO or maybe a powerful lawyer or high-priced financial advisor. He probably had a janitorial staff that was bigger than this classroom contingent. "Thank you for coming," he said in a wavering voice. "Now before we get started, I'll open with a word of prayer."

Everyone bowed their heads; I followed suit. This was something new. It was my first exposure to corporate prayer that wasn't said before a meal, as part of a small group, or during a church service.

Chuck didn't speak in some gothic, high-and-mighty tone, just down to earth and friendly, like having a conversation with your next-door neighbor. "Dear heavenly Father," he began, "thank you for bringing us all together today on this glorious October day. You surely can't beat the colors you have given us. We thank you for Pastor Caslett's sermon and ask that we apply it to our daily lives. We thank you, Father, for the opportunity to learn more about you through your precious Word. I realize that it is indeed a major responsibility to convey your teaching here this morning. I pray that you use me as a worthy messenger to teach only what you want taught. And for there to be no misrepresentations or misconstruing of your holy, majestic Word."

The prayer was real and personal, straight to God and straight from the heart. It had no flowery embellishments or stultifying rote elements. It was organic, free-flowing, and immediate. It was offered up to God as if he were right here beside us, and spoken with a humility I had rarely heard before.

"I now commit this classroom to your Holy Spirit, dear Father, and ask for the love of Jesus to be in us. Thank you, Almighty God, in the name of your magnificent Son, Jesus Christ. Amen."

Most everyone echoed "Amen." And the class suddenly became alive.

I slowly opened my eyes realizing I felt differently after that prayer. A lot of things drained from me, primarily my anxiety. I tuned out the pressing demands of the world—including that unfinished equipment list back at the office. Now I was eager and receptive to learn about the Book of Luke.

Then everything went haywire.

My desk got rear-ended. Someone intent on wanting to make their presence known—or to register their displeasure—had launched the front of their desk into the back of mine. This was followed by persistent, and hugely annoying, foot-tapping on the horizontal brace beneath my chair. I got a feint whiff of perfume—even the scent was agitated—leaving no doubt who it was.

Chuck didn't acknowledge the new arrival because he wasn't looking at any of us. Instead, he addressed the wall in back of the room. Haltingly, he laid the groundwork for the study of Luke, explaining that the author was a physician of known stature. We learned that, in addition to being a man of science, Luke was a Greek citizen, meaning he was quite interested in detail. According to Chuck, Luke's goal was to focus on the humanness of Christ as someone who was all God and all man.

But with the distraction going on behind me, I barely paid attention. What kind of message was Collette sending based on her seating choice—and seating manner? There were certainly other available spaces in the classroom. Was this a plea for me to acknowledge her in some way? Should I dare even think about getting involved with her? After the sum total of women I'd dated, was she finally the one? Maybe even placed in my life by God?

Who really knew?

"So, without further ado, please turn with me in your Bibles to Luke 10:38-42, where we will begin studying the relationship between Martha and Mary and our Lord Jesus." Chuck dutifully repeated the verses, and pages were quickly flipped in unison.

I tried to make it look like I knew what I was doing—mainly to impress Collette. I was sure she had already pinpointed the passage.

After Chuck finished reading from Scripture, he looked up. "So here you have a younger sister and an older sister, just like the Prodigal Son parable, but, of course, without all the debauchery and drama." As I nodded my understanding, Chuck forged on. "And like so much of what we see in the Prodigal Son, this story also stresses the importance of relationship building."

The phrase caught my ear: relationship building. I wondered if that was the key point of life: cultivating, nurturing, growing, and expanding relationships. I heard on the radio recently that God created each of us to have a relationship with him. If we rejected God, there was an undisclosed hurt within us. We hurt whenever we pushed God away because we knew, deep down, instinctively, that God loves us with all his power and all his might. Denying God is contrary to our nature. But we do it because of our rebellious, sinful birthright.

Chuck provided more insight from the passage. "So Martha, the older sister, is rattled that Jesus has shown up for dinner and she's chasing around like a chicken with its head cut off. Here we can guess that the twelve disciples, and possibly some of the women who supported Jesus' ministry, might also have been at the dinner."

My eyes tracked the ceiling tiles. There were those twelve disciples again. Pastor Caslett had mentioned them in his sermon earlier. I wondered how many I could name. Well, we knew about Peter, who tried walking on water. Then, of course, Judas was in the mix; everyone was familiar him. Then you had Doubting Thomas, and I think at least one named John—and after that I was drawing a blank. Maybe I should just turn and ask the resident toe-tapper to name the others. I was dead certain she could fire them off in record time.

It got me to thinking, though: I was kind of whacked in my priorities. The disciples were real men who had actually interacted with Jesus—God among us—and I couldn't even name half. These were obviously some of the most prominent figures in history. To put the whole thing in perspective, I could name every college team in the SEC, Big Ten, ACC, Big East, Big 12, Pac-10, and the Western Athletic Conference. I could name every NFL team and its respective conference and division. The same for Major League Baseball, the NBA, and even the NHL.

Of all those teams, I could name a boatload of starters—past and present. Yet I couldn't come up with the names of the twelve disciples who helped shape the world in ways we cannot remotely understand. It made me wonder: on Judgment Day, was God going to be excited that I could recite every World Series winner over the last decade—and yet come up woefully short on basic biblical issues?

I started naming teams in the Big East, beginning with schools in the north. *Let's see, we have Syracuse and BC, Pitt, Temple . . .*

I may have passed out briefly because the next thing I knew, Chuck was wrapping up his spiel. He was the most impassioned I had seen him yet.

"Never, ever lose sight of who we owe our entire existence to. Without Jesus coming to deliver us . . . coming to save us . . . coming to redeem us . . . we are irrecoverably lost. There would be no hope, no promise of eternal life in God's glorious kingdom. Let us never forget what Jesus did for us on the cross, and let's tell others about it. Time is running short, ladies and gentlemen. The end is almost upon us. We owe it to our family members, our neighbors, our coworkers, and our fellow man to let them know we owe our absolute everything to Jesus Christ!"

Someone murmured "Praise God" as Bibles were shut.

After Chuck's closing prayer, the room echoed with a loud and affirmative "Amen!"

As people started to get up, I took a deep breath. This was the moment I'd been waiting for the entire class. Rehearsing one last time, I planned to keep it light with Collette, asking how things were going, feigning ignorance about her current status with Laird. I didn't want to come off as too aloof or too eager, just genuinely concerned.

My heart raced as I turned in my seat . . . but all I saw was an empty desk and the sway of her backside as she strode from the room.

I sighed and turned forward again. Watching Chuck collect his notes, I asked, "Did you get a load of that musical chair demolition derby thingamajig?"

"You mean Collette?" Chuck smiled. "If I didn't know better, I'd say she likes you."

"Who's nuts now?" I got up from the desk and followed Chuck out of the classroom, realizing I knew next to nothing about the twelve disciples—but even less about my feelings for Collette.

CHAPTER TWENTY-TWO

TYPICAL HALLOWEEN HIJINKS

Sancho Panza in a Speedo. Yes, there are some things the human psyche should not be forced to endure.

As I strode through the studio on my way to the parking lot, I got the feeling I was observing one of those gauzy photos from a Hollywood back lot circa 1930 where the cafeteria was overrun with gunslingers and royal highnesses. I guess that's what happened when Halloween fell on a Friday: it gave everyone license to get even wackier than usual.

Across the studio, Jules, the inimitable Rock 'n Roll Plumber, was rehearsing a new spot. All was currently forgiven with Jules. One of the songs he'd recorded in Nashville on my dime, "Bad Day on the Bidet," had actually become a hit single. He was more than able to pay the station back for past-due invoices, plus bring us some national PR in the process.

Decked out in full regalia, his skintight chartreuse jumpsuit showed more of his personal plumbing than I would have preferred. Purple hair, red wristbands, and a matching headband completed the garish ensemble along with a pair of white knee-high patent leather boots.

Raking the strings of his turquoise Fender Stratocaster, Jules screeched into the mic: "You got a clog, baby / it's some kinda log / you need some help / it might be kelp!" He fingered a clean lick and wrapped it up with more reverb than a set of Talladega tailpipes.

In the adjacent studio, Felix Fenton, the Slip-and-Fall Ninja, cavorted in his bright yellow leotards and fancy red cape. The diminutive attorney killed time while waiting for his production team, flailing at a displaced moth with his trademark nunchucks.

High above, Cabana Clarence Harkridge—sporting the bandana and busted-open shirt that earned him his nickname as a swashbuckling thespian—adjusted lights while perched atop an oversized step ladder.

It was half-past Crazy Rancheros and I needed to get out of there *immediatamente*.

I pushed through the wide set of soundproof doors, headed down an unfinished hallway, and out to the parking lot. Now that daylight savings had ended, it got dark much earlier. Shadows grew in the late afternoon heat. A thin breeze blew across the valley from the tree-lined mountains, kicking up dust eddies in anticipation of a good old-fashioned All Hallows Eve.

I checked my watch as I headed toward my car. With any luck I'd be on time for dinner. Was there any doubt traffic would be heavier than usual on this exceptionally celebratory occasion? Friday night combined with Halloween . . . *hello?* I could hear the *ca-ching* of cash registers. This town would be bursting at the seams with thirsty ghouls.

Mired in stop-and-go traffic, I finished checking messages on my mobile phone. My stomach churned as I started having second thoughts about this little caper. Billy Whatcom had put me up to it a couple of nights ago. The guy I was supposed to meet,

Martin Slosser, was married to a pillar of the church, the esteemed Florence Slosser. Martin, who did not attend church and who I'd never met, had apparently run into a dead end at work, which was now causing friction on the home front. Florence had reached out to Billy for guidance, and Billy figured if anyone could help lift Martin's spirits and provide some useful insight, it was me.

I wasn't so sure. Having never counseled anyone in a ministerial way before, I didn't know what to say or how to act. The pressure was on not to let anyone down.

As I navigated traffic I thought back to Halloween of one year ago. So much had changed over the last twelve months; my life was now as different as trick or treat. Last year, during the afterglow of an agency shindig, I had met the enigmatic tax maven, Verona Shrevesworth, whose passion for the occult, I was coming to find out, was bad for business in the biblical sense.

Flash forward to this year: I was ministering to a struggling soul in the name of Jesus Christ.

It was now all about accountability. I was the CEO of accountability, striving to be a worthy role model while toeing the line. Of course, I still had mishaps; the difference now was the presence of God in my life. As long as I grew in this relationship and put God first, things were going to be okay—even though I still fell down on the job seemingly every step of the way.

And then the burning question: where did Collette fit in? Time would tell. It was all up to God. I vowed not to push it or speed things up, as I would have in the past. I was well aware of the pitfalls created by a lack of self-control. I had a PhD in lack of self-control.

Driving into the shadows of the Ninth Street Bistro, I had a wacked thought: this being Halloween, what if I had dressed in character? Since I was ministering to someone, maybe I should have rented a priest's getup. It would come complete with one of those smoking buckets that swung on the end of a chain. I pictured myself strutting through the restaurant to greet Martin Slosser, shaking holy water off the tip of a lightsaber wand onto unsuspecting occupants at nearby tables.

As I slid from behind the wheel, I wondered if Slosser was expecting me to read from the Bible or spout memorized verses of Scripture. I criticized myself for not consulting Billy more in preparation for this meeting. I was totally clueless on the nuanced procedural issues. For all I knew, Martin Slosser needed the services of a theological giant, and I was coming to the table ill-prepared. Man, I was on the brink of dispensing some really bad juju.

I thought about grabbing the owner's manual from the glove compartment to make it look like I had a Bible in hand. Talk about a cheap trick. What if he really wanted to hear something from John 14 and all I could cite were the manufacturer's parameters for replacement of the intake manifold gasket? I chided myself for not filching a copy of the Gideon's Bible from the last hotel room I'd occupied.

As I handed my keys to the whistling valet, professionally made up like Zorro, I hustled through the scented shadows across the glazed terrazzo tiles. Just past the flowering gardens I saw costumed people on the veranda that overlooked the backside of the city. There I was—without a clue, without a game plan, and without a costume—feeling vaguely disconnected. What else was new?

Pausing at the vacant front desk, I scanned the expansive, minimalist restaurant. It was still relatively uncrowded at this early hour. I spotted a patron who could have been Martin

Slosser at a corner booth sipping a drink. From a distance he looked calm and decent, though I'd been warned by Billy that he was a piece of work.

The maître d' strode officiously around a phalanx of potted palms. He was decked out as a credible Tin Man. Like his Zorro counterpart, the costume appeared professionally rendered. I wondered how much people spent dressing up like fictional characters and figments from the graveyard. It was not for me to judge, but I was definitely looking at the whole notion of Halloween through a brand-new filter.

"Do you have a copy of the Bible handy?" I asked as we headed to the table where Slosser sat.

The Tin Man turned stiffly and gave me a pained expression. "You mean the *Bartenders Bible of Mixology*? Perhaps you'd like to look up the ingredients in a drink you wish to order?"

"No, I'm talking about the *actual* Bible." I gestured. "You know what I mean . . . the holy one?"

"I'm pretending I didn't hear that," he whispered caustically out of the side of his silver mouth. "Are you going to be a problem?"

"Look, just forget it, okay?"

Martin Slosser was already two fingers down on a Manhattan on the rocks. The Tin Man gave me a dirty look and Slosser appeared indifferent. Wow, this was shaping up as a swell night—and on the holiday that celebrated death and mayhem.

My quick assessment of Slosser concluded he was harmless. He wore an immaculate suit and appeared poised and confident to the point of being cocky. In his mid-to-late 40s, he had a receding hairline and somewhat pinched features. An accountant or attorney, take your pick—I didn't really know what he did.

According to Billy, he derived no satisfaction from his place of employment. The problem stemmed from his new supervisor, who had come from a startup in Boston. Apparently, she had all the answers; all one had to do was ask her. Realizing his department was being squeezed to the max, Martin didn't know if he wanted to tell her off and risk being fired, or just quit altogether. Neither scenario had much of an upside.

Since I knew something about business, I was more than capable of navigating the murky waters surrounding the man's shaky job status. My goal was to give Martin a lift up and get him looking at the glass as half full instead of leaking like a sieve.

That did not allay some of my creeping second thoughts, however. Though I'd counseled friends, neighbors, coworkers, and acquaintances in the past, this was a whole new ballgame. This was not about me throwing in my two cents' worth; it was about me being a messenger of God.

Billy had stressed that my meeting with Slosser need not be a heavy-handed counseling session. I recalled his words: "You'll be fine. Just go there and show up. Nine times out of ten, all people want is a sounding board. They just want someone to listen. So don't go there trying to fix everything. Let God do the heavy lifting."

That was still a little counterintuitive. I was used to shouldering the bulk of the responsibility. This "giving it over to God" thing was still foreign. I understood it in principle, but putting it into practice was daunting. It was so much easier to impose my will on a situation than to let God do the right thing.

As I zeroed in on the table, I suddenly had a gut feeling this was a colossal mistake.

Too late now.

Slosser could barely muster the enthusiasm to shake my hand. As I sat and faced him, he folded his arms defiantly and looked away. "I'm contemplating taking her to court. What do you think?"

"Huh?" I was taken totally off guard. It was obvious we weren't going to open by talking about sports. "Take *who* to court? What are you talking about?"

"My boss, of course," he said. "And it's 'whom.' Take 'whom' to court."

"Ohh . . . kay." I needed someone to take my drink order.

"I believe her incompetence and recalcitrance are costing the shareholders innumerable opportunities in the Asian market."

"I, uh . . . " I swallowed, realizing I didn't even know the industry we were here to discuss. Some basic facts would help before diving headlong into a lawsuit. "I'm no lawyer, but I don't have to tell you, the minute you drop the hammer, it's going to get expensive."

He tilted his head like a dog anticipating a treat.

I ignored that. "The first question is: can you win? And if so, what's it worth to you?"

"Of course I can win. What kind of nitwit do you think I am?" The slight man tugged on his wire rim specs. "You think I haven't counted the votes before going into the chamber?"

"What chamber are we talking about?" I was already tired of this creep's snide antics.

"It's a political figure of speech." He examined me, stupefied. "You realize, of course, you never introduce a bill on the floor of the House unless you've already got the votes in hand?"

"That's very reasonable." I nodded vacantly.

"Reasonable?" He sneered. "Don't you do that before every shareholders meeting?"

"I don't have, um . . . I guess . . . a real reason to do that," I said with a shrug.

"What's your deal, man?" Exasperated, Slosser banged the tabletop. "I thought they were putting me together with a real hotshot, not some schlub from the second string."

Okay, now Slosser had hit a nerve. The reference to the second string dredged up all my gridiron failures. Wanting to smack the cocky jerk into the next county, I fantasized about overturning the table and ramming it into his gut, not stopping until he was hinged at the diaphragm. My blood coursed and temples pounded.

Then I had to remind myself: this was not about me. This was all about God. I couldn't take it personally, but needed to summon every last ounce of self-control. *Oh man, oh man is this tough!*

The waitress showed up, fashionably disguised as the Bride of Frankenstein, and I was finally able to order a beer.

Martin leaned heatedly into the table. "What kind of settlement do you think I'd get if I leveraged a figure based on a percentage of overseas sales for the next five years?"

"A percentage of overseas sales . . . " I glazed over. So now I was supposed to be a CFO or cost accountant? How was I possibly going to frame an answer without getting into round two with this creep? I'd had enough and decided to show him a little of the underbelly. "Did you ask to see me tonight because you wanted some moral support or because you wanted a corporate raider to rake the company over the coals?"

My beer came and he appeared to struggle at being civil. "Maybe you're right. It's not fair to ask someone with limited capabilities to weigh in on these nuanced issues."

Nuanced issues, my flaming three-car garage! Breathing hard, I was ready to come after this prim moron with renewed vigor. Then I pulled back, realizing he was merely pushing my buttons—and deriving great pleasure in doing so. I tried to calm myself. "Let's talk about your boss." I spread my hands on the table. "Tell me the reason you're in these straits to begin with."

"You mean the Death Stalker?" he asked haughtily.

I flashed him a glance. "Come on, you can do better than that."

"Don't give me that sanctimonious attitude," he spat. "It's one of the deadliest scorpions in the world. It's what she calls *herself* for crying out loud!" He gestured angrily. "And that doesn't even begin to describe her."

"Okay, okay." I leaned back in my seat. "What's your problem with her?"

"It's quite simple. She wants to cut R&D to the bone."

"That's never a good thing," I offered.

"Well, what do you know?" Slosser nodded snidely. "You might actually have a thought in that muddled, pathetic head of yours after all."

"Hey man, can we have a little understanding here?" I worked very hard to contain my rage. "The more you open that big trap of yours, the more I see where the problem is coming from."

"What's that supposed to mean?" The small man was startled. He wasn't used to getting called on things.

"If you're this abusive with me—someone, believe it or not, who's actually trying to help you—there's no telling how you come off to others, your superiors and coworkers. So why not stuff a sock in it for the time being, and let's see if we can get to the bottom of this."

That seemed to do the trick; no guarantees, though. I trusted this jerk about as much as a viper with hemorrhoids, but at least we had the semblance of a truce. Soon thereafter we ordered dinner—without a fight.

We had a cordial evening the rest of the way. The more he divulged his company's plans, the more my interest was piqued.

I made the decision to expense the meal because I felt his firm might ultimately become an advertising client.

I gave the Bride of Frankenstein my credit card and leaned back, sipping the last of my coffee. "Just remember," I said, "the minute you give in to your emotions, you've lost the game. The more I hear about your stake in this company, the more I'm behind it. You're an incredible asset, and they need you more than you realize. If you give up now, I think you'll regret it. Hang around a little longer. What do you have to lose?"

Slosser nodded. "Thanks. It's never been explained to me in those terms before."

The Bride returned with my card. I overtipped her and signed with a flourish.

"I guess I owe you one. But that sounds a little trite." Martin tugged the cuffs of his tailored shirt.

"Happy to be of service," I smiled, patting his shoulder. We had gotten through this. I felt better about this guy.

Striding through the restaurant, we were both reminded that Halloween was in full swing. Just about every kind of costume, from elaborate to chintzy, was on display.

A thought suddenly struck me: I had come as a chameleon—just not dressed the part. The whole evening was predicated on me giving Slosser insight into a relationship with Christ, and I had failed to make even a passing reference to the promise of salvation. Now in the waning moments, I was finally getting around to the main course—and yet it was nothing more than an afterthought. Talk about misplaced priorities.

I sucked it up and took the plunge. "You know, the welcome mat is always out at our church for you. If, of course, you're so inclined." *Man, was that a weak finish.*

"Real good," he said, totally blowing me off. He turned sharply at a booth filled with ghouls and trolls and marched with renewed urgency toward the front door.

I rolled my eyes and quickly caught up with him.

"Now that you brought church into the conversation," he said brusquely, not looking at me. "I've got a question." He pushed through the front door.

"You bet," I said, following him outside. "Shoot."

"Are you having an affair with my wife?" He asked the bombshell question matter-of-factly, not missing a step.

I jerked to a stop. I'd been blindsided by a sucker punch. My teeth grated—a nasty, telltale sign from my deep and sometimes dark past, signaling that a beatdown was imminent.

My blood pleasure shot through the roof; I gasped to keep from hyperventilating. My mind exploded with venom. All I saw was red, pulsating corpuscles blinding my vision as this impish little man, so self-important and full of himself, sauntered stupidly ahead of me.

"Hey! You can't accuse me of that and just walk away!" My voice echoed off the flagstone walls as we entered the portico.

He made a little wave without turning.

I was going to crush him, but how? I couldn't start hammering on him with his back to me. "Come on, Slosser. You asked for it. Let's get it on."

He stopped walking when he reached the valet stand.

I kept pressing in. The plan was to mash him into the front of the stand and start driving. Hopefully he'd feel the pain and turn to ask for mercy. Once he did that, it would be open season and I'd start wailing on his face.

"Is this guy giving you a hard time?" The muscular attendant appeared through the doorway from the garage. He was still Zorro, just now smoking a cigarette.

Slosser turned, assured he was protected, and sized me up like he was king of the roost.

I froze, realizing my temper had gotten the better of me. If I so much as laid one finger on this peacock, my whole life would come to a sizzling halt. Hello, prison. Good-bye, career.

I was not out of the woods yet. Slosser held all the cards. He could summon the cops with one sideways glance, one subtle nod.

It seemed like an eternity as the attendant and I waited for an answer . . .

"Hey man. I don't have all night!" Zorro ground his butt on the pavement and blew an agitated column of smoke. He glanced my way, looking at me long and hard, wanting any excuse to put me in a hammerlock.

I made a mental note: if I got out of this little imbroglio alive, I would tip him more than the national debt was worth.

Slosser bored me with his dark, beady eyes, sneered, and turned back to the stand. He reached for his wallet and presented his ticket. He made it look like he was a big-time poker player cashing in.

The attendant grabbed Slosser's ticket and hustled into the garage. Over my shoulder, I glanced as Slosser pivoted arrogantly to give me a piece of his mind.

Only I was gone.

Retiring to the men's room, I hunched over the granite counter at one of the big sinks. As the stinging ice-cold water sluiced over my fevered face, I began to calm down. It was good I'd walked from the scene, not wanting to be alone with that rat. Left to his own devices, there was no telling what he could cook up. It was his word against mine, and I was the one who had lost his temper.

Flicking my fingers, I looked in the mirror. I envisioned Slosser whisking away in his car, probably a Mercedes C-Class. He was the kind of guy who would lay in wait somewhere until I left the premises. Then he'd start following in close pursuit, tailgating me until I pulled over, and then the fun would begin.

I wondered if he was carrying.

I was ticked that I hadn't been the one to leave first, because that was surely the ploy I would have used against him.

CHAPTER TWENTY-THREE

Hyperconnectivity at the Speed of Sight

It was not shaping up as the greatest Monday morning of all time. Traffic on the West River Skyway was at a near standstill. And I was running late for a meeting at the Thurlingate dealership to finalize details for their annual "Thanksgiving Price-Slashing Trot."

It had been a bad weekend—a bad, bad, weekend.

Friday night's encounter with Martin Slosser still had me in knots. I couldn't shake the feeling of betrayal when he'd accused me of having an affair with his wife. I replayed the scene at the valet stand, dissecting my every move, wondering what would have happened if the attendant hadn't shown up when he did. Would I have followed through with my beatdown of the snide jerk? If so, what would have happened to me? Where would I be right now?

Saturday morning, I woke up like I'd been on a bender. The hateful poison had consumed me. I now realized what people meant when they talked about God's courtroom: you didn't have to kill someone physically to be a murderer. I saw the sick, villainous nature of my heart—the same heart that God saw—and it was not a pretty sight.

Here I thought I'd done such a good job of putting my past life behind me. Then it came rushing back at the first hint of provocation.

I was a sinner in need of a Savior.

Yesterday at church I'd felt like a deviant interloper, averting my eyes from Florence—Mrs. Slosser—the alleged object of my unfounded advances. I even avoided her friends, feeling somehow compromised by the fallout from the sordid accusation. I didn't tell Billy Whatcom, because then he'd be in the middle of something he had absolutely no control over—and why would I want to give wings to such an asinine falsehood to begin with?

Hopefully I would finish my meeting with Junior in time to run things past Arnie. I welcomed his unbiased appraisal. If anyone could put this mess in perspective, it was Crusher.

Guys from the parts department rode a bucket tuck in the main lot stringing industrial Christmas lights overhead. Sliding from my car, I thought to myself that it was a little early for decorations, but who was counting? Halloween was over; let the laborious holiday season begin.

I finished meeting Myron Jr. in record time and hightailed over to Arnie in fleet sales, anxious to find out if I was overreacting to Martin Slosser's false accusations.

Stepping from his office, Crusher wore a starched white shirt and blue silk tie. His cuff links were probably more expensive than my entire suit. He brightened and motioned me to the break room. "Good of you to stop by, Brother Vance. I've got something to ask you, and this saves having to make a call."

I followed him through the fluorescent glare of the red-and-white tiled confines. "I need your advice, man."

Crusher turned over a broad shoulder. "Hit me."

"Last Friday night I met this guy for dinner. He's the husband of one of the pillars at our church. Anyway, he's not making headway at work, kind of down on his luck, and I was supposed to, you know, counsel him. Billy Whatcom, our associate pastor, had asked me to lend him my ear. That sort of thing."

Crusher kept his stride, looking straight ahead. "Is he a believer?"

"How should I know?" I shrugged. "What difference does it make?"

Crusher stopped and pivoted sharply. "It makes all the difference in the world. You should know that by now." He made a pained face.

"All right, forget the technicalities. Just hear me out." I hustled to keep up once he started walking again. "We didn't hit it off at first, but by the end of the night we were getting on pretty good. Then, just as we're leaving, he turns to me and asks if I'd been sleeping with his wife. Can you believe that?"

"Well," Arnie said, turning casually from the overworked coffeemaker. "Is it true?"

"Of course not! She's a church matron, for crying out loud!" I gestured frantically. "Who do you think I am? It's not like I even know her that well, and her screwball husband—my accuser—apparently can't get along with people if his life depended on it." I put hands on my hips. "And I'm supposed to be ministering to him about career advice." I looked for something to kick. "You just never know! Right?"

The whole business was so distasteful; all I wanted to do was stuff it in a trunk. But I was finding it especially difficult to excuse Martin Slosser's nonchalant arrogance. It was just another day at the office for him: the office of boldface lies and baseless accusations.

"Could he have been any less tactful?" I went on. "It just came out of left field." I slapped the counter and shook my head. "Totally blew me away."

Arnie nodded thoughtfully. "That stuff happens." He poured steaming coffee into a Styrofoam cup and cradled it in an oversized hand. "So what did you tell him?"

"What did I tell him?" I sighed. "I don't know, I don't even remember. I was so hacked. I just wanted to lay him out."

"Did you feel like killing him?" Arnie shook in some sugar.

"Who knows? I was definitely seeing red."

"You need to take that to the Lord and confess it. You need to do that right away."

"It's already done. That's how I spent the weekend, playing it over and over in my head. I never should have lost it like that." I nodded dejectedly. "I'm just glad the valet guy showed up when he did to defuse things. And don't worry. I've already thanked God for protecting me from myself."

"All right." Arnie shook powdered creamer into his cup. "At least you've made your peace on that score." He came up beside me. "Do you realize the progress you've made?"

"Well, if your idea of progress is wanting to kill somebody, I guess you could say that."

"I'm talking about what you did with it, how you handled it." Arnie appeared impressed. "It's only been a few short months, but you're light-years ahead of where you were. And light-years ahead of a lot of people who've been at this a lot longer than you."

I reflected on this while pouring my own coffee. "That's the part about growth, I guess, huh?"

"Right. What good would living be if there was no growth?"

"Even though it hurts."

"When you look back at it, you'll see God's fingerprints all over it." Arnie smiled. "It will all make sense."

I set the pot down. "But concerning my accuser. Him . . . I can't deal with."

Arnie stirred the contents of his cup. "The thing you gotta watch when dealing with snakes: if you come outta the gate too hot, they'll think you're trying to hide something." He sipped his steaming coffee and winced. "Best thing is to keep them guessing. Just walk away and don't let it get to you."

"Easier said than done."

"Nobody said it would be easy." Crusher led the way to a table in the middle of the room where he settled his muscular girth on a sparkly, red vinyl chair. The stainless steel frame groaned under the pressure. "So how did Dallas do yesterday?"

"Come on, man. Y'all know they beat the Niners." I mocked him with a fake Texas drawl. Arnie knew just about everything worth knowing about the Cowboys. Dallas had been one of a handful of NFL teams that showed an interest in him coming out of college. In the process he had become a lifelong, inveterate, and insufferable Cowboys fan.

"You think Michigan can run the table?" he asked.

I ignored Crush's attempt to change the subject and dove back in.

"Should I have hauled off and hit the guy? I mean, really. The whole thing destroyed my weekend." I felt myself getting all worked up again. "What gave him the right? Where was he coming from anyway? You just don't cast aspersions like that without dealing with the ol' five-knuckle fallout."

"I take it you didn't pray with him?"

"*Pray with him?*" I made a pained face. "Are you *nuts?* Pray with a guy who's throwing you under the bus?"

Crusher just blinked. "You're joking, right?"

"Dude, I wanted to coldcock him!"

Arnie tilted his face to the ceiling. "What am I going to do with you?" His green eyes made intense slits. "Are you telling me you don't know the power of prayer in that kind of scenario?"

"We're talking heat of the moment, snap decisions," I pleaded feverishly. "Who's got time for prayer?"

"We'll just see about that." Arnie grabbed the smudged house phone, his booming voice echoing over the PA system. "Belle to the break room. Belle to the break room. Code Delilah."

"Belle?" My kneecaps turned to meringue. "What's she got to do with this?"

"She's a prayer warrior of the highest water." Arnie set the phone down and ran thick fingers through his sculpted blond hair. "She'll make you forget all about doubting the power of prayer. Trust me."

Alleviating my nervousness, I sauntered over to the coffee-maker and topped off my cup. I didn't dare glance at my watch because time was really getting away from me. I took a long sip as I headed back to the table. "What was it you wanted to talk to me about?"

"Oh yeah, right." Crusher snapped his fingers and straightened up. "The Fellowship of Downtown Christian Businesspersons. I'm the chair this term. Ever hear of them?"

"Fellowship of Downtown Christian Businesspersons . . . " I shook my head. "I don't know, maybe. Not that I'm aware of."

"It's been around awhile. We meet for breakfast once a month to get a Christian perspective on current events, politics, sports, entertainment, the economy, that sort of thing."

"Okay, right. Got it." I figured Crush was going to invite me to their next gathering. I didn't really want to go, but if it meant showing support for him, I was all in.

"The annual Advent breakfast is right around the corner, and I've penciled you in as our guest speaker."

"Huh?" Surely I had misheard him. "I don't get it. What are you talking about?" My heart pounding, I felt beads of cold sweat. All aboard for the next anxiety attack!

"I'm not asking for much. Just a brief update on the TV industry. Give your testimony, answer any questions. You know the drill. Twenty minutes, half hour tops. I'll need your bio for the liner notes. Bring it home by telling them how you invited Jesus into your life."

A hundred thousand doubts flooded my thoughts. Was Crusher nuts? I didn't measure up! Who in their right mind would want to hear what I had to say about coming to faith? "I don't know, man," I said. "I'll have to see if I'm in town that week. With this new workload of mine, the balls are always up in the air." I was backpedaling like crazy.

"Don't give me that." He waved me off. "I'm giving you enough advance notice. You can work your travel around it."

I wanted to give Crusher a laundry list of reasons why I wouldn't be available. Then all of a sudden, nothing mattered anymore.

"Vance!" Belle lit up the shabby little room. She wore a burgundy dress, dark stockings, and spike heels. Her curly, honey-blonde hair was immaculately coiffed.

I nearly knocked over the table in my haste to stand. "Hey Belle!" If I'd known it was this easy to get an audience with her, I would have questioned my prayer life a long time ago.

"What's up?" Belle smiled sweetly at me and then Arnie.

"I believe our friend here is not giving prayer its full due," Arnie said stoically.

"Oh?" Belle looked at me with concern. "How so?"

"Let's not make this into a Mount Rushmore kind of thing, okay?" My eyes darted warily between the two of them. I could have mentioned the breakthrough prayer in Las Vegas, but I figured the extenuating circumstances would have raised more eyebrows than it was worth.

"Come on, Brother Vance." Crusher nodded all knowingly. "We've called in the reinforcements. Don't hold back."

Belle took my hands in hers. "You can tell us." She searched me with her majestic blue eyes. "Do you doubt the power of prayer?"

"No. Of course not." I shrugged, hoping Belle did not detect my heavy breathing, definitely not the impression I wanted to convey to the stunning prayer princess.

"Sit . . . please," she said, releasing my hands and gesturing across the table. She pulled out a chair and sat gracefully without once taking her gorgeous eyes off me.

Exhaling, I sat.

"Vance had an episode last Friday night," Arnie said. "I won't go into the details, just that he was accused of something he didn't do. Following a near altercation, he leaves the scene without offering up a prayer for the wrongdoer."

Belle nodded. "That won't be the first—or last—time something like that happens."

"How could I pray for the dude?" I asked. "All I wanted to do was slug him."

"Don't worry," Arnie said to Belle. "He's already made his peace with God. It's his accuser we're talking about."

Belle nodded and looked at me with concern. "You know, Vance, prayer changes a situation because it changes you, the person saying the prayer."

"Okay." I pretended to get it while I didn't get it at all.

Belle spread her hands on the table. "Tell me something. Do you think God's too busy to listen to your prayers?"

"I don't know." I leaned back. "Like all of us, he may have his peak times."

"Okay, then." Belle gave it time to sink in. "Are your prayers too insignificant? Does God not answer your prayers because he doesn't like the way you phrase them?"

"You got me." I shook my head. "I'm sure there are some styles he prefers over others. Especially those with a rich, lyrical flavor."

Belle shook her head. "The answer to all of the above is a resounding no. And the sleazy author of all those wasteful thoughts is none other than Satan himself. He wants nothing more than to cast doubt on your relationship with God."

I nodded. "I'm getting a real feel for those relational aspects."

"That's what it's all about," Arnie said. "You're entering into an everlasting relationship with the Creator of the universe."

Belle nodded. "Do you want to know the surest way to defeat Satan? Pray this prayer: Father God, please cast out these doubts and fears. Please shine your brilliance on me and let me give you your full glory. I call upon the name of your incomparable Son, Jesus Christ, to shut this monster down. We know the victory has already been won. Please just silence the serpent so we can lead our lives the way you intended, now and forevermore."

I closed my eyes and tried to follow. When she was through, I mumbled an "Amen."

"There's no way to overstate this," Belle said. "Prayer is the single-most powerful tool known to man. We can't comprehend the force one prayer packs. For all we know it's like detonating a neutron bomb in some celestial battlefield."

"Right." I nodded. "I like it."

"Never forget," Belle said. "God loves prayer. But . . . " She raised a little higher in her seat. "There is one condition in particular."

"Okay," I said.

"You can't just pray for anything." Belle gestured to the ceiling. "I could pray for five million dollars to drop out of the sky today. You think that's going to happen? Not if it's against God's will. I could pray for any number of things. Unless God is behind it, it's not going to happen."

"Don't put your wants ahead of his," I offered.

"That's right." Belle nodded. "Treat prayer like a personal conversation. How would you like it if someone called you on the phone every morning and said the same thing, time after time, even if your situation had changed since you last spoke?"

Arnie leaned into the table. "Okay, so how does our brother here ramp up his prayer life and hit the ground running?"

"Start small," Belle advised, turning back to me. "Your goal at the end of the day is to talk to God in a personal way. Since God is with you at all times, you should be talking with him non-stop. That may not be feasible in a practical sense. So as you go through your day, just be aware he's there for you constantly. Talk to him as much as possible. Make him a part of the conversation."

I nodded, trying not to overanalyze what Belle was presenting.

She continued. "When I first started out I prayed in as many places and as often as I found the time. The more I did it the more I realized I wasn't merely mouthing words. I was speaking directly to Almighty God, maker of Heaven and Earth. Think about it: the one who created the universe actually cares enough to listen to you—and answer your petitions!"

I hearkened back to the fateful night in Las Vegas when I had done the same thing. I was living proof of what happens when you communicate your needs, thoughts, desires, and feelings directly to God. "And so it's okay to pray before going into a contentious meeting or something mundane like that?"

"Right," Belle said. "About the only time you'll let him down is when you don't pray when you know you should." Smiling, she went on. "It's what I always tell people: prayer is like the most unbelievable phone call you'll ever make. The connection is absolutely perfect. There is never a dropped call, never any static, and you will always reach your heavenly party no matter what hour of the day or night."

"And no hidden fees," Arnie added.

"Definitely not," Belle said with a smile. "God wants to hear from you early and often. He wants to hear from you when you need him, when you don't think you need him, in times of strife, and in times of exuberant celebration. He wants to help you make decisions large and small. He wants to be intimately involved in every aspect of your life. Prayer blows the lid off everything with the force of a hundred million determined angels."

"God listens to prayers. All prayers. Got it?" Arnie added. "The main thing is to include him in the process of your life, both for the big and the little things."

"So true, Crush," Belle said, again smiling. "When you pray, you honor God by showing him you trust him enough to bring him your problems. You are asking for his eternal help. And he is thrilled to come to your assistance in ways you could not even remotely begin to predict."

"Believe it or not," Arnie said, "God knows what's best for you. And he wants the very best for you. Prayer helps mesh his gears with yours."

Belle drew back just a bit. I figured she saw my eyes glazing over. She exchanged a knowing nod with Arnie. They must have realized I'd reached my limit.

We all stood. Before anyone left the room, Belle prayed over me, asking that I should understand the true meaning of prayer and make it a major part of my life.

Halfway through her impassioned petition, my cell phone rang. Though I didn't answer it, it kind of disrupted the mood.

I don't think it was God on the other end, either.

As I drove from the dealership I phoned my next client to apologize for running late. Navigating traffic on the Four Islands Bridge, I checked in with the office. I was reminded about today's lunch with the city councilmember promoting the expanded enterprise zone. I passed the turnoff for the Golden Lawns Bar and Grill. Tonight's *Monday Night Football* was a grind-'em-up tilt between KC and Pittsburgh. I would definitely be in attendance for at least the second half.

My thoughts turned to Collette: I needed to sort out my feelings for her. Resisting the urge to turn on the radio, I listened to the hum of the tires against the newly surfaced road. Then, without the least bit of thought or deliberation, I launched headlong into an audible, spontaneous and unashamed prayer.

"Dear God, heavenly Father . . . I don't know where I stand with Collette. I don't know what I've done to make her dislike me. I guess I'm asking for a sign. I don't know whether I'm coming or going with her. I don't even know if I have any feelings for her. I don't think I've ever experienced anything like this before. That is why I'm asking for your help. I need you to straighten this out and show me what end is up. Maybe she wants to get back with Laird. Who knows? If she does, so be it. Just let him do a better job next time. We all deserve second—and third and fourth—chances." I sighed, vacantly tapping the steering wheel. "Okay, God. I guess that's it. Thanks for listening."

As I rolled on without the radio, I felt vaguely refreshed, at peace with the world. I wondered whether I should ask Collette to join me at the Golden Lawns tonight. I wondered if I should pray on it. Nah, I wouldn't bother God at this point; things would just have to take their course. If God wanted us together, and if he wanted Collette at the game tonight, he'd figure out a way to put it together.

Amen?

Amen.

CHAPTER TWENTY-FOUR

Turkey Day with Satan

It was Thanksgiving Day, 1997. A spectacular afternoon, the sun radiated from a cloudless backdrop, filtering through stands of majestic hardwood trees, their scarlet, orange, and burnt yellow mantle forming a supernatural collage that captured the last vestiges of autumn.

My palms sweated as I gripped the steering wheel. Why so nervous? I should have been thankful. It was, after all, Thanksgiving. Instead, I was filled with trepidation.

Turning onto the frontage road, my pulse quickened. I had volunteered through our church to work the second shift in a soup kitchen that afternoon, serving Thanksgiving dinner to those who were alone, homeless, and otherwise in need. Not knowing what was expected of me, I figured the biggest thing was just showing up. It represented the next step in my spiritual growth—even though I secretly wondered if I was worthy of the assignment.

Traffic was exceedingly light as I drove across the causeway to the west side of town. I had just come from an abbreviated game of golf at Mohonnigan Acres Country Club. Members of my foursome had bailed early, all saddled with Turkey Day commitments; go figure. I had sunk a nail-biter of a five-foot putt on the tenth hole, but that was nothing compared to the raw nerves I felt right now, realizing what I was about to do.

I tried to control my breathing. Anything to calm myself down. I had half a mind to scuttle this whole plan and hightail it over to the Golden Lawns sports bar. I wondered who was there at this hour. A group of us without a set place to go made a tradition of celebrating Thanksgiving at the Lawns with doubleheader football action on the multiple widescreens. All day long, it was a sprawling open house with people coming and going as they pleased. But I couldn't turn back now; I had made a commitment.

My adrenaline pumped as I turned into the parking lot beneath the garish neon sign. The restaurant, "To the Max!," was situated in a West Valley neighborhood a few blocks from the Historic District. The area was already submerged in shadows even though there were still a couple hours of daylight left.

The front parking lot was moderately full as I rolled toward the auxiliary spaces behind the building. Apprehension gripped me. Was I on the verge of a panic attack? This was totally out of character. I was understandably anxious, but really—this was not that big of a deal. Wanting to do the right thing for the right reason and with the right attitude, I took a deep breath and broke into prayer. *Dear heavenly Father, I don't know why I'm so worked up about this afternoon. I am more than capable of handling the assignment. Thank you for the opportunity to serve. Please help the men and women, the children, and the families in need that will be lifted up. Bless them all, Father. In your holy name. Thank you. Amen.*

As I strode across the parking lot, I remembered a recent installment of *The Sinners for Beginners Show*. Wanda and Wallace, the perpetually exuberant hosts, had been discussing the concept of service, the giving of one's time, energy, and resources to outreach programs. I remembered a caller to the show who was brand new to the church scene. Wanting to flex his muscles on the service front, he spoke of stepping out of his old life and smack-dab into his new passion. This occurred the evening he started volunteering at a seniors' center. He made it sound like he was giving up everything for this monthly two-hour commitment. He was actually taking the first step to giving more time to God and less to himself. And guess what? He liked it so much he started volunteering two nights a month instead of one.

God used Wanda and Wallace as messengers to convict me about serving others in the name of Christ. It entailed backing up one's faith with a bold statement of service. Wanda cautioned that you couldn't buy your way into Heaven by amassing a balance sheet of works designed to blow God away. She did concede, though, that some form of mission work, if undertaken with a humble heart, was a vital component to a growing walk with Christ. That was key: a humble heart.

Taking a deep breath, I swung open the rear door of the restaurant and entered the fray, assaulted by the clatter of plates and the bustle of controlled culinary chaos. The aroma of turkey and fixings wafted about the warm, humid air.

I recognized some of the people from church working the line behind the counter and waved. The establishment was a functioning restaurant that had been converted to soup kitchen status for the day. Between tables and booths, it must have seated around 150; I estimated it was about a third full.

One of the helpers stormed from behind a steam table poised to attack me with a long-handled spoon.

"Is that all the better you can do?" she accused.

"Collette?" I blinked in disbelief.

She wore an apron that dragged on the floor and an ill-fitting chef's hat. Appearing totally out of sorts, she wiped her greasy face with a yellow-gloved hand that gripped the menacing utensil. I tried not to burst out laughing. *God, you're surely kidding. This is your sign?* I asked myself, remembering the prayer I'd said three weeks ago after the meeting with Belle and Arnie. The Lord had come through in a big way, completely wiping Collette off my radar. I hadn't thought about her, pined about her, or wondered about her since. I sincerely hoped that she and Laird were back together again.

Case closed. At least I thought . . . until now.

What was she doing there? I hadn't seen her name on the signup sheet. Had she signed up at a later date as a legitimate volunteer—or was she stalking me?

Worse, did I still have feelings for her?

"Go figure!" she cackled. "You just waltz in here all fresh from the links wearing your golf duds." She shook the spoon at me. "Is this what you call 'par for the course'?"

This broken record was really getting old. What was her problem? I may have made mistakes in the past, but what about the here and now? What part of forgiveness did she not understand? I was one cross-eyed minute from having it out with her. But I kept my temper in check; such an outburst would accomplish absolutely nothing at this upbeat, Christ-centered event.

The restaurant owner rounded the corner and clapped me smartly on the shoulder. "Reinforcements!" he shouted above the din. He was a stocky man, a Romanian, proud beyond measure, and grinning extravagantly. "I'm Max," he said.

"Hey Max. I'm Vance Chelan. It's a pleasure to meet you." We shook hands warmly.

"Yes, and as you can see, he dressed for the part," Collette sniffed.

"Please go back to your mashed potatoes or wherever you came from, my dear," Max said with a thick accent.

Now that was what I liked: a man who could put a lunatic in her place. I nodded with gratitude as Collette retreated in a huff to her station behind the counter.

"Now you . . . " Max sized me up like a prized side of beef. "Perfect."

He gave me an apron that fit only marginally better than Collette's and led me into a side room with a mountain of dirty pans, dishes, bowls, cups, and glasses. He squeezed a stainless steel nozzle dangling from the end of a suspended hose. "Ever done this before?"

"I take it I'm not cooking." I tried not to look disappointed.

Max showed me how to load soap in the industrial dishwasher. "Once you catch up you can start bussing tables. As of now you have the most valuable job on the floor because we're running out of plates and silverware."

I was totally into it. I realized I was representing the church and, ultimately, God. I sensed that the Lord was right there in the dish room beside me. I made doubly certain I was a model volunteer. There was no way I was going to dog this detail.

As the afternoon progressed, I had a pretty good run of it. The whole scene began to have an ebb and flow all its own. People came, people ate, people left. The last meal was served at about 4:30, meaning everyone in food prep was free to leave. Somehow Collette schlepped out the door without hurling further insults my way, which was just fine. Good riddance. Left to my own devices, I made short order of the bus work.

Developing a rhythm, I enjoyed myself immensely. I was thorough, efficient, and cheerful in dispensing my duties, working as hard as I would at any other enterprise. For those in the restaurant partaking of this delicious Thanksgiving repast, I was on display. These people needed to see someone representing Christ who was going above and beyond. I owed them my very best because God had given his very best to me.

Time passed quickly. I barely noticed it was growing dark. If the rest of the job went this smoothly, I'd be sprung in time for the Tennessee at Dallas pregame show.

But, of course, Satan had his own plans.

"He took my food!" A young woman stepped back inside from the rear porch where she had been smoking. She was angular, wore no makeup, and had soft brown hair. Her red T-shirt advertised an ammo company. Hands on jeaned hips, she stood over her table and scowled at me.

I stopped on my way to the kitchen and turned. "Sorry about that," I said. "I thought you'd already left." I hefted the gray bus tub on my hip. "I'll see that you get a new plate."

The crowd started to take an interest in this exchange.

Ratcheting up the stakes, the woman feverishly glanced around. She pointed at me and shouted, "Hey, you stole my purse!"

"*What?*" I nearly dropped the tub. Everything in me wanted to charge the table and refute this wayward chick. How dare she? Yet I was on display; I had to hold back, I had to keep my cool. "I'm sorry, but you are very mistaken. There is no possible way I stole your purse."

"Yeah, what about her purse?" asked a longhaired geezer seated at an adjacent table who wore a Mets cap backwards.

She nodded at him in a gesture of solidarity.

Other people started getting into the act. This had all the elements of an uprising.

I rested the bus tub on a Formica countertop. Sweat beaded on my forehead as I cautiously approached the glowering woman. Giving her plenty of space, I observed all the non-confrontational tactics for standard crisis intervention. "It's obviously been misplaced. I can assure you, I did not touch your purse." The calmness in my voice belied the chaos inside me.

"Thief!" screeched an elderly woman behind an ersatz potted palm.

"I seen it in his thieving eyes!" shouted a man from the mezzanine level. "I swear, he's got them crazy, thieving eyes!"

"Thief! Thief! Thief!" The crowd erupted in a rabid chant, fists raised to the drop ceiling.

Hearing the commotion, Max hustled out of his office. The place was up for grabs. "What's going on here?" the outraged Romanian screamed.

In the deafening silence you could hear a bent fork drop. The distraught restaurateur turned to me. "You want to tell me what this is all about?"

"Sure." I glared at my accuser and nodded at Max. "She was outside having a butt. I accidently cleared her plate, not knowing she was coming back. That made her upset. I told her we'd get her another. Then she accused me of stealing her purse."

"She accused you of stealing her purse?" he said tersely, barely containing his rage.

"That is correct," I told him.

"Well, *did you?*" He drilled me with unblinking black eyes and the most accusatory tone he could muster.

"*What?*" I was in a state of disbelief. I gave him a deer-in-the-headlights expression. How could he even think such a thing? "No, man. Of course I didn't!"

Fuming, Max quickly surveyed the situation. The crowd was close to mutiny. He turned back to me. "I think it's time you left."

"I don't believe it. You really think I did it?"

"Don't forget to leave the apron." He snapped his fingers, staring at the floor.

Patrons cheered wildly. The restaurant rocked as customers stomped their feet, banged tables, and swapped violent high fives.

Pulling the apron over my head, I couldn't believe what was happening. The humiliation was overwhelming. I collected my things and prepared to leave. Max was hard on my heels, escorting me to the door.

I sat behind the wheel of my car before starting the engine. I replayed the whole sorry scene in my head. Had this been my fault? Had I handled it wrong? No, I had been ambushed by a young woman who, for whatever reason, may not have been completely in her right mind. None of it may have been her fault, but even so, her problem had become my problem. Then I had suffered further humility when everyone sided with her. What else was new? Could I really blame them?

I banged the steering wheel. *How could it have gone so wrong? I was only trying to help.* How could something so good have become so polluted and perverted? I vowed never to do anything like this again.

I flashed back to the meeting with Belle and Crusher at the car dealership. They had encouraged me to pray for my accuser, Martin Slosser. Until then, that had been the most recent example of being accused of something I hadn't done—having an affair with another man's wife. Today I'd been accused of stealing. Different day, same old lies. I sent up a prayer for the woman who claimed I'd stolen her purse, plus a prayer for Max and everyone else inside the restaurant. I prayed for myself that I'd make it through this ordeal without coming unglued, and I thanked the Lord for giving us a free country with the freedom to worship as we choose.

Today was Thanksgiving. It was a day to be thankful.

Amen.

Rolling out of the parking lot, I turned on the radio and listened to the pregame show. I was unaware of it at the time, but I had just withstood a full frontal attack by the Great Deceiver, the embittered enemy himself. He didn't want me volunteering for causes like this so he made sure I thought twice about ever doing it again. He succeeded in leaving a bad taste in my mouth, but that was the extent of it. I got over it by the time I pulled into the sprawling parking lot encircling the Golden Lawns Bar and Grill.

As I swung from behind the wheel and savored the crisp night air, I was feeling stronger and more confident than ever. Normally I'd stew on an altercation like this for weeks, playing it over and over again in my head, chiding myself for not having done this or that differently, upset beyond reason for being in that position to begin with. Now, however, I was actually defending everything I'd done, a total departure from the status quo.

Ultimately, this episode was Exhibit A in my deepening relationship with God. There was no better proof that I was making headway. I knew God had my back. He was fully aware of everything that had transpired in that restaurant and would not hold me accountable. So why was I beating myself up after the fact? I felt increasingly comfortable speaking with God—even though I still couldn't see him—because I knew he was more a part of my life than any mortal ever could be. Without God, I would spin my wheels trying to figure out how to fix things on my own. With God, it was an absolute joyful partnership and an honor to work out life's problems and challenges together.

It did not help the enemy's cause when Max called the following Monday morning to let me know the woman had come clean about misplacing her purse. In a full *mea culpa*, the apologetic Romanian gave me a one-year gift certificate and purchased a lucrative sponsorship package in our weekly high school sports show.

I thanked Max for his business but told him he needn't go overboard. I had put the experience behind me, I said.

And if another opportunity to serve arose in the future, I told myself, I'd snatch it up.

You bet I would—in less time than it took a bent fork to hit the floor.

CHAPTER TWENTY-FIVE

Public Speaking with Your Mouth Full

Could they make this coffee any weaker? I wondered if hotels had a universal recipe for brewing flaccid coffee. Maybe it was the water. And they'd better not be trying to slip me decaf.

From the head table, I glanced across the elegant ballroom. With the lead-up to Christmas in full swing, decorations were everywhere—huge wreathes adorned frescoed walls; gigantic multicolored orbs cascaded from chandeliers.

I'd been revving my engines for this opportunity ever since Arnie had asked me last month. This was the biggest event of the year for the Fellowship of Downtown Christian Businesspersons. The annual Advent breakfast was always a crowd-pleaser. Catered by one of the region's top chefs, it resulted in a ballroom bursting at the seams.

More than five hundred men and women—civic leaders and titans of commerce—enjoyed each other's fellowship along with a savory breakfast buffet. I knew a smattering of these people from the local business community; most, however, were an unknown commodity. This was not exactly the kind of people I'd been rubbing shoulders with my entire adult life.

I closed my eyes trying to keep everything straight. This assignment had me twisted in knots. On the one hand it was a straight-up industry talker, while on the other it was my personal testimony. Though I was no stranger to gassing about the media at chamber functions—I could do these speeches in my sleep—this one was different: for the first time I'd be sharing my faith with an audience of more than two, the majority of whom were strangers.

Tension grew as members of the wait staff dutifully cleared tables. Anticipation in the festive ballroom was palpable. To many in attendance, it was now time for the main course: me.

I choked back some of the fruit I'd been nibbling on and washed it down with lukewarm coffee. Butterflies bombarded my gut. Key points of my speech knocked about in my head as I engaged in mental editing.

When Arnie walked stiffly to the podium I felt the bottom drop out. Adrenaline pounding, I listened as he read from the bio I had furnished that expounded on my personal qualifications. It now sounded embarrassingly over the top in its self-serving platitudes.

"And I can tell you, having known Vance for this number of years . . . and—" He turned to me as I looked up with a swallow. "I don't think you'll mind me saying this, will you?"

Riddled with confusion, I gave him a clueless shrug.

He turned back to the audience with a confident nod. "I've seen the Lord do a powerful work in this man during the past few months. A powerful, powerful work."

Enthusiastic applause was punctuated by hoots and whistles.

"If you could have only known him before!" Arnie thumped the edge of the podium, lost in wistful contemplation. "Well, enough said. He'll tell us all about it himself." Arnie gestured grandly. "Please welcome Vance Chelan, the man in the middle of the media mix!" Clapping his huge hands, he encouraged the audience to follow suit.

Amid the raucous reception, I cleared my throat, flattened my tie, and headed for the podium. "Thank you, Arnie," I said, pleased with the audio levels of the floor mic. "Thank you, members and organizers of the esteemed Fellowship of Downtown Christian Businesspersons for including me in the program this morning. Believe me, it's an honor to witness the difference you are making in people's lives. I thank Arnie for introducing me to this great and benevolent group, and I definitely look forward to future involvement."

I glanced across the sea of attentive faces, impressed with the diversity of age and ethnicity. What would Collette think if she saw me right now? Would she be proud of me? I thought about the first Sunday I'd met her at church. It's true: I'd been instantly attracted to her. I had buried all those feelings, however, even after she'd broken up with Laird. Was there ever going to be anything between us? I took a deep breath and—inwardly—dedicated this talk to the most beguiling, mysterious, frustrating, and confounding woman I had ever met.

I glanced at my outline, lightly laid my hands on both sides of the podium, and began. "I can talk literally for hours about utility frequencies, electron-emitting cathodes, and equalized signals—and it all starts sounding like so much hot air." I metered the audience, fighting my runaway adrenaline. "We could talk about beam currents, transformers, generators, power grids, chrominance, bandwidth, video fields, pixels, and interlace scanning." I looked up and nodded. "But at the end of the day, it all comes down to God. Even though man figured out how to harness all these elements to create what we know as moving electronic pictures across the little screen, God still bestowed upon the inventors the intellect, resources, drive, and experience to make all those integrated systems work. And God created all the natural resources needed to successfully pull it off. So the next time you turn on the television to watch your favorite show, just remember the miracle—albeit a man-made miracle—that makes TV a reality. Bottom line: take nothing, and I mean nothing, for granted."

On a modest roll, I was either making sense or had lost them altogether. I trotted out the usual chestnuts, including the difference in the television biz between the sixties and the go-go nineties. Then I talked about the genesis of cable and how it grew to become such a force. That was followed by a description of the current regulatory state of the broadcast industry, including an update on the status of newspaper/television cross-ownership rules.

Everything was back on track and resonating smartly—right until the jarring digression about how I invited Christ into my life. Things became muddled after that, and I was never able to recover. The more I tried folding my coming-of-faith speech into the canned industry gasser, the more I realized I was losing it. Air wheezed from the tires, and before long I was belly up on the Boardwalk of Butchered Talks.

I should have just kept to the facts. Staying on topic would have allowed me to address digital compression, national broadband initiatives, 1080p versus 720i hi-def modes, fulfillment of public interest standards, the future of subscription services, and media consolidation. Then, at the very end, I could have raved about how God had spectacularly and undeniably transformed my life.

Instead, I made a clumsy mess of it. In a meandering mishmash, I talked a little about the digital revolution, and at that point a lot of people were on the edge of their seats because, as business leaders, much of this was going to hit them in the pocketbook. Then, instead of moving on to the next TV-related topic,

I launched into a soliloquy about Heaven and Hell and the absolute need to develop a rock-solid relationship with God. Before I could stop myself, I was comparing the calamities of hellfire and damnation to deleterious Nielsen ratings. People grew agitated, uncomfortable.

Oblivious, or perhaps just stubborn, I continued proclaiming, "There's no such thing as a fence-sitter. God is very specific about that. You either give your life totally to God or you don't." I grabbed at every spiritual concept I could think of. None of my notes contained any of this burning-in-Hell hypothesizing. My dalliances into the throes of eternal torment may have been a little rich for this early morning gaggle; Arnie, on the other hand, seemed to be relating.

I shifted into a backwoods preacher's rant. "It's your choice. When all is said and done, you can have all the trappings, you can be worth billions and be known the world over. But if you don't have a relationship with God, and if you haven't claimed Christ as your Lord and Savior, there will be a day of reckoning. Your sins will be clearly exposed to God, who cannot condone rebellion. He sent his one and only Son to earth to atone for our sins. But if you don't recognize Christ for what he did, if you don't humble yourself to the Father of the universe, then you make it clear you don't want any part of the inheritance."

I felt I was pretty much nailing it. That was, of course, if you were talking about nailing a coffin lid shut. Some of the attendees nodded at each other, glanced tactfully—or not so tactfully—at their watches, and appeared to grow restless.

Crusher made a little sign to speed it up. I cut to the chase and offered a gushing testimonial about the transformation God made in my life after bursting upon the scene.

As the speech wound down, the whole exercise devolved into a haphazard rant. Talk about awkward. I finished weakly, didn't provide a call to action, and forgot to thank everyone for coming.

Applause, what little there was, was not nearly as loud or heart-felt as when I'd first taken the podium only a few minutes ago. *Weird how much damage you can do in so little time.*

As people politely filed from the ballroom, I sat alone at the head table pretending to run through voice messages on my mobile phone. It was imperative to avoid eye contact during times of wound-licking. Down the hallway, I spotted Arnie jawing with the organization's executive director, probably assuring her that a stiff like me would never again be booked as guest speaker.

All I wanted to do was hit the road. I had rarely, if ever, felt so weak and ineffective following a talk. The enemy was goosing me good. He was laughing at me, telling me how pathetic I was, how I should never agree to do something like this again.

"Hey, man. You got a sec?"

"Huh?" I looked up. One of the waiters stood over me. He was a fresh-scrubbed kid, probably not yet twenty. "Yeah, I'm done." I pushed everything toward him: plates, saucers, glasses, the works. I gulped the last of my cold coffee and handed him the cup. *Boy was I done.*

"I got a question." He paused while stacking plates. "It was something you said in your talk."

"My talk," I said thickly. "You mean the part about hi-def TV with the 1080-progressive scan capabilities?"

He appeared impatient. "Not that. It's what you said about fence-sitters."

"Fence-sitters?" I made a face.

"Yeah, you know. You said that fence-sitters think they have it made in the shade, when in truth it's just the opposite. They aren't as golden as they want to believe."

"Well . . . " I felt sheepish, like I had to walk it back. I never wanted to come off as holier-than-thou. "What I meant to say was . . . life is full of decisions. And your eternal life is dependent on the biggest decision of all, whether or not to accept Jesus Christ as your Lord and Savior."

"That's what I don't understand." The young man was perplexed—and frustrated. "According to your definition, a fence-sitter doesn't commit to God one way or another. If that's the case, count me in. I'm fine with somebody worshipping whoever or whatever they want. It's none of my business. Plus, God is totally in agreement because I'm being tolerant of others."

I tensed. It had taken me this long to get over my bruised ego. Realizing this kid was engaging me in a conversation on which all eternity hinged, I snapped to attention. "What's your name?" I stood at the cluttered table.

"Kyle," he said, startled that I had taken such a sudden interest in him.

"Okay, Kyle, that's great. It's a real pleasure to meet you." We shook hands as I summoned every remaining shred of energy. "So tell me. Have you made the conscious decision to deny Jesus just so you won't offend others? Or is it because you don't want to submit to him as your Lord and Savior?" My voice cracked under the weight of the question.

Kyle grew defensive. "That's just it, man. That's such a canned posture. You people claim that Jesus is the only way to Heaven. Hah! That's only because that was your God growing up. I'm sure the world is filled with people who grew up Muslim or grew up Hindu, and they all swear by those religions as well."

Fumbling for answers, I hit on a passage of Scripture that was discussed at Bible study just last week. "John 14:6," I said, snapping my fingers. "Are you familiar with it?"

"How should I know?"

"When Jesus was speaking to his disciples, he said, 'I am the way and the truth and the life. No one comes to the Father except through me.'" I metered Kyle to see if anything registered. "Pretty much spells it all out, don't you think?"

"Big deal. You know a verse or two." He shrugged.

"Then answer me this: of all the other religions, can you tell me which one had their leader die and then rise from the grave, defeating sin, death, and disease forever? And can you tell me which one features a living God who desires a *personal* relationship with me and you? Out of all those religions, can you tell me which one promotes loving your fellow man and promises eternal life if you put your faith and hope in the one who came to earth to die for you?

"Give it a rest." He gestured offhandedly. "I hear that from my mother all the time."

"Look, I'm not here to ram anything down your throat. All I can tell you is what happened to me."

"Yeah," he said, almost in a dare. "And what was that?"

"I was living my life for the moment. I didn't have a care in the world. I knew there was probably a God out there somewhere, but I made a career of kicking him in the teeth every chance I got. Then I heard this simple question—at a funeral, of all places: when we die and go to meet God, what are we going to say for ourselves? When God asks why he should let us into his glorious Heaven, what will our response be?"

"That's easy," Kyle said. "It's lights out when we die. Ashes to ashes, dust to dust. We'll just fade away and never wake up again."

"I see." I nodded. "No consciousness after this life. I guess that means we don't have eternal souls, right?"

He sneered. "Sounds like a winner to me."

"So, in other words, the Bible has it all wrong."

"There you go with the Bible again!" Kyle hooted. "Give it a rest, man. We all know that thing is a piece of fiction."

"A piece of fiction, huh?" I mused. "Tell me something. Have you ever read it?"

"I don't have to," he scoffed. "There are some things I just know."

"Like what?"

"When I die, things will take care of themselves," he said.

"I thought you said we were all just gonna go to sleep."

"Okay!" Kyle put his hands up defensively. "Enough already." He stiffened, seemingly hankering for a fight. "Here's the deal: I'm working real hard right now. I hold down two jobs while I'm going to school. I treat everyone like I want to be treated, and I don't stand in the way of anyone's freedom." He glared at me. "So why should I be punished just because I'm not simpatico with God?"

"I was the same way until just recently." I scrambled to come up with something he could identify with. "You can be the nicest person on the planet, you can have the best-tended front lawn on the block, you can be well educated, have above average income, be a major charitable donor, and the proverbial life of the party. But unless you understand that God is at the very heart of everything, you will be missing the whole point of life. The reason we're on earth is to build a relationship with God and glorify his existence. And the only way we can have that relationship is by the work of his Son, Jesus Christ, who died a brutal death on the cross to redeem our rebellious souls and assure eternal life for anyone who believes in him."

Kyle fought on. "That's the whole point: how could a God of love do that to *his son*? How could a God of love allow a place like Hell?" Kyle was growing more heated by the moment. "I don't want anything to do with a God like that. He's just like my own dad—before he decided to bail on us. Demanding and unforgiving, selfish and nitpicking. I have no time for that garbage."

He struck a nerve. Growing up, I didn't know how lucky I'd been to have a loving, forgiving father as an earthly role model. "I'm sorry to hear that, Kyle. I'm really, really sorry. I can't imagine what it must be like to have to deal with that."

Kyle knotted his fists. "You know something?"

"What?"

"You remind me a lot of him."

Great! So much for this attempt at witnessing!

So this was what it had come to: yet again I was being accused of something I didn't do. Over the last two months, guilt by association had been my ongoing nemesis. First it had been Slosser accusing me of being an adulterer, then it had been the woman at the soup kitchen accusing me of being a thief, and now Kyle was accusing me of being a deadbeat dad.

I was too tired to put up a fight. If Kyle wanted to take a few years of aggression out on me, so be it. I'd be his human punching bag. No problem. I could see it now: I'd be laid out on one of the tables, bloodied and bruised, lights out in a bed of dirty, broken plates.

Kyle defused the moment when he started laughing quietly. It was difficult to tell if it was good-natured laughter or bitter laughter. "You and my mother should get together. She's single for the third time. She's looking again." He glared at me. "I'm sure you're her . . . *type.*"

I pulled up and decided to give it one more honest go. "Look, there's a difference between God and our earthly fathers. Believe me, we're talking about a God of love. Did it ever occur to you that the cross represents an act of supreme love? God did the unthinkable, sacrificing his own Son to save us from the torment of eternal damnation." I tracked Kyle's eyes, even when he tried looking away. "He loves us unconditionally. Incomprehensibly. All he wants is to give us the desires of our heart. And if we want nothing to do with him, he'll respect that, severing ties with us for all eternity, even though it rips his heart out."

"You can't help yourself, can you?" Kyle was now gesturing furiously. "You've made me feel worse than before. This Bible-thumping business can be dangerous. You lord it over people who don't have what you have and make them feel like second-class citizens. It's not fair."

"Do you think that's what your mother does?" I asked. "Lord it over you? Or does she witness to you out of genuine love?"

He looked at me more confused than ever. "Yes, she loves me. I won't ever deny that."

"Then how are we going to leave this?" I glanced down at the debris-filled table.

"I don't know." He started halfheartedly shoving plates across the tablecloth.

"I'll tell you where we'll leave it. If you'll let me . . . "

He riveted me with a confused, angry glare.

"Prayer," I said. "Can I pray for you?"

Tension drained from every muscle. His eyelids fell heavily. "What's the point?" he sighed. "Do what you gotta do if it makes you feel better. But don't make it any longer than it has to be, okay?"

Closing my eyes, I made sure he had settled down. I laid a hand lightly on his shoulder. "Dear heavenly Father, it's just the three of us: Kyle, you, and me. I know you've been planning this meeting since time began. Father, we know you love Kyle to no end and want the very best for him. We ask that you bless his paths and make his direction apparent. If Kyle hasn't given his heart to you yet, we pray that he does so soon, while there's still time in your holy kingdom here on earth. We thank you for Jesus and the unthinkable work he did on the cross. We bless Kyle's mother and her faithfulness to you and look forward to the day when Kyle gives his life to you, when there will be dancing in the streets of Heaven—not to mention in his mother's heart. I pray this in the name of our holy Savior, Jesus Christ. Amen."

I opened my eyes to see Kyle's head still bowed. I pumped his shoulder. He took a deep breath and sighed, almost in resignation.

"That's the Holy Spirit coming alive in you," I whispered.

He nodded.

I collected my things. The room was totally cleared out. Arnie was nowhere to be found. My watch said it was a full half hour later than the last time I checked. Before I left, I handed Kyle a business card. He paused before lifting a stack of plates.

"I want to hear from you. Day or night. Anything going on in your life you want to talk about, call me."

"Sure thing." He inspected the business card before pocketing it. "Thanks."

We shook hands and then . . . hugged.

As I headed across the ballroom, I watched Kyle disappear through the service door. I wondered if Collette would be proud of me. But neither Collette nor I had anything to do with this. This was between God and Kyle. I was nothing more than a conduit.

Shuffling through the ornate lobby, I had rarely—if ever—felt so tired.

Yet never as fulfilled.

CHAPTER TWENTY-SIX

PUBLIC SPEAKING WITH YOUR EYES CLOSED

"Today we turn our attention to one of the most endur-ing passages in all of Scripture, Philippians 4:7, where the Apostle Paul writes about the 'peace that surpasses all un-derstanding.'" Pastor Connelly Caslett stared out across the large Chorus Lake congregation and began his sermon for Sunday, January 11, 1998.

"Peace comes in many flavors, many shapes and sizes." The dapper preacher made a sweeping gesture. "You can have peace of mind, peace and quiet, peace and security, and inner peace. You can rest in peace, yearn for peace, go in peace, and make peace. Real peace, though, true and meaningful and lasting peace, starts with the perfect, pure, unblemished, and incompre-hensible peace that Jesus Christ achieved for all eternity when he died on the cross in atonement of our sins."

I stared at the floor where a stray pine needle or two remained from the recent removal of the church's Christmas decorations. Everything had been taken down and stowed for another year. It had been a good Christmas. For the first time in my life, I realized the true meaning of the season. The birth of Jesus, the greatest gift of all, was reason enough for peace.

"Why was that gruesome sacrifice needed in the first place?" Pastor Caslett asked. "The central point is the eternal, abiding peace that Jesus secured for us with God. As we are born into sin, we are at odds with God from birth. Though he loves every one of us with a love that knows no bounds, he hates our sinful nature with an equal amount of passion. Jesus is the answer to fuse us together with God—if we accept Christ as our personal Lord and Savior. Once we do that and give our lives to him, the peace we attain defies description."

I thought about the genuine peace I now felt and the absolute thrill of knowing that once I leave this earth, I'll forever be in God's ever-expanding kingdom of infinity. There will be no more uncertainty, no more things wearing out, no more self-doubt, no more nagging questions, and no more separation caused by the sting of death.

"Of course, that battle still rages in people who have not accepted Christ as their Lord and Savior," Pastor Caslett said. "Only Jesus can obliterate the bonds of sin that separate us from a relationship with God. Where do you stand on the matter? Does the nonstop infighting between God and you still tear you apart? Are you skating a perilous course of letting your rebellious sin nature dictate your ultimate eternal destination?"

I furtively checked my watch, not the smoothest of moves in the middle of a sermon. I was still in good shape to get to the airport for my afternoon flight. What had compelled me to attend church this wintry January morning before hopping a plane for Seattle? Had my commitment to the Christian faith become so deep-seated that I now sacrificed professional aspirations for the chance to spend more time in worship? As I gained a greater understanding of what Jesus endured for us, the answer was yes:

I desired to spend more time offering my gratitude for his everlasting love.

Pastor Caslett rapped the podium. "Now there's a big difference in the peace that God gives and the peace the world tries to offer. Don't confuse the two. The world would have you calculate a counterfeit peace in comparing yourself to your neighbor. You know the drill: 'I'm better than so-and-so who just got dinged for shoplifting.' Don't fall into that trap. The world's peace is temporary at best and needs constant replenishing. The world gives you peace based on half-truths and manipulation. This is not the design for God's peace at all."

I considered the ways that peace was impacting my life: I was at peace knowing I had a personal relationship with God. I was at peace knowing that I am mightily loved by God. I was at peace knowing I no longer needed all the attention, and that all of my accomplishments—all of them—are made possible by the grace and gifts of God. I was at peace knowing I didn't have to prove anything to the world anymore. I was at peace knowing that I couldn't do anything to make God love me any more—or any less.

Pastor Caslett concluded his sermon with a flourish. "God wants us to have that peace nonstop. He wants us to rest peaceably in his arms, realizing that he has taken care of every last one of our needs. We have a total, pure, enduring, unconditional peace knowing that, in Christ, we are everything God wants us to be. And when we have that unbreakable peace, the rest of the world looks at us with scorn and derision. Our peace makes no sense whatsoever to those in the world who snub God. It looks downright foolish to those who put all their stock and faith in worldly things, so that's why the apostle Paul says it surpasses all the world's understanding."

Following the benediction the sanctuary emptied quickly. The vast majority headed for the parlor. The line of people waiting to shake Pastor Caslett's hand was almost nonexistent.

"Vance, how goes it today?" Pastor Caslett's handshake was strong as ever as he riveted me with those intense blue eyes.

"I'm headed to Seattle this afternoon." I said.

"Ah, I see." His smile dazzled. "A little rest and relaxation?"

"Close," I chuckled. "We're acquiring a property out there and I need to find a tower site."

"You sure do get around." He nodded with an amused smile. "Before you hop on that plane, maybe you'd like to stick around for our Focus on Missions presentation."

"Nah, I've got to hit it." I concealed the real truth: I wanted to catch the kickoff of the AFC championship game between the Broncos and Steelers at 12:30. So I fed him a line. "No telling what the weather's going to do, and I don't want to miss my flight." He probably saw right through my chintzy ruse, but who cared?

"Sure, sure." Pastor Caslett nodded. "You know what you're doing. Safe travels."

"Yeah, same to you, man."

I grabbed my overcoat from the expansive cloakroom. It was weird; a few hundred coats and jackets were still in place. It reminded me of those scenarios where a third of the world suddenly vanishes. Where did they all wind up? As I headed for the front door, I reviewed my schedule for the day: I could watch the first quarter of the game from the airport lounge before boarding my flight. Then, with any luck, once arriving at Sea-Tac I could watch the tail end of the NFC championship game featuring Green Bay and San Francisco.

Wind whipped my face as I headed across the fully packed parking lot. It was growing dark, like a snow squall was approaching. When I reached my car I was shivering against the wintry blast. I paused to look back at the church. Brilliant light spilled from the bank of massive windows and I imagined the people inside, enjoying each other's company while they learned about missions. It struck me as an analogy of Heaven and Hell, being left all alone out in the cold versus being part of a nonstop family of love. There was absolutely no question which was more inviting. Suddenly I was compelled to rush back to the warmth.

I hustled through the parlor without stopping for coffee. The place was deserted, meaning the presentation had probably already begun. I followed the signs down the long hallway to the lakeside auditorium. I squeezed through a knot of people congregating around the entryway and surveyed the packed hall. Chuck Simmonson, seated on the portable stage, smiled broadly when he saw me and motioned to a vacant seat—the only one left in the house—right up front. I pointed at myself, wondering if he might have been signaling to someone behind me. That was not the case. It was as if he'd been waiting for me.

The program was just about to start as I navigated my way none-too-gracefully to the auditorium's front. Pastor Caslett, Chuck Simmonson, Collette, and a handful of other people from the missions committee sat on the stage facing the teeming throng. As I squeezed into my seat, Collette remained glued to her notes. I hoped she didn't presume I was trying to curry favor with her by sitting so close.

I had to admit: being in such close proximity of Collette was intoxicating. As much as I tried to put her out of my mind these days, I couldn't help thinking about her. Constantly.

One of the fallouts of Collette's breakup with Laird—in addition to a sautéed ego—was the need to reenter the labor market. She was now rumored to be working in the media department of a rapidly expanding convenience store chain that was looking to go national.

I had to watch myself on this one. It made perfect sense for my company to align with hers in their expansion efforts. With a growing stable of TV outlets coast-to-coast, we could supply an arsenal of advertising, promotional, and production services for the burgeoning convenience store empire. But if Collette thought for one minute I was leveraging our church relationship to drum up business, it would be all over. She'd raise such a stink I'd be kicked to the curb faster than you could spit.

It made me realize, though, just how much I'd changed in a relatively short amount of time. In previous eras I would have instantly leapfrogged her in the corporate hierarchy and gone straight for the financial jugular controlled by her superiors. Now, however, I didn't feel like putting her, or myself, in such a compromised position.

Collette neatly tamped the edges of her notes as she stepped to the mic. She engaged in meaningful eye contact with people in various sections of the crowded hall—except, of course, me.

"Well, good morning, everyone!" Her voice resonated with just the right amount of warmth and enthusiasm. She quickly hit her stride. "The Chorus Lake Missions Committee welcomes you to its quarterly installment of Superchargers Sunday. What a great event we have planned for you this morning. Our guest speaker is none other than Mr. Herb Fendustrade, a beloved personality affectionately known as the Place Mat Pal."

During her introductory remarks I saw a different side of Collette: she had improved remarkably as a public speaker since the Carpet Rodeo debacle. She appeared more relaxed, somehow more approachable. Her brunette hair was swept back from her elegant face and she wore hardly any makeup, a marked improvement over her seemingly brutal penchant for eyeliner. She wore dark dress pants, a red silk blouse, and heels, and appeared to be passionate about her role as moderator.

"Needless to say, he's a man on a very special mission," Collette continued. "You might already know something about him: from humble beginnings on the outskirts of Wichita, Kansas, Mr. Fendustrade utilized the place mats in his father's diner to make the case for Christ."

My eyes tracked stage left on the dais to the guest of honor. The slight, unassuming man wearing highwater pants and a frayed herringbone sport coat sure looked the hayseed part.

"If you haven't seen one up close, a whole slew of them are on the table against the back wall." She held up an example of Mr. Fendustrade's signature product. "Each place mat has six panels, three on top and three on the bottom, just like the Sunday comics. They are seasonally themed and address a growing number of spiritual issues and topics."

I studied the colorful series of panels that Collette held above her head. I couldn't discern the message it conveyed, but the artwork was definitely top-notch. Collette saw my heightened level of interest and handed me the place mat. It dealt with the issue of lust at the supermarket checkout line.

"Well, that's enough from me," Collette announced. "Let's give the inimitable Place Mat Pal a warm Chorus Lake welcome and get the ball rolling." She gestured for the timid man to take center stage. "Ladies and gentlemen, I present to you Mr. Herb Fendustrade!"

The eager crowd gave it up for Fendustrade, the Place Mat Pal. You would never guess that the shy, middle-aged man from Wichita had the heart of a disciple-warrior. But he did.

The applause reached a crescendo punctuated by whistles and cheers. The bumbling Kansan grappled with the mic. He soon proved his ineptness at public speaking. "Good evening, ladies and gents. My name is Herbert Fendustrade. Friends call me the Place Mat Pal. Family members call me late to dinner. Sometimes." He rocked back on his worn cap toe Oxfords. "I meant to say good morning. I do have an engagement with another church this evening, I guess I jumped the gun. Sorry." You could see he was starting to break out in a sweat.

I wondered if I should hand him back his place mat on supermarket lust so he could mop the sweat from his face. Ol' Herb settled for the worn sleeve of his herringbone sport coat.

"My daddy ran a diner in El Dorado. El Dorado is about a half hour outside Wichita. You get there by bus or you drive. But you must know something about Daddy, may he rest in peace. He was a big believer. By that I mean devout. His main concern in life was knowing that his customers heard the Gospel." Herb gestured uncomfortably, at odds with what to do with his hands. "While you're munching away at your food, you know, well . . . you're pretty much a sitting target. So Daddy had the local printer make place mats that had passages of Scripture on them. That's not all, because he then had his customers agree to give their used place mats to people they met in the street. Even if they had ketchup, mayo, biscuit gravy, or barbecue sauce on them. I don't mean the street people having ketchup and mayo on them; I'm referring to the place mats. You know how nasty they can get."

I felt a wave of slumber about to overwhelm me. This was possibly the most boring dude I'd ever encountered. But I could ill afford to nod off now. Not in front of the missions committee. Not in front of Collette. Everyone in the auditorium would know what happened.

"So I embraced Daddy's concept and expanded on it," Herb droned on. "I basically took a place mat and made a miniature tract out of it. I had always been pretty good at drawing; this just came natural to me." The downtrodden man forced a weak smile. "Today I have six volunteers involved in the design, production, and distribution of place mats. We ship to diners, restaurants, and taverns throughout the US, including Alaska and Hawaii."

Needing a double-barreled jolt of charisma, Herb's relentless monotone encouraged everyone to seek deep and satisfying somnolence. As he yakked on, attention levels waned and eyelids drooped.

"To date, we are rolling out an extensive test market in Ireland." After an uncomfortable silence, he shuffled papers and coughed nervously.

As the crowd grew restless, the rumpled visitor ratcheted up the torturous afterburners and started infusing numbers into his gaping yawn-fest.

"Okay, the distribution figures into Ireland and the corresponding constituencies look like this: Carlow-Kilkenny, 179 cases of assorted topical place mats to 268 pubs and sixty-three restaurants. Then we have fifty-two cases of seasonal place mats to Dublin Fingal, representing eighty-six pubs and ninety-three restaurants. Or is it ninety-three pubs and eighty-six restaurants? Whatever. We have a whopping 452 cases going into Donegal, so keep your eyes on that one . . .

This guy was *killing* me. Soon I'd be picking my eyeballs off the floor. And it just went on and on. " . . . eighty-two cases into Galway East, fifty-seven cases into Dublin Mid-West . . . "

Enough with the stats, Slim!

I fantasized what he'd look like getting a wedgie.

Two could play this numbers game. Pulling a cheat sheet from my suit coat, I studied the report that had kept me up last night until 3:00 AM. It entailed my search for a tower site in the Seattle-Tacoma market for the new TV station we were purchasing.

My number-crunching began with the premiere Seattle location atop Queen Anne Hill: 915 feet above mean sea level, 850 feet above average terrain, 484 feet above ground level . . . then I reviewed the crosstown site atop Capitol Hill on East Madison Street: 810 feet above mean sea level, 692 feet above average terrain, 410 feet above ground level. This was followed by analysis for a site atop Gold Mountain on the Kitsap Peninsula . . .

While I mulled these stats, the prince of place mats kept blabbing on with his nonstop, mindless spiel. Both his and my figures began to coalesce and morph until I was drowning in a sea of stupefying calculations.

It was a chaotic maze of dueling decimals!

The Kansas snore king mercilessly interrupted his mind-numbing report to ask if there were any questions. In the wake of his excruciating data dump, it was a wonder people were still coherent. Chuck Simmonson was glancing at his watch with increasing frequency, indicating that the shaky purveyor of place mats was on borrowed time. I was anxious to hear one thing: how the meek little man would close the deal when he delivered the call to action and solicited donations.

Sweating profusely, Fendustrade pointed to the back of the room. "You will see the full tabulation in the handouts you can pick up at the door that contain your pledge envelopes. These handsome collections of place mats spell out a person's eternal salvation in a variety of compelling, eye-catching ways. If you have any reservations about the effectiveness of the place mats, I wholeheartedly encourage you to pick up a stack and see how fast your local diner gobbles them up. I guarantee, for a nominal monthly fee, you will make inroads for the kingdom you never thought possible."

Chuck and Collette exchanged a furtive glance. Chuck cinched the clasp of his bolo tie and stood slowly.

The wisp of a speaker gripped the sides of the podium like he was on the verge of toppling over. "With that, I'll let you pray about how much you're prepared to give in support of this vital ministry. Praise God for your faithful financial outpouring and your prayerful partnership."

Spirited applause erupted as relief swept across the crowded room; everyone was glad the ordeal was finally over. I maintained that the dude needed some PowerPoint muscle to hold people's attention. I wondered if I should take him aside and talk a little PR sense into him. Maybe our video services could add some pop to his presentation. There was no telling what graphics and other creative embellishments could do in making his message come alive.

Chuck stood solemnly at the podium and prepared to close us in prayer. *Great, let's get this over with and bust out of this sardine can!* I vowed to give Chuck a hard time. He always forced me to sit at the head of the class to make sure I stayed awake, and here I caught him nearly nodding off a couple of times himself!

I bowed my head, just hoping I'd stay awake for the duration of the petition. Then I heard the words that made me freeze: "Vance, would you please close us in prayer?" Chuck's voice grated like day-old razor burn in my suddenly inflamed eardrums.

What are you doing to me, Chuck! Thanks a million, goombah!

I went into full panic mode as the mic was handed to me. Was Chuck *nuts*? What did I know about praying in public? Sure, I'd grunted some lines to myself, but nothing on a grand scale.

My head may have been bowed, but I was wide-eyed. I heard myself breathing heavily into the microphone. Breaking into a cold sweat, I realized this wasn't getting better with age. There were no notes, no comfy script. Nothing!

Belle! Belle! Belle! Where was Belle when I needed her!

I tried hearkening back to what she'd taught me. But I had no time to think; all around were muffled coughs and creaking chairs. This was getting more embarrassing by the second. Running out of options, I was bereft of excuses. Most people would have been halfway through the thing by now. Where was I even supposed to begin?

Just wing it! Dive in and get the show on the road!

I remembered hearing my voice, but I was clueless where the words came from. "Heavenly Father, uh . . . wow. What a beautiful day you've given us here . . . right along the shores of Chorus Lake. Even on a gray day like today, we know the sun is burning brightly somewhere. We appreciate the geese flying by, or maybe they're blue herons. God, we also appreciate this guy who gives a rip—I mean, who cares enough—about his fellow man to spend his time, talent, and energy getting these place mats and other stuff into people's hands. He's got a lot of passion, doesn't he? Ireland, who woulda thunk it? I ask you, God, to make his finances such that he can continue to keep this up, and bless his ministry, Father. Bless those he serves, bless the ones who will help out in the production and rendering and distribution of these materials . . . bless those who read these place mats—especially the ones who take them out the door and deliver them to someone in the street, even if they later discard them on the sidewalk—in whatever event, please let people discover and discern your eternal Word, Father, and your love, dear Jesus. And I pray for this church and all the people in it. I pray for a blessed week and safe travels coming and going on the highways and byways. Thanks again, God. You're the greatest."

I forgot to say Amen, but there was a whole chorus behind me shouting it. This was followed by raucous whistling and foot-stomping.

I opened my eyes straight into the last person imaginable: Collette. I didn't do it on purpose, and if I had to do it again, I would have looked in the opposite direction. But that was not the way God intended it.

Collette stared back at me. I had never seen anyone look quite like that before. She conveyed an expression of absolute bewilderment. And there was maybe, just maybe, a hint of something else, something deeper. If I were a betting man, I'd say it was a burning devotion, a flaming, impassioned desire. But how much of that was wishful thinking?

I wasn't sure about much of anything anymore.

As people started filing out of the auditorium, I made a face at Chuck. He flashed a big canary grin like it had been prearranged to put me on the spot like that. Ordinarily, I would have given him a piece of my mind, but I didn't feel the need to get exercised. I was sky-high after saying that prayer. This was the best thing that could have happened to me. Now I understood what people meant when they said they were "moved by the Spirit."

There had been a definite force working inside me. Something, or someone, more powerful than I had delivered those words, intimately telling me how to pray and what to pray. I may have gotten off to a rocky start, but God was not going to forsake me. He had started a work in me and wasn't going to stop until he was done.

I stood from my chair, wanting to compliment Collette on her presentation. She was already engaged in an animated conversation with the Place Mat Pal, which I didn't want to interrupt. Hopefully, she was telling him how to punch up his presentation. Checking my watch, I realized I was, now, officially running late for the airport. My talk with Collette would have to wait for another day—if at all.

It was obvious she didn't feel the same for me as I felt for her. And maybe that was just as well.

CHAPTER TWENTY-SEVEN

ETERNITY COMES IN ONLY TWO FLAVORS: WHICH WILL YOU CHOOSE?

It was my first cigar in months. I blew a plume of sweet smoke toward the arched Victorian ceiling, then tried not to make a face when my nostrils started burning. The thing just didn't taste right. Who knew, maybe it would be my last drag ever.

"Whoa, that's a new one." Norris Turson watched as I carefully tamped the embers and laid the cigar to rest in the Art-Deco ashtray.

"What?" I asked, trying not to appear bilious.

"You feeling okay?" He nodded at the unfinished cigar. "I've never known you to give up that early. Is the blend not up to your exacting standards?"

I leaned back with a smile. "Naw, nothing like that." I sighed deeply. "Things have changed a little since I saw you last."

"How's that?" Norris sipped after-dinner cognac from a heated snifter. He was a likable film salesman from LA. We first met when he was a rep for a small animation outfit in Glendale; he had since graduated to a major distribution company.

I nodded. This was the moment of truth. How much should I tell him about the difference God had made in my life? Norris was a pretty tough customer, so I had to pick my spots carefully. "Well, life is exceptionally good. I can tell you that much."

"No one's going to argue that," Norris said. "That promotion of yours is a game-changer."

"Yeah, well . . . " I sipped my coffee, stalling for time. "It's more than professional platitudes driving the train." I was approaching my one-year anniversary of when God tapped me on the shoulder in that funeral parlor and said, "What about me, Vance?" So much had happened in the ensuing months to transform my life. As I continued to build my relationship with God, I felt positive changes in ways I never dreamed possible. Yet there was still much room for improvement.

"That's funny you should say that." Norris lifted his snifter in a mock toast. "It's always been about the career with you. And the women, of course."

"Of course," I whispered hoarsely, looking away.

"So what's changed?"

I glanced at the beached cigar, wondering if I should retrieve it. Norris and I hadn't seen each other in two years, not since the big blowout. He'd awarded a popular first-run sitcom to my former crosstown nemesis, Lorna Bongles, without giving me right of first refusal. The sting of betrayal had been too much to bear. I boycotted all programming buys from his company from that point on. But now it was time to put all that behind us.

"Norris, on my way over here tonight, I didn't know how I was going to react when I first laid eyes on you after all this time. I thought about hauling off and smacking you." I tried not to get overly emotional. "Just for old time's sake."

"That was real gentlemanly of you."

"So you know what I did?" I lowered my coffee cup. "I said a little prayer."

"You did . . . *what?*" Norris stopped loosening his tie and gawked skeptically at me.

"You know. I took it to God in prayer." I pointed to the opulent ceiling. "I asked him to help me do the right thing."

"Wait. I can't be hearing this correctly." Norris could barely curb his disdain. "You actually put your hands together and . . . *prayed?*" He even gestured in a mocking way.

"It's not that big a deal," I calmly said. "I do it all the time now. Well, not all the time. Not as often as I should. But a lot. I pray a lot."

"To whom?" Norris asked. "Or should I say, to what? The gods of the tree-lined fairways? Or maybe the creator of the holy stock option?" Incredulous, he sipped cognac and shook his head. "I can only imagine what those disjointed petitions sound like."

"Oh, it works great," I nodded. "Prayer really works. You should try it sometime."

"You're serious?" Norris narrowed his eyes. "You've actually bought into this higher power nonsense?" He lifted the glass stonily. "How long has this been going on?"

"About a year now," I said. "I guess a lot of stuff has happened since the last time I saw you. We haven't really spoken in quite a while."

"And whose fault is that?" Norris pressed his back into the leather wing chair.

"Look, can you find it in your heart to forgive me?" I brushed ashes from my suit coat. "I'm sorry for the way I acted in the past and hope—no, I pray—you won't hold it against me."

"I could easily forgive you," Norris said with a jaundiced chuckle. "But now that you're bringing religion into the picture, I don't know."

I smiled. "I'm feeling better already. I've carried this resentment around for so long, and allowed it to do such a number on me . . . for what? All it's done is eaten away at my happiness. And the only one who can change it is me."

Norris glanced at his snifter, swirling its contents. "That might be the healthiest thing you've said all night." He relaxed, managing a deflated smile. "And I'm sorry for doubting your intentions. If you've found something that works, by all means, keep at it."

I settled back in my wing chair, basking in the peace of the moment. I studied my friend, wondering how far to take this conversation about God, explaining the profound and lasting difference he's made in my life. I nodded thoughtfully. "It's all about relationship building. I've developed deep friendships with people from the church where I attend . . . people who I never thought I'd see eye-to-eye with in a million years." I went on, gaining confidence. "It's just like running a business. It comes down to trust and openness. Only in this arena, we're playing for keeps."

"What arena is that?" There was a glimmer of interest in his eyes.

"Eternal life," I said. "We're all going to live forever, no matter what side of the equation we're on. It's our choice about where, and how, we want to spend it."

"And you're getting this font of information from whom?"

"Personal experience," I said. "I can speak directly on how my life has been—and continues to be—transformed." I told Norris how God had retooled me, shining a blinding hot spotlight on offensive personality traits such as greed, lust, covetousness, and anger. During tonight's dinner, I had patched things up with Norris by confronting toxic twins from the past, pride and jealousy, defeating them with a healthy dose of forgiveness.

"You really have gone off the deep end, haven't you?" Norris observed coldly.

"No, man, I'm giving it to you straight. For the first thirty-four years of my life, I was lost and misguided, living for temporary highs that could never be sustained. It was not until a funeral that God reached out to me and let me know the score."

"And what score is that?"

"He loves us so much his heart bursts. And he's waiting to work with us, each and every one of us, in whatever we're doing. He knows our station in life, our predicaments, even better than we do. He's just waiting to come to our aid and assistance at every turn in the road."

"Vance, Vance, Vance . . . I can't believe we're having this conversation." Norris appeared to get hot under the collar. "As a friend, I'm suggesting that you dial this back. Not everyone feels the same as you. Trust me."

"But it's the truth, Norris." I sat on the edge of my seat. "If you want to know how much God desires to work with you, just ask him."

"You really don't get it, do you?" Norris glanced at his watch.

"The only way he can work with you is if you come to him and tell him what a sinner you are," I said. "Tell him how you can't figure out your life by yourself and ask him to be your guiding light for now and all of eternity."

"That does it. I'm outta here."

"No, don't go." I gestured ardently, moving farther forward in my seat.

Norris drained his cognac. "I've got an early flight out in the morning and still need to touch base with the West Coast." He stood from the wing chair and reached for his briefcase.

I stood with him. "Look, there's something I need to ask you."

He ground his jaw. I had seldom seen anyone as hostile-looking. Maybe Iris Halfontaine at the Mid-City media mixer.

Here it was, the chance of a lifetime: I summoned my courage and prepared to tell my good friend about the eternal choice that was right then within his grasp—meeting God by placing his hope, faith, and trust in Jesus Christ. God was preparing to use me to change Norris's life forever and ever. But what if Norris wasn't ready to accept Jesus Christ as Lord and Savior and instead got belligerent with me and refused to go forward with the deal we were trying to hammer out?

I did something I'd regret for a long, long time: I changed the subject.

"Look, I've got this guy at the flagship station who wants to syndicate a car show," I said.

"A car show." Norris seemed to relax now that we were back on more solid footing. "Come on, we both know car shows are a dime a dozen."

"Right, I know. But I think this guy's on to something. He's producing a pilot with his own money. I've blocked him for a long time now, discouraged him every way I can, but he won't take no for an answer. And you know what? I think he's got a product we can push."

"Okay. When the pilot's finished, send it to me." Norris nodded stoically. "No guarantees, though. Got it?"

"Right," I said. "No guarantees."

Norris stuck out his hand and we shook warmly. "It's nice doing business again."

"I've missed you," I said.

"Vance," Norris sighed, "you never make it easy. Do you?"

Fireflies peppered the succulent night air as I drove leisurely along the deserted country road. It was unseasonably warm and the full, expansive moon shone brightly across the meadows, backlighting the mountains in a gauzy lunar haze. The flickering lights of the luxury hotel where I'd met Norris for dinner receded in my rearview mirror.

In the unrelenting silence, I cranked up the radio for a sports update. The big programming note tonight was no Bulls game. They had just beaten Charlotte in the Eastern Conference semifinals to embark on yet another deep run at the championship. On paper, the Bulls looked like they had the tougher path to the finals than Utah did, but who knew? That's why they played the games.

When the station went to a commercial break I punched up the second hour of *The Sinners for Beginners Show*. "Here's a little Q and A for you, Wallace," Wanda said. "What's one of Satan's favorite words?"

"What's one of Satan's favorite words?" Wallace mused. "I don't know, there's probably a whole slew. Is this a trick question?"

"I assure you it's not a trick question," Wanda said. "Even though the biggest trickster known to man, the enemy himself, is at the bottom of it."

"Wow, now you've got me really going," Wallace said. "Is it the word 'lie'? Is that what you're looking for?" He snapped his fingers. "Or how about the word 'hate'? Satan surely has a special place in his singed heart for that word."

"Those are good choices, dear," Wanda said. "But I'm afraid you're veering a little off course."

"Then I might need some help," Wallace said. "There are a lot of strong possibilities regarding the squalid character of the author of deceit."

As I motored along the winding road, my cell phone rang. I glanced down at Billy Whatcom's number on the call screen. I let it go to voicemail, more concerned with the discussion on the radio. I'd call Billy back later. He'd understand.

"Okay, drumroll please . . ." Wanda wound herself up. "One of the favorite words in Satan's hate-filled vocabulary is . . . are you ready for this? The word . . . wait."

"Ah ha, the word wait. Very good," Wallace mused. "Subtle but deadly."

"Yes, and just think of the ways he can use it to his twisted advantage," Wanda said. "People say they'll wait until they're retired to start serving at the homeless shelter; people will wait until their lives are all cleaned up before setting foot in church; people will wait until they've achieved a certain income level before giving to missions. And here's my choice for the most debilitating of all . . . people will wait until the 'right time' to share the Gospel of Christ with others."

"Ouch," Wallace said. "That last one is a real indictment."

"It most certainly is, Wallace. But I'll bet if we're all honest with ourselves, there's not one among us who isn't guilty of that one. Me being at the top of the list."

"Me too," Wallace said.

I dumped the volume. Reaching for my mobile phone, I retrieved Billy's message. He'd called to remind me about the men's retreat next week; I needed to mail in my deposit to reserve a space. I had to laugh: in years gone by, mere mention of a men's retreat would have elicited mockery and derision. How times had changed. Now I was just thankful my schedule allowed me to attend.

The second part of the message was not as neat and tidy.

"Don't forget, man. . . . Josie wants to know about that dinner with Collette. Have you called her yet?"

I clenched the phone, realizing it was the moment of truth. Two weeks ago I'd promised Josie that I'd invite Collette to a dinner party Josie was hosting. I took a deep breath. On the verge of hyperventilating, I glanced at the display screen and scrolled down for Collette's number.

Suddenly, flashing lights pulsated across the front seat. I gasped, snapping to attention. My heart pounded as I gripped the wheel and swerved, narrowly avoiding an ambulance that had turned out in front of me.

I took a deep breath, regaining composure. I chided myself for my lack of awareness. Pumping the brakes, I increased the cushion between me and the emergency vehicle. I noted that it had exited the grounds of an exclusive retirement community. Based on the nature of the facility, the person being transported was probably elderly—and wealthy.

I wondered what was going through the individual's mind, especially if this was their last trip. If it were me, would I be ready to meet God? I said a brief prayer for the patient, hoping they were not in any pain.

Questions swirled in my mind: what kind of life had the person led? Were they looking forward to leaving Earth? Were they proud of all their accomplishments? Had they filled their days with everything *but* God, figuring they were doing enough in the community, that God would take care of them when the time came? Had they failed to realize God had been caring for them all along? Had they bothered to give him one iota of acknowledgment the whole time they had been drawing a breath?

What would their imminent meeting with God portend? When they had nothing left but their buck naked souls, would they experience a joyous homecoming with the prospect of magnificent reunions and the unbelievable majesty of God's infinite love speeding into time zones where time did not exist? Or would they instead experience the realization that the God they had disdained, marginalized, ignored, vilified, and defied—yes, *that* God—had only their best interests at heart all along?

Now, however, possibly after a lifetime of kicking him in the teeth—with no repentance in sight—time was running out. How many breaths remained while they could still accept Jesus Christ as their Lord and Savior . . . before succumbing to an irreparable, horrific demise?

God's heart would still burst with love for them, only now it would be broken because this person chose to reject his offer of eternal life, and it was now too late to do anything about it. The person's soul would be separated from God for all eternity—because wasn't that what he or she wanted in the first place? No hope forever and ever, all because the person wanted nothing to do with God.

I studied the ambulance up ahead as it negotiated an elongated curve. Something didn't add up. If the person inside hadn't yet given their life to Christ, wasn't that the biggest emergency of all: a person near death with no knowledge of a saving faith in Christ, a soul about to depart from Earth with no peace with God? Where was the monumental sense of urgency?

Shouldn't the siren be wailing?

It is often said that we have a hole in our soul that only God can fill. And if we try plugging that hole with anything *but* God, our efforts will prove vapid and counterfeit. Some people pump drugs and booze into the ravenous chasm; some fill it with jobs and promotions; some idolize education and scholarly papers; others worship cars, houses, parties, and friends. The list is endless. I know I've more than held up my end of the bargain on multiple scores.

We go to great lengths to shore up the emptiness in our souls at a massive cost of time, money, energy, and resources. We frantically search for ways to satiate that aching void, yet the more we get of something the more we desire. Unless God is at the very core of our existence, we'll spend a lifetime pursuing false leads, meaningless goals, and unresponsive idols.

The answer, however, is right inside us. Our one true reason for living is to build an everlasting relationship with God Almighty, Maker of Heaven and Earth. We need to strike an accord with God, made possible by the death and resurrection of Jesus Christ, and allow him to use us for his eternal purposes. When we finally fill that hole with his majestic peace and contentment, we can accomplish great things in this life in preparation for the next.

I flashed back to when I was a youth and sides were being chosen for a pickup baseball game. Unless you were one of the tall, strong kids who were fleet of foot, things could get pretty tense. Remember your heart sinking as one, then another, and another, kid was chosen ahead of you? Hey, wait a minute! You were better than at least half these guys!

Weren't you?

Hopefully you wouldn't be chosen last; you didn't think you could endure the humility. Or, worse, you wouldn't be chosen at all.

How great is it that God doesn't operate that way! He gave us the ability to make all the choices on our own. We can choose to have a relationship with him—or choose not to. But nowhere are we subjected to the queasiness of waiting around for some corny, razzle-dazzle guy to choose us—or not. We can make our choice anytime—the sooner the better—and our ticket is immediately punched, no questions asked. God has already seen to it. We first just need to ask him into our lives.

There are many absolutes in this world: open and shut; black and white; true or false; night and day; hot or cold. But the single-most important distinction is the one demanded by God: are we with him—or not?

The same fate awaits each and every one of us. Which eternity will we encounter once we leave the planet for good: the eternity with God or the one without him? The eternity brimming with hope or the one riddled with incalculable despair? The eternity overflowing with infinite light and love, or the one plunged into nonstop darkness in which we're perpetually alone, forever and ever?

If that were me in the ambulance right now, how would I view my imminent eternity? Would I be ready for the biggest reality of all?

Gripping my mobile phone, I took a deep breath. *So weird.* Why was I getting all worked up over a lousy call? I was only asking Collette to a dinner with friends. It didn't even qualify as a legitimate date.

Plus, I was sure Josie had already run interference. There was no way she or Billy would set me up for failure or create an uncomfortable situation.

Maybe that was the problem: this was more of a sure thing than I wanted to admit, and it scared me. Maybe I was afraid this relationship would blossom into something that, eventually, I would be incapable of handling.

Hey, it's only a dinner party.

I paused before punching the call button, praying I would have the wisdom and patience to let this play out the way God intended. I had to keep reminding myself that this was all his show. My relationship with Collette was a work in progress. Or, maybe more accurately, a mystery in progress.

What would the final outcome be? A life together or . . . a life not together?

What's it going to be, God?

Trust was always a tough one for me.

As I waited for the first ring, I glanced up at the heavens stretching across all eternity.

An odd peace came over me as I realized this was exactly what I was supposed to be doing at this exact moment in time.

YOUR PERSONAL INVITATION

You've made it this far. Congratulations! Thanks for hopping aboard and taking a read through this novel. If something regarding Vance's journey has stirred within you the desire to take a deeper dive, there's no better time or place than right now to start attending a local house of worship where the Bible is taught and the Lord's love felt.

If you have any questions, doubts, or concerns about embarking on your newfound journey of faith, please don't hesitate to drop me a line at georgem@screamingscripts.com. I pray for the knowledge, wisdom, and understanding to answer any comments or criticisms you may have.

In the unspeakable, incomprehensible name of Jesus Christ, Amen!

ACKNOWLEDGMENTS

While God rightfully receives all the praise, accolades, glory, and honor, I would like to gratefully acknowledge the time, talents, gifts, and energy supplied by so many in so many different ways: Larry Carpenter, Chairman and CEO of Christian Book Services, LLC, a remarkable man and true visionary, who believed in this project from the very start and made it a reality; the capable, helpful and resourceful staff at Christian Book Services, including Shane Crabtree, President and COO, and Jeff Carpenter, Vice President of Production—thank you for your efficiency and congeniality; many thanks to Suzanne Lawing for her artistic eye and talented layout expertise; and my deepest appreciation for the insight, patience, thoughtfulness, and creativity of my editor, Bob Irvin.

My sincere gratitude to Dale Wynn Davidson, the talented and multidimensional host of *Las Vegas Tonight*, who is one of the bright burning lights of Sin City and a consistent oasis of peace, grace and compassion in a town that so desperately needs it; who pushed me from the very start and never let up on the gas pedal. My heartfelt thanks and appreciation for his unswerving support, loyalty, and encouragement that never flagged, not even during his hospitalization for a brutal case of COVID-19.

Additional Las Vegas support from Tim Berends, Pastor Danny Daniels, and Guy Williams—thank you for your early marketing help and for being such exceptional role models and inspirational champions for Christ.

Mahalo to best-selling author Dr. Jay Carter, whose invaluable insight, nurturing, and support were the source of great inspiration that fueled me on my journey every step of the way.

Kudos for the cover art rendered by the talented design team at Damonza.com.

With deepest thanks and appreciation to . . .

Rachelle Gardner, whose wise, cogent, and experienced counsel opened up tremendous new possibilities that led me in all the right and rewarding directions;

Jim Hart, who provided a much-needed wake-up call—thank you for your wisdom and compassion, and for your enthusiasm, generosity, and genuineness;

Marlene Bagnull and her capable staff at the Greater Philadelphia Christian Writers Conference—thank you for the bountiful resources and for always being there to help;

And to all of my family, friends, colleagues, and loved ones who nurtured and supported me so patiently, unconditionally, graciously, and indefatigably—my sincerest thanks. I praise our dear heavenly Father for bringing each and every one of you precious souls into my life.

About the Author

George Mattmiller has worked in a number of television markets, from Anchorage to Philadelphia, where he was primarily involved in management, operations, content development, and production. On the creative side, he has scripted promotional spots and corporate capabilities videos from coast to coast.

He has written scores of radio and TV commercials that deal with everything from soap-saving devices to mountain climbing gear. For print applications he has supplied articles and content across trade publication, promotional, and newspaper platforms. Two of his scripted documentaries received awards. His fictional blog, www.screamingscripts.com, details dysfunctional media shenanigans in a post-apocalyptic world.

George has participated in street ministries and is affiliated with Media Fellowship International, which serves the entertainment industry. He attended Carthage College and is a graduate of Columbia College-Chicago.